To Henry

Happy Reading!

THE
PICKMAN
PAPERS

BEING A COLLECTION OF THE TALES
AND REMINISCENCES OF THOSE MOST
AUGUST MEMBERS OF THE PICKMAN CLUB

Edited by R Poyton, Esq.

www.innsmouthgold.com

THIS IS AN INNSMOUTH GOLD BOOK

ISBN 978-1-7391756-4-1

Copyright@ 2023 R Poyton.

www.innsmouthgold.com

Cover and interior art by
Shelley De Cruz
Copyright@2023 Graveheart Designs
www.facebook.com/graveheartdesigns

Contents

I was thrilled, at that very first meeting, to be called upon to recall one of my own rather singular adventures

THE PICKMANITES

In setting out these papers, I cannot help but be reminded of the very first occasion on which I met the esteemed Mr Samuel Pickman. I say esteemed not because he was a prominent politician, nor a celebrated novelist, or philosopher. Neither a famous artist, nor a noted philanthropist. He was none of those things, yet Mr Pickman was, without doubt, held in high esteem by the widest spectrum of people, due to his formation and continued overseeing and organising of what came to be known as The Pickman Club.

Indeed, it was at a meeting of that august group that I first encountered him. At the time I was a reporter on the *Morning Chronicle*, then under the ownership of William Innell Clement. It was the novelist Lady Mindy Geres, author of *The Curse of Livemere Hall*, who drew my attention to the group, whose existence I had been singularly unaware of, despite their meeting place being but a short stroll from my Fleet Street office. Lady Geres, knowing of my interest in the bizarre and unusual, mentioned the Pickman Club in passing and, curiosity aroused, I made enquiries.

So it was that, two weeks later, I found myself in the George and Vulture on Lombard Street, squeezed into a back room with a group of men of various backgrounds and origins. Ah yes, for unlike many gentlemens' establishments of the day, the doors of the Pickman Club were open to all. In that respect, old Samuel was quite the progressive, the main criteria for acceptance being an interest in sharing strange tales and experiences rather than being possessed of gentlemanly means. Indeed, a mere journalist such as I, had no prospect, beyond, perhaps, marrying well above my station, of gaining entrance to the portals of the newly founded Athenaeum Club, for example, let alone the venerable and even more exclusive Whites.

Do not imagine, though, that the room was filled with ruffians or bad-hats. No, for already I recognised a number of men of distinction; Sir Brian Hicks of the Bank of England, the landscape architect Gideon Clarke, the French painter Lee Le Blanc and various others. Indeed, the main talk that evening was from the Cambridge mathematician Alexander Zebediah Loudon, who spoke of the recent work of one Franz Taurinus on something called "non-Euclidian geometry." I freely admit, much of that talk proved far beyond my meagre levels of understanding.

Thankfully, the following talk on Egyptian history, from a Mr Thomas Kirby, was rather more within my intellectual grasp, and I was thrilled, at that very first meeting, to be called upon to recall one of my own rather singular "adventures," centred around the investigation of reports of hauntings at the Oxford Arms on Warwick Lane. Such was enough for me to effect entry into that most convivial of companies known to one and all as *Pickmanites*.

Samuel Pickman himself was a jovial fellow of early middle years. One might be mistaken, in viewing the balding head, circular spectacles, and modest attire, for taking Pickman as a minor clerk of some kind, a man of little consequence. Yet, that placid exterior concealed a pin-sharp intellect, and a busy, enquiring mind that was never happier than when engaged in some form of investigation or research. And, despite becoming the beneficiary of a considerable sum of money on the death of his wife, Pickman stayed on in his position at the solicitors, Tweedie & Prideaux, where, I understand, he carried out work of an investigative nature.

However, that pecuniary good fortune did not completely go to waste, for Pickman invested it in new club premises. No more the crowded, fug-filled back room of a London tavern. No, the new club premises were both more spacious and luxurious, being part of a recently constructed edifice at 10-11 Carlton House Terrace, St James. The building had been designed by the eccentric architect Ernst Von Steiger, famous, or infamous, perhaps, for his design of the new Bethlem Hospital in Southwark, which some termed "the most opulent mental asylum in the world."

Still, Pickmanites could now take their ease in the comfort of large armchairs, in front of blazing fires, with a dedicated dining room, and various, smaller, private rooms. The Club also gained a body of servants, run under the joint steely gaze of Mrs Lisa M. Gargano, Housekeeper and William Hodgson, Butler. While Mrs Gargano was largely an unseen presence, Hodgson, resplendent in his morning jacket with black, calico sleeves, was ever on hand, supervising the various doormen, waiting staff and servant boys.

And so, we come to the collection before you. In all bar this one meeting, I had to curb my journalistic impulses, and neither breathe nor lay down in ink even a single word of those experiences shared at the Club (such was one of the few terms of membership.). But that autumn night in 1826, on the occasion of the Annual Dinner, I had an inkling that something strange was in the air. My instincts were to be proven correct. So it was that, contrary to all previous occasions, I surreptitiously kept notes on the proceedings. Now, so many years further on, I feel I can release those notes, written out in full by myself, and printed by Shane, Ardley and Sons of Pall Mall.

I trust you will find them of interest.

- *Moses*

*The magician set the box on the table, with the
lens pointing to a spot on one of the walls*

THE AMAZING THOTH

MIGUEL FLIGUER

Before dinner was called, as the club members were still standing, mingling and chatting, sipping aperitifs, Mr. Pickman gestured and made an announcement.

"My friends, a very special guest is coming to the Club tonight and will be with us shortly. He is unable to partake of dinner with us, but we shall not take that as a lack of courtesy. He has a previous commitment of which I cannot speak... suffice it to say, royalty is involved, and it was, therefore, inescapable. He expressed his apologies to me earlier, and also a special wish... that he shall remain anonymous until his arrival. So I implore your patience. I promise it will be amply rewarded."

The club members discussed the identity of the mysterious guest, as they moved to take their usual positions in the various Chesterfields and sofas, sipping coffee and puffing on cigars. Mr. Pickman stood near the fireplace and cleared his throat to gather their attention.

"There is something else I must request of you, my friends. When our esteemed visitor arrives, I ask you not to greet him with a handshake, for I believe he follows a religious restriction against physical contact with people not of his faith."

"Never heard of that before. Is he by chance a Mohammedan?" asked Mr Allen.

"No. As far as I can tell, he professes something else, something much older," replied Mr. Pickman, and the strangeness of the reply greatly inflamed the curiosity of everybody in the room. Suddenly the barking of dogs was heard on the street, which was unusual for that high hour of the night... something had roused them out of their sleep, something other than the ordinary pedestrians and late-night drunkards to which they were used.

The doorbell rang, and a moment later Hodgson, the butler, appeared at the doorway and, as Club protocols demanded on special occasions like this, he resoundingly proclaimed the arrival of the guest: "Mr. Harley Patton, KCB!"

Mr. Pickman greeted the newcomer warmly, but without shaking his hand. Then he led him into the room, and introduced him thusly.

"Esteemed friends, it is an honour of the highest order to have with us tonight Mr. Harley Patton, Knight Commander of Bath, *tria iuncta in uno*. He is an accomplished entertainer, who has enthralled kings and peasant crowds alike all across Asia and Africa with his astonishing feats of magic and science. He has just arrived in England for a one-time show at Drury Lane, before embarking on a tour of the Continent. It is then, for us Pickmanites gathered here tonight, an incredible privilege to have a small preview of his fantastic act. Gentlemen, I present you, Mr. Harley Patton, the Amazing Thoth!"

The club members acknowledged this speech with a lukewarm salvo of applause, for the gentleman standing next to Mr. Pickman didn't seem to live up to the expectations they had been building, nor to that bombastic announcement. He appeared to be a regular fellow... bespectacled, a bit on the portly side, with affable looks and a genial demeanour. He carried a small, black suitcase with "The Amazing Thoth" neatly engraved on the leather on one side, and the stylised head of an ibis painted on the other. He bowed slightly at the applause and set his suitcase on a table that Hodgson had prepared earlier to that end. Mr. Patton walked behind the table and faced the expectant crowd. He remained still... only his eyes moved as if sizing up his audience.

He suddenly opened the suitcase with a deft, well-practised movement. The spectators nearer to the table could only see a gaping, black void inside. Mr. Patton drove a hand into the valise, up to his forearm. He seemed to be rooting around the contents, but suddenly he went further in, almost to his shoulder, and the audience gasped in astonishment, for he was now clearly exceeding the physical depth dimension of the suitcase, and his hand was now in an impossible place under the table. Was that a trick of the light? Mr. Bellingham, who was seated a few feet in front and had a good view of the proceedings, started to get up for a closer inspection, but the magician raised his other hand in the air. As if obeying an unspoken command, Bellingham sat on his couch, but his gaze remained fixed on Mr. Patton's arm disappearing into that twisting blackness.

"Ah! Here you are!" exclaimed the performer. With a flourish, he quickly removed his arm from that puzzling suitcase... and his hand was grabbing, by the nape of its neck, a jet-black panther cub! Everyone gave cries of excitement, and a few members rose to have a closer look and to try petting the beautiful, small beast. Upon seeing them, the cub let out a loud, profound growl that didn't quite correspond to its minute size, which quickly drove everybody back into their seats. Mr. Patton smiled, but his grin had lost the genial attitude and now seemed a shade sinister. He set the cub on the table, and to the member's surprise, the little beast licked his hands.

"My young companion, from the jungles of Burma," whispered the magician, and there was a coldness in his voice that translated to the smoky atmosphere of the room, and some of the more impressionable spectators shivered in discomfort. Mr. Patton gently led the cub to the suitcase, and the little feline dove inside with determination, as if returning to its mother's lair. Mr. Pickman led the applause, this time stronger and more sincere than before.

Mr. Patton bowed slightly, and once again introduced his arm up to the elbow into the apparently bottomless suitcase. He rooted about for a moment as if looking for something - or perhaps for theatrical effect- and then extracted a very strange contraption, the likes of such no-one present had ever seen. It was a white rectangular prism or box of slightly larger dimensions than the valise, which again puzzled the spectators to no end. The prism had a short, black, cylindrical protuberance on one side, tapered with a glass lens the type seen in optical experiments. The magician set the box on the table, with the lens pointing to a spot on one of the walls, devoid of furniture and decorations. He conducted these operations with an unsettling grin on his face that made most of those present quite uncomfortable.

"I have brought this to you FROM THE FUTURE! And I will show you YOUR FUTURE!" he proclaimed. With a dramatic gesture, he pressed something unseen in the back of the box. A shaft of bright white light shone from the lens and formed a glowing rectangle on the wall. Almost everybody in the room was astonished, even Mr. Pickman, and some gave cries of incredulity, but then the always sceptical Mr. Bellingham rose and, unable to contain himself, exclaimed,

"Pah! This is surely a better version of Humphrey Davy's electric arc bulb! I have seen one in his laboratory years ago, and this one seems to be more powerful, perhaps it is combined with a lens like those Mr. Faraday has been working on. It is physics, my friends, natural philosophy... there is nothing magic about it! And also..."

Suddenly he froze in mid-word. On the wall, images had formed... moving images! All members, as one, rose from their chairs and couches and approached the singular phenomenon, which defied the comprehension of even those learned minds. How could it be? Where is that? Are we all hallucinating?

Meanwhile, the moving images began to show astounding scenes, the meaning of which was not entirely clear to the astonished Pickmanites. There were birds' eye vistas of an immense parade of what undoubtedly were enormous armies, the size of which dwarfed anything the war veterans among the members had ever seen. Interspersed with the hundreds of thousands of marching men, there were gigantic machines, moving apparently of their own volition, with the undeniable aspect of deathly engines of destruction. There was no sound, but that somehow made the shifting images even more terrible to watch.

Soon the images changed to a grey sky, where immense metallic winged things flew in formation, their glide powered by unseen forces that defied the club member's comprehension. And from those strange airborne engines dropped a myriad of odd-shaped objects that fell to the ground far below and exploded with unimaginable violence... The vistas shifted once again to what was apparently the aftermath... a vast landscape of ruins and rubble among the remainders of what was once a city... desolate faces peering from behind crumbling walls... corpses scattered on what was left of the streets... a nightmare of devastation...

The room abruptly darkened, the many candles extinguished by a wind that was not there, and the light on the wall took a different quality, a sickly jaundiced tone that some of the club members tried to avert their eyes from, but seemed unable to do so. Mr. Patton laughed from his spot behind the table, a chilling reminder of his presence as master of that mysterious ceremony. He bellowed, "There is MORE! Behold, PUNY HUMANITY!"

Suddenly, from behind him erupted a flurry of blindingly white sparks, which gave his head a demonic halo and his eyes a malignant phosphorescence. From some unseen quarter, there came a sound... a beating of drums, soft at first but quickly growing louder, almost deafening. And the tobacco-infused atmosphere of the room became rank, as if mephitic, invisible vapours had seeped into the chamber without warning.

The moving imagery now showed a single flying machine, stark against a backdrop of churning skies, releasing another of those obscenely shaped devices. But this time the explosion dwarfed anything they had seen before... it was a colossal pillar of smoke that reached the clouds and mushroomed there, its unimaginable power erasing out of existence everything on its way. Mr. Patton's shadow seemed to grow two enormous wings that spread across the wall on his back, and his cackling laughter rose above the frenzied din of the drums. Suddenly, with an uncharacteristic lack of fortitude for a veteran of the Gorkha War, Mr. Wilkins screamed, "Make it stop! Please, I beg you!"

Mr. Patton, or the entity that had possessed him, was seemingly satisfied by that pleading request. He touched the white box and the noxious light extinguished. The cursed vision of that mushroom cloud vanished from the wall, leaving, however, a chilling afterimage on everybody's retinas. The thundering drums were gone too. The darkness and the silence were total, save for a soft whimpering from someone in the crowd, and the heavy breathing of most of the present.

Steadying himself, Mr. Pickman called for Hodgson. The butler immediately barged into the room, as he had evidently been eavesdropping, leaning against the door in profound confusion and distress from what he was hearing.

"Hodgson, old chap, kindly light up this pit of a room, and open a window to clear the air."

As the butler complied, Mr. Pickman turned to the magician, who had seamlessly morphed back into his harmless, affable persona. He had put away his white box of wonders back into his unfathomable valise, which lay closed on the table, looking just like an ordinary suitcase now.

"My friend, this was outstanding! Pickmanites! I bid you to give this man the ovation he deserves!"

"That was indeed stunning," said Mr. Cooper to the magician. "I have dabbled into magic parlour tricks and scientific experiments for the masses, but never have I seen anything approaching the nature or scale of what you have shown us tonight, or even remotely conceived them. I bow unto you, Sir!"

Mr. Patton's grin clearly widened upon hearing that. He softly replied to Mr. Cooper, "Sir, no reaction to my performances satisfies me more than those heartfelt final words. Thank you, and I now predict we shall meet again."

There came a thunderous applause from all the members. Even Hodgson, who had not left the room and remained spellbound by Mr. Patton's voice, applauded without understanding. But soon he came to his senses, and announced to the assembly that dinner would be served. Mr. Patton politely declined and, after another round of applause and cheers of admiration, left the premises.

As the club members took their seats in the dining room, the barking on the street was heard again, but this time the Pickmanites understood what the dogs were reacting to, and they looked knowingly at each other. Finally, Mr. Bellingham excitedly broke the silence:

"I say... is this... wizard, or sorcerer, for lack of a better word... is he really going to perform at Drury Lane? In front of three thousand people? A performance like the one he showed us tonight... He is going to cause a commotion! There will be riots in the streets! The constabulary should be forewarned!"

"Fear not, my friend," replied Mr. Pickman. "I have read chronicles of the Amazing Thoth's performances in other nations. As I said earlier, he had shown one form or another of the feats we witnessed tonight, in front of royalty and also for the crowds. And something exceedingly strange seems to happen after those shows. Once people leave the venues, they slowly forget what they just saw, and only a vague uneasiness lingers... a sort of spiritual nausea, that never really abates. It is something remarkable, and I'm confident it will happen to us too, after tonight. But rest assured, for there had been no riots, no wars, no royal dynasties overthrown in Mr. Patton's wake."

"I agree his act is a wonderful display of stagecraft trickery," said Mr. Bellingham. "The man is a master of his trade. But still, I worry..."

"It was indeed amazing," added Mr. Kirby, our resident Egyptologist, as he unfolded his napkin. "And you are right about that strange effect. I feel like I am already forgetting the nastiest bits of his presentation. But something else intrigues me when I think about it... Harley Patton... It's the strangest sensation, those words stir a vague memory that I am unable to fully call to mind. A title or name, perhaps, or the hint of a name... Oh well, it eludes me for now. I imagine it will surface at some point,. Ah, here's the first course!"

*Reaching the terminus of the path in a
squalid cul-de-sac, Wallace confronted
an ominous chapel*

THE DARK CLIFFS OF BLACK VEN

LEE CLARK ZUMPE

After an unusually quiet meal, Tavish Cartwright stood and prepared to address his fellow Pickmanites. He cleared his throat, wore a solemn face, and ruffled papers upon which he had collected his notes.

"If I may presume to ask for your consideration," he began. "Not every tale of the Pickmanites can be promptly divulged, as specific circumstances may warrant a certain degree of discretion. In the matter of an impetuous and momentous proceeding in which some of our illustrious members found themselves entangled in an emphatically implausible series of incidents - each succeeding episode less tenable than the former - prudence led those participating to document their summation of the experience in writing only, while withholding this adventure's singular revelation from the troupe to protect the credibility of an important devotee of science, whose contributions to the emerging field of palaeontology are as significant as they are undervalued by the smug elitists of the London scientific community. Because of her expertise, her integrity, and her earnestness, we agreed to make an unanticipated sojourn to Dorsetshire at her urging.

I should add that her request was less a casual invitation than an urgent entreaty. While this account has been subject to necessary concealment for more than one year, recent developments have made it compulsory to share the details of this adventure, with the mandate that all Pickmanites join in a conspiracy of silence - for the benefit of Miss Mary Anning, noted fossil collector of Lyme Regis, and to prevent panic amidst the faint-hearted and unschooled of London who are so prone to fits of panic and delirium."

---

i.
Unquiet Slumbers

Clifford Balfour, geologist and paleontologist, shambled across the floor and gazed into a mirror above the washstand before splashing water on his face in a futile attempt to banish from his mind the reverberations of an unpleasant night of insufficient slumber - the third such experience since he and his colleagues departed London on their impromptu excursion. This latest eventide had been spent in Bridport, an old Saxon market town found at the confluence of the River Brit and the River Asker. Thankfully, Bridport would be the final stopover before the party reached Lyme Regis, their destination, just a short jaunt down the rambling road.

Balfour cleaned himself as thoroughly as his accommodations allowed, scrubbing and wiping and mopping the accumulated dirt and sweat from the previous day's travel. By the time Tavish Cartwright summoned him for breakfast, he felt satisfied he had attained an adequate level of cleanliness and that his companions would find him at least presentable, if not fully revitalized and reinvigorated.

"How do you find the lodging in the low country, Clifford?" Cartwright stood outside the door of his overnight billet, a knowing look on his face. A portraitist of distinction whose work revealed him as a master of character, Cartwright came from one of London's wealthiest families. He was among the charter members of the Pickman Club, and a close personal friend of Samuel Pickman, the club's founder. "Did you attain any peace in your dozing crib?"

"Less restful than the night before, which was equally disagreeable to the one that preceded it," Balfour said. "If I slept two hours out of eight, I would be surprised."

"My night was similarly discouraging. After a few hours of tossing and turning, I abandoned any attempt at repose and opted to bridge the hours between dusk and dawn reading one of the academic tomes you recommended."

For emphasis, Cartwright tapped the selected volume, tucked beneath his arm. Though its title was hidden in shadow, Balfour recognized it as *Visitations from the Unseen World*, a rare 18th century manuscript. "Quite an interesting inventory of obscure folklore and inconspicuous mythology. It is fascinating how history omits details, either by accident or intention."

"There are as many gods and monsters as the men whose dreams and nightmares spawn their ilk," said Oldfield Godolphin, a noted historian and author of many books, including his recent well-received publication *The History and Antiquities of Dorsetshire*. Balfour had insisted upon his inclusion in their modest adventure because of his familiarity with - and appreciation of - legends and traditions associated with South West England.

"I trust you both slept soundly?"

"Not in the least," Balfour said with unintended vexation. He managed a smile as he continued. "Only unquiet slumbers for these sleepers, regrettably. Were you able to doze?"

"Deeply and without interruption," Godolphin said. The oldest member of their entourage, his faced flushed with sudden amusement as he noticed a distinct lingering weariness and dishevelment that had settled upon the faces of his friends. "I must have had the quietest chamber in this Bridport inn, or the softest bed - or the most tranquillising nightcap."

"Perhaps a digestif after dinner would have helped," Balfour admitted. "By early this afternoon, we should arrive at our destination. I have faith that our bed and board in Lyme Regis will be a more pleasant stay."

These three members of the Pickman Club found their fourth constituent gobbling down a gargantuan breakfast consisting of porridge, fish, eggs and bacon. Roland Wallace sat on a bench outside the inn on a wide porch overlooking a small herb garden. He loomed above an overcrowded plate of food perched precariously on his lap. Crumbs cascaded down his frock coat. The youngest of the group, Wallace had only recently relocated to London after serving more than a decade as an agent of the East India Company, working as an administrator at the Trincomalee harbour in Ceylon. His time there had been punctuated by periods of chaos and clamour, with sporadic episodes of rebellion threatening to dislodge British troops from their garrison in Colombo.

Seeing him as source of many interesting tales, Mr Pickman had recruited Wallace for the group. As yet, the 38-year-old had held fast to whatever yarns he might be capable of spinning, showing a patent disinclination to share his experiences in the British Crown Colony - other than to report one evening, after a few too many pints of stout, that he had witnessed unspeakable atrocities throughout the struggle between British forces and the Kandyans who controlled the island's interior highlands.

"Apparently our initiate's appetite was so great he could not wait for the rest of us to feast," Cartwright said with a hearty laugh. "No worries, lad - we older folk find that approaching the day somewhat surreptitiously, with caution and discretion, prevents us from becoming cynical and cantankerous before midday."

Wallace grinned at the comment, but could not articulate a direct response due to the amount of smoked haddock and fried eggs he had just stuffed into his mouth.

A short time later, Balfour, Cartwright, and Godolphin joined Wallace on the porch to devour their own morning meals - each one consuming a fraction of what the former East India Company agent had procured from the inn's busy kitchen. As they cleaned their plates, they turned their attention to the letter that had precipitated this adventure.

"Do you think she's expecting an ensemble cast to appear on her doorstep?" Cartwright wondered if Balfour's contact in Lyme Regis was prepared to house four visitors. "In her letter, she asked for your assistance. She did not extend an invitation to your colleagues."

"I responded, sending word that I would be travelling with companions," Balfour said. "My association with Mary Anning has always been cordial. I do not anticipate any problems when we arrive. As to our accommodations, I have a distant cousin - Algernon Glyndon - who owns a sizable estate not far from town. He would gladly welcome us in his home, or put us up in the hotel he recently acquired."

"What do you think she is so eager to show you?" Cartwright scratched his grey whiskers. "In the past, has she not been content working through representatives of the British Museum?"

"As well as private collectors," Balfour said. "There are plenty of people willing to pay modest sums for good specimens. Buyers from Paris and Vienna attended a recent auction, hosted by Lieutenant-Colonel Thomas James Birch to raise funds for Miss Anning."

"I've seen the famous Ichthyosaurus she pulled from the fossil beds along the coast," Cartwright said. "So why did she reach out to you directly in this instance?"

Balfour pulled the envelope from his coat pocket and withdrew the epistle, unfolding it carefully before sharing it again with his colleagues. These were its contents:

My dear Balfour: Should you wish to be witness to something extraordinarily inexplicable, I implore you to pay a visit to my precious village at your earliest convenience. I discovered something quite unnatural and unnerving in a remote vista along the dark cliffs of Black Ven. It is like no other structure I have encountered, fashioned from material not found in this region, and assembled in such a way that it is only visible at certain times and under specific meteorological and astrological conditions.

The thing possesses a striking quality of unearthliness, leading me to believe it is - much like the fossils that are my stock and trade - something from a bygone age, not dreamed of by modern man. I wish I could offer more than this rudimentary depiction to express the urgency of my request, but I am hindered by the fact that its distinctiveness makes it quite indescribable - and its high strangeness inhibits me from further investigation, despite my natural curiosity.

Make haste, Balfour: I cannot predict how long this phenomenon will persist.

Mary Anning

"Not to be critical, but it is likely some Roman remnant that has emerged from obscurity following a cloudburst," Godolphin said. "Those cliffs are prone to accelerated erosion. This girl likely hasn't seen the carcasses of old colonies that date back to antiquity."

"This *woman*," Balfour said, "is far brighter than you might imagine, given her limited education. She reads and writes, and, I am told, she follows every scrap of scientific literature she can obtain that is connected to the fossils she recovers and passes along to the scientific community."

"In that case, I look forward to seeing whatever she has uncovered." Godolphin happily conceded the point. "And I am grateful that this woman, Miss Anning, has invited us to be the first to set eyes upon it."

ii.

The Arrival

The carriage journey from London to Lyme Regis took the better part of three days with frequent detours and nightly lodging. Clifford Balfour chartered two Hackney coaches to ferry his audacious company and their accoutrements. Though roomy and elegant, the transports exuded an air of diminished stylishness, as if whatever heights of respectability and dignity these aging relics had enjoyed when owned and employed by the British aristocracy had been deliberately depleted by overuse and neglect. These particular conveyances had deteriorated to the point of near collapse, and each day one or the other had to stop to make some roadside repair.

That the company arrived without a single broken bone amongst them was a source of celebration when the Pickmanites finally reached Lyme Regis.

At once a quiet little fishing village and a bustling hub of idyllic commotion, picturesque Lyme Regis sat on the south coast overlooking Lyme Bay, flanked by lofty cliffs of shale and clay. The Hackney coaches bounced along Broad Street, the main thoroughfare, before arriving in the small business district adjacent to the Harbor. It took little time to find someone willing to point them in the direction of Anning's Fossil Depot. In the glass storefront, Mary Anning displayed her inventory, including invertebrate fossils such as ammonites and belemnites - marketed as snake-stones and devil's fingers, respectively - along with a few select vertebrate specimens, including a recent find she had tentatively dubbed a "flying dragon."

"That marvellous specimen alone was worth the trip." Clifford Balfour muttered as he gazed upon the unique vestige of a former world. Tucked inside a wicker basket situated on shelf inside the window, he also took an interest in an elongated, oval-shaped, blue-green fossil measuring at least 12 inches long and 4 inches wide. Its surface bore strange swirls and striations, along with scars and pockmarks that hinted at its great age. "I hope Miss Anning is willing to sell these to the British Museum."

"As intriguing as her stock may be, that is not why we are here, Clifford." Cartwright, finding the door locked, vented his exasperation in a muffled grunt. "No one tending the store on a Saturday afternoon, apparently."

At Cartwright's prompting, Oldfield Godolphin and Roland Wallace strolled along the lane looking for local points of interest. Across the street from Anning's business they found the Pilot Boat Hotel which advertised daily coach service to and from Bridport. Just a few doors down was Brown's Stores, selling a variety of staple food items and household goods. The Pickmanites discovered a forge, the fires of which had likely been burning for hundreds of years. The clang of hammers striking the anvil echoed through the nearby neighbourhoods. Other businesses clustered in the district included a tobacconist, a barber, a cobbler, a tailor, and a chemist.

At some point, Wallace went off on his own, wandering down a shadowy cobblestone lane lined with dismal buildings of a much earlier age, fronted by weed-grown doorsteps and filthy windows that hinted at generations of squalor and decay.

The air was tainted by some unidentifiable putrescence, causing the 38-year-old to cup a hand over his nose and mouth as he proceeded. As he descended the slender path, the ancient structures stooped unnaturally, their disintegrating gambrel roofs and unsymmetrical wooden gables pitching clumsily, all threatening to collapse at any moment into a mountain of foulness and palpable degradation.

A light rain fell as he continued, and water dripped from every eave and awning. The rainwater absorbed the ubiquitous rot of these dilapidated domiciles, trickling down the sloping roofs, and dribbling onto the ground - and onto any passersby - as if the buildings salivated at the intrusion.

Reaching the terminus of the path in a squalid cul-de-sac, Wallace confronted an ominous chapel, its stone walls covered with archaic symbols. An uncanny radiance oozed through broad windows, highlighting several peculiar figures whose outlines could not be convincingly characterized as either fully human or beast. What Wallace first thought might be worshippers singing praise to God quickly became a muddle of horrible discordant voices - unearthly voices - chanting unintelligible words punctuated with sporadic yaps and yelps. A quick glance at the weedy patch of ground between the cobblestones and the building showed meandering trails of three-toed footprints.

Though he felt the urge to approach that awful, unhallowed shrine, and to peer through its mucky, encrusted windows, Wallace hurriedly retraced his steps and rejoined the other Pickmanites in a more hospitable section of Lyme Regis.

By this time, Balfour had managed to squeeze down a narrow alleyway trying to find some other way to access the

Anning residence. He knew that the fossil collector lived on the second or third story of the building. His efforts, however, proved unsuccessful, and he reconvened with his colleagues on the street in front of Anning's Fossil Depot.

"A quaint seaside resort, Clifford." Cartwright's perpetual impatience most often manifested itself in bursts of wry sarcasm. "Perhaps we can enjoy sunbathing on the beach while we await Miss Anning's imminent return."

"We will catch up with her," Balfour assured him. "She does have a business to run. She may be collecting samples as we speak."

As the Pickmanites loitered at the storefront, they turned their attention to the inhabitants of Lyme Regis. The townsfolk formed small cliques as they negotiated the narrow, winding streets beneath grey skies. Not far in the distance, dockworkers scurried along the quay, consolidating the bounty of the sea delivered by fishing boats. Seagulls filled the air with their insistent squawking, begging for charity or plotting a daring robbery.

After a short time, a handsome gentleman approached the out-of-towners. He wore a navy-blue reefer coat, white trousers, and carried a yachtsman's cap. His expression revealed neither familiarity nor aloofness. He paused halfway across the street to remove his eyeglasses and polish the lenses. Replacing them, his face broke into a crafty grin.

"It is you, Clifford!" Algernon Glyndon, Balfour's blood relative, threw open his arms to welcome the Pickmanites. "Miss Anning told me you might be arriving in town. She left meticulous instructions on how to greet you. She insisted on showing you the finest hospitality. I have a room ready for you."

"Thank you, Algernon," Balfour said. "Would it be an imposition to ask if you might also be able to accommodate my companions?"

"Of course, I can find rooms for your companions," Glyndon said, introducing himself to Balfour's party. "Any friend of yours, cousin, is a welcome guest in the Pilot Boat Hotel."

"It is good to see you again, cousin," Balfour said, mildly embarrassed by Glyndon's boisterous enthusiasm. "It has been some time."

"Decades, cousin!" Glyndon leaned forward, embracing his relative. "We were both unruly urchins, no more than 10 years old when last we plotted anarchy and pandemonium. We caused monumental turmoil that summer in London at your father's estate. 'Masters of bedlam,' your governess called us."

"I have not forgotten that summer." Balfour shrank in his skin, feeling Cartwright's eyes upon him. He had not realized that Glyndon might be eager to share stories about his youth that he would prefer to keep secret. "Though I confess, I am not proud of some of the mischief we achieved."

"We were young and undisciplined." Glyndon patted his cousin on the shoulder. "Best to rid oneself of those wild impulses before the appalling malaise of terminal adulthood sets in, I think. One should have memories of wanton disorderliness and wild intractability to reflect upon when the countless hardships of life besiege us."

None of the Pickmanites had noticed that the grey skies had grown menacingly black. Though each member of the group prided himself on a keen capacity for observation, none of them detected the gentle breeze had increased to a persistent gale. None of them read the telltale signs that warned of an oncoming tempest. The light rain that had been falling on and off for the last hour at that moment transformed into a soaking deluge.

"Follow me," Glyndon shouted as the winds continued to increase. "I will send someone to collect your luggage from the coaches and have the horses taken to a stable for the duration of your stay."

The group scrambled across the roadway, jumping over a stream of runoff water surging down the thoroughfare toward the harbour. Inside the lobby of the Pilot Boat Hotel, Glyndon spoke with the manager of the inn and asked him to take care of Balfour and his associates.

"This is Joseph Leach," Glyndon said. "He will see to your rooms and your gear. I will join you in the dining room this evening for dinner."

"At your service," Leach said. A thin, genteel-looking man, fetching save for his prodigious bulging eyes, he forced an unconvincing smile as he nodded his head. "Please let me know if I can assist you in any way."

As Leach took his leave to prepare their rooms, Wallace caught a whiff of an unpleasant stench - an odd odour he had encountered a short time earlier as he explored that crumbling neighbourhood saturated by some unidentifiable putrescence.

"Thank you, cousin, for your hospitality." Balfour shook Glyndon's hand. "I look forward to reminiscing with you as soon as I meet with Miss Anning. Do you know where we can find her?"

"I am going to search for her now," Glyndon said, a worried look on his face. "She was hunting for fossils on the beach. I only hope she was paying more attention to the sky and saw this storm approaching. With those crumbling cliffs, her vocation is dangerous work on any given day - but when the weather turns foul, like this, someone caught unaware on that narrow strip of shoreline can be buried in a mudslide without warning."

iii.

An Ancient Ruin

Night had fallen before Algernon Glyndon returned to the Pilot Boat Hotel. He traipsed into the lobby, sopping wet, his fine clothes caked in mud and seawater. His face showed his exhaustion, and his hands busied themselves with brushing aside layers of muck that fell to the floor only to reveal additional stains.

"Good Lord!" Balfour spotted Glyndon first, looking up from a book that had held his attention for hours. "Are you all right, man?"

"I am," Glyndon said, tentatively smiling. Somehow, his smile only accentuated the grime that enveloped every inch of his exposed flesh. "And I bring good news: Miss Anning is fine. She found shelter long before I arrived. I intended to be her saviour, but it was she who saved me, leading me through the darkness back to town after nightfall. I owe her my life."

"Please, Mr. Glyndon, do not consider yourself indebted to me. I have enough obligations and assurances to commit to memory." Mary Anning strolled through the front door of the inn, depositing a cumbersome umbrella near the entrance before surveying each member of the Pickmanites with scrupulous inquisitiveness. Unlike Glyndon, she showed no visible sign of being left the worse for wear after the afternoon cloudburst: not a speck of mud on her clothing, not a hint of dishevelment in her appearance, and not a note of tension in her demeanour. After examining the group, her gaze finally settled on Clifford Balfour.

"You, sir," she said with unambiguous authority. "Though we have never met face to face, I presume you are the honourable Clifford Balfour, geologist and paleontologist associated with the British Museum."

"Yes, ma'am." Balfour confirmed her deduction. "I am honoured to make your acquaintance."

"Thank you," Anning said. "And I yours." She paused, turning to Glyndon who continued to shed enough water to generate a broad puddle on the floor. "Should you not go and find clean, dry clothing, Mr. Glyndon? I will not have you stand here freezing and inviting some respiratory malady to settle in your lungs after I risked my own life rescuing you."

"That seems like sound advice, ma'am." Glyndon summoned his employee with a snap of his fingers, causing Leach to spring into action from his alcove behind the reception desk. The lanky fellow disappeared into a nearby alcove, presumably to fetch clean clothing for his employer. "Give me an hour to rid myself of this filth and we can all have something to eat."

"Be back in less than 30 minutes," Anning commanded. She glanced toward the fireplace and took note of the time reported by the mantel clock. "It is already nearly 10 p.m. If we are to reach Black Ven by midnight, we must leave shortly."

Anning spoke with such confidence and authority, no one thought to question why she felt it necessary to make the trip in the middle of the night. As they waited for the return of their host, Balfour took the opportunity to introduce his associates to Anning.

"I hope you do not mind that I invited these gentlemen," Balfour said, worried that Anning might be aggravated with him. "We are united in a certain fraternity. They share my curiosity and may be more equipped to solve the mystery you described in your letter."

"I welcome anyone who will view it with an open mind." Anning plucked a small ammonite fossil from her pocket. "This relic represents the organic remains of a previous geologic era. Though I recovered it, it is not my property. I do not view it as a possession. Obviously, I make a living selling fossils - but the prices I assign to each piece are for the time and labour that went into procuring my inventory, and for my knowledge and experience."

"I understand," Balfour said. "You believe everyone should have the opportunity to see prehistoric relics."

"Yes, though I do acknowledge some limitations that may restrict access to some individuals." Anning eyed her visitors, half expecting someone to blurt out their opinion that women had no business partaking in scientific endeavours. Of course, Anning did much more than act as an enthusiastic participant: She was a prolific contributor to the field. "Just as one would not give a fragile piece of antique porcelain to an infant with no comprehension of its value, it would be absurd to entrust the discovery of an archaic archeological site to rural residents whose religious affinities might inspire them to acts of defacement or destruction."

"Indeed," Cartwright said, nodding as he stood and approached Anning. He could not disguise the mix of bafflement and respect he felt at meeting such an interesting figure. "That is a remarkably wise consideration."

"For a woman?" Anning studied him, searching his eyes for signs of either deep-seated bias or sincere acknowledgment. She expected tolerance at the least, but hoped for genuine recognition. "I suspect you do not often show appreciation for any females in London who make an effort to be something other than wife and mother, and show interest in anything beyond etiquette and manners."

"Perhaps I should introduce them to you, Miss Anning," Cartwright said. "They could certainly learn a few things."

Cartwright's response evidently pleased the renowned fossil collector, and she rewarded him with a modest smile and a hint of redness in her cheeks.

"Have no fear of Tavish Cartwright, Miss Anning - his querulous deportment is a façade to dissuade the unenlightened from attempting to engage him in mindless banter." Balfour retrieved from his coat pocket the correspondence that summoned him to her small town. "Should I infer from the contents of your letter and from what you have said here this evening that you have not revealed your discovery to anyone else in Lyme Regis?"

"You may," Anning said. "Mr. Glyndon knows I found something of interest, but I have not shared any details with him - for doing so would be tantamount to printing it upon exhibition handbills and posting them around town." Anning's suggestion amused her guests, and she joined them in laughing at Glyndon's expense.

Following the aside, she grew more serious. "As I reported to you, this structure - be it an ancient temple or burial mound or part of some megalithic ceremonial complex - is unlike any other I have seen detailed in history texts. Just from the small portion that can be seen protruding from the cliff, it features asymmetrical design and unorthodox architecture, and seems dependent upon principles of geometry that clash with every axiom mathematicians regard as self-evident."

A moment later, Glyndon reappeared in the lobby of the inn. "Unless anyone objects, I think we should respect Miss Anning's advice and dawdle not a moment longer," Balfour said. Cartwright nodded in concurrence, and Roland Wallace was already on his feet and moving toward the front door. "If you would be so kind, Miss Anning: Please introduce us to this ancient ruin."

"Just one moment: Although I am eager to investigate the site," Godolphin said, "I must exempt myself from this evening's foray. The journey took its toll on this old codger's rickety frame, and the thought of even a short hike fills me with unease. This time of year, there seems to be too many hours in a day. I grow weary."

"Find yourself a soft cushion in a comfortable room at the inn, Oldfield." Balfour empathized with his companion's fatigue. Should he allow himself the luxury of relaxing in a snug chair, closing his eyes for just a passing moment, Balfour knew he would drift off into a sound sleep. Only the excitement over glimpsing the ruin kept him from succumbing to drowsiness. "We will report back to you in the morning."

Had any townsfolk happened to gaze out the window that night, they might have seen Mary Anning escorting the Pickmanites - Clifford Balfour, Tavish Cartwright, and Roland Wallace - and the local innkeeper, Algernon Glyndon, through the darkness. No one invited Glyndon, but he found himself an adjunct to their adventure.

It took no more than 45 minutes of travel, walking at a brisk pace through the sleeping town and then along the shoreline, to reach Black Ven. The sand beneath their feet quickly gave way to an endless stretch of pebbles. Anning assured them that the tide would not return until dawn, so they faced no danger from rising water and swirling currents. Tidal pools gathered in basins along rock ledges that appeared at irregular intervals along the water's edge.

Glyndon supplied each member of the party with a lantern that glowed with ample luminosity. With their combined light - added to that of a waxing gibbous moon hanging low in the black dome of night and glimmering on Lyme Bay - even the darkest shadows showed reluctance as they traversed the twilit path.

Beneath that resplendent moon, Black Ven seemed far less ill-omened than its name and reputation implied. The cliff face bisected one of the many hills which divides the valleys of the Char and the Lyme stream. Its seaward countenance revealed parallel veins of compacted layers cataloguing bygone ages. Clays and limestone bordered yellowish brown sand, which lay adjacent to soil and subsoil, and black and dark green loams. One specific stratum held all those treasures Anning had pursued for most of her life: the preserved remains of once living organisms, their bodies buried in sediments after death, concealed from scrutiny for countless millennia, conserved and eventually exposed again by a perpetual interplay of biological and geological cycles.

"Be wary, and mind the cliff's expression," Anning said. She scanned its bulk, taking interest in heaps of fallen mud dislodged in the recent downpour. Rivulets of runoff continued to spill over the escarpment, creating a series of cataracts tumbling down the precipice. "You can sense when an avalanche is imminent. None of you want to find yourselves in close proximity to the cliff at the moment of earthfall."

Anning led them along a tortuous route that lacked an evident destination. Her tedious, meandering course reminded Balfour of a wretched drunkard wandering the streets of Pimlico, a district of London noted for its brick pits and its alehouses. Despite the aimlessness of Anning's progress, none of the Pickmanites questioned her leadership: She advanced with such poise and certitude that they entrusted their fate to her as she escorted them ever closer to the cliffs at the back of the beach.

"Here." Anning stopped suddenly, holding out a hand to caution her guests. Before her, a great crag projected from the pebble beach, its height and bulk and curious configuration reminiscent of certain dolmens scattered across the English countryside - though this formation was more colossal in scope. "This is where I found the structure."

"I fear this may have been an unnecessary sojourn, Clifford," Cartwright said, quickly concluding that Anning had been mistaken in her assessment. "This is nothing more than a common scarp, young lady. Just a peculiar bit of chert stone, jutting through the ground, perhaps recently exposed after part of the adjoining cliff collapsed into the surf."

"Give her a moment, Tavish." Balfour had more confidence in Anning than his mentor. "In her letter, she explained that it is not easily perceived by an untrained eye."

"That is correct, sir." Anning presented her hand to Balfour.

"If you would allow me - "

Balfour nodded and took her hand in his. She stepped cautiously as she skirted the crag, searching for the right position from which to view it. As they proceeded, Balfour watched as its contours transformed. Its configuration seemed dependent upon their vantage point, so that each step brought some significant alteration in its silhouette. Then, abruptly, Balfour saw it: an arched temple door, plagued by shadow, beckoning from deep within a slender fissure within the rock. Steps had been carved into the stone along a narrow path that ascended the crevice. The lantern light illuminated archaic symbols along the walls.

"Tavish," Balfour said, gasping. "Tavish: You are going to want to see this. And, I believe you owe Miss Anning an apology."

"Indeed," Cartwright said, his tone now jubilant. He and Wallace quickly joined Balfour at the breach.

Anning refused to enter the natural corridor, alluding to her previous attempt at further exploration which left her unnerved and anxious.

"I simply will not put myself in that position again," she said. "There is something unsettling in that place. You will feel it, too, once the shadows envelop you and the world behind you starts to fade away."

Glyndon volunteered to stay on the beach with Anning, though no one believed his insistence that he only did so to safeguard her. One by one, the Pickmanites entered the slender gap in the rocky protrusion, climbing its polished steps, shifting their bodies into awkward and contorted poses to negotiate the constricted passage. Their lanterns splashed light into cracks and clefts that had gone unseen for countless ages. Their fingers brushed against unfamiliar glyphs that no scholar could begin to decipher. Their eyes surveyed the darkness beyond the temple door, trying to ascertain how such a voluminous sanctuary could be contained within the limited bounds of the outcropping.

"The pathway stretches farther than my cursory assessment projected," Cartwright said, half whispering his growing trepidation to Balfour. "Either some optical illusion is at play, or there are forces at work here that I do not understand."

"No matter which phenomena explains this enigma, it was worth the journey," Balfour said. "And we have yet to see what treasures await us inside the antechamber."

"Treasures?" Wallace, the last in line as they traversed the passage, sounded dismayed. He recognized the symbols etched into the stone. He recognized the stench of an unidentifiable putrescence, its loathsomeness only slightly surpassed by the pungency of seaweed and other marine life that comprised the coastal ecology. He even thought he glimpsed a brief twinkling of uncanny radiance spilling through the arched temple entryway, and perhaps a fleeting echo of discordant voices muttering blasphemous hymns.

"I would not expect treasures in such a place," Wallace said. "I would expect to find something not meant for discovery - something ancient and monstrous."

Before either Balfour or Cartwright could respond to Wallace's pessimism, a more palpable peril confronted them. Overhead, the glimmering stars visible through the narrow fissure disappeared behind an ominous, black mass. Thunder rumbled across the beach, and the crag shook with violent tremors. Realizing what was happening, the men froze in their tracks for a moment before scrambling toward the temple door as fast as their feet would carry them.

Mary Anning screamed the last word they heard as they clambered for shelter. Her warning echoed along the corridor. "Earthfall!"

iv.

The Old Religion

Morning brought Oldfield Godolphin back to the lobby of the Pilot Boat Hotel, though he felt no sense of urgency in greeting the new day. He selected a few items from a bountiful breakfast buffet, engaged in conversation with fellow guests, and inquired about where he might find someone capable of repairing a hole in one of his shoes. Though he made repeated inquiries at the reception desk as to the whereabouts of his colleagues, he found no one able to provide him with an update.

Waiting in the lobby, the historian finally encountered a man of similar age who seemed equally isolated and eager for some distraction to lift him out of boredom. After brief introductions, the two men discovered a shared affinity for folklore.

"I have found these folk to be a superstitious lot," the man told Godolphin. "As beholden to local legends as to any modern church. I believe some of them may secretly embrace pagan gods from some forgotten religion that was practiced before the Romans arrived on these shores."

"You would be surprised at how common that is around Europe," Godolphin assured him. "There are pockets of cultists to be found in any country. Adherents of ancient creeds are as common as crofters who make offerings to fertility deities."

"I am told that the people of Lyme Regis have a unique cycle of stories involving creatures from the sea that emerge from dormancy once or twice each century," he explained. "Even now, their town elders blame recent livestock mutilations and a few unexplained disappearances on these small, amphibious beasts."

"That is very interesting." Godolphin recalled a local legend he had once researched. "This place is not far from Weymouth and Portland, and the perilous banks of Chesil Beach, where locals claim to have found a monstrous finfolk hag washed up and decomposing on the shifting pebbles of the coastline not more than three quarters of a century ago. I'm told there are a few lifelong residents, now at an advanced age, that witnessed that particular horror."

"Perhaps the events are related," the man said in a serious tone. He then laughed, amused by the charm of such unbelievable stories. "Or, perhaps the inhabitants of both locales indulge in the same hallucinogenic toadstools when constructing such tales."

At that moment, Algernon Glyndon burst through the front door of the hotel, covered from head to toe in mud.

"We need help on the beach." His eyes gleamed with panic. His face showed a mix of fatigue and dismay. "People are buried on the beach. Part of Black Ven collapsed. Miss Anning and I escaped, but others are trapped in some kind a rock formation that is now resting beneath the landslide."

"Bloody Balfour and his adventures," Godolphin said, rising to his feet. "How will you get yourself out of this one, old friend?"

As Glyndon rallied rescuers in the street, a thin, genteel-looking man - a man with prodigious bulging eyes - approached the only member of the Pickmanites who had avoided the overnight calamity.

"Mr. Godolphin, a word if I may. I cannot overstate the danger your friends currently face." Joseph Leach spoke with a degree of dramatic intensity that filled the historian with sudden dread. His voice sounded oddly different, deep and sharp, with a strange frog-like croaking underlying each syllable. "They are likely still alive, but they will not survive long given their situation. I believe I can assist you in locating them, if you are willing to do what I ask."

"Of course," Godolphin agreed. "Whatever you need."

"Then follow me, quickly." Leach grabbed two lanterns from behind the reception desk on his way toward the door. "Be aware that our route will take us through a network of underground passages filled with hibernating creatures. Silence is critical. Should we rouse them, none of us will see the light of day again."

Leach led Godolphin down a shadowy cobblestone lane. The edifices in this neighbourhood differed from those elsewhere in Lyme Regis. The dwellings predated the community that had blossomed around them, and centuries of neglect and stagnation hinted at both their antiquity and at the vileness of those who populated the homes. More than disrepair and dereliction maligned this neighbourhood. The very composition and design of each abode contradicted basic architectural motifs and opposed the laws of physics. The geometry employed undermined logic and, if viewed continually over an extended period of time, might destabilize one's grasp on reality.

In a squalid cul-de-sac, they reached some form of depraved

chapel. The morning sun, now climbing toward its midday zenith, failed to dispel vast patches of shadow encircling the house of profane worship. Leach passed through a gate before arriving at a doorway. From his pocket, he plucked a key that fit the lock, giving them access to whatever wickedness held sway within the building. Inside, strange symbols covered the walls from floor to vaulted ceiling.

"I have never seen these markings." Godolphin hesitated for a moment, his eyes searching for a single familiar character that might help him understand their derivation. "How old is this place?"

"It is believed it was here before the Romans came," Leach said. "And the labyrinth below is far older." Leach arrived at a trapdoor in the floor of the chapel, sealed with a heavy bolt. He slid the bolt aside and used a winch to roll back a chain, opening the access point just enough to reveal a series of steps leading down into darkness. "We must move quickly. They will stir at nightfall, but they sometimes leave watchers to guard their nests."

"Who lives in this subterranean world?" Godolphin took the lantern and reluctantly peered down into the cavern. "What are these creatures?"

"The remnants of an old civilization," Leach said. "Their merchants once engaged in commerce at trading posts in the subterranean realm of K'n-yan, and with scrounging exiles ejected from Y'ha-nthlei and Y'lu-Y'loa. Their explorers once catalogued the black idols of Tsathoggua found buried in grim caverns of N'kai. Their diplomats once decreed an alliance with distant Mnar, long before the fall of that empire's famed capital."

"I have not heard of any of these kingdoms," Godolphin said.

"From what source have you learned of their history?"

"They existed before our eldest ancestors had developed the tools and the skills to communicate, much less record history," Leach said. "We are left only with the scraps of their documents, most of which remain undeciphered. That - and the brutish inheritors of their legacy, perverted by millennia of inescapable disease and degeneracy."

"And this place?"

"This place serves to keep them confined to their fetid underworld," Leach said. "The earliest settlers of this land built this shrine, both to imprison them and to furnish them with sustenance by making ritual offerings from time to time. Over the centuries, their custodianship somehow deteriorated into shameless worship. Instead of fish or poultry, the zealots began throwing their own children into the pit."

"And the townsfolk did nothing to stop this madness?"

"Other than the families that live on this street, the residents of Lyme Regis have no knowledge of this abomination," Leach said. "They refuse to see it - just as so many people in your great city turn their gaze from ubiquitous scenes of poverty, intolerance, and cruelty." Leach began descending the steps into the darkness. "Come with me, and keep quiet. If my memory of this warren is intact, I should be able to find your friends - assuming the creatures have not already claimed them as their next meal."

Having been entombed in the temple following a landslide, it only took the Pickmanites a few minutes to come to a consensus on the best course of action. Clifford Balfour and Roland Wallace agreed that it might take days - if not weeks - for the residents of Lyme Regis to remove the debris and reach them. None of them knew for certain that Mary Anning and Algernon Glyndon had even survived the calamity, or that they were in any condition to make the return hike back to the town and raise an alarm.

"We may well die in this sepulchre, fellow travellers." Balfour maintained his characteristic composure, unruffled by the disastrous event that might bring about their doom. "If death is fast approaching, at least I have an interesting milieu to explore as I await it."

"Always eager to put your quest for knowledge above self-preservation," Cartwright said, chiding his friend. "Although I will agree that this discovery is unparalleled. Still, I should inform you that if I do die here, I intend to return as a spirit and haunt your family members as retribution."

The Pickmanites shared three lanterns, each with a limited span of usefulness. They possessed neither food nor water. They had unlimited time, assuming the air within the chamber did not grow too thin or foul to breathe, and they found they had much to explore.

From the temple's antechamber, a long corridor stretched into infinite darkness. Its direction suggested that it followed a linear path inland, beneath Black Ven and back toward Lyme Regis. The passage's low ceiling meant they had to bend at the knees and proceed cautiously, but the possibility of additional access points scattered amidst the Dorsetshire landscape gave them some amount of hope.

"Imagine how long it has been since men have wandered this passage," Balfour said as he stared down the corridor. His lantern light failed to expose any immediate revelations. Its radiance seemed to infuriate the clustered shadows, and they mustered in the distance as if preparing to repel any attempt at incursion. "Shall we conduct what may be our final investigation?"

"Let me go first," Wallace said, stepping into the corridor. "I have seen tunnels like this before, in coastal villages in Ceylon. I have an idea of what may populate this grotto." He stooped low, holding his lantern before him. "If I am correct, then it is entirely possible that men have never set foot in this place."

Joseph Leach and Oldfield Godolphin maintained as brisk a pace as the elderly Pickmanite could endure, though even now his legs ached and his lungs burned. At Leach's insistence, they did not deviate from the main corridor, though countless spur trails branched off at regular intervals on either side. At times when they came upon a fork in the path, Godolphin could not understand why Leach chose one over the other. He could discern no difference between any two channels.

Godolphin glanced down one or two of the smaller tributaries, scanning as much of those passages as his lantern light illuminated. He saw clear evidence of predation in the form of animal bones picked clean of flesh and meat. He saw foul pools of filth in spaces that may have been designated as communal latrines. He saw signs of perpetual tenancy, as though countless generations had come and gone, gradually declining from their civilization's peak in the distant past into the perverted, parasitic clan of savages that persisted only because of the misguided veneration of an ancient cult. He saw along the route countless objects crowded into inexplicable burrows: elongated, oval-shaped, blue-green formations that seemed too numerous and too uniform to be geologic anomalies.

And Godolphin saw the creatures, too - in a myriad of malodorous lairs scattered along the corridor, each horror curled in upon itself in an embryonic affectation, their slimy bodies twitching as they dreamed of unspeakable excesses and violence, their three-toed feet jutting into the air, their hideous faces twisted into appalling veneers that blended ferocity with unintended innocence. Something about their descent into uncultured barbarism made Godolphin suddenly feel sorry for them. In their slumber, he saw traces of simplicity and naiveté, and of forgotten grace and decency.

In that instant, he questioned whether humanity might be equally inclined to eventually lapse back into uncivilized brutishness.

"I see a light in the distance," Leach whispered. He slowed his gait and thrust a hand against Godolphin's chest to bring him to a halt. "Yes, it must be your friends."

"They must see us," Godolphin said, smiling. "They seem to be hurrying to reach us."

Both men suddenly realized that it was not in recognition of their salvation that they made haste: They were being pursued. Cartwright, Balfour, and Wallace raced down the length of the corridor, grunting and gasping for air, their lanterns swinging wildly and frequently crashing into the walls. Each sound stirred more creatures from their slumber, adding to the number of predators scrambling to catch their prey. When conscious, these mindless beasts thought of nothing other than filling their bellies. Hunger drove them to madness, leaving no room for thought of strategy or cunning. That attribute gave the

Pickmanites a fair chance at eluding them. But as more and more creatures joined the pursuit, the good fortune of those being hunted diminished.

Wallace felt one at his heels. He spun around and pounded his fist into the thing's chest. He felt its brittle bones snap upon impact, and it uttered an awful squeal as it fell to the floor. Immediately, half a dozen of its cannibalistic brethren surrounded it, tearing it apart even as it continued to howl. The things ripped its limbs from its small body as others snapped at its head, its neck, and its torso. Within seconds, its final cries subsided, and the ravenous beasts had all but devoured it.

Realising that the others could be delayed if presented with a corpse, Wallace grabbed two of the creatures and shoved them headfirst into the wall, causing their skulls to burst. He tossed them at the oncoming horde before resuming his flight.

By the time the Pickmanites reached Leach and Godolphin, the creatures had encircled the small party. They lingered along the periphery of lantern light, desperate to satiate their hunger but hesitant leave the sanctuary of shadow, even for a moment.

"They will not approach," Leach said. "The light prevents them from doing so, for now."

"These lanterns will not last forever," Cartwright said. "If you have any thoughts on how we can escape this catacomb, now would be a good time to share them."

"We walk," Leach said. "Slowly, carefully, we walk down the corridor, remaining in a circle, holding our lanterns aloft, maintaining this pocket of illumination. I will lead us back to Lyme Regis - if they will allow it."

"If you are capable of such a feat, we will all be indebted to you, Mr. Leach," Balfour said. "But these corridors form a formidable maze. I cannot imagine how you will find your way out this place."

"These corridors are etched into my memory, Mr. Balfour, because I once dwelled in amongst them." Leach kneeled and removed his shoes. He displayed his misshapen, three-toed feet, which matched those of the creatures. "I was a born into this nightmare, along with many other unfortunate people that live in an isolated neighbourhood of Lyme Regis. These creatures are our shame, our remote past, and - sadly - our family."

Upon recognizing Leach as a distant relative, the creatures receded slightly into the shadows, though they did not entirely abandon their hopes of picking one or more of the outsiders from the group as a luscious repast. They trailed the small party for some time, gradually slipping further into the darkness, until finally, they disappeared altogether.

Leach made good on his promise, delivering the Pickmanites back to the Pilot Boat Hotel, much to the delight of Algernon Glyndon and Mary Anning.

After a celebratory meal and a night of much-needed sleep, Clifford Balfour and his friends prepared for their return to London. Before departing, he visited Anning's Fossil Depot, hoping he could persuade the fossil collector to sell him a few choice pieces from her inventory.

"I apologize for bringing you here and putting you and your friends through such a trial," Anning said. "I am afraid that the town does not possess the manpower or the equipment to excavate the temple."

"I am not certain that it should ever be uncovered again, Miss Anning," Balfour said. "I am not sure it is something that should be brought to the attention of the masses. Its existence may be best left a guarded secret."

"I am surprised a man of science should wish to conceal knowledge." Anning glanced over Balfour's shoulder. "Your cousin is beckoning you."

"He can wait." Balfour directed Anning's attention to the fossils on display in the storefront. "I wonder if you might be willing to part with one of these exquisite pieces, as a memento of my visit."

"I am afraid the flying dragon has already been acquired by another collector in London," she said. "Should I find another, I will give you the opportunity to purchase it before contacting anyone else."

"That is gracious of you, Miss Anning." Balfour eyed the elongated, oval-shaped, blue-green object resting in the wicker basket in the window. "And what about this piece?"

"That is available," Anning said. "And I will let you have it at no cost, if you promise me to make me an honorary member of your little fraternity."

"The committee might not approve." Balfour smiled.

"Which makes me all the more willing to accept your terms. I will see to it as soon as we return to London."

"Thank you, Mr. Balfour. I look forward to meeting you again someday." Anning raised an arm and waved. "Your cousin is growing a bit impatient."

"I think my cousin may be smitten with you."

"His starry-eyed adoration has not escaped my attention," she said. "Sadly, I have little time for romantic entanglements. I have told him this repeatedly."

"I hope he does not bother you so much that you find it

distracting."

"Mr. Balfour: Nothing distracts me from my work."

———————

Tavish Cartwright, still standing, surveyed the room. He surmised that the Pickmanites found his tale as engaging as it was inimitable, but could sense among them an element of bemusement. He anticipated their unspoken queries:

"As mentioned earlier, this account was subject to concealment for more than one year," Cartwright explained. "Last week, Clifford Balfour brought to my attention an internal memorandum issued by the British Museum. It presents an account of an incident involving an unidentified artefact, described as an *elongated, oval-shaped, blue-green object*' the surface of which displayed *swirls and striations* as well as multiple stress fractures. Because it was not part of a current exhibit, the object was secured in the museum's extensive collection area. The memorandum reads:

On the morning of November 17, a museum employee found the object on the floor, shattered. The museum launched a routine investigation to determine how the object - which was housed in a small wooden box - was destroyed.

Though the comments do not appear in the memorandum, Clifford Balfour states that the employee who discovered the object also stated that he observed a trail of crusty, three-toed footprints. He followed the trail into a subbasement in the museum, where they subsequently disappeared..."

*As he poured first a white powder, and
then a night-black one into the bowl, the
apothecary spoke*

GOODBYE, CRUEL WORLD

MIKE SLATER

Jacob Bell strode into the Pickman Club that evening as though he owned that venerable building, and something in his stride forced the august gathering therein to take heed. "At least he's wearing trousers tonight", sneered one worthy to another as the young apothecary passed; but it was not said loudly enough that the subject might hear.

The upstart looked around, greeted a few known close allies, and stood, pharmacist's chest heavy in hand, listening politely to the end of old Cartwright's tale with all appearance that he cared. While the applause of the gathered echoed around the room, Bell the Younger busied himself at the long table full of hors d'oeuvres. Having eaten lightly of the offerings there, he moved with purpose toward the bowl of crimson punch sat like a pool of fresh blood in a squat crystal bowl.

A servant brought a small round table draped in white to the centre of the room. Hodgson the butler, called, "Alec, Joey, see to the chairs," and a pair of serving lads wrestled padded armchairs into near rows arranged in concentric semi-circles around the table. Bell deposited his travelling chest behind the table, and then went back to the long table and its waiting punch bowl. Encircling it with his arms, he lifted it and carried it with careful steps to the small table that was now the very epicentre of the Event. Under Hodgson's watchful and credulous eye, he set it down, like a circus strongman would set down a hefted boulder. Some of the onlookers, already in their cups , almost applauded.

Straightening his vest and tie after his exertion, the master apothecary (at such a young age!) stooped over his chest, which opened upward to sprout four compartments in floating tiers. Each held tiny glass phials, corked in coded colours and bearing powders, waxes, and liquids known only to the owner of the chest. Perhaps another expert chemist could have identified some by sight, but perhaps not.

Bell swiftly plucked one container from each, and placing them with respective flourishes upon the table, he then arranged these at the cardinal points around the punch bowl. Now, reaching to the yawning darkness of the chest's depths, below the floating compartments he grasped something else with a theatrical intake of breath, and held aloft a lump of matter so singular that mutters of speculation immediately rippled about the room.

The light of the crystal chandeliers graced its upper surface with white glintings and streaks. From below, it seemed to gather the sanguine hue of the bowl and its contents.

"There are two of these. They are precious beyond reckoning. Tonight, I share a portion of one of them with each of you!'

Retrieving a syringe of delicate silver and glass, Bell punctured the small object and withdrew some viscous humour that in the weird way it gathered light, seemed to swirl of its own accord. The object, which had looked like an over-firm grape bearing trailings of its stem, deflated a little. This was reverently returned to the depths of the burlwood chest. Onlookers closest in noted the thin trail of strange vapour that followed it down into that darkness.

As he poured first a white powder, and then a night-black one into the bowl, the apothecary spoke.

"I found this, and its twin not far from this very place, as travellings go. Close in distance, but separated by vast gulfs of privilege and propriety! Such is the lot of the scientist. We like to think our work is the staple of immaculate laboratories and the sterile halls of academia or hospital theatres; but as many of you might attest, it is hardly always so. In amazing squalor, exceeded only by the astounding circumstances therein, did I find what I shall share with you tonight so intimately, that any who refuse it should not only have their membership revoked by this august club - but they would themselves surrender it upon hearing the accounts of their fellows after this night!'"

A waxy blob from the third phial, and a coarse umber paste from the last went into the punch. Producing a whisk from inside his vest, Bell the Younger stirred the darkening fluid sternly as he gazed out upon his Pickmanite peers. He took each of them by turn in his furious gaze, prejudging something only he could know. The crowd shifted uncomfortably.

Laying down the whisk on a clean white napkin bordered in lace filigree, he held the syringe above the bowl like some mad priest about to plunge a dagger into the heart of a hapless, bare-chested girl. With slow deliberance, the youthful scientist depressed the contents into the still-swirling mixture. They fell with a strange gravity, almost floating at first as if unwilling to fall - like the held breath of the guests arrayed about the low table and the man who presided over it. Then, in some strange preservation of momentum and Newtonian requirement, they accelerated downward to smash thunderously into the red cyclone below them. Some of the the gathered looked at the windows for corroborating bolts of lightning, but there were none. The viscous stuff tore itself apart and dissolved instantly into the, quite literally, doctored punch.

Barelworth shouted, "Surely you don't expect us to drink that, do you Bell?"

Like clockwork automatons, the boys appeared once more, with tiny crystal goblets in hand, pressing one into each member's grasp. Under strict orders to acknowledge no hesitation or refusal, they boys mutely ensured every man present took one. The last went to Bell himself, who, with something like reverence, dipped it into the churning liquid.

Raising his glass of blood-black elixir in salute, he said, "And now, you shall see what I have seen. You see it by my labour of two years to understand what this is. Live another's life - and thereby, at the end, cherish yours all the more!"

Bell upended the glass into his gullet and swallowed languidly. His eyes fluttering, he sank into the chair placed behind him, as, spellbound, those gathered marched like church-goers to the Eucharist of Sunday Mass to receive their measure, and return to their places to sample the gift of wondrous vision it bestowed. Bell's exhortation about membership still ringing in their brains, to a man, they quaffed that ineffable brew and sank into the arms of their chairs, where they dreamed memories not their own...

The cobblestones were wet and slimy with a variety of hideous fungi, and Archie hated each of them individually, the mouldering spaces between them even more. Greenish-black hairs and filaments reached up out of those spaces, soft-looking but seeking always to pierce his bare filth-encrusted feet and inject their transmogrifying venom. He hurried along, anxious to get himself to the smoother, poured-stone curbs his nimble form could balance on, keeping him floating above the hated cobbles like an angel's feet rejected the touch of base Earth.

His parcel was nestled under his patchwork of shirts, which made him look like some sort of diminutive hunchback, scampering between pools of sulfur-yellow light. Few people went abroad in this neighbourhood after dark, and his friends whispered, not softly, that it was because of his patron. The parcel squirmed in the burlap under his motley attire. Anyone seeing this would have averted their eyes, at the least, if not emptied their gullets, at the appearance of hideous deformation. Would any have been comforted to know it was only a drugged street cur of negligible size stuffed under his tattered clothes? Archibald Noname, as the slumlord who owned the place where he slept called him, thought not, and decided he could afford to hurry on before any explanations became necessary.

His surrounds were exemplary only of the poorest and most squalid places London had to offer. If there was a karmic sewer where human filth flowed on its way to whatever damnation it deserved, this place was the clotted gutter grate where some of it collected for a while before being sluiced out into oblivion by the leaden and spasmodic rains that came too infrequently to cleanse so much detritus.

Violence between strangers was more-or-less given. The best shields were to avoid being seen, or to be so fearsome as to instantly dissuade common predators. Up ahead, the flickering orange light of a dirty, homemade candle beckoned him toward the battered boards of his employer's hovel, a street-level apartment jammed between two even older buildings. Archie suspected it had once been an alley that ran between them, and that Mr. Torvik had wrestled some blocks of stone from the crumbling church abandoned some streets over to make the place. Some of those blocks also had the look and thickness of ruined tombstones, but he had never had the nerve to look for evidence of engravings or embellishments in their surfaces. Scarred and gigantic, old Torvik had then simply laid claim to the place - and none would have gainsaid him.

Casting a quick look over his shoulder at a shadow that should not have moved, Archie rapped quickly on the broken, patched, and re-broken boards of the door, and then let himself in. None without firm business here would dare do such a thing, so he slipped in without waiting for acknowledgement, and closed the makeshift door on the grime and shadow behind him.

Within, amidst the water-stained ceiling, cracked floor of wooden patches, laid stone, and half-disintegrated remains of mismatched rolls of carpet, there was the hospital smell of Death held in abeyance. A near-shapeless mass filled one corner of the appalling room. It had been no less than four mattresses, lashed together with interpenetrating belts of leather and sailcloth. He who slept in it filled the opposite corner of the room, as vertically voluminous as the mattress was haphazardly horizontal. His breathing seemed to empty the room of its foetid air, and then push it back out into every corner and crack, moist and worsened for having given sustenance to its source. Archie stood rigid and silent until the red-rimmed eyes with their cavernous pupils raked across him, and then lowered themselves upon the odd vase held in hands the size of the boy's quivering ribcage.

"You've brought it, or you would not be here," his master said, in a voice like shattered pottery being ground to sand at the bottom of a haunted well.

Archie nodded stiffly, once, and shuffled off his top four shirts. Perhaps together they made one complete shirt, but they'd not been complete for many long months or years. Spinning to catch it, the languidly squirming parcel dropped into his hands. He peeled back the filthy canvas to reveal a dirt-smeared dog, little more than a large rat in size and appearance. Its hair might have once been the tawny colour of port swirling in a rich man's goblet, but it was now the mottled grey and charcoal black of mildew growing in soot.

Only the eyes seemed clean and bright, though the laudanum he'd rubbed on its tattered gums had robbed it of control and volition. Mr. Torvik need not know that the remaining bit he'd not used, had bought him a decent meal of poached fish from the old monger whose only usual non-piscine topic of conversation was the torture his back and feet inflicted upon him. One could easily be forgiven for wondering if the old man thought them parasitically attached imps, that existed only to inflict anguish upon the rest of his wizened and decaying body.

Looking away, he offered the shaking cur to his benefactor, who accepted it in his own massive paw. When he looked back, Mr. Torvik had, himself, turned away, as was tugging one-handed at a stone in the floor that two men could not have moved with both of their hands. The crackle of the smoky fire in the middle of the rear wall that kept the place a tolerable temperature in this London winter, seemed to grow on cue to cover the soft grinding of the moving stone concealing the rough hewn stairs sloughing down to a basement. Archie again wondered how such a thing could have been dug, or how long it would have taken. He had been here before, and down there before, though then he'd been sure it was to be the end of him. But, Mr. Torvik had proven to be good to his Word, and the boy had remained perfectly safe, if somewhat shaken by what he had seen.

The walls, like the steps, were hewn earth, strangely painted with thick white plaster and braced with leaning beams of roughly stripped wood jammed in place with a force that showed in the troughs dragged and battered into the floor and ceiling. These, too, were slathered white with slovenly smeared thick plaster, or perhaps a clay of some sort. The room had a briny smell, and Archie suspected it came from whatever Mr. Torvik had used on the walls and pillars. Perhaps it was dredged from the sea? Sausage-sized finger markings showed that the stuff had been applied and smoothed by hand.

The glass "vase" tucked under the giant's arm turned out to be one half of an artefact whose other component was a series of oddly tinted panes, each a different hue and shape, that fitted over the "vase" components like a shade might fit a lamp. These were assembled and then put aside.

"You've not yet been with a woman, I surmise," rumbled his master. It was not a question, but a statement daring refutation. Archie was somewhat shocked at it, and the idea that for a boy his age, in this age, it could be otherwise.

"N-no, Sir," he stammered. An answering rumble that was probably the only laughter Archie had ever heard from Mr. Torvik ricocheted off the thickly plastered walls for a moment, and then seemed to be drawn thirstily in by them.

"Good, good. Saves a lot of trouble." Archie wasn't sure if he meant presently, or in general, if he was to judge by the moping and angst of some of the older boys and men back at the flop house.

"Use this. Don't let it touch anything else but your flesh. Three drops." Archie's eyes widened at the scar that went all the way around the man's wrist as his hand, holding a stout hatpin upright by the pearl, snaked out of the drooping sleeve of his coat. He took the pin mutely, and steeled himself, driving it into the heel of his other hand as commanded.

Mr. Torvik produced a small, shallow dish of some cloudy, polished glass. A white powder with yellow flecks in it lay in the dimple at its centre, and it was into this that Archie shed three fat drops of his blood.

Snatching the pin back from him with a speed and precision it was difficult to credit to such a behemoth, Mr. Torvik began to stir together the contents of the dish. A kind of smoke or vapour arose from the now greyish paste, and it was then that his master bellowed out three words whose volume and nature hurt Archie's ears.

"Orgth! Korumn! Odhqlonqh!'

With this, he not-ungently pressed between the back teeth of the dog to force open its mouth. Shaking the glass dish over the little thing, a dollop of paste seemed to roll against gravity, hang in space a moment, and then plunge down between the dull yellow pegs of the dog's teeth. Mr. Torvik pinched that mouth shut with two fingers, and blew into the creature's face. With an *ulp*, the dollop went down, and almost instantly, some life seemed to come back into the little dog's limbs. With haste, the beast went face first into the waiting glass apparatus, which turned out to be constructed exactly to admit something this size. Mr. Torvik loaded the now progressively more agitated cur into it like a tiny, shaking cannon ball covered in matted fur and street filth. No wonder he had been so specific, Archie thought.

Already bug-eyed, as was the nature of its kind, the vermin-ridden creature's black orbs seemed to swell like ripening grapes. Likely, it was some magnifying effect of the prismatic glass it now resided behind. Still , it gave the thing the manic aspect of a jungle lizard ever vigilant for both insectile prey, and marauding predators.

It was then that Archie noticed the faintly but meticulously formed figures scratched into the walls. He couldn't read, but he knew what regular letters looked like - and these were nothing of the sort. Each twisting and self-recursive knotted line headed a column or row in a vast sort of chart that covered the central part of each wall. The floor and ceiling bore similar markings, and the giant and the hapless glass-encased terrier were now at the center of all of them, revolving slowly.

As Mr. Torvik's brobdingnagian feet shuffled in circles, he

raised, lowered, and inclined the wretched thing. It yapped madly all the while, but the frenzy of its cantata definitely varied as it was pointed about. Their master seemed to nod and incline his own head as if listening to the changes in pitch as they moved, using the dog-prism apparatus almost like a water witch would use a dowsing rod. Now and then, the pin in his other hand flashed out, and made a mark in one of the columns or rows, his unreasonably long arms putting him in reach of all four walls and the ceiling without causing him to leave the diagram on the floor.

As they moved and the marks multiplied, Archie saw that the space in which they could operate was being steadily constricted and somehow defined by the pattern of marks, as if each became the limit of a new border that could never be re-crossed. Yet the noise from the high-pitched yips of the captive dog seemed to be traversing some cavernous space he could not see. Something about the prism focused and filtered not only light, but also sound; and the sounds were so markedly energetic now, that flashes of lumescence seemed to accompany them within the pulsing, shuddering glass of the strange artefact.

With a whoop of final inhalation, and an exhaled stream of barking yips so fraught with panic that Mr. Torvik stopped, the glass shattered as the nose of both dog and apparatus came to rest at one particular spot in the northwest corner of the room, at the very limit of that wall's eldritch diagram. Excepting its swollen eyes, the little beast seemed to fold inward upon itself, as most of the glass exploded outward in a shining cloud. But the giant was past noticing. With an animal grunt, he reached into the wall at that precise place, made a monstrous fist, and pulled back on something that wasn't there. Archie cried out as part of the world came away, pivoting like some stone block in a secret temple, to open upon...somewhere, wholly, else.

"What is that? What IS that?!" he heard himself shrieking. The voice was distorted, and he was unaware of consciously forming the words or willing them to be released into the shuddering air. His lungs burned with the effort of forcing words through air too thick to be gaseous, and cold too dire to be Earthly.

Shedding the heavy coat and threadbare shirt beneath to reveal a massive, and massively scarred torso that seemed composed more of sutures than plain flesh, Mr. Torvik shook the blood from his stovepipe forearm, grinned raggedly and said, through the gale from another world, "Cykranosh? Umnahquah? It matters not. A place where neither my nature nor my provenance have meaning to anyone else."

Heaving a great sigh at the motionless boy, the formidable architect of this fantastical tableau growled, "Are you coming?"

Archie looked back up the earthen staircase. He could feel London's cold breath sighing into the room, closing its fist around the little fire. He thought of his empty belly, empty prospects, and the bruises around his ribs and shoulders, earned defending the stump of discarded roast that was to have been his first dinner in days. The lamp device lay at his feet. Two quivering orbs that had absorbed all the wild thoughts and events of the evening clung to a few shards of the shattered panes, gluing them together and seeming to fix him with horrid accusation. With a shiver, he followed the Monster into the hole they'd made in the world, into the searing cold that burned his skin in the transition to a place with a red sky and silver mountains like perfect pyramids that savaged the bloody heavens...

It was nearly thirty minutes between the ending of the vision and when the first of the Pickmanites stirred in his dream throne. Perhaps inured by previous experience, or simply owing to his youthful constitution, Bell roused first. Hodgson and his squadron of lads stood guardian over them all, at a respectful distance. Their discipline was astounding, given the fact that they were all likely one-time urchins no better than the boy of the vision.

There was no languor or other stupefaction associated with wakening from some surfeit of wine or laudanum. They came alert within moments of each other, and their limbs obeyed their commands almost as soon as their eyes finally focused on the recessed alabaster ceiling tiles above. Immediately they fell to amazed and urgent conversation. Each a luminary of fields of various sciences, they agreed quickly that somehow they had all experienced the same life-fragment of another soul. Bell gazed out over them like some chirurgeon watching a crippled patient rise and walk for the first time. He was silent, but the suppressed smirk that thinned his lips even further, told any who glanced at him that the chemist prodigy was extremely well-pleased with himself.

No one spoke directly to Bell. By his order, the crystal bowl was set before him by the butler, and later he was brought a series of metallic camp decanters in which to pour the contents. A particularly brave boy approached at one point as asked if he might remove the bowl and its residue, but Bell half-playfully, half-sternly slapped him away, jealous of even those precious drops, which he then sopped up with his napkin. Perhaps he feared what would happen to an unsupervised administration of even the smallest amount of his arcane elixir. Perhaps he was afraid some rival would use it to his own advantage and fame.

We do not know, as he spoke no further word that evening, but only smiled when Mr. Pickman rose suddenly from his chair at one point, slapped his thigh, and shouted in revelation. "That's what happened to that devil! I knew our good Captain Walton should have been sure it went into the ice!"

*Once prepared, I sat cross-legged in the
centre of the circle, drained the glass,
and waited for the drug to take effect*

THE HUNTERS
OF THE HIGHWAY

TIM MENDEES

"It is our melancholy duty to record another most woeful calamity, in which a whole family has been again most savagely butchered!" -The Star, 20th December 1811

"I fear it is my duty," Thorndike began, "to inform my fellow Pickmanites of the unfortunate passing of one George Mulgrave, reporter of *The Star* newspaper, delver into the outré and uncanny, and fellow member of The Pickman Club."

He reached for a steadying gulp of brandy and fidgeted nervously in his wing-back chair. "I had occasion to run into him not three nights since and have learned this very morning, through a mutual acquaintance, that he has been brutally shaken from his mortal coil."

A low murmur spread through the assembled members of the club. Thorndike raised a hand for silence. "I can report that he was in, shall we say, a disordered state of mind when last we spoke. A series of murders in Wapping, which you will have no doubt read about in the papers, had him in a state of severe agitation. You see, honoured guests, Mulgrave believed that he had hit upon the solution, not only to these crimes but several others. One of which is somewhat notorious, I'm given to understand. In an effort to quiet his agitated soul, I stayed with him throughout the evening of the seventeenth and listened to his monstrous tale unfold. He had me take voluminous notes in case any misfortune may beset him. In light of the morning's disquieting news, I can't help but wonder if the poor fellow had received a premonition or had otherwise gleaned some prior knowledge pertaining to his ultimate fate. As you will see, this is far from being out of the question... if the deceased is to be believed, that is. In any case, I have spent the morning ordering his somewhat fragmentary delivery into a cohesive narrative for your dubious delectation.

Before I begin, however, I have news of the inquest should any of you wish to accompany me. I took the liberty of paying a visit to the coroner, a passing acquaintance, being in a similar line of work to myself, and he informed me that it will take place three days hence at The Pear Tree public house in Wapping. An ironic decision, as I'm sure you will agree in due course. Very well, if everybody is ready, I will begin. Here is the terrible tale of George Mulgrave..."

Keeping out of sight, George peered through the filthy plate glass window at the rear of number eleven Ratcliff Highway, his square graphite pencil scratching out what he could see on his notepad. The chill December air cut through his threadbare overcoat, chilling him to the bone. It took a supreme effort of will just to stop his teeth from chattering and betraying his presence to those he spied upon. The room beyond was lit by the dim lambency of a guttering candle that cast looming shadows over the scene... and what a scene it was.

The window looked out over the squalid shop-front belonging to a purveyor of cats' meat. Various acquisitions from the nearby knackers yard hung on rusty hooks above a deeply-scarred chopping block and an assortment of boning knives and cleavers. The single glassy eye remaining in the rotting skull of a decapitated mare hanging inches from the window peered out at the observer sending waves of nausea through his slight frame. Towards the centre of the room, next to a wooden basket lined with newspaper and filled with festering horse meat, lay the body of a middle-aged man. Above him stood an older gentleman with a lustrous silver moustache and a nauseous-looking member of The Thames River Police.

As the dapper gentleman began to speak, George pressed his ear to a crack in the window frame. "Christ, what a mess," the man took a handkerchief from his pocket and dabbed his lips, "what time were the bodies discovered?"

Bodies? Plural? George's mind raced and his pencil risked catching fire as his furious scribbling intensified.

The constable shuffled nervously, "I ain't sure, Mr Capper, about an hour ago, I reckon. The charwoman, Miss Lloyd, found them when she came to do for the family around six. I reckon it would 'ave taken her a few minutes to find the night watchman. He was in 'is cups again..."

Mr Capper, the magistrate for the borough of Wapping, cursed under his breath and produced a gleaming fob watch from his jacket. "Everything's how you found it?"

"Aye, I ain't touched nothing."

Wincing at the double negative, Capper crouched to get a better look at the victim. The crumpled ruin of humanity lay in an undignified heap. The man's face contorted in fear and his skull split. There was a laceration that had severed the carotid artery but it was oddly bloodless. Capper sighed and shook his head, it was all too familiar. "Are the others the same?"

"More or less."

"How many?"

"Seven in total, sir. This poor bugger, his wife and two sons, and a lodger by the name of Jessop, an artist, and his nude model, a local unfortunate by the name of Mary."

Seven! Good Lord above... George's pencil worked so quickly that it nearly shredded the paper. The situation had a ring of *deja-vu* about it that he couldn't yet discern.

Capper nodded curtly as if his suspicions had been confirmed and once again retrieved his handkerchief from his breast pocket. This time, he folded it into a square and pressed it to the deceased man's chest. As the policeman raised an eyebrow, he palmed the cloth, stood and turned his back before taking a look. Neither George nor the puzzled constable could see what was on the cloth, but the stream of invective that spilt from Capper's maw told them that it was what the magistrate had expected to find... and it wasn't good.

"What is it, what did you find?"

Capper turned sharply and snapped, "never you mind. Go and see if the coroner has arrived, and not a word of this to anyone, understand? If the papers get wind of this there will be pandemonium."

George couldn't help but smirk. The constable muttered assent and left via the street door, no doubt relieved to get some fresh air after the noisome odour of the squalid dwelling. Capper crouched again and gently lifted the victim's head.

George couldn't see from his angle but the grimace of revulsion that passed over the magistrate's face told him all he needed to know. Raising and moving over to the counter, Capper examined the edge and nodded silently to himself. Moments later, the door opened and a portly gentleman with mighty mutton chops clad all in black entered. George recognised him instantly, it was the coroner, John Wright Unwin.

"Robert," Unwin nodded, removing his wide-brimmed hat, "We don't often see magistrates at crime scenes, scared of dirtying your finery, I'd wager, it must be bad. I'd say it was good to see you but under the circumstances... Are they the same as the others?"

Capper nodded. "Eight years to the day, and before that..."

"You need not remind me, I assure you, I remember well our first meeting. The scenes are etched into my mind. As I recall, it was but four doors down."

"The Marr family, yes," Capper led Unwin around the basket of meat towards the body. "The wounds are consistent, I'm sure you will agree. The back of his head is mush. I think the poor chap was knocked back as if pounced upon, and struck his head on the counter. As to the cause of death, I'll leave that to you."

"I was told there were multiple victims?"

"Seven in total."

Unwin crossed himself. "So, we are due one more," he muttered darkly.

George frowned as his mind raced. One more?

"The others, have they been dispatched in the same manner?" Unwin asked.

"I have not as yet had time to examine them. I was on my

way up there now. From what the River Policeman who discovered the slaughter said... yes, I'm afraid so."

"Then, it is as we feared."

"One more thing. I found this on the deceased man's clothes." Capper took out his hankie and showed it to Unwin. They turned and stepped towards the street-level window to get better light. George cursed silently. Again, he couldn't see what had been discovered. To make matters worse, the two men were whispering and he could no longer hear what was being said. He had been lip-reading to fill in the blanks. Clearly, what they discussed was of import due to the animated gesticulations.

George repositioned himself, moving his ear from the frame to the glass. Unfortunately, the pane was loose and rattled against the worm-eaten wood. Instantly, Capper snapped his head around and spat an oath. "Blast it! Someone's lurking in the yard," snatching up a meat mallet that had been sitting next to a pile of festering offal, he swept towards the rear door. Taking to his heels, George raced to the rear of the yard and hopped the fence.

Dashing over an expanse of waste ground separating the backs of the Highway dwellings from those of a parallel street, George ducked through an alley and onto a narrow lane. Turning left back onto Ratcliff Highway, he quickly crossed and took another alley leading to the churchyard of St Georges in the East. After checking that he hadn't been followed, though he was certain the ageing magistrate would have been instantly stymied by the fence, he found a quiet place to catch his breath.

As the low-lying fog that had rolled in off the river coiled around his ankles, George took out his, now crumpled, notebook and tried to process what he had overheard. Though colloquially known as a pea-souper, this close to the river the miasma lost its greenish tinge and more closely recalled his landlady's lukewarm porridge oats that he had forced down over breakfast. This memory, coupled with the grisly details in his notes, made his stomach churn.

Seven victims, he mulled over and over, seven victims and due one more? *What did they mean, due one more? They mentioned two previous cases, one eight years ago and another. He mentioned a name, Marr, wasn't it? That rings a bell.*

His internal monologue was silenced by the striking of the church bells. The hollow notes reverberated through his frigid bones. One thing was for certain, there was a story here, a big one. The sort of story that a chap could build a reputation upon. He needed more information. Details on this latest atrocity shouldn't be too hard to come by. He had a friend of a friend that worked at the mortuary, his information was always well worth a shilling and there was always a Runner or two with alcohol-loosened lips in the local alehouses if one knew where to look. What he really needed was information about these prior incidents. After a brief deliberation, he figured that his editor would be as good a place as any to start and he knew which pub he would be in at lunchtime. He had plenty of time to walk the two miles to The Tipperary on Fleet Street.

Taking the northern exit from the churchyard onto Cable Street, George started to amble in a Westerly direction. He had only gone a handful of yards when he heard a commotion followed by the clatter of a watchman's rattle. Quickening his pace towards the crossroads where Cannon and Cable Streets intersected, he squinted to see what was happening. Through the ever-increasing gloom, he could see four men engaged in a scuffle in the centre of the crossroads. Two shabbily-dressed men armed with shovels were standing off against two less-than-burly watchmen.

Coming to a halt next to the oyster shop on the corner, George was just in time to see one of the watchmen walloped over the head with a digging implement. As he dropped like a sack of potatoes, the two miscreants took flight and disappeared towards the docks. As the upright watchman tended to his fellow, George sidled up to a match-girl that was loitering on the corner.

"What in God's name was that all about?" he asked, dropping a farthing into her grubby paw.

Shrugging as she smiled through the grime, the young urchin passed him a box of Lucifers. "Bloody ghouls, sir."

"Pardon?"

"Ghouls. Grave-robbers."

"I'm afraid, I don't catch your meaning, Miss. This is far from being a graveyard."

"That's where yer wrong, mister. I've 'eard it said that there's a man buried at this 'ere crossroads. A right rotter. Murderer, or some such. I 'eard those two roughs sayin' that Williams was up to his old tricks down on the Ratcliff Highway and they wanted to make sure he was still down there. They stared trying to dig up the bones. Mad as March hares, if you ask me, sir."

"Thank you, miss," George passed her another coin before departing.

As he continued towards his destination, he took out his notebook once more and scribbled down the name, Williams... After shovelling an oyster into his maw, Alfie Budnery, the portly editor of *The Star* newspaper, wiped his mouth on the back of his hand and took a gulp of porter to wash it down.

"Sounds like a right old production you've discovered, George, my boy," he grinned after a mighty belch, "so it begs the question, why are you here bending my ear and not out there interviewing the players?"

George's nose wrinkled as the pungent aroma of masticated seafood and sour beer reached his nostrils. "I wanted to ask you some questions. Mr Capper mentioned something about a case on or near The Highway exactly eight years ago."

Alfie thought for a moment, scratching his mutton chops. "Eight years, let me see. Ah, yes, he was probably talking about the incident at Walpole and Son's."

"The shipping company down at the new dock?"

"Aye. Nasty business. There was some kind of accident. As I recall, a winch broke free from its mooring, eight men were mangled by a falling consignment of plough blades... messy. At least, that's the official version."

"Oh? You think there was more to it?"

"I know there was. One of my boys, a young lad like yourself, talked to the poor sod that stumbled across the carnage. He reckons that there was no sign of any fallen anything, just a bunch of men with their throats slit and heads bashed in. He wrote up the story but your man, Mr Capper, put his foot down. Sequestered the lot. Made him write up the accident story and threatened to lock him up on a charge of sheep molestation if he didn't keep mum. He left town shortly after. Said he felt like he was being followed."

"By the police?"

"Maybe, he didn't say. Personally, I reckon it was all in his head. The man was an arsenic eater, so take his testimony with a pinch of salt."

"Did he tell you anything else about it?"

"Only that the bodies were covered in some sort of slime. As I say... pinch of salt."

Silence fell over the corner table of The Tipperary as Alfie continued eating and George jotted notes. His mind was mulling over the alleged slime. Is that what Capper found on the cat's meat vendor's clothes? Finally, George continued his questioning. "Capper mentioned another case, something about a house four doors down. Something to do with someone named Marr?"

Alfie nearly choked. "Bless my soul, Mulgrave, have you been living under a rock these past fifteen years?"

"Fifteen years ago, I'd have been but three years of age, Mr Budnery."

Alfie chuckled, "a mere whipper-snapper! Still, you must have heard about the Ratcliff Highway murders of 1811?"

"Vaguely. What can you tell me about them?"

"Well, fifteen years is a long time... but you don't need me to tell you about it. You can read all about them in Blackwood's Magazine. I assume you've heard of Thomas De Quincey?"

"The opium eater?"

"The very same. He recently had a satirical essay appear in that austere publication. *On Murder Considered as one of the Fine Arts*, I believe it was called. Caused quite a bit of a stink in polite society."

George beamed, "Marvellous. Do you know where I can lay my hands on a copy?"

"I can do better than that, dear boy. I happen to know that, right this minute, Mr De Quincey is over the road at The Olde Cheshire Cheese, smothering a parrot with Coleridge and Lamb. Freddy Fotheringhay has just finished interviewing Lamb about *The Pawnbroker's Daughter*. He mentioned that the other two were with him and that the absinthe was flowing like water. I think the poor chap was somewhat out of his depth. If he doesn't buck up his ideas sharpish, I'll put him back on agriculture where he belongs. If you get a move on, you'll be able to hear it from the horse's mouth before they end up insensible."

"I'll go over there this instant," George shot from his seat like he'd sat on a wasp and shook Alfie's hand, rather over-enthusiastically, "thank you!"

"Don't mention it, just get a good story out of it. I'm counting on you, George!" Alfie called out as George navigated the tables on the way to the door. As the door closed behind his exuberant employee, he shook his head in amusement and returned to his plate of steamed molluscs...

While The Tipperary had been calm and subdued, The Olde Cheshire Cheese was a bustling hive of revelry, despite the sun not being long over the yardarm. Its surprisingly large interior was a labyrinth of oak panels dividing dark rooms and shadowy booths that harboured all manner of citizens in varying degrees of intoxication and debauchery. George had been prepared to check each and every nook and cranny in search of his quarry, but, as it happened, Thomas De Quincey proved to be an easy chap to locate.

Holding court on a large central table in the main bar area, De Quincey and his two companions had been joined by several other poetic and literary types. He was in the process of ordering more wine for the table by bellowing from a standing position behind his chair at the harassed-looking landlord when George arrived. Though he had never seen so much as a picture of the man, he knew instantly that it was him that he sought. Skirting the table to avoid the more inebriated of the party, he hoved in on De Quincey before he could resume sitting.

"Mr De Quincey? I wonder if I could have a moment of your time?"

De Quincey waved a hand airily. "Make it quick, dear boy, and call me Thomas, only the worst kind of prig calls me Mr De Quincey. You're not a prig, are you, Mr..?

Thinking fast, George spotted the trap set out before him. "George," he answered with a smirk. "I don't consider myself a prig, no."

Thomas roared with laughter and clapped George firmly on the shoulder. "Bravo, young George. You would scarcely believe the number of slow-witted fellows I have ensnared with that one. I feel it my duty to keep the self-righteous, sober, and stupid away from intellectual gatherings such as this. Now, what can I assist you with?" He looked George up and down. "Newspaper man, eh? One of Budnery's Boys, I'd wager?"

George nodded.

"Well, keep it quick. I can't have gutter-sniffers such as yourself impeding my date with oblivion."

"Um," George shuffled nervously and cleared his throat before looking at the larger-than-life character in his bloodshot eyes. "It's about the essay you recently printed in Blackwood's magazine."

Thomas smirked and opened his mouth to deliver a sermon
on his narrow-minded critics, but George, wisely, cut him off. "More specifically, I'm looking for information on one of the cases you mentioned.

"Go on..."

"Specifically, the Ratcliff Highway murders of 1811."

Thomas De Quincey's smirk twisted into something more unsettling. "Ah, a connoisseur, I see. Come," he steered George to a corner booth and thrust a glass of wine into his hand, "I do not wish to sour my companions' drinks with talk of John Williams and his alleged crimes."

George hadn't even had time to extract his pencil, and already things were getting interesting. "Alleged? You don't believe he was the culprit?"

Thomas shrugged, "he never stood trial, therefore is innocent in the eyes of the law."

"There's more to it than that, I can tell."

"You're a shrewd one, George, and no mistake. First, let me ask you this, what is your interest in such a macabre episode?"

George thought about lying, of spinning a yarn about an editorial, but decided against it. A man such as Thomas De Quincey would have seen through such an unsophisticated ruse.

"There have been similar murders, four doors along from The Marr residence."

"Ah, I see."

"I overheard the magistrate, Mr Capper, talking to a coroner by the name of Unwin. It appears they think there is some connection."

"Overheard?" De Quincey winked. "Capper and Unwin, eh? The dour duo reunited. Very interesting. Capper rarely comes down from his ivory tower, so there must be something in what you say," he took a draft of red wine and stretched, feigning tiredness. "So, what is it you want from me?"

"I wonder, could you give me a brief outline of the events of 1811? If I can compare them to what I know about the recent case, and another, I may be able to weave the threads together."

De Quincey's face darkened. "Another?" He stroked his whiskerless chin for a moment. George couldn't tell if he was trying to remember or weighing up whether to reveal his knowledge. "Ah, the warehouse..."

"You know about that?"

De Quincey held up his hand. "So many questions, so little time, I fear. Yes, I will tell you about those dark December nights, if you promise to keep your lips buttoned until I am done, do we have an agreement?"

Knowing De Quincey's penchant for tricks and traps, George didn't speak. Instead, he simply nodded his head.

"Very well... The horrors began just after midnight on the seventh of December 1811. 29 Ratcliff Highway was home to a draper by the name of Thomas Marr, his wife, Celia, and their infant son, also named Thomas. Also present was Marr's young apprentice, James Gowan. As they were finishing for the day, Marr sent his maid, Margaret, out to buy some oysters for supper and to drop a payment in at the nearby baker's. This she did with all haste, but became delayed by around twenty minutes at the bakers and missed the oyster shop closing. Fearing a scolding, she returned to the Marr residence with lead feet and a heavy heart.

Upon arriving, she instantly felt a prickle of unease. The door was bolted and the light extinguished. Fearing she had become locked out, she set about hammering on the door. This, in something of a minor miracle, aroused the night watchman from his drunken slumber. He came and joined Margaret and noticed that, while closed in haste, the shutters hadn't been bolted. Sharing the maid's unease, he joined in trying to rouse the family.

All this commotion roused a neighbour who hopped the fence and discovered the back door ajar. Cautiously entering the eerily silent abode, he discovered sights that will, I have no doubt, give him nightmares for the rest of his life. Marr, Celia, and James had all been brutally dispatched. Throats were torn and craniums smashed. The very walls were plastered with fragments of skull and brain. This, it turns out, paled in comparison to what lay above...

This neighbour, Mr Murray was his name, let the watchman in and together they went to check the upper floor. I won't linger on the grisly details. Let's just say that the baby's crib was covered in blood... or so Mr Capper's statement at the inquest states. Poor Thomas, a mere babe a few weeks old, had been exterminated in the same manner as his parents."

"Good Lord, how abominable."

"Quite. You see now, George, why the case is so well remembered."

George nodded, all the colour drained from his pinched cheeks.

"The horrors didn't end there, however. Twelve days later, on the eleventh of December, another property was targeted and its occupants dispatched. This time, it occurred at a public house just off The Highway on New Gravel Lane, The King's Head, you know it?"

"I do. I passed it this very morning."

"Then you know it isn't far from the Marr residence. The two crimes were so similar and their proximity meant that the collective force of magistrates, parish constables, river police and Bow Street Runners, who had until that point been capering all over Wapping like headless chickens, had no choice but to connect them. As you will see, the similarities are striking.

A parish constable doing his rounds heard a cry of 'Murder' as he turned into the street and was nearly struck dumb by the sight of a near naked man descending from the upper floor of the hostelry using a rope hastily fashioned from knotted bed sheets. As he dropped to the street, the constable approached and asked him what in God's name he was doing. The man, John Turner, explained that he was a lodger at the establishment and had heard a struggle followed by the anguished cries of his landlord. Fearing for his life, he had fled via his only escape route, the window.

By now, a crowd had formed and forced their way into the pub in an attempt to nab the miscreant responsible. Their attempt proved fruitless. All they found were the lifeless bodies of the landlord, John Williamson, his wife, Elizabeth, and their servant, Bridget. As luck would have it, their granddaughter was asleep in one of the rooms on the top floor of the two-storey building. Her distance from the bar, no doubt, saved her life. It appears that the attacker was unaware of her presence. As you would imagine, there was uproar. The public demanded action.

As it so happens, earlier that day, Capper and his merry band had hit upon what they considered a breakthrough. At the scene of the Marr atrocity, they had discovered a ship's maul that the maid didn't recognise. Being a heavy implement, the investigators put two and two together to make five and declared that this was what had been used to bludgeon the unfortunate draper and his fellow departed. The fact that there was grey matter on the edges of the counters and walls seems to have slipped their notice. In any case, the suspected murder weapon provided them with a clue. The handle had the owner's initials carved into it.

Faced with a fresh slew of bodies to clutter up the mortuary, Capper set out to find the owner of the maul. Unfortunately, the tool's owner, a sailor by the name of John Peterson, was away at sea that very moment and had been since before the Marr attack. Undaunted, they traced Peterson to his lodgings at The Pear Tree public house and found his sea chest. According to a friend of Peterson's, the chest was missing said maul.

Again leaping to the most convenient solution, they quickly focused their suspicions upon another lodger, John Williams. The case was slim, to say the least, and hung on access to the postulated murder weapon, the fact that he had money after the Marr killings but not before, that his shirt was bloodied, and that he was a friend of Thomas Marr. Despite the paucity of evidence, the fair-haired fellow was duly arrested and taken to Clerkenwell Gaol."

As De Quincey paused to wet his lips with a full-bodied red, George frowned at his notes. "That's seven, Capper said eight. Where's the final victim."

"Ah," De Quincey reclined in his seat, tapping his nose with his forefinger. "That's the big question, isn't it? You see, Mr Williams allegedly hanged himself on the twenty-eighth. It was the fact that Capper considers Williams to be another victim of the true killer that first sent me on my own investigation."

"Then, you also believe he was innocent?"

"Alas, I cannot say with certainty, I lacked the courage to take the final leap, but I would have to say... Yes."

George frowned, De Quincey's strange aside had caught him off-guard. He opened his mouth to question but was silenced by a raised hand.

"First, allow me to refute the so-called evidence. The maul, one could reason, if one were inclined, could have been lent to Marr by Williams for some household task. The fact that the maid didn't recognise it is neither here nor there. The fact that Williams had borrowed it, can be explained away by this supposition. Perhaps Marr had asked his friend if he had a suitable tool for effecting repairs? The money and the bloodied shirt? Williams claimed to have won the money in a game of cards which then turned violent. As the man was a notorious gambler, this is also likely. That doesn't leave them with much now, does it?"

"Slim pickings, I have to agree."

"Well put, George, I fear your talents are wasted on a rag

such as *The Star*."

George shrugged off this praise for fear of blushing. "You made your own investigations?"

"Of course! I kept my findings out of my essay, you understand? Though the essay was satire, I deemed it prudent to stick to the official version for fear of ridicule. It doesn't do for one such as I to stray from so-called established facts. The critics are lean and hungry, constantly sharpening their knives. You get so much as the colour of a lady's bloomers wrong and they pounce!

What prompted me to investigate was a conversation with Mr Capper. I had approached him for information on the case as research for my essay, as the details released to the public had been scant, to say the least. I was immediately struck by his reluctance to even mention the case. When he did, it was a mere parroting of what had been printed. It felt rehearsed, a well-remembered yarn to be trotted out over dinner. In short, the fellow was shifty. I picked up on it instantly, he was hiding something. I left his office no more enlightened than when I had arrived.

Deciding to change tack, I recalled that the coroner assigned to the Marr family, Mr Unwin, was a chap, not unlike myself, who was partial to the odd libation and that I knew his favoured hostelry. I ambled along with due haste and proceeded to ply him with drink. He was reluctant to talk, at first, but I am well-versed in the arts of loosening tongues with in-toxicants. After the third bottle, he was spilling secrets like a gossip-starved washerwoman. What he told me, sent me down a path that I am lucky to have returned from. Had I not faltered at the final gate, well...

Mr Unwin disclosed that he never seriously considered the maul to be the murder weapon, not the crowbar found at the King's Head. He was almost certain that the skulls of the victims had been shattered upon contact with a hard surface. As though the victims had been pounced upon with such force that their craniums had split and the contents pulverised. It was a startling revelation. I asked him if it was possible, realistically. His answer will go to my grave, *not by human hands...*

By now, I was determined to ferret out the truth behind the Ratcliff Highway murders and continued to press Mr Unwin. It was now that he divulged information about the accident at Walpole and Son's. I assume your Mr Budnery has told you about that one?"

George nodded.

"I assumed he would. One of his boys nearly landed in hot water over that one. Well, Mr Unwin said that the wounds were the same. Their heads bashed in and their throats slit. It was here that his tongue slipped and he mentioned that, while the artery had been severed, there was no blood. In fact, all the victims, little Thomas included, had been almost completely drained of blood. Sucked dry! Can you credit it?"

George shook his head, he was completely dumbfounded by De Quincey's narrative.

"I instantly leapt upon the fact that the papers had reported that the crib had been soaked in blood. Unwin replied darkly that it had been soaked but not with blood..."

"What did he mean by that?"

"Alas, he wouldn't say. His hands became tremulous and his face drained of colour just at the thought of whatever he had discovered. Fearing that the interview was on the verge of reaching an abrupt conclusion, I asked him who he thought was responsible. He muttered that it wasn't so much a case of who but what. As he began to rise, I asked him if he could tell me anything more. All he was able to tell me was that the answers I sought could be found at The Pear Tree. As a parting gift for filling him so masterfully with wine, he gave me a name... William Ablass."

"I take it you went to The Pear Tree?"

"I did indeed. Ablass' name was known to me from the newspaper reports. He was an-other lodger at The Pear Tree and lives there to this very day. He wasn't a hard man to find. Long Billy, as he was known, had also been a suspect in the murders and was a known companion of Williams, therefore, known to Mr Marr. Ablass was a known brawler and had once participated in a mutiny aboard a ship he was serving upon. With this knowledge in my mind, I approached him with care for fear of provoking him.

In the end, I needn't have worried. Despite being a cutthroat and a villain, Ablass proved to be a garrulous sort that was only too happy to tell his tale in exchange for a few tankards of ale. As countrymen, both were Irish, he and Williams had become fast friends when they sailed together aboard the Roxburgh Castle. Another of their crewmates, you will be interested to learn, was none other than Thomas Marr. The trio remained close after departing the vessel and often drank in The King's Head.

I asked him whether Williams was guilty, to which he replied in the negative, though he did say something rather queer. *Guilty, no, but not completely without blame.* I asked him to elaborate but his lips became uncharacteristically tight. After a few moments of painful silence, he informed me that Williams' alibi of the card game was indeed true and that it was none other than he who had bloodied his friend's nose. Apparently, Williams had a touch too much to drink and became insufferable. I asked him who committed the crimes but he merely shrugged. I feared my investigation had come to an end.

It was here that things took a turn for the outré. Completely out of the blue, Ablass asked me if I had ever heard of a drug called Liao?"

"I can't say that I have."

"This may come as some surprise considering my, ahem... reputation, but nor had I. Ablass told me that he first encountered it while employed by The East India Company. Several men from China were aboard the same vessel and introduced him to it with the promise of seeing the past and future. I must have rolled my eyes or produced some other facial tic that betrayed my scepticism as he suddenly leaned in close, grabbing my lapels. His eyes were wild and his breath stung my retinas as he hissed, *It's true, I tell you. It works. It really works!*

Brushing his grubby paws from my garments, I asked him the point of this little diversion. He replied that if I wanted to know what happened on those fateful nights, all I needed to do was take the drug and see for myself. Naturally, given my penchant for such enlighten-ing substances, I was intrigued. So much so, that when he produced an old snuff tin contain-ing a fair amount of sticky blue grains, I quickly handed over the remuneration he desired. Ablass gave me the vaguest of instructions. I was to dissolve a grain or two in a libation of my choosing and sit in a circle composed of exactly eight candles. I asked him why the specificity but he merely shrugged and reiterated that it must be a circle. On no account must there be any right angles. His words committed to memory, we parted company with Ablass issuing a warning as a parting gift. He told me not to go too deep and to avoid linger-ing in those places where the corners are dark and filled with shadow..."

George was sitting forward in his seat, so rapt was he by De Quincey's tale. "Did you take it?"

"I did," his companion sighed, "a terrible experience, all told. First, though, I did a little digging around the local public houses about our friend, Mr Ablass. It turned out that he, Williams, and Marr were known for peddling this drug around Wapping. They had a con-tact, an old shipmate, who had recently settled in the Limehouse area. It was from him that they got their supply. They had a small exclusive clientele that included the now-deceased landlord of The King's Head, Mr Williamson and Marr's young apprentice.

On my wanderings, I encountered an artist acquaintance who lived on The Highway and was, it turned out, a devotee of the drug. He extolled its potency and he jotted down for me a series of chants and meditations to employ in order to achieve the maximum effect. On his blasé assurance that there was no danger, I returned to my rooms in Holborn and pre-pared myself. First, I lit candles, cleared a space on the floor, and arranged them in a circle as instructed. It was a chill night, so I donned a heavy overcoat for fear of catching my death. Once prepared, I mixed two grains of Liao with a glass of brandy and sat in the candlelight ring.

I had, per the artist's instructions, set up a carriage clock in the circle with me along with the newspaper reports of the Marr killings. I was to focus on the date and location while counting down the number of years I wished to travel, in this case, sixteen. Once prepared, I sat cross-legged in the centre of the circle, drained the glass, and waited for the drug to take effect. It didn't take long to enter my blood, in no time at all the shadows cast by the flickering candlelight lengthened and the confines of the circle became indistinct. I commenced counting."

"Did it work?"

"Oh, yes, it worked. I experienced sensations such as I have never felt before as the winds of time surged around me. I felt like a marker buoy on the high seas, cast adrift from its mooring and taken by the current, swept away to uncharted lands. Colours and patterns rushed and whirled as the very substance of reality dissolved to allow my consciousness passage to the past. I felt at once a mixture of awe and panic. As if I knew, in my heart of hearts, that what I attempted went against all natural laws and that if I wasn't careful I would be crossing the Rubicon, so to speak.

It was the oddest thing, I seemed to experience those sixteen fleeting years simultaneously as I tumbled through abyssal depths of time. I saw life happen around me as I, a detached observer, lurked on the threshold, unable to interact, barely able to comprehend. It was almost too much. The artist, and Mr Ablass, had given me a way of escaping the trance. I needed only to reverse the count and think of home. A simple escape route that, I confess, I nearly took at that moment. I persevered, however, and found myself standing in the cold

December air outside Thomas Marr's shop.

It was a dismal night, one fitting for a tragedy such as I had gone to witness. As I huddled in my heavy flushing coat, the door opened and a young woman emerged, herself huddled up against the frigid mist that hung low over the street. I recognised her at once from descriptions in the reports. It was Margaret Jewell, the Marr's maid. As I stood and watched, she turned and appraised me with a suspicious eye. I panicked, buried my face in my collar and hurried off in an Easterly direction. I hadn't expected to be visible. It was something of a shock to know that I was there in a corporeal sense.

After a minute or so, I stopped and checked behind me. Jewell had continued on her er-rand. I turned tail and returned towards the Marr residence. Keeping to the shadows, I approached the frontage in time to see Thomas Marr closing the shutters. I knew that he never bolted them... it was almost time. I was about to see the truth of the murders. I felt a thrill of anticipation as the moment dawned. Then... something strange started to occur.

From nowhere, an oppressive shadow settled over the drapers like a funeral pall. I hate to be over-dramatic, but I can describe it in no other way. An odd tingling sensation coursed through my extremities and my hair began to stand on end. There was a foul odour too, one that I can only compare to the charnel stench of a freshly opened grave. It was so over-whelming that I found myself trembling, though I knew no tangible reason why. It's hard to put into words, but I felt as though I was being observed, as though something lean and hungry was poised in the dark corners of the street, ready to pounce. Every darkened door-way and gloom-enshrouded alley exuded a menace the like I have never experienced before or since. It is a wonder I didn't cry out and run for my life.

Nevertheless, I strived to maintain control. In a desperate attempt to quiet the unease that screamed in my ears, I focused once again on the details of the case. Facts could keep me anchored when the tides of hysteria threatened to sweep me away. Thinking back over the reports, I recalled that Margaret Jewell had reported seeing someone loitering in front of the shop, though I had seen not a single soul.

It was with some horror that I realised that the suspicious character she had spotted was none other than myself. My panic returned tenfold. I was a recognisable figure, all it would take is one person to recognise me and I'd be joining Mr Williams at the crossroads. I had horrible thoughts about winking out of existence like a dying star. If one could interact with the past, could one also come to harm? If I was identified and executed in 1811, I couldn't yet live in 1826, could I? The idea was chilling, so I fled along the highway, counting myself back to the present as I did."

George's face crumpled into a dark frown. "So... you didn't see what happened?"

"Alas, not. My nerves got the better of me, but it wasn't so much the fear of being recognised, but something altogether more intangible. Something was drawing near."

"The assassin?"

"Perhaps... Perhaps, not. I hate to talk in such Biblical terms, but there was a presence abroad that night that was evil, Satanic, almost... I don't expect you to understand."

De Quincey's whole demeanour had changed. He had

gone from being the life and soul to a frightened child. In a second it passed and was replaced by something equally alien in someone of his character, embarrassment. Instantly, he rose from his seat, flustered and visibly sweat-ing. "I trust that was enough for your article? Now, if you will excuse..."

"Thank you, Thomas," George rose with him, "one more question if I may?"

"Go on."

"This drug, Liao, what did you do with the rest of it?"

"It's locked away in a drawer back at my rooming house, I meant to return it to Mr Ablass with a firm rebuke but never got around to it, why do you ask?" His eyebrow raised as he figured out the answer to his own question. "You don't mean to take it?"

"Well, if you don't want it?"

"It's sheer folly, dear boy!"

George rummaged in his pockets for some coins and deposited them on the table. "I can pay."

"Out of the question."

Realising that De Quincey wasn't to be that easily swayed, George changed his approach. "You know that I'll just go and get it from Ablass if I don't get it from you."

De Quincey stopped in his tracks, his shoulders sagged and a sigh of resignation escaped his lips. "Very well, if you want to charge off down the path of oblivion, who am I to stop you? I'd rather you stayed clear of that miscreant, just don't say you haven't been warned!"

"Thank You, Thomas."

"Don't thank me. It is not a good turn that I do this day, and make no mistake about it." De Quincey snatched George's notebook and his pencil and scribbled an address across one of the half-filled pages. "Call on me here after breakfast on the morrow. Now, my own sweet oblivion awaits in an earthy green liquid... good day to you."

As Thomas De Quincey rejoined his companions, George Mulgrave smiled to himself. If Thomas was telling the truth, he would have two good stories by the end of the week. The identity of the Ratcliff Highway murderer past and present, and a new wonder drug that could allow men to see into the distant and veiled past. He left the pub and returned to his lodgings for an early night. He would need all of his mental strength for the day to come...

Returning home with the four candles he had purchased from a local trader named Arkwright, he supplemented the four he had already snaffled from his landlady and placed them in a wide circle on the floor. After once again imploring that he abandon the reckless idea, Thomas De Quincey had given him the artist's notes along with the drug. After that, it was a simple matter of heading to his newspaper's offices and digging out the edition for the eighth of December 1811. Once spread out in the centre of the circle, he lit the candles and positioned himself cross-legged and took out his dented pocket watch.

"Christ," George gasped as he opened the tin and caught a whiff of its malodorous contents, "I don't even want to think about where this stuff comes from." It was a good point, he knew next to nothing about the mysterious blue substance. Still, that wasn't going to stop him from ingesting it.

Using a pair of tweezers, he extracted two viscid grains

and dropped them into a glass of the rough Scotch he kept by the bedside to combat the winter nights. They fizzed, danced, and capered on the surface before dissolving into the peaty amber.

Focusing on the yellowing newspapers spread out before him, George gripped the glass in his right hand while clutching his watch in his left. With one well-practised motion, he threw his head back and poured the whiskey down his gullet. Grimacing as it burned a trail down to his guts, he read the report and muttered the odd chant that the artist had written down for Thomas De Quincey. In no time at all, the shadows lengthened and his surroundings started to dissipate, revealing the vertiginous abyss of time beyond.

Tumbling out of his body, George's spiritual form was sucked into the time eddy and dragged down towards an ever-increasing pool of blue light. As it closed in around him, he felt a jolt as the membrane pierced and he found himself on the streets of London, specifically The Ratcliff Highway. It was just as De Quincey had described, he stood motionless and impotent as time wound back around him. From the previous morning when he had skulked at the rear of number eleven, he watched day become night over and over in a dizzying montage as the lives of the denizens of one of London's busiest thoroughfares reversed before his eyes. Men became boys and boys became infants. It was terrifying to see all the horror and drama of daily life condensed into just a few heartbeats. So overwhelmed was he that George screwed his eyes up tightly and prayed for it to end. Eventually, it did.

As time stabilised and his head cleared, George found himself a few doors down from the Marr's drapery shop. The last line in the newspaper he had read mentioned St George in the East so that's where he was. Staring up at the sixteenth-century Hawksmoor church as a gibbous moon, framed neatly by the twin pepperpot towers, glowered through the fog, George huddled in his coat against the night air. Recalling De Quincey's similar experiences, he turned and stared in the direction of his ultimate destination. With a sudden shock, he watched as Thomas materialised and staggered around in bewilderment. George panicked. He couldn't be seen by De Quincey and vice versa. To escape this awkward situation, he ducked down a side street and, remembering the open back door from the report, hurried around to the rear of number twenty-nine.

The wood of the rear fence was slimy with moisture as George clambered over and dropped silently into the yard. It was an almost complete replica of the rear of number eleven down to the tangled weeds that sprouted from around the doorstep. Pausing halfway down the path, he was struck by an anomaly, the door was firmly closed. Scratching his head, he moved to the rear window nearest the door and pressed his ear against the frame. Mr Marr was closing the shutters and telling his wife that Margaret shouldn't be long with their supper. Everything seemed normal... until he heard counting and chanting.

The noise came from the cellar window that sat at his right ankle. The chant was wholly familiar and filled him with dread. He knew what was happening but he had to make sure. Crouching down, he used the cuff of his coat to clear away the grime and saw the apprentice, James Gowan, sitting in a ring of candles clutching a pocket watch and a sketch of an old woman in a bonnet. As George watched on in confusion, the corner of the cellar started to blur and smoke. James went rigid as panic seized his soul. George himself let out a stifled cry of alarm as something started to appear from the fabric of reality.

James Gowan screamed and rushed for the stairs as an angular snout protruded from the smoking corner. Composed of a strange protoplasmic substance with a dripping proboscis protruding from the end, the unearthly creature tasted the air. Letting out a hungry howl as it caught the scent of James' fear, the abomination flew from the corner in a liquid motion and chased the fleeing youngster.

George, unable to fully comprehend what he had just seen, stood and stared through the ground-floor window. He was just in time to see James race from the cellar door with the creature hot on his heels. Grabbing the maul off the kitchen table, James spun and prepared to stand his ground. It was no good, he never stood a chance. The hunter sprung upon him with such force that he was thrown backwards and the back of his skull was shattered against the wall. Quick as lightning, the creature plunged its proboscis, dripping in blue slime, into James' neck and sucked him dry in a second.

Alerted by the hideous cries and slurping sound coming from their kitchen, Thomas and Celia Marr appeared on the threshold of the doorway. Catching the scent of their fear-borne adrenaline, the creature discarded its first meal and pounced upon poor Celia. She too had her head smashed against the wall and her blood drained. George covered his mouth with his hands and backed away from the window. That was when he heard the baby...

Something about the infant's plaintive wails awoke a

paternal instinct in the young reporter. Without thinking, he flung open the back door and prepared to attempt a rescue. Considerations about altering history didn't enter into it, he was going to try and save the baby and hang the consequences. All his good intent evaporated, however, as soon as he put a foot on the kitchen tiles. By now, Thomas Marr had joined his wife in eternity and the creature was looking for a fresh meal. As its dripping snout loomed around the doorway, George screamed and backed into the yard.

His survival instinct kicked in, and he started to count himself back to the present, all the while attempting to focus on his rooms. The creature sniffed the air and, tasting George's terror, started to flow and undulate towards him. Again unable to fathom the creature, George shut his eyes and continued to count. He could hear the odd mewling and slavering that the creature produced as it closed in for the kill.

As George reached zero, it pounced on him with all its might. He was knocked off his feet as he tumbled forward through time. Awaking on the floor of his room covered in blue slime, George screamed himself hoarse for the better part of a minute...

Thorndike finished packing his pipe, struck a match and lit it. The assembled members of The Pickman Club waited in silence while he took a few puffs and sank back into his chair.

"Finally coming to his senses, George removed his soiled garments, bundled them up in the newspaper articles, took them downstairs and tossed them onto the fire that raged in his landlady's grate. The old woman was deaf as a post and hadn't heard his cries. He explained his singular actions away to the bemused spinster by spinning a yarn that his clothes had become covered in blue paint while visiting a painter friend. She smiled and nodded, whether she had heard a word of his imagined narrative is another matter altogether.

"It was while he was concocting his falsehood that the near-gibbering Mr Mulgrave was struck by a terrible realisation. De Quincey had mentioned an artist on Ratcliff Highway that experimented with Liao and one of the victims of the latest atrocity, the lodger, had been a painter. It didn't take an extraordinary mental leap to deduce that these two were one and the same. Finally, all the pieces fell into place. The Marr household, the landlord of the King's Head, the artist... all had taken or were around those who had taken, Liao. He would also have put a hefty bet on one or more of the warehouse workers had taken it. In short, Liao was not only the key to the mystery but its potential cause. More than that, he realised with horror that the creature he had so narrowly escaped was also linked to it in some way.

Upon leaving the landlady's abode, George saw a wisp of smoke beginning to appear in the corner of the room and he detected a distant mewling cry. The creature had his scent and was in the process of hunting him through time! Fleeing into the night, he knew he was now a hunted man and if he stood any chance of survival, he would have to get some answers. First, he needed to know exactly what it was that hunted him so relentlessly. If he was to find a way to evade death, he would first need to know what he was dealing with. As it turned out, he knew exactly who to ask... the despicable Mr William Ablass. A hound Ablass called it." Thorndike took a puff on his pipe and blew bluish smoke into the air above the assembled members. "Though it bore little resemblance to Man's best friend. George had, as expected, found the perfidious peddler of Liao drinking himself silly in the back room of The Pear Tree. When approached directly, Ablass feigned ignorance. Infuriating George with a knowing sneer and a mocking laugh. This was the straw that broke the camel's back. George, it pains me to say, lost all reason and resorted to drastic actions.

Leaving The Pear Tree incandescent with rage, he sloped around the back to the waste ground and searched the undergrowth for a weapon which he found in the form of a half-brick. Returning to the public house, he lay in wait by the outhouse and waited for nature to take its course. As mentioned, Mr Ablass had imbibed enough liquid to float a boat so he didn't have to wait long. As the lumbering Irishman concluded his business and backed out of the foul-smelling structure, George leapt from the shadows like the creature that hounded him, clubbed him insensible, dragged him onto the waste ground and pinioned his arms with his belt. Kneeling on the man's chest, George slapped him back to the land of the living.

Despite being at another's mercy, Ablass still refused to talk... at first. He quickly changed his mind, however, when George embraced his inner Torquemada and got, let us just say, *creative* with his pencil."

Thorndike paused to wet his lips with a sip of brandy. "Let this be a lesson to you all, never anger a writer, they will get their revenge in the most inventive of ways! I will spare you the details, but Ablass was soon singing like a lark. He,

Marr, and Williams had first en-countered the creatures that he referred to as hounds when aboard the Roxburgh Castle. The reported mutiny was nothing of the sort. Despite the warnings of the Chinese chap that had introduced them to Liao, they had ventured too deep into the past and been detected by these predators that stalk the angles of time.

Neither I nor Mulgrave fully understood what he meant by this peculiar phrase other than that Ablass said that time was made up of a jumble of curves and angles. We live on a curve... they live in the angles. I am a man of medicine, not mathematics but I think I get the gist of his meaning. Needless to say, venture into one of their hunting grounds at your own peril. If they get your scent, you are forever marked. A total of eight men were killed aboard the ship before the hunter was satiated. The three thought that the sacrifice of their fellows was enough to save them but they were sorely mistaken.

The creatures returned eight months later demanding more. From that moment on, the trio unwittingly entered an un-spoken agreement with the beast. As long as they provided it with a sacrifice whenever its angle intersected with our curve, they would be spared. Marr was unfortunate to have been around one of the sacrifices and Ablass chose to give up Williams for fear he would spill his guts to the magistrate. How he got the Liao into the man's water will have to remain a mystery.

Unsurprisingly, Mulgrave saw red at this callous revelation and battered the murdering swine to death in a fit of rage. Filled with hopelessness and shock at his actions, he fled the scene and called on a trusted friend to seek advice. To say that I was shocked by his bloodied garments and wild aspect would be a monumental understatement. Before he had rid the world of William Ablass, he had asked him what was significant about the number eight. He had wondered if it had some numerological meaning. Ablass had attempted to shrug before saying that curves were anathema to the hounds... and what has more curves than a figure eight?

So ends the tragic tale of George Mulgrave. I have little more to add other than to say that after he had concluded his story, he fled into the night screaming after seeing a phantom puff of smoke in the corner of my room. I tried to tell him it was from one of the candles, but I am far from certain. I wasn't sure whether to believe his fantastical ravings or label them as a product of a disordered mind. I suppose the inquest will be the final judge of that.

Maybe he fell foul of a cut-throat or some accident? Loathed as I am to admit it, I fully expect him to have had a shattered skull and a laceration in his neck. I will speak to the mortuary attendant after the official verdict. If he confirms that his clothes were soaked with blue slime then we will know to stay away from Liao at all costs..."

In the thickest part of the gloom, pushed back in the corner, a small, hunched figure sat in a large, winged chair

EVENTS IN THE CITY OF NORWICH

TONY BRADBURY

"Gentlemen, gentlemen, thank you. Now, who shall be next to tell us of a strange adventure?" Mr Pickman's gaze took in the room. A young slender man in a once well tailored suit, stood. "Thank you Mr Shadbolt. Gentlemen, I give you Mr Padget Shadbolt."

The tale I have to tell involves a trip to the City of Norwich, an encounter with the miscreant and a possible foreshadowing of the future. We had reports of a similar creature to this "Spring Heeled Jack" that has been seen in London also sighted in Norwich, and so I had decided to investigate these particular reports, not to mention that I had a yearn to visit Norwich.

I had considered a steam packet to get me to Southwold, thenceforth travelling to Norwich, but both the price and thought of a trip through the Broads and down the Wensum filled me with dread. The intervening landscape is a stinking morass of marsh and river channels, its inhabitants subsistence farmers of the poorest type, and along the coast the fisherman are of the hardiest and gruffest sort. All are known to distrust strangers. Still, hardly more inviting was the ensuing coach trip which took several days and was uncomfortable in the extreme. I alighted in Whitechapel and changed at Ipswich however, at its end I was abed for two days in the boarding house room I had secured at very short notice.

This establishment was run by a Mrs Rosie Chiddock, a stout elderly woman who, it seemed, had an inordinate amount of extremely comely daughters, all of whom were at great pains to tell me about the latest gossip in the city - including the tales of "the jumping monster with hellfire eyes," along with many other things of a more "delicate" nature.

I later discovered that the coachman had misunderstood my accent and intent and taken me to a house of ill repute, this was much to the amusement of some of my fellow travellers as this was a well known establishment within the city. However I found Mrs Chiddock's "daughters" to all be sweet tempered intelligent girls, good company and of a good honest nature. There I have said it, and I shall speak as I find!

I took to the streets that night, armed with my trusty sword stick and an ash truncheon as you know I have an aversion to firearms, since that incident in Cardiff with the sheep! My search began in the area this creature had been known to frequent. Sybil, one of the "daughters" had told me it had been seen by an acquaintance of hers three nights previously in this very place. The streets were dark and foul smelling with the gables of the houses almost touching at the top stories, so close that I can believe the old stories of occupants shaking hands from their windows.

I was making my way between hostelries on Bethel Street heading towards the Market Place, a warren of stalls and food places open even at that late hour, when I heard a noise coming from a side alley. Thinking I could be accosted at any moment, I put my hand into my coat pocket and gripped the truncheon tightly. From out of the alley strolled a battle-scarred, and evidently pugnacious cat. It was obviously the Lord of the Alley and wanted me to know as such! The feline glared at me with its one good eye sat down, and started to wash itself. Just then, a medium size dog of indiscriminate heritage rounded the alley corner and approached me for a morsel of some kind. The cat stopped its washing and glared at the poor hound, which tucked its tail between its legs and fled post haste, this cat was evidently known and feared - in fact it put me in mind of a childhood pet, a magnificent white Cornish Rex I named *Ghostcat*... but I digress!

This feline strolled towards me with no fear, came to within a foot or so, then me and stopped stock still, looking wide eyed past me. It emitted a low, its ears went back, it bared its fang (it only had one) and hissed at something behind me. Now, since it is popularly believed that felines can see things humans cannot, I was, I must admit quite concerned. This concern was heightened when the said Lord of the Alley fled, howling and spitting, back down, the alley at high speed, knocking a bin over in its haste.

I turned slowly, and there before me in the gloom shone a pair of red eyes, at approximately knee height to a tall man - as you know I am over six feet tall. However the eyes rapidly ascended in height from the ground and I found myself looking up at them slightly. This menacing figure was wearing a cowled garment of indeterminate colour. On instinct, I drew my truncheon and swung at him roughly where I thought its skull might be. My attack was batted aside with the ease of a seasoned fighter. I felt the sudden stinging impact of a limb of some sort striking my arm, so I endeavoured to grab the limb with my other hand, in order to twist it as I had been taught by my old Sergeant. Yet the thing was preternaturally quick and I found myself thrown to the alley floor with ease. Muck spattered my clothing, the truncheon was torn from my hand, thrown a considerable distance, clattering away down the alley.

The creature turned away apparently losing interest in the combat, as if I was no threat to it . Angered by my assailant's contemptuous manner, I rose, gripped my swordstick, and drew the blade. The noise as it hissed out of the cane caused the creature spin back towards me as I lunged, my attack hitting home, straight into its chest. I had been expecting it to reel backwards with force of the lunge, yet was like striking a heavy training dummy, it moved back not an inch! Sword embedded in its chest, the thing backhanded me down the alley and I slipped, crashing to the muck-filled floor again. As I gazed up in shock, it gripped my sword by the blade, pulling it out of its body with no sign of pain, nor any sound at all. A toss of the hand, and blade followed by club in clattering down the alley.

The creature advanced, I pushed myself away with my legs, trying to back away from my approaching doom. Yet, as I looked up, the creature paused, looking past me into the darkness at the end of the alley. It suddenly span on the spot and leaped, straight up, landing sure footed and with uncanny precision on a corbel supporting part of an upper story of the tenement.

From there, it leaped again, turning midair to land on a steeply tiled part of a gable window, from there vanishing over the roof. Other than the clattering of loose tiles as they slid to the ground, the creature had made no sound whatsoever during the whole encounter

Rising quickly I made to follow it, running to the end of the alley hoping to catch a glimpse of it in flight. I heard a noise like a click of a door latch, then realised there was another figure in the darkness of the end of the alley, this one was far smaller and was dressed what appeared to be a dark suit. It stared at me with a quizzical expression on its thankfully human face for a few seconds, then advanced, with a hitch in its gait, favouring the left leg. It appeared to be holding a rather large , peculiar looking pistol in its hand. A buzzing, as of a swarm of bees, suddenly surrounded me, outside, also in my head. Then came a blue flash, like summer lightning, and I knew no more.

I awoke, or more correctly regained consciousness, feeling as if I had been beaten with a cudgel. To my surprise, I was not restrained in any way, laying on a cot bed in a dimly lit room, the source of said illumination being a single, small window set high up near the beamed ceiling. From its construction I surmised I was in a flag-stoned cellar of some kind. It was gloomy, damp and dank, off to one side a set of steps lead up. I gingerly arose, there was barely enough room to stand without striking my head on the beams. Through the gaps in the boards above, I made out a dim light and could hear low voices and movement.

Although I thought I had made no sounds, the trap door was pulled opened and a man's voice called down to me.

"We know you are awake. Would you please join us Mr Shadbolt? We know who you are and why you are here in Norwich."

I was dumbstruck, as I had told no-one of my mission or its reasons, not even Mrs Chiddock's "daughters." How had this been known? How had I betrayed myself?

I ascended the steps into what appeared to be a rude farm kitchen, a lit range sat to once side providing warmth, a plank table with plain food and drink on occupied the centre of the room. A tall, stocky man, with the aspect of a farm labourer stood in front of the only door, his hands held loosely by his side, a slight smile on his face. No exit that way, I quickly surmised.

The fellow who had called my name stood by the trapdoor. I recognised him as the small, neatly dressed man I had encountered in the alley, the man who had rendered me unconscious with his dammed "lightning gun." His voice was cultured and well spoken, with a slight hint of an Indian accent.

"Help your self Mr Shadbolt." He gestured at the food. "It helps the body recover from the effects of being stunned by one of their weapons. Please, you will be free to leave soon. My..." he hesitated, "supervisor just wants to talk to you. Please, take some sustenance. You will be returned to the city by dawn. You have my word."

I turned sharply. "How dare you imprison me thus! I have been scared half to death, attacked, have run something through that just took it on the chin, so to speak. Oh, and been shot with a lightning bolt and apparently kidnapped and am now being held prisoner! And your *supervisor* just wants to talk to me?" I raged at him, making to step forward. The smaller man did not move, excepting for a restraining hand to the muscular chap, who had stepped forward, hands raised, to intervene.

"No Mr Jenks, no need. Let him be, he will not harm me." Jenks nodded and stepped back to stand impassively once more in front of the door, arms crossed. The other glanced up the narrow staircase to an upper floor and gestured.

"You will go up alone, but do not be frightened. He will not harm you, though he is quite capable of doing so. It is dark, but with enough light to see by. For your own protection, do not move out of the circle of light. This merely stops you seeing my supervisor clearly, whilst allowing him to see you. He is somewhat sensitive about being seen by outsiders, that is all." He gestured again and, with little other option, I started the ascent to the upper story

A thin rickety door stood at the top of the stairs, upon opening it, I was struck by a wall of frigid air. The temperature in this room was several steps lower than the kitchen below. The room itself was gloomy, with a circle of dimly flickering lamps set around the door. In the thickest part of the gloom, pushed back in the corner, a small, hunched figure sat in a large, winged chair. It was swathed in what appeared to be dark robes or perhaps a blanket of some kind, the whole effect being I could make out no details of the person. The scene held for a moment, then a thin papery voice whispered,

"Ah, Mr Shadbolt, so nice to meet you at last. I do hope that we can reach an understanding to our mutual benefits. You see, my associates and I need your help in a delicate matter, one that, should we fail, will impinge on us all. You see, I have limited," the thin paper voice paused slightly, "resources in this place, and as an invalid have virtually no mobility. My associates also have their limitations. Lamsal was injured in my service, and despite my best efforts will not heal in time. As for Jenks, well, Jenks is a blunt instrument, useful when one is needed, but at present I require a scalpel. Which brings me to you, Mr Shadbolt. We have, I believe, the same aim. To either apprehend, or at least stop, the being you call Spring Heeled Jack."

There was slight rustle as he shifted position in the chair. "You see, I cannot go to the authorities, as I wish this matter to be kept most private. But make no mistake, Mr Shadbolt, this creature is dangerous in the extreme and will, I am certain, bring ruin and death to this place, as he has in other cities. For a long time we have tracked him, and we now know that he is near to here. I entreat you for aid. I can call for assistance from my kind, but it will not be forthcoming in time to be effective. Matters are coming to a head, it must be stopped now, at any cost."

I stood looking into the shadows beyond the light. Fantastic as they sounded, I sensed the underlying truth of his words, though was certain he was not telling me all of the tale. "Why do you need to capture this Jack?" I asked, "What has he done?"

He is a an aberration. His behaviour threatens the future of my," again a short pause, "*family*, shall we say?" The halting cadence of his speech was confusing, as though he were translating a foreign language in his mind, then relaying to me in English. The papery texture to the voice, its breathlessness, made it thin and weak, and hard to follow. He spoke again.

"Its sole purpose is to spread violence and destruction. At present, its psyche is at war with itself, and i fear it will succumb to its more baser urges. It escaped from confinement killing five of what you might call its handlers, and fled to this country. It has been roaming your cities ever since, I do not know why"

"If I agree, what do I gain from this venture? What is in it for me" I asked firmly

The shadows seemed to sigh, "As ever, the same question from your kind,. What do I gain, what is in it for *ME*? Do you seek monetary rewards? Knowledge? Power? All of this is possible, of course. Or will my gratitude and the gratitude of my... *family* suffice? Perhaps the gratitude of Mr Pickman, and the adulation of your cohorts in your quaint circle of friends would be enough for you? Or, perhaps a satisfied ego, knowing that you have apprehended a dangerous miscreant? Don't look so surprised, Mr Shadbolt. I have a far more powerful intellect than you can possibly imagine, and I discern with ease who and what you are. But time grows short. If you do not wish to help me that is understandable, but I will not allow you to hinder my stated purpose either! I will have Lamsal return you to your lodgings, unharmed as promised,. Of course, he will have to stun you again. Well Mr Shadbolt your decision, if you please?" The thin papery voice rose in tone slightly, as if agitated

"What guarantee is there that you are telling me the truth, Mr ...how can I begin to trust if I don't even know your name?" I exclaimed

A thin, papery wheezing , which I took for laughter came from the shadows.

"I forget that there are other methods of determining social bondings. My kind are not tied to these strictures, yet I understand your people are hide bound by social etiquette. My profound apologies, Mr Shadbolt. My name is Yarnwood, and I am what you would call a scientist, although my kind have an entirely different understanding of the term."

I stepped back and mentally reviewed the conversation. My captor, for there was no doubt I was a captive, had peppered the conversation with phrases such as "your people " and "my kind," also referring to Spring-Heeled Jack as a "being", not a man. Yarnwood's obviously powerful intellect, that weapon Lamsal had fired at me , this all was like nothing I had ever experience or heard of, it was damned perplexing.

"Mr Yarnwood, where exactly are you actually from? You are not from these shores are you?" I queried politely "I cannot place your accent. Are you from one of the Southern States of the Union, Louisiana perhaps? I will not co-operate at any price if this is a covert operation against my Government!"

The wheezing laugh again, even more breathy this time.

"Calm yourself, Mr Shadbolt, it is nothing so prosaic as that. You see I am not from anywhere that you will have heard of, indeed, your limited intellect could not understand the vast distances involved or the method by which my kind have travelled here. Nor do the petty politics of your world concern me in the slightest. You see, I am not a native of this world, and am hunting a byblow of an unauthorised experiment that has escaped confinement. As I mentioned, it has the potential to cause a great deal of harm, for my kind, as well as yours. Also, if discovered and examined, by even your primitive technology, its unusual origins will be plain for all to see."

My mind struggled to take in this information. *Beings from other worlds?* Yet more shocking revelations were to follow.

"We have been on this world for aeons, but it is only since you have developed civilization that we have concerned ourselves with your kind. It is predicted by our savants, that in approximately one hundred revolutions of your planet around its star, you will develop the technology to effectively fight back against us. This is inevitable. If our presence becomes widely known, it is also predicted that the pace of your technology will accelerate exponentially, and we will merely doom ourselves all the quicker. Our technology is far superior in every way to yours, but we do not have the numbers to either destroy your kind completely, nor to rule the survivors of any such a war. In short Mr Shadbolt, I need your help to stop a catastrophe, for all our sakes, for such a war would kill billions and likely render your planet uninhabitable forever."

I stared into the shadows "Does Lamsal know all this?" I asked quietly. "Surely he is human?"

"Lamsal is a valued servant. His people have served mine for thousand of years. In return, we have guided and enhanced them, they are superior in many ways to baseline humans. Faster, stronger with a better capacity to learn," stated Yarnwood matter of factly,

"And no doubt reliant on you as well" I said quietly

"There is that of course" he wheezed dryly

"How do I know you are not lying to me to get what you need from me?"

Yarnwood fell silent, evidently thinking, "There is a way, I can let you see into my thoughts, but it is dangerous for both of us. For me, linking with such a primitive mind could have unforeseen effects. For you, there is a possibility of overloading your mind and damaging your brain permanently. It will not be pleasant for either of us, but it will allay your concerns of duplicity on my part, of that I am certain"

I nodded, replying, "I agree to this, with reservations, for I see no choice. I certainly have no desire to be a party to

Armageddon. How do we go about this Mr Yarnwood, what do I need to do?"

"I would suggest you sit down in the chair behind you."

I glanced round A similar wing back chair sat empty in a darkened corner. I was moving to take a seat in it, when the floor smashed me in the face.

Yarnwood's papery voice echoed in my mind.

"Just relax, Mr Shadbolt, just focus on the images. What you will be seeing is a recording, the racial memory of my kind on your planet, or at least a version of it that you will be able to comprehend without going insane."

I saw the great lizards that are being described in the latest scientific journals, but of vastly more variety than currently known to human science. I witnessed the continents cracking and moving, vast ice sheets growing and shrinking across a vastly different map of the world than we know today.

There came a race of strange beings with starfish-like heads, wielding terrible weapons against flying creatures that appeared a cross between crustacean and intelligent fungus, I intuited, somehow, that the latter were Yarnwood's kind. This all occurred aeons before any life was present on Earth. Indeed, they speculated that all Earthly life was nothing more than an experiment of the starfish-heads spiraled out of control! Yarnwood's race came from other colder, more arid, worlds by methods not made clear. They engaged in terrible wars that lasted for thousands of years for possession of this globe, it being a relatively rare world, in that it could support life without the expenditure of a lot of precious resources.

After long and prodigious wars in which neither side could

claim victory, both races retreated. The starfish heads to the the deepest parts of the Ocean, where they built cyclopean cities, forever wreathed in darkness. Yarnwood's kind retreated to the tops of newly forming mountain ranges, to high, cold plateaus where they built prodigious cities of stone, in ages long past, all trace of which has now vanished. The detritus of failed experiments from both races spread across the Earth, living and dying, engaging in their own proxy wars, never knowing their origins.

Further aeons passed, the age of the Great Lizards was long gone, ending in fire, dust, and then extreme cold. This badly affected Yarnwood's kind, being surface dwellers. The starfish heads,retreated to the sea bottom and cities deep within the Earths crust, survived relatively intact. Still, internecine wars eventually destroyed their original civilization, leaving their created servants in possession of their technology, living amongst the ruins of a civilization that they did not understand and could not possibly replicate.

Humans now made their first appearance in this tale. Yarnwood's people tried to influence them to be willing servants, to no avail and further wars raged across the planet, further culling Yarnwood's kind. They came to be forced back to the highest and most desolate mountain ranges, where they became more introspective, reclusive and paranoid

Still, their advanced medical technology had made them, barring a violent death, functionally immortal. Some cabals within their population continued attempting to manipulate humans, in effect breeding us like cattle in their damnable vats. All to make humans "better," even crossbreeding humans and other more unsavoury things to create a soldier that would follow orders without question. This, I know understood, was what Spring Heeled Jack was, a purposely bred and engineered killer, capable not only of cleansing humanity, and any other beings, from the face of the Earth. I do not claim to understand the methods used, but it appears that they had taken human child, possibly from its mother's body before birth, and altered and changed it like some kind of puppet to suit their dammed purposes. I therefore felt I had little choice but to ally myself with this Yarnwood to stop this devilry. At this thought, Yarnwood's voice came back into my head.

"With that, I take it you will aid me in my endeavour, Mr Shadbolt, I thank you and so I will return you to your own psyche. Goodbye, I will likely not see you again."

Although this part has been long in the telling, it took only minutes at most for me to assimilate all this information. I came to on the floor,with a blinding headache and bleeding copiously from the nose and tear-ducts. I struggled to sit up, wincing at the bright lamp Jenks now brought into the room.

"The miscreants hiding place has been discovered, we know where he is " said Lamsal, following.

"You will have to give me a moment, and I will need to clean up. Do you have a kerchief I can use?"

Jenks produced a belcher from his pocket, soaked it in the ewer on the small table and passed it to me. "Wipe thy face man," he said in a north country accent. " No man should go into a fight looking like they already lost previous one"

Lamsal explained he had received word that the miscreant had recently been sighted near the asylum in Thorpe Hamlet. I knew the place, a large imposing brick building, it had off to one side a small group of cottages rumoured to be of ill aspect. These were the old leper almshouses, shunned by locals, and not used by the asylum. A weirdly-hunched figure had been spotted going into one of the cottages. With all due haste, we set out for Thorpe Hamlet.

In silence, the three of us crept along the road toward the row of cottages. They were dilapidated overgrown, thatch gone. In the darkness, the exposed timbers had the look of shattered ribs poking up.

"It all seems deserted," I whispered. "One might expect local indigents to take advantage of such accommodation."

Jenks snorted "They used to be leper cottages, built on old priory ruins , in the grounds of an asylum. Personally I can't think of a more ill- omened dump in all Creation. No wonder Jack chose it. And anything strange is seen, who would believe the poor inmates of an loony house? Not a soul. That's cunning that is,"

"He is certainly that and highly dangerous, besides. Do not underestimate him or we shall surely fail in this endeavour," warned Lamsal. He stepped back and seemed be distracted for a moment. "Mr Shadbolt, you may need this," he said, handing me a firearm , which I recognised as a twin to the lightning gun. "Be careful, it has more than one setting."

"How does it work" I asked. He merely shrugged.

"I do not know, at least not in any detail. It works, that is all, and it is a powerful weapon be careful."

"Jenks not having one?" I responded, and Lamsal smiled.

"Mr Jenks prefers a more... classical approach, " he said gesturing. Jenks revealed a large woodsman's axe. "

"Bessie here can cut down anything," he boasted, hefting it

over his shoulder. We approached the cottages.

"You see anything, anything at all?" I asked .

"We are being watched," hissed Lamsal. "We must beware"

There was a slight silence in the still air, like a drawing of breath, and then it all went to ruin!

"What was that" Jenks queried, turning slightly. At another noise in front, he span back, whip fast, axe hissing wickedly as it arced down. It was stopped dead in the air by a hand, that seemingly came out of nowhere, It effortlessly tore the axe from Jenks' hand, reversed the grip, and smashed the blade through Jenks' skull as though it were a porcelain bowl.

I was frozen with fear, but Lamsal moved aside putting some distance between us, and drew his weapon, firing at the creature. Blue lightning arced and spat, grounding itself on the cottage walls, knocking me breathless, though not stunned, to the ground. Through the pain I saw the creature stagger, but not fall. Lamsal fired again, the creature lurched forwards and backhanded him hard across the face, sending him crashing into the cottage wall, where he slumped without a sound. The creature turned to me, red eyes glowing balefully, its dark clothing rent, and smoking with the effects of Lamsal's gun." It took two of paces forward, I could hear it crunching through the remains of Jenks' skull.

I remained rigid with panic as the thing leant forward, grasped me by the lapels of my jacket and hauled me up to its face, without any apparent effort. My feet barely touched the ground, the thing's breath was foetid in my nostrils, I felt myself gagging at the odour. Yet, over my assailant's shoulder, I saw a slight movement from Lamsal, saw him raise the weapon again, saw him aiming it at us.

At this point I must admit to have despaired, for there was little doubt that I was doomed. Lamsal fired the gun, I screamed in pain and the creature convulsed in agony, its hands opening, dropping me to the ground. Lamsal feebly and desperately gestured to to me, and I realised I had not attempted to fire my own weapon. I drew it, looking across at Lamsal, to see him mime turning the barrel assembly. I looked down at the assembly and saw markings on the gun barrel that seemed to be set at one end of the range. I twisted it frantically, up to what I hoped was the maximum amount.

The creature had regained some of it faculties and was advancing on Lamsal again, clearly intent on taking out its rage on the person that had caused it so much pain. As it reached for Lamsal, he fired at point blank range, but only a low buzz came from the weapon, I guessed it had been discharged of its lightning store. In my fear, I hastily aimed and fired. I do not know what I had expected, there was no noise and certainly no recoil as from any other hand gun I had ever fired. The weapon held steady on the creature and a blue white bar of light struck the creature in the back, punched through, and exited its torso, barely missing Lamsal. The creature dropped to its knees and folded over onto the ground, cored through, the wound burning black, and smoking.

Lamsal staggered over to me, bleeding profusely from his wounds.

"Again, shoot it again," he urged. "Aim at the skull!"

I fired again, and the head vanished into a steaming hole in the ground, the smell of which made us both retch. My companion limped over and slumped down at the side of Jenks' crushed ruin of a body.

He remained silent for a second, then said, "We must deal with his remains as well. There can be no trace for anyone to ask questions over. This is imperative."

He appeared distracted for a moment, then looked me in the eye, nodding his head slightly, looking past me and gesturing with his chin. Without thinking, I turned to see, and a blinding pain enveloped my head. Once again, I knew no more.

I came to sometime later in the alley near my lodgings, with a bump the size of an egg on the back of my head, bloodied, as if I had been assaulted and robbed. Had that indeed been the case, was all I experienced nothing but an imagining while I lay here senseless in a stinking alleyway? It checked through my pockets. My effects remained intact, and I found a folded note. It read:

I am sorry, for this outrageous betrayal, but we cannot afford to attract any attention. All remains have been disposed of, there is nothing to be examined at all. Jenks will be buried in a paupers grave nearby the asylum. Again, we cannot have any scrutiny from the authorities. For what it is worth you have my thanks.

It was signed in a bold hand simply *Lamsal*.

"That, gentlemen, is the conclusion of my tale. The miscreant known as Spring Heeled Jack, should trouble the good people of this land no more, there is no body to find or examine, he is gone."

A brief round of murmurs and congratulations, palms slapping on tabletops, rippled around the room.

"What of this Yarnwood, what happened to him? You do

not mention him, after your melding of mind," exclaimed Weems from his seat.

"I do not know what happened to him. As I have inferred, he appeared to be weak bodied and was possibly an invalid of some kind, nevertheless possessed of a prodigious intellect. I had assumed he left the physical aspect of the chase to myself, Lamsal and Jenks. Though I did notice that at several points Lamsal became distracted, seemingly in silent conversation with another. Is it possible they were mind linked, as I "heard" Yarnwood's voice in my head? Further than that I cannot say."

Pickman interjected at this point. "We have made extensive enquires since Mr Shadbolt's return to the capital, and can find no trace of either Yarnwood or Lamsal. Whilst it is most probable that Lamsal was entirely human - he did bleed copiously during the final encounter, after all - he has now entirely vanished, and we are perplexed in the extreme by this turn of events! We can only speculate that the being called Yarnwood has likely fled the country by means unknown, to parts of the globe, as yet undetermined. However, I do not think we have seen the last of his kind. In the coming years we will need to be vigilant. Even if he was helping us on this particular occasion , we cannot expect that will be the case if we encounter them again. Humans, it would seem are easy for them to manipulate in many diverse ways,"

Le Blanc took over. "The derelict mill where Mr Shadbolt was held captive was burned to the ground a few nights after the incident. Admittedly, not an uncommon fate for Mills in that area, as they are often used by tramps and footpads. The local constables examined the ruin of the mill and informed us that as no bodies were found, they have put down as an accident. Mr Jenks has been buried in the asylum graveyard. Our enquiries reveal that a drunken brawl took his life, at least that is the official account."

"A poor reward for a brave man," Pickman sighed. "Still, an excellent story, my boy, you have the thanks of the Pickmanites. And what do you plan to do now?"

Shadbolt pondered for a moment. "As you may imagine, my friends, such an experience, such encounters, such revelations have somewhat shaken the very foundations of my beliefs. I have a mind to travel. I believe in India there is a high mountain range the Hindoo call the *Himalazias,* which they believe is the roof of the world. Some also claim there is a city within these mountains where people can "live forever." They legend goes that the beings that live there have great knowledge of the past, and great wisdom. Is it possible that this was one of the places Yarnwood described to me, a refuge of his kind? I must admit, I feel a strange compulsion to explore there. I wonder what I may find?"

*It was an eerie journey, illumined by the
uncanny glow of the coastal lighthouses
and a gibbous moon that limned the
sandhills' flanks with silver*

A SINISTER INTERLUDE

GAVIN CHAPPELL

1 The Village

My ability to report on eerie matters in the far flung corners of the kingdom was greatly enhanced when I departed London to take up employment with the Liverpool Dockyard Police. This tale of the wilds of Cheshire which I will relate to members of the Club, including our esteemed president, will, I think, be of the greatest interest to all Pickmanites present.

My *quondam subordinate*, Police Constable Hector McAndrew, languishes in Lancaster County Asylum, ranting frantically of lands under the wave and squamous mermaids. I fear that I am in some way responsible for his sorry plight, since it was I, in my position as Commissioner of the Liverpool Dockyards Police Force, who despatched him to that fishing village whence came he by the mental aberration that plagues him still. Since McAndrew's sinister interlude on the Cheshire coast is not without elements of *grotesquerie* and the bizarre, I have thought fit to report to you on the matter, outlining his supposed experiences.

You may or may not be aware that the Cheshire coast is infested by wreckers of notable cruelty and mercilessness, far worse than those for whom the counties of Cornwall and Devonshire are notorious. Those latter prey upon the Bristol traffic; these of Cheshire wax fat upon the wrecks of ships sailing into or out of Liverpool, second city of empire. Due to the laxity of ship owners in ensuring that vessels are subjected to costly maintenance, not to mention the storms that assail the coast in wintertime, it is seldom necessary for the wreckers to lure vessels onto the rocks using the false lights employed by their Cornish counterparts.

Entire families have forsaken their grandfather's profession of fisherman or crofter to thrive by preying upon wrecks. This occupation is in direct contravention of the 26 Geo. II, which states that plundering a vessel in distress (whether wreck or no wreck) is felony without benefit of clergy, punishable by death by hanging. However, without hard evidence it is a difficult matter to bring any such felon to trial. So it was that I despatched McAndrew, in the unlikely guise of a poet seeking inspiration, to dwell in a cottage in the tiny fishing village of Hoose, near the Hoyle Lake, on the Cheshire coast.

According to his first report, which I received by post shortly after his arrival in the village, he rented a room in a thatched dwelling house of whitewashed sandstone belonging to one Broster, a gangling, angular, surly peasant with an unhealthy cast to his skin and severe alopecia not wholly concealed by a broad brimmed hat, who lived almost alone in the decaying cottage, attended to only by his daughter, Polly.

"We're reet grateful to take on a lodger, sir," he explained to my agent. "Since me wife and me eldest were lost to th' sea, I con fish nay longer. I would be on th'parish, sir, or in th' workhouse, without thy money and th'elp o' moi daughter."

And yet there was a sullenness to his tone and a look to his watery eye that implied McAndrew's presence, if not his money, was distinctly unwelcome.

"I seek inspiration amidst this bucolic setting," McAndrew explained. My agent was a genial Scot with a dry sense of humour, and I believe that his guise of wandering poet, in the mould of the late Lord Byron, was his own notion. Before seeking employment with the Liverpool Dock Police he was a government spy, and had infiltrated such seditious groups as the Luddites and the Blanketeers. He was no stranger to subterfuge.

A cursory examination of the cottage, which was surprisingly well furnished for a poor fisherman's dwelling, seemed to belie Broster's protestations of poverty. Sundry items of mismatched furniture and garniture adorned the place, much of it betraying signs of having spent time in the sea, and McAndrew surmised that they had been cast up on the shore, if not in fact plundered from wrecks. Yet amidst that strange setting, Miss Polly Broster was a jewel, as winsome a coquette as any Parisian belle.

"I'll 'elp 'ee unpack, sir," she said, assisting McAndrew with his luggage, taking it through into the room he was renting.

In his report McAndrew waxes lyrical on describing the young lady, and I fear that he was smitten by her rustic charms. A pleasant spoken Cheshire girl, Miss Broster was a delightful creature with remarkably big, pretty eyes, lacking the ill looks or rank, fishy odour of her father; buxom and forward, with nice tricks of manners, sidelong looks, and a laugh as infectious as the smallpox. McAndrew stood talking with her some while after unpacking, and I gather from his words that he found her most appealing, a stark contrast with her surly parent.

However, she had her work to attend to, going by what she obliquely referred to as 'shanks' pony' (i.e. walking) to fetch water from a nearby well. McAndrew assisted her, accompanying the girl on a perambulation of the sand hills that line the coast. These, a veritable range of sizeable dunes, can also be seen upon the Mersey shore, and are said to have appeared in the space of one night after a storm many years gone.

A strange landscape, its sparse acres are sandy and its slopes fringed with star grass. Amidst this herbage and the towering dunes a wanderer may encounter small cottages, dwarfed by their environs, with fishing nets drying outside to show the avowed pursuit of the inhabitants. In such a barren setting farming would seem to be of limited facility, apart from the grazing of livestock.

The wind sighed mournfully amongst the grass and blew grit into McAndrew's eyes. Wading to the top of one sandhill, he looked out upon that anchorage they call the Hoyle Lake. Here ships rode at anchor. Miss Broster was able to name several of them, and their captains, since they were habitués of the region, it being much frequented by ships awaiting the turn of the tide, not to mention the fishing vessels of her neighbours and kinsmen. Further off, the grey waters of Liverpool Bay extended amidst sandbanks and reefs before commingling with those of the Irish Sea.

On one hand, the smokes and fogs of Liverpool tainted the air. In the opposite direction, the peaks of the Welsh hills stood out starkly against blue skies, while closer by a small island stood off from the shore. Looking towards Liverpool again with some longing, McAndrew remarked a lighthouse a mile or two off, one of several along the coast, and beyond it a curious octagonal tower. Miss Broster identified the latter as Mockbeggar Hall.

Before he could learn the derivation of this quaint sobriquet, McAndrew stubbed his toe on something almost wholly buried in the sand and fell flat. Stifling curses, he allowed Miss Broster to help him hobbling to a place of rest on a cast-up ship's timber, beseeching the girl to determine the nature of his stumbling block. To his surprise, the girl showed little inclination to return to the scene of his downfall, but rather urged him to hurry home with the buckets once the pain from his toe subsided.

It was then that McAndrew noted a gig from one of the ships drawing ashore, rowed by a pack of villainous looking sailors. He would have remained behind to watch their progress but the girl grew distraught and he permitted her to lead him back to the cottage.

During his brief acquaintance with the sand buried obstacle, McAndrew had gained the impression that it might be a keg, of the kind that contains rum or brandy. This notion preyed upon his mind, and on returning he quizzed Broster about the discovery. The fisherman grew more than usually sullen, going as far as to warn McAndrew off.

"I don't doubt," said the fisherman morosely, "that there were a reason for what 'ee found to be where 'ee found it. Nor do I doubt that little good will come o' fowk poking their noses into what is o' nay concern to 'em."

Fearing that if he asked further questions Broster would suspect the true nature of his work, McAndrew made no more inquiries, but instead spoke at length of the beauties of nature he had witnessed while walking with Miss Broster, using tones of rapture such as he supposed a poet might adopt. Broster scowled and directed his daughter to ladle out the 'tater hash', a hodgepodge of potatoes and rabbit that was their evening meal, washed down with a spiced homebrewed ale. After several draughts of the latter, Broster grew quarrelsome, and his daughter enjoined upon McAndrew to seek his bed. Her father would be himself in the morning, she explained.

McAndrew lay abed that night in his rented room with no intention of sleeping. When certain that Broster and his daughter had both gone to their own beds, and after a suitable space had passed to ensure they slept, he slipped from his bed and dressed himself. As silently as any Red Indian he departed the cottage, leaving the door on the 'sneck' (latch) and made his way across the sandhills, following the same winding path by which the girl had taken him during the day.

It was an eerie journey, illumined by the uncanny glow of the coastal lighthouses and a gibbous moon that limned the sandhills' flanks with silver. The night silence was broken only by the occasional croaking of a natterjack toad. Reaching the sandhill where he had stubbed his toe, he sought cover behind a tuffet of star grass.

Several dark figures had gathered round the same spot, wielding spades and digging deep. McAndrew saw they were unearthing several objects that resembled kegs. In his eagerness to see more clearly this scene of moonlit skulduggery, he must have dislodged a pebble from amongst the grass for it went skittering away down the side of the dune. Whereupon the men started, seized their loot, and shambling, hopping, and leaping, vanished in different directions amongst the sandhills. Some even sought refuge in the spreading waters of the Hoyle Lake.

2 The Sunken Forest

McAndrew remained where he was. The exodus had been so rapid, it had passed like a dream. The sandhills were deserted under the light of the moon, as if no one had been there. He rose, and went to investigate. Quite a sizeable excavation had been dug, but there was no indication of what had lain in it. In their flight, the men, smugglers, wreckers or whatever they had been, had taken their loot with them. It would be dangerous to remain here, deserted though it seemed to be. He hurried away.

Returning to Broster's cottage some while later, he slipped within and found his own room where he undressed in the darkness and then slid himself between cold sheets. His mind was a whirl of surmise and it took him some time to fall asleep.

In the morning, after breakfast, McAndrew posted his report to me, then borrowed a sturdy nag of Broster's and rode with the sandhills on his right hand and the mudflats and sandbanks on his left. The sea was busy with shipping, but dark clouds surged on the horizon and he disliked the look of the weather.

The tide was out, and as he galloped along the strand he saw what resembled the stumps of trees in the sand below the highwater mark, as if a whole forest had been felled ere it was inundated. Passing the lighthouse, he crossed the sandhills to see meadows and marshes stretching away in the direction of two low ranges of hills. Another lighthouse was visible on the closest of these prominences.

The octagonal tower was his destination. As he drew closer, he saw that Mockbeggar Hall stood in its own grounds in the lee of the sandhills, surrounded by several outbuildings and lawns with ornamental flowerbeds, a far cry from the meagre dwellings he had hitherto seen. This, he told himself, must be the home of a gentleman. Dismounting and flinging the reins to the stable-boy who appeared from an outbuilding, he approached the door and rang the bell.

After handing his visiting card to the butler who answered, he was shown through into a library. He was inspecting a carved piece of wood on one wall, on which someone had inscribed the enigmatic words *From Birkinheven unto Hilbre / A squirrel might leape from tree to tree*, when the door was opened. A woman's voice said, "In the old days this was forest as far as the eye could see."

He turned to see an elderly lady leaning on a stick. She entered, and sat down on a chair by the fireplace.

"You may sit," she added graciously, and McAndrew did as he was bidden. Introducing herself as Mrs Boode and welcoming him to Mockbeggar Hall, she added, "We seldom have visitors at this time of year, Mr McAndrew. May I ask what brings you to this coast?"

"I am a poet," McAndrew said, "and I am staying in a nearby cottage while I seek inspiration amongst scenes of unspoilt nature. I live in Liverpool, and the city's hurly-burly is not conducive to poesy."

"Indeed," said Mrs Boode. "I fear your work has yet to come my way. How may I help you?" She rang for the maid and drinks were served.

"You mentioned a forest," McAndrew said obliquely. "On my ride here I went along the shore. It was low tide, and I seemed to see tree stumps going out a long way, vanishing into the sea itself."

"This coastline is eroding at a rapid rate," Mrs Boode said. "The old rhyme you were reading refers to a forest that once stretched from what is now called Birkenhead, newly a scene of the most ardent industry, to Hilbre, the small island off the coast. Once it was not an island, and land stretched much further. Sometimes, when there has been a storm and the tide is low, whole villages have appeared from the sand and mud, whose lanes show the ruts of wheel tracks and the prints of boots of a kind worn hundreds of years ago. I have heard that if you swim a short way out from the shore due north of the nearby lighthouse, it is possible to find gravestones beneath the water, as if some churchyard stood there at one time, since flooded. Amongst the tree stumps of the forest you saw have been found the antlers of Irish elk and other extinct creatures. Furthermore the wood has become stone, so it must be very old. This library is ornamented with petrified wood taken from the forest."

"How very interesting," said McAndrew politely.

"Oh, the vicinity is rich in folklore," Mrs Boode added with a laugh. "Some say that it was on this shoreline that King Canute bade the sea 'come not hither nor wet the sole of my foot', and a mermaid is said to appear by the so-called Mermaid Stones nearby when the moon is full. The local people are most inventive in their legends."

"I am staying with some of them," McAndrew commented, "a fisherman named Broster and his fair daughter."

"I fear I have not made his acquaintance," said Mrs Boode a little frostily. "I would counsel you to be wary of the natives. In my youth I went to live with my husband on his plantation in the West Indies, when pirates were still not unknown in those waters, and yet it is the denizens of the Cheshire coast who I find to be the most rapacious and cruel saltwater thieves."

"I believe I read something to that effect in the *Liverpool Mercury*," said McAndrew airily. "Are they truly more black hearted villains than the likes of Calico Jack and Captain Morgan?"

"They are wreckers, Mr McAndrew," said the old lady. "During winter storms, whenever a ship founders off this coast, the people of all the neighbouring villages come down to seize what they can take a hold of. By ancient custom, they maintain that a man may claim anything washed up from the wreck if he puts his foot on it and declares 'This is mine.' Anything can be claimed—as long as the owner is dead. And if he isn't..." The pause gave sinister emphasis to her words. "I have done what I can to ameliorate the savagery of my neighbours. Whenever a ship has been wrecked, I have done all I could out of Christian charity to see that the crews were rescued and given every comfort in my home. I am cordially loathed and detested as a busybody by villagers all along the coast, but I have no fear of them."

After taking his leave of the hospitable old lady, McAndrew mounted his horse again and continued his ride along the shore. From time to time he found cottages or small villages whose inhabitants watched his passing with eyes that glittered, he now fancied, with a murderous menace and avarice. Mrs Boode's words only confirmed what he already knew, what I myself had told him when I sent him on his mission. But otherwise his peregrinations that day were fruitless.

It was growing dark when he rode back towards the village of Hoose. The wind blew amongst the star grass again, but it was growing to an angry howl, lashing up the surging foam of the sea, and all he could hear otherwise was the thudding of his nag's hoofs on the sand. The glow from the nearest lighthouse was his only source of illumination when he detected a sound of stealthy movement from all around him.

Dark figures appeared from the sandhills, converging silently on him and his plodding horse. A clammy hand snatched his ankle, another the tail of his coat, and he was dragged from the saddle. Fists and feet punched and kicked him, and a man struck at him with a heavy stick. He fought desperately against his unseen assailants, hearing his nag whinny as she galloped away.

3 The Storm

"Knock the spy on the sconce and fling 'im in th' wayter," one of his assailants growled.

"Wait!" cried another. "Look out t' sea! T' sea, mon! To sea!"

The storm was growing. McAndrew saw the dark figures gazing out to sea, where a ship was battered by the howling winds. She was an Irish packet ship by her lines, carrying mail and passengers to Dublin, and he could see her heeling over as her mast shook and trembled in the storm wind and the crew struggled to lower the mainsail. With a crack that was audible even ashore, the mast snapped and vanished overboard.

Now with only mizzen and bowsprit, the ship was driven towards the sandbanks. Excitedly, voraciously, the wreckers began running towards the water, McAndrew forgotten in the heat of the moment. One man went sprinting up the strand, as if bearing a message. Taking this as his cue, my man fled.

He knew, as he floundered over the sandhills, that the wind was growing, that it would batter the coast, that ships would be driven onto the sandbanks and the shore itself. He knew that if things ran true to form the local villagers would come down to the strand to seize whatever they could get their hands on. He should be on hand to witness it, or else he should send for help. If he returned to Mrs Boode, perhaps word could be sent to Liverpool and the Dock Police.

But he was dazed and battered from the fight. He needed a mount if he was to reach Mockbeggar Hall in time, and the only horse available to him had galloped away into the night. He had a shrewd suspicion, however, that he knew where she would be making for, and so he turned his steps in that direction. Towards Hoose.

When at last he saw the lights of the village amidst the dark shadows of the sandhills, the storm wind was reaching its height. He stumbled blindly, arms bent to shelter his face from the stinging grains. When he found his booted feet clattering on cobblestones he lowered his arms to find the village a scene of the utmost fervour and excitement.

Men carrying lanterns crowded the narrow lanes, accompanying other men and even women and children with handcarts or barrows or horses or asses; every means available for transporting ill gotten gains. They were moving en masse in the direction of the coast. McAndrew stood in their path, staring at them in a daze.

"Out o' th' road, mon!" someone yelled, and he staggered into the shelter of a thatched cottage as the villagers flooded past.

Seeing Broster and his daughter among this rout, the former leading his lost nag, McAndrew grabbed the man's arm.

"What's happening?" he shouted.

The good folk of Hoose were singing as they eagerly traversed the few sandy acres leading down to shore. "Looks loike there'll be a wreck afore mornin'," Broster shouted back, not breaking step so McAndrew was forced to follow him. "Thou'd best be gaddin' 'ome. Bain't for th' likes o' 'ee."

"We was afeard for 'ee when th'owd nag come back without 'ee," said Polly pertly. "Did she throw 'ee?"

"You mean to plunder the vessel?" McAndrew cried, not heeding the girl.

"Only if she founders," said Broster. "If not, there'll still be rich pickin's alung th' strond."

"You can't take your daughter out in this storm," said McAndrew. "Or with this gang of villains."

"Oi towd 'ee," said Broster. "Gad back to th'ouse. Dur's on th' sneck. Don't 'ee come wi' us."

"I'll come with you," said McAndrew, suddenly inspired. "You'll need help carrying your booty back home."

Broster looked at him in surprise, studying him as if he saw a stranger, rather than his lodger. "That be reet good o' 'ee, sir," he said. "Never thought a poet like 'ee would 'elp us. Too like a mardy choild, beggin' thoi pardon, sir."

By the time they reached the shore near where McAndrew had been ambushed, fires had been lit in the lee of the sandhills and their sporadic light shed illumination on a ghastly scene. The packet ship had foundered some little way off shore; its mast and rigging was all that could be seen jutting from the turbulent water, but the strand was strewn with a litter of goods from its hold. To McAndrew's horror, he saw the bodies of crewmen and passengers mingled with the flotsam and jetsam.

Already people from the surrounding villages had descended upon the shore and were busy hauling items of cargo up out of the water. McAndrew saw men and women carrying timber, bales, boxes, and sundry other items cast up by the foaming wave. Little remained for the Hoose folk when they got there. Broster fell to cursing at this dearth, but mercifully the roaring of the wind obscured his oaths.

McAndrew saw three dark, drenched shapes clamber up out of the surf, crawling on hands and knees as the wind battered at them. Several men approached, and for a moment McAndrew rejoiced, thinking they would become the castaways' saviours, but it was not to be. On encountering a pair of ill shod feet, the first of the escapees looked up. A man raised a cudgel, it swooped down and the castaway fell flat in the surf, a dark stain blotting the water.

Another man scrambled to his feet and began to flounder away, but the men followed him, one seizing him by the legs, another belabouring him with his cudgel until he moved no longer. The third castaway got as far as the sand before the mob beat him and flung him back into the water.

"We con keep whatever we foind," Broster explained to the horrified McAndrew, "as lung as th' mon who owned it be dead. 'ee shouldn't have come," he added. "This bain't for th' likes o' 'ee."

"Is it for the likes of your daughter, man?" McAndrew demanded harshly. "What kind of example are you giving her?"

"Polly's a good girl," said Broster. "Not soft gutted like some Oi could mention. What's that ye've found, lass?"

Polly looked up from her inspection of a drowned woman's body. The clothes, though thoroughly drenched, were costly and in the height of fashion. The face was one of remarkable beauty, and long tresses floated around her half sunk head like seaweed. A ring glittered on one finger and earrings dangled from the corpse's earlobes.

"Looks loike gowd, feyther," she said with an impish grin. "'ee take th' ring and Oi'll have th' earrings."

McAndrew was shocked. "You see how your upbringing of her has blighted the girl's morals?" he stormed. "If her mother were still here..."

"If 'er mayther were still on droi lond," said Broster, "she wouldn't be wasting toime loike this." He produced his knife as if to cut off the finger, ring and all.

McAndrew grappled with him, seizing his knife hand. "In the name of Christian charity!" he exhorted the fisherman.

Broster thrust him aside. In his weakened state, McAndrew was helpless, and he landed painfully on his side in the wet sand.

Standing over him, Broster laughed. "'ee prate to me o' Christian charity!" he yelled. "But 'oo is it led us 'ere but th' parson?" He indicated a well dressed man who was loading an ass with valuables cast up by the waves, and McAndrew saw that this was indeed a man of the cloth.

Broster seized the finger of the dead girl and began to saw through flesh and bone. Morbidly fascinated, McAndrew watched the grisly process, sickened by what he saw. All around, the strand was a scene of bacchanal as the wreckers caroused, singing 'Admiral Benbow' and 'Spanish Ladies' while they harvested the bounty of the sea. A keg of rum had been hacked open with an axe and a group of men was passing it from mouth to thirsty mouth. McAndrew saw the man Broster had called parson drinking deep as he held the keg precariously to his lips.

With a chuckle, Broster lifted up the severed finger. One end was bloody, the other was graced with an elegantly manicured fingernail. In its middle was the ring, a band of gold containing a gem that resembled a ruby in the fitful firelight. He stripped it from the finger, consigned the latter to the yeasty waves, then slipped the ring on. He held it up and examined it gleefully in the firelight.

"Feyther," grumbled Polly, tugging at the corpse's earrings, "'ow do Oi get these off?"

"Do as thoi mayther would 'ave done," said Broster.

And Polly knelt down beside the body, the wet skirt of her gown clinging scandalously to her slender legs. For a wild moment McAndrew thought she was kissing the corpse goodnight. Then she lifted her head and he almost vomited, seeing the trickle of blood run down her lip. In one triumphant hand she held an earring, which she had torn away from the corpse's earlobe with her own teeth.

4 Beneath the Wave

McAndrew awoke with a dry mouth. He was gazing up at a sky in which drifted early morning clouds, and seemed to be lying in the sand. Turning his head confusedly, he saw the tide was out, a long way out. He was very cold.

When he sat up, his clothes moved stiffly on his skin. They had partly dried out on his body as he slept but still retained moisture. Salt was crusted thick on them. He broke off in a fit of coughing. He had no recollection of falling asleep.

To one side of him were the sandhills, to the other the beach stretched as far as the distant sea, which glimmered bluely on the horizon. Over the dunes the morning sun was rising. A few broken fragments of wood lay scattered on the churned up sand. Black circles showed where fires had blazed last night, and here a few embers still glowed. In the near distance, the broken timbers of a ship lay half sunk in the sand.

Crawling nearer to one of the patches of ash, he found enough unburnt wood and sufficient embers to start a new fire. Once it was burning merrily, he stripped off his still wet clothes and propped them up on sticks by the fire. Clad only in his drawers and his shirt he sat waiting for his clothes to dry. What had happened?

He remembered the revelling wreckers, his fight with Broster, the horrifying scenes that ensued. Then all was a blank. Had he fallen asleep where he lay? It was the only explanation. And then the wreckers had all returned to their dwelling houses. As soon as his clothes were dry, he would make his way back to Liverpool and file his report.

He heard laughter like the mocking call of a gull. Turning,

he saw, atop a sandhill, Polly, her long hair, her gown, and her shawl all fluttering in the breeze. She ran down the side of the dune as barefoot as any gypsy wench.

"There 'ee are!" she said. "Feyther thought Oi would foind 'ee here. We lost 'ee in th' festerment last neet."

McAndrew, like most Scotchmen, was prudish to a fault, and felt mortified to appear before a young woman in only his shirt. But what he remembered of the night before filled him with righteous wrath.

"You have been led astray, Miss Broster," he said severely. "Your father, all the other villagers, they have led you into sin. I must take you away from here, shield you from further temptation."

She laughed, gazing down at him. "Mr McAndrew, Mr McAndrew," she chided. "Oi could not leave moi village. We are aw one family in 'oose. Aw th' same, Oi miss Mayther, ond moi brother." Brightly, she added, "Feyther says it is toime 'ee met Mayther."

McAndrew gazed sadly at her. "Miss Broster," he said awkwardly, "your mother was lost at sea long ago, your brother with her. I will never have the privilege of meeting that good lady."

"O' course 'ee will!" she said eagerly, seizing his hand. "Come wi' me. We'll go to see Mayther."

Protesting, he allowed himself to be hauled to his feet, but withdrew his hand from her grasp. "Miss Broster," he remonstrated, "I must be going..."

"Not yet!" she insisted. "Oi must take 'ee to see Mayther. Come on! Oi'll race 'ee." She ran across the sands in the direction of the distant surf.

McAndrew stood by the little fire, gazing anxiously after her. What did she mean to do? He tested his clothes again, but they were still wet. Hoping no one else was abroad on this cold morning, he broke into a run, following the line of footprints Polly had left in the deep, rippling sand.

Soon his shoes, the leather already thick with saltwater, became unwearable, and he paused to unbuckle them. Once he had done so he looked up. Polly was but a tiny dot on the horizon. Gasping for breath, feet bare, he shambled after the girl. He found her shawl lying half in and half out of a tidal pool. Picking it up, he stared at it in bewilderment, then ran on. Further along he found her cap. Then her gown, discarded beside a spot where her footprints had halted a while. When the marge of the sea became more distinct he saw that she stood a little way out into the water, with the foam rushing around her ankles. She wore only a chemise.

"Miss Broster, I must beg you to come away from the water," he said uncomfortably. "And I insist you put your clothes back on!" He placed them all in a neat pile by the water's edge.

"They'll only get in th' road when we gad to visit Mayther," said the girl, and to his horror, she reached down and pulled the chemise up over her head. "Oi see thee come ready," she added, "but thou'd be well instructed to doff thoi undergarments. Follow me!" She turned and waded further out, then as the water began to reach her waist, dived as sleekly as any otter.

It is at this point that Constable McAndrew's report grows unreliable, for he maintains that in that flash of bare flesh he saw for the first time that her creamy skin was freckled with a multiplicity of tiny, dark green scales. Despite this uncanny vision, he feared for her life. It was cold and the sea would be icy. Struggling out of his shirt he ran after her, wallowing through the surf and diving into the water. At first he saw nothing under the surface but rising bubbles and a distant green glow. Then she was there, naked as the day she was born, her legs threshing like flippers. She seized his hand, and together they swam through the green depths.

The water was warmer than he had anticipated, and the wintry sun danced above them as she led him deeper. Now, extending across the sandy sea floor as far as he could see, he saw the stumps of trees like those he had noticed closer to the shore. The pair swam over the felled forest, passing occasional wrecks, ships of ancient design; an Elizabethan brigantine here, a Viking longship there, even a quinquereme, and a curraugh of the ancient Irish lay half shrouded in sand and festooned with weed. It must be noted that he had no trouble breathing during a lengthy period submerged, but such fantasies are to be expected from the ravings of madmen.

Next he glimpsed drowned buildings. Medieval houses of wattle and daub through which swam dog fish, cod, pollack, even a conger eel. Beyond the medieval houses squatted mud huts such as the Saxons dwelt in. Beyond them he says he saw half toppled towers built of drystone like the brochs that can still be seen in many parts of McAndrew's 'ain countrie'.

Amidst this prehistoric city lurked a broch larger than the rest. Out of it swam fishlike forms with bulging eyes and squamous skin, yet shaped uncommonly like men, if deformed and of abysmally savage type. And something else lurked inside the broch. Something Polly called Mother. She urged him to swim under the stone arch.

At the mere sight of that tentacular horror, McAndrew broke frenziedly free from the girl's grasp, shuddering in fear. She reached out to seize him but succeeded only in slashing him across the face with a hand that now was sharp with talons. His last sight of her revealed the disappointment written upon her green hued face as he began to swim, swim, swim desperately for the surface. Shoals of fishlike men pursued him avidly through forests of weed, and he fled them for a nightmarishly long space of time...

The next he remembers is waking up in a bed between crisp, starched sheets, with Mrs Boode's concerned face peering down at him. He was shivering with cold. A smartly dressed maid helped him to sip from a hot drink and he coughed violently.

"Mrs Boode!" he cried. "Madam, what am I doing here? Is this Mockbeggar Hall?"

"Why, yes, Mr McAndrew," she said, "or should I say constable?" Seeing his bewilderment, she added, "You have spoken a deal in your sleep. Much of it I could not understand, but now I know that you are employed by the Liverpool Dock Police. You were found cast up on the shore after high tide and my servants brought you in, fearing for your life. There was a storm last night and at least one ship went down. I fear the wreckers claimed the lives of those wretches who were spared by the sea. But how did you come to be in the water yourself?"

Had it all been a dream? It must have been, he told himself, for it had been low tide when he followed the girl into the water. He felt a twinge of pain from his face. Reaching up with a tentative hand, he encountered the linen of a dressing.

"You seemed to have been attacked by something," Mrs Boode informed him. "Something that left four slash marks like the claw marks of some large creature. The sea can do strange things to a man's body."

Epilogue

When he was brought back to Liverpool McAndrew was sufficiently *compos mentis* to write down what he had seen in an official report. But what I read gave me no qualms to call in an alienist of my acquaintance, and after many efforts to calm the madman, he was committed to Lancaster County Asylum.

No arrests were made amongst the villagers of Hoose, neither Broster nor his compadres were hanged at Gallows Hill as they so richly deserve, for no judge would listen to evidence provided by a man who has been condemned to the madhouse. But I am determined that one day we will break these wreckers, these land pirates who stole from me one of my most able officers by driving him out of his wits. The Lord grant that I live to see that day!

There came a rustling from the far end
of the cellar. A shape lurched into view

THE ACCOUNT OF MALCOM CONRAD, Esq.

B. HARLAN CRAWFORD

I will not recount the circumstances or details of my transportation to Australia and my difficulties there. Nor will I recount how I was exonerated and returned to Cornwall where I became embroiled with that horrid affair with the Pictish fetish-hammer, as my fellow Pickmanites have assured me I have rehashed those accounts with such frequency that they have grown tiresome.

Let me instead relate the details of a later affair.

After being dismissed from my position with Nupkins and Braithwaite after a misunderstanding around a discrepancy of some three hundred twenty pounds and sixpence, I found myself once again at my leisure, wandering the environs of the Forest of Dean. Word had reached me that an old schoolmate, Sam Meagles, was engaged in building a coke-fired furnace in that area using a novel design of his own invention. I was not surprised to hear Meagles was undertaking such a project. He was an imaginative lad in his youth prone to flights of fancy that often intruded on his perception of the realities of life.

The locals directed me to his operation with many a wry glance. I gathered they found Meagles amusingly eccentric. It was situated deep in a sparsely travelled area of the forest. I followed a narrow pathway for some miles before I arrived.

The furnace itself dominated the clearing in which it was constructed, and its design was indeed novel. Even with my desultory smattering of engineering knowledge, I could tell that once in full operation it would without doubt revolutionize the steel industry.

However, as I gazed upon it, it became clear to me the furnace had lain idle for some time. Foliage had encroached upon it, and rust had formed on some of the more exposed areas. Perplexed by this, I proceeded to the crude shack erected near the furnace where I assumed Meagles and his crew made their abode.

I rapped heavily upon the door with my stick and receiving no reply, I called out. "Meagles! Meagles, it is I, Conrad! Are you there?"

From within, I heard a faint stirring and a muffled thud, as if a heavy slab were dropped to the floor. After a rattling of multiple latches and the door opened, and at last I clapped eyes on my old friend.

He was in a remarkable state of dishevelment, his hair and moustache were wildly disarrayed, with the remainder of his face unshaven for a week or more. His stained shirt was without collar or cuffs, and his demeanour was one of the utmost agitation. Still, he seemed genuinely pleased to see me and greeted me warmly.

"Conrad? Can it be? It is you! Conrad my good fellow! Come in, come in."

He ushered me into the shack. The interior consisted of one large room, spartanly furnished with a large table, several straight-backed chairs, and a few rows of bunk beds meant to accommodate a crew of workers. A cast iron stove sat near the center. Adjacent to this was a heavy trapdoor no doubt leading to a cellar. I surmised this had been the source of the booming noise I heard upon my arrival. The whole place was filthy and cluttered with empty bottles, cans, and other detritus.

"Are you alone here, Meagles?" I enquired. "Seems like a big operation for one man."

"Alone? No. I sent my assistants away... a while back. I have suspended work with the smelter. Another project has presented itself that occupies my full attention. No, I am not alone."

Meagles was agitated and his wide eyes rolled about alarmingly. They ceased to flit when he fixed them upon me and stared with a burning intensity.

"Conrad, we haven't seen one another since our school days, but I always remembered you as a fellow of strong character. I must confide in someone lest I go mad. Can I count on your discretion?"

I assumed he had devised some sort of invention that he feared may be co-opted by a third party. "Of course, Meagles, my lips are sealed."

"Very well. I will give you the facts of the matter, then show you what is in the cellar."

Meagles shuffled to the stove and fiddled with it nervously before continuing.

"I found him hiding amongst a wagonload of coal brought in for our experiments."

"Him?"

"Yes. A child. Cowering naked in the coal wagon. I don't

know how he came to be there. Perhaps he took shelter in the wagon. At any rate I discovered him and brought him inside. Secreting him in the cellar so as not to alarm the others. You see, the lad has many... peculiarities that the less discerning among us might find distressing."

"Surely you informed the authorities and made enquiries as to the boy's next of kin?"

"That had occurred to me, but the child is so extraordinary I felt that would be counterproductive. I believe the lad is a feral child, born of the wilderness and untouched by civilization. "

In a burst of frenzied energy, Meagles abruptly wheeled from the stove and snatched open the trapdoor. I was taken aback by the strength thus exhibited. Taking up a paraffin lamp, He stood panting over the open trapdoor. He gestured to the opening then to his ear. I gathered he wished me to listen.

I will refer to the sounds I heard as speech, for it describes the sounds as well as any other word in my arsenal, but it was like unto speech a is the warbling of a bird or whimpering of a dog. It consisted primarily of a droning high-pitched rattle, occasionally my mind would try to put the sounds into words and language, but the effort soon set my temples to pounding.

"Clearly he was never taught to speak" stated Meagles. "Come and meet him."

I followed him down the steeply inclined stairs of roughhewn timbers into the basement. The name glorifies what was basically a roughly oblong pit dug out beneath the shack. It was filled with various crates and barrels containing sundry supplies used by Meagles' group.

"Charlie!" Called Meagles. "Charlie, come out and meet Mr.

Conrad!" Meagles turned to me with a wink. "I call him Charlie."

"So I gather."

There came a rustling from the far end of the cellar.

A shape lurched into view. It was indeed about the size of a boy of perhaps six years of age, clad in a suit of workman's clothes, inexpertly tailored to fit its smaller frame. Its skin was of a sickly bluish pallor.

A bulbous hairless head perched atop a long curiously crooked neck. Without projecting ears or nose, it had the look of a rotten gourd or pumpkin. Large lidless black eyes leered at us above a pulpy lipped mouth that worked over the yellow irregular pegs of its teeth. A ceaseless litany of droning nonsense streamed from it.

The hands were incongruously large and broad for its stature, tipped with thick spatulate nails and filthily encrusted with dried mud and clay. It waddled toward us on short, bowed legs with a gait that was hideously comical.

"Meagles." I croaked. "I don't believe that is a child."

"Nonsense. He suffers from deformities, but this should not be cause for us to deny his humanity! It is our duty to see he has a chance to contribute to society."

Charlie stood before us, arms akimbo in an attitude of confrontation, his droning growing louder and insistent. My nerves were reaching a breaking point.

"Let's go back up Meagles, and we can discuss it."

We went back up and I seated myself at the table. After I had fortified my nerves with two glasses of brandy, I questioned Meagles as to what he intended for the creature in the cellar. He stood and paced the floor with one arm behind him, as though he were a professor addressing his classroom.

"Obviously, he cannot stay here. I will arrange to have him brought to Monmouth, where I have rented rooms. There I will educate him, at least to the point where he can communicate and comport himself in a reasonably respectful manner, then I will arrange for his formal education."

"Have you considered consulting a doctor, or perhaps a... zoologist?"

"Don't be silly Conrad. Such over-educated jackanapes would only hinder the lads' education."

"See here Meagles! I don't believe it is a child, it seems to be... to be... perhaps an orang-outan, rendered hairless in some way. It may have escaped a menagerie."

Meagles waved a hand dismissively. "An Ape? Charlie is nothing of the sort. I thought you were more compassionate, Conrad."

"I assure you I am, but I am more concerned with your wellbeing. You seem unhealthily fixated with this creature. Perhaps you fancy yourself Lord Stanhope to his Kaspar Hauser?"

Meagle's face reddened, and his hands curled into fists, I feared he might strike me. But suddenly he sighed and relaxed.

"Forgive me Conrad, it is true the matter has agitated me to the extreme. Let us not speak of it further until morning. I will pour more brandy, over which we will confine our conversation to old reminiscence."

This we did, we finished the bottle as we merrily discussed our school days. I became so relaxed that I barely registered the gibbering from below.

After some time, we grew weary and retired to the bunks. The soporific effects of the brandy had quieted the agitation of my nerves. I was untroubled by the muffled tittering and scratching coming from the basement. Indeed, these served almost as a lullaby and soon sent me into slumber. I am unsure how long I slept, but I next found myself in that half-slumbering state that sometimes proceeds full wakefulness.

My gaze fell upon the trap door. A ruddy glow emanated from the gaps around it. I watched as the gaps widened, flooding the shack with crimson illumination. I was not alarmed. I think I felt the whole proceedings were part of a dream. The illumination flickered as thick spatulate fingers wedged into the gap. The door was opened, and Charlie emerged from the basement. His pulpy bulbous head swivelled on his gangly neck, looking to and fro. When his eyes settled upon Meagles his face split into a wide toothy grin. Clambering out of the basement Charlie scuttled across the floor.

Behind him another figure emerged. It was a duplicate of Charlie in many ways, but rather than the outsized workman's costume this creeping homunculus was naked save for a filthy rag wrapped about its nether regions like a crude kilt. In its massive, outsized fist it gripped what I would call a pickaxe, though one of foreign and extraordinary design. Its bare feet were as incongruously large and robust as its hands, with heavily nailed hammer toes. Thick hairs, like those upon the legs of a fly, grew upon the tops of the feet, comprising the only visible hair on the thing's repulsive body.

A third dwarf emerged, and a fourth, followed by more. It was as if the earth vomited forth an endless stream of these stunted abominations.

Yet I took no action, I lay under a lassitude that left me a passive observer to the phantasmagorical events playing out inside that crude shack. I now observed how Charlie gripped a serrated knife of the same outré make as his fellow's pickaxe, and he closed in on the slumbering Meagles.

My mind screamed for my body to act, but I was immobilized by unseen fetters. As one part of my mind strove against spectral bonds, another opened like a cauldron into which poured cosmic truths rejected by men for centuries. Charlie was no child, deformed or otherwise. Rather he and his brethren were those stunted, burrowing troglodytes who have lived alongside man since he was cast out from Eden.

As man's forebears reared great towers into the sky, Charlie's delved deep and wide into the earth, making obeisance to primordial god-things in subterranean tabernacles. We above have always known of them, cloaking their true horror in whimsy and folklore, yes, but we have always known them.

By some misadventure one of these infernal goblins found himself in the coal wagon and fell into the hands of Meagles, who in his ignorance had heaped indignity upon it. Now Charlie wished revenge.

Charlie crept toward Meagles who lay as though stupefied. Charlie clambered up onto the bed and stooped over Meagles' face like a clerk stooping over his ledger.

I sought to scream, to wake Meagles to the approach of doom, but I could do little more than shudder and emit a muffled squeak. Thus, I could only watch as Charlie cut Sam Meagles' throat from ear to ear.

The deed done, Charlie began a recital of squeals clicks and titters that left no doubt as to its celebratory mood, he paused this only to occasionally lick his reddened blade with a long purple tongue that wrapped about the knife like the arm of an octopus.

Whether it was through an act of will, or through the shock of witnessing the horrid fate of Meagles, the paralysis that held me faded. I bounded from the bed and faced a brace of goblins who stood before me brandishing their bizarre pickaxes. Lacking a weapon of my own I seized the frame of the bunk and with all the power my panicked muscles could muster, I hurled the affair toward them. They scrambled out of the way giving voice to inhuman, guttural howls.

I made a mad dash to the door but was arrested when one of them grasped me about the knees and endeavoured to bowl me over. It was incongruously strong for its stature. Casting about for any means of defence I snatched the paraffin lamp from the table and smashed it repeatedly into the pallid orb of the goblins head. The glass chimney shattered, slashing open the things head which then oozed a sickly black ichor.

Guided by desperation or panic, I hurled the undamaged base of the lamp hard against the stove. It shattered and spilled its contents upon the stove. In seconds, it belched tongues of flame and a billowing cloud of acrid smoke.

The fire and smoke vexed the goblins and they shrieked and wailed. I strove once more for the door. They belaboured me with their knives and pickaxes, succeeding in dealing me several wounds, but none serious enough to stop me. The flames and smoke no doubt hindered their efforts at ending my life.

I staggered out of the shack into the first rays of the dawning sun and fled as though the hounds of hell were upon my heels. Perhaps I became unhinged, for I spent some days living as a wildman in the forest until stumbling upon a rail line. I waited alongside it until I was able to leap upon a slow-moving freight car which eventually delivered me to Gloucester. There, having recovered my senses, I secured a situation as a stevedore.

It was nearly two months later when I came upon a newspaper account of the mysterious disappearance of Meagles. As it happened some of his assistants returned to the site to inquire after him and discovered the shack destroyed by fire. No bodies, human or otherwise were discovered. The police professed bafflement and had no persons of interest in the matter save for a "vagabond" some locals recalled asking after Meagles prior to his disappearance, needless to say I made no effort to illuminate the authorities as to the identity of this person.

That, Fellow Pickmanites, is the long and short of it. I am hopeful that my account has both amused and enlightened you.

He stepped over the low remnants
of a wall. Ahead stood angular
shapes between which the grass grew
thick and unruly

THE FEASTER FROM AFAR

GLYNN OWEN BARRASS

"Greetings gentlemen." Edward Williamson stood as he addressed the room. "Many of you are aware I am a detective in the City of Glasgow police force. Now, this may appear a rather exciting position, yet it was only when I departed Glasgow that I encountered something so strange I have trouble believing the events I witnessed first-hand."

He nodded towards Samuel Pickman. "This good man has a nose for the strange, for it was on his recommendation my superiors despatched me down to the north east coast to investigate two most bizarre deaths." Williamson held a bundle of papers in his hands. He examined the eager faces around him, unfolded the bundle, and began his reading.

"My journey involved travel by three carriages. After beginning in my home town, I stopped off in Gretna Green for the night, taking a second cab to the town of Newcastle..."

He'd remained in Newcastle a short while, a bustling centre of shipyards and industry. Just long enough to stretch his legs really. The smoggy air had reminded him of Glasgow. The carriage, nearing his destination according to the time on his pocket watch, currently passed through the Yorkshire moors. Beyond the window, a beautiful, untamed wilderness of purple bracken and hills sprawled off into the distance. Longing to walk that moorland plateau, feel the rough country under his feet, he wondered if he'd have time to visit them during his sojourn.

"Not bloody likely," he said under his breath, and instantly regretted it.

"Ah, I see you are admiring our moors, sir. It is very mild there you know, even at this time of year."

Williamson looked to his companion, nodded politely. The gentleman had joined him in the cab at some point after Newcastle. The man had florid cheeks, a wiry blonde moustache going to grey. With his stout boots, walking stick and thick jacket, he looked ready for the moors himself. Williamson cringed at the thought of having the insufferable man as a companion there.

Stainsby, as he'd introduced himself, appeared to be awaiting an answer. The man had nearly talked him to death at the start of their journey. He wasn't going to fall into that trap again.

"The Romans visited all over the moors you know?"

It seemed Stainsby couldn't be perturbed. "Arrived in AD Seventy-one, built signal stations all along the coast at Scarborough, Filey, Ravenscar, and Hunt Cliff."

Williamson's attention pricked up at the mention of Ravenscar, his destination.

"You are quite a fount of knowledge, sir," he replied.

The man grinned, his moustache bristling. "Oh just a dabbler in local knowledge really. You know-"

"Excuse me," Williamson interrupted Stainsby and leant forward in his seat. A change of scenery was visible outside. Beyond the untamed moors, he saw uneven cliff edges, and beyond these, the metallic blue of the ocean.

"Ravenscar Peak!" the driver boomed. "All off for Ravenscar Peak."

Stainsby, who'd leant over to look out the window himself, said, "You know that the name comes from -"

The carriage came to a quick halt. Williamson used the opportunity for a swift escape. "Time to dash!" he said, turned and offered his hand. "A pleasure to meet you sir, pleasant journey."

"A pleasant journey to you too," Stainsby replied. His hand felt warm and moist.

It came as a relief that Stainsby wasn't getting off with him, and Williamson exited the cab and closed the door behind him. He stepped upon gravel. A small wood-panelled structure stood before him. Probably somewhere for folk to rest in this way-station in the middle of nowhere. An elderly man, sat on a bench beside the building, stared at him lazily.

"Master Williamson, sir" a voice said behind him.

Williamson turned. The carriage driver, a burly man with worn features, had his case. He passed it over, and Williamson dug into his pocket, removed some coins and slipped them into his hand.

"Thank ye kindly," the man replied. He sent Williamson a toothless grin and shook the horses' reins, taking Stainsby and the carriage away with him. Williamson began walking. A white fence followed the road with an open gate a little ways along. Beyond stood shrubbery, and trees. Hurried footsteps sounded behind him, and a voice shouted, "Sir, sir?"

Williamson turned on his heels. It was a lad in his teens, wearing an oversized grey coat and a top hat.

"Supposed to be here to greet you sir." The lad panted as he spoke. "My apologies. You must be the policeman yes? I can tell by your bearing."

Williamson placed his case to the ground, said, "Inspector Edward Williamson, a pleasure to meet you, er..."

"George is the name sir, Georgie for short," the lad said and shook Williamson's proffered hand. "Lord Ravenscar's people sent me along sir, to pick you up and take you to the village, I am his odd-job man and messenger."

Lord Ravenscar, an old school-friend of Samuel Pickman's, and part of the reason he was here.

"All right Georgie," Williamson said, "Is it a long walk?"

"Oh no sir," the lad grinned, "There is a carriage waiting." He stepped forward, took the case, and added, "Follow me."

Georgie rushed past Williamson and headed through the gate. *Another carriage, simply marvellous*, Williamson thought and trailed the boy.

Beyond the gate lay a dirt road covered in horse and cart tracks. A large, boxy-looking blue carriage stood nearby. The wheels and lower sides were coated in a light brown dust.

"This is his Lordship's carriage," Georgie said as he approached the vehicle. "Pride and joy. I polish her, feed the horses."

Williamson started in shock at the driver. His head appeared impossibly large. It took a moment to realize the man wore a black turban. He had a dark complexion, a black beard streaked with grey.

"This is Bimalinder, our driver. Bimalinder, meet Inspector Edward Williamson."

"Sir," the man growled.

Georgie patted the carriage as he passed then opened the door, depositing Williamson's luggage inside. He turned to Williamson with a smile. "All aboard!"

Williamson paused to examine his surroundings. A large brick building, what could be a guesthouse, stood nearby. A few miles behind the carriage he saw rows of grey slate roofs, their chimneypots pumping smoke into the sky. *Ravenscar*, he thought, and nodded thanks to Georgie as he climbed into the cab. The lad closed the door behind him with a slam. Without any delay, the carriage started moving, the sudden jolt pushing Williamson back in his seat. He turned to see Georgie's reaction, but the lad sat staring out the window, his expression one of excitement. Williamson didn't share his enthusiasm. The road beneath them was terrible, nothing but potholes and rocks. He planted himself firmly into the seat and looked out the window himself.

They passed hilly scenery for a short while, then a row of low cottages came into view. Pedestrians stopped what they were doing to stare at the cab as it travelled onwards. Williamson turned to Georgie. "Where am I going first? Parish constable?"

"He will not be in," Georgie replied with a thoughtful expression. "Constable Foggitt is also our postman." He pulled a pocket watch from his coat. "Erm... I think he will be back soon. You might want to see the bodies first anyway sir, at the doctor's office. If he is there."

Williamson raised his eyebrows, wondering what other

occupations the doctor might have.

"You may want to find somewhere to stay, too," Georgie continued. "There are two lodgings, but I recommend the Bawdy Rook, that is the pub, sir. It has the best nosh in the village."

"Bawdy Rook it is, then," Williamson replied. A sudden change in direction jolted him in his seat. A moment later, Williamson saw a man in the road waving his fist angrily at them.

"I see the doctor, just heading to his surgery," Georgie said quickly. He stood and rapped his fist on the roof of the cab, which slowed to a stop. Georgie turned to Williamson. "Best catch him before he goes back out. That's him over there, burly fellow holding the gun and the dead birds. We shall take your case to the pub, eh?"

"Yes, certainly," Williamson replied. "Thank you ,Georgie."

Williamson left the carriage and stepped onto the dirt road. He barely had time to close the door before the carriage sped off in a cloud of dust. He'd been deposited in the village square, an area of flattened dirt with a small hexagonal stone fountain at its centre. Scanning the surrounds, he saw women and children walking past shop fronts. Across the square moved the figure the young lad had pointed out. Tall and hatless, the man had a thick black beard, a shock of black hair streaked with white. He held a gun over one shoulder of his tweed jacket, and a brace of pheasants dangled from his other hand, the birds strung by their necks. He moved purposefully along the cobbled pavement, then paused before a one-story building.

Williamson checked for carriages before crossing the

square. It was an action for the busy thoroughfares of Glasgow though, not here.

"Doctor?" He called.

The man turned, watching Williamson's approach with a grimace. He didn't appear to be too happy at this intrusion to his day.

"I am Inspector Williamson, Glasgow Police," he said, and reaching the pavement, offered his hand.

The other man raised thick eyebrows and smiled. "Oh, yes, yes! No wonder Ravenscar sent his driver out in that death trap of a carriage. Follow me please."

The doctor turned, and, having ignored Williamson's hand, bustled into the building before them. Williamson stopped short just inside the door; the other man had paused to stamp his feet on a rug. The doctor continued, and out of politeness, Williamson brushed his heels against the rug.

The office was large, and cosy looking. It had green wallpaper, a varnished wooden floor and ceiling to match. The windows behind Williamson filled the room with afternoon light.

"Bloody nuisance eh?" the doctor said, and deposited the birds and gun on the large desk . He pulled a pipe from his jacket and placed it in his mouth, removed his coat and placed it on a stand by the front door .

"Oh, I forget my manners," he said. "I am Harold Britton-Jones, the town doctor."

They shook hands, the man's grip strong in Williamson's own. Britton-Jones turned and headed towards a door set in the centre of the far wall.

"I have no morgue, you will understand," he continued as

he walked, "Been storing the dead in the cold room at the butcher's. No disrespect intended. We would have buried them had you not been summoned." Britton-Jones harrumphed, opened the door, and stepped inside.

The following room had similar dimensions to the first but quite different decor. Walled with whitewashed bricks, it had a white wood-panelled ceiling and floor. Two windows, on the north and the east walls, provided illumination. Cabinets and tables lined the walls, clean and filled with surgical instruments and bottles. Williamson's attention went to the two tables at the room's centre. The content of each lay hidden beneath a pristine white sheet. *Body-shaped contents*, he thought.

"This kind of business never happens here. Never." Britton-Jones said, and vigorously shook his head. "That is why Ravenscar pulled some strings, had a police chappy come investigate, yes?" He stepped towards the nearest table, paused and turned to Williamson.

"Yes, well... My acquaintance Samuel Pickman pulled the strings. He is a friend of my Chief Constable, as is Lord Ravenscar."

Britton-Jones nodded, beckoned Williamson over. As he approached, the doctor pulled back the sheet. The removal revealed the pallid face of a dead man. Clean-shaven, his eyes and cheeks were sunken, the black hair on his head a greasy-looking mop. Williamson caught the sickly scent of decay. He removed his hat, out of respect, and clenched it between his hands.

"This poor fellow is Justin Whateley," the doctor said, pointing with the stem of his pip. "The village tinker, discovered by the vicar on a Saturday morning, out on the moors. No obvious signs of foul play, but..." He lowered the pipe, and tapped the white forehead with the bowl. The tapping produced a distinctly hollow sound. "His head probably sounded like that before his unfortunate demise." Britton-Jones smirked, saw the empty look on Williamson's face, and cleared his throat. "Now this one," he continued, and moved to the next table, "Is a real tragedy, struck down in her prime, yes?"

Britton-Jones pulled the second sheet down, uncovering a young woman's face. Williamson grimaced. Her hair had been crudely shorn off, leaving blonde chunks and wisps on the scalp. An ugly looking laceration circled her head, reattached with rough stitching.

"My God! Did the killer do this?" He felt horrified.

"The incision and the hair? No, no." Britton-Jones stepped back. "That was I, getting into her blasted head to see what had been done."

Williamson's horror only diminished a fraction, thinking, *this man is a butcher*.

"The mother, of all people, found this wee girl," Britton-Jones continued, "Discovered stumbling into town last Friday morning, two days before Whateley." He tapped her head with the pipe, eliciting the same hollow sound. "Carrie-Anne Fisher; a maid at the Sunny Nook boarding house. With no real outside signs of foul play, I found a small hole in the back of her skull, like something a sharpened pick would do. I felt around there and discovered it empty. Further exploration," Britton-Jones waved his pipe over the ugly cut, "Revealed a brainpan completely drained of contents. Who would do such a damned thing?"

"Wait," Williamson said. "You say the girl was walking in

this condition?"

"Yes, yes, according to the mother," the doctor replied, sounding defensive. "But I cannot believe it myself."

Head hacked open, brain removed. A maniac, Williamson thought. Britton-Jones gently replaced the sheet over the girl's face. Williamson folded his arms. "I would like to see the witnesses of course, and see the places these victims were found."

"Oh, righty-ho." Britton-Jones returned the pipe to his mouth. "Mrs. Fisher is gone, I am afraid, down to Colchester to stay with in-laws."

"The constable should not have allowed her to leave. What about the vicar? Has he also absconded?"

The doctor scratched his beard, and tilted his head in thought. "Reverend Cannon. No, if not at the church he will be at those blasted Roman ruins. It's the remains of an old signal station, up on the moors. In fact I know he is there, as I bumped into him earlier."

Williamson put his hat back on. "In that case, I shall go seek him out. Goodbye, sir."

"Of course, yes. I shall see you out," Britton-Jones replied, and stepped forward.

Williamson shook his head, raised his palms. "No need for that, please." As he turned to leave the room, he felt Britton-Jones's stare burning into him.

Williamson got his wish of exploring the moors, but not in as pleasant a manner as he'd envisioned. His shoes weren't built for the terrain, nor his coat. As such, he walked on aching feet with his collar pulled up.

He travelled on a path, of sorts, a hiker's trail he hoped would lead him to the Roman ruins. Back in the village, a gentleman had shown him the way, pointing west and saying a trail lay that way. He'd thanked the man, but wasn't thanking him now, or himself, for heading out so unprepared. He blamed his own damned eagerness. If Georgie had been around, he could've tried for a lift in their carriage, if a road went this way. Or he could've just waited for the vicar to return.

Regardless of his regrets, the scenery looked beautiful. Purple bracken covered the low green hills and valleys, with the occasional rock outcropping and stone mound jutting up between the flowers. *This is nature at its most primal,* Williamson thought. There was poetry to be written about this sweet desolation, poetry waiting for a man better with words than himself to take pen to paper.

When Pickman had asked the club members to travel to places of interest, Williamson had thought his work wouldn't allow for such a venture. Still, once word from Lord Ravenscar, concerning this peculiar case reached Samuel Pickman's ears... Now he was here, with the dual goals of solving these murders and finding something interesting to tell Pickman and the club.

The trail had gone uphill before levelling off for some distance, before rising again, quite to his chagrin. After several minutes walking, the scenery began to change. Swaths of untamed grass, swaying in a low wind, replaced the delicate purple flowers. The distant sound of crashing waves reached Williamson's ears, carried along by a growing wind. Across the uneven fields ahead, he spied shapes that appeared manmade, and beyond these, jagged wedges of cliff he guessed held a precipitous drop. Beyond the cliffs, the sky hung littered with grey clouds. Those nearest the horizon had reddish-purple undersides. Sunset already? He removed his pocket watch and checked the time. It was nearing five o'clock. Sunset was approaching.

The path, nothing but padded down grass now, felt easier on his shoes at least. The cold ,however, had successfully leeched through his coat. Williamson tucked his watch into his waistcoat and held his hat secure on his head. Somewhere beyond the cliff edge, a lone seagull issued a melancholy cry. The ruins were a dozen steps away now. The only Roman ruin he'd seen before had been Hadrian's Wall, hence, this was something new. Well, old new.

He stepped over the low remnants of a wall. Ahead, stood angular shapes between which the grass grew thick and unruly. A square enclosure stood nearest, constructed from the same white stone he'd just crossed. Another, smaller square enclosure stood to its left, with a third just beyond it. The stones were weathered and ancient, worn down by the elements, lichen and moss growing within their crevices. These were foundations, he surmised, the remains of Roman towers brought down by the centuries.

A mound of rocks, enclosed by a makeshift fence, lay just the other side of the nearest foundations. The fence was crude, constructed from wooden poles and ropes, a boundary for the excavation work, he assumed. It rattled gently in the wind. As he headed on, Williamson noticed another wall, close to the cliff edges. Far to his right stood the circular foundations of a tower. He reached the mound, stepped over the fence, and looked around.

Two chairs stood behind the mound, next to a table piled

with rocks and small tools. *Must be base camp*, he thought, and headed towards it.

"Hello?" he asked, scanning the area for the vicar. No reply issued back to him, and certainly no one was in sight. To the northeast stood a low, square stone enclosure surrounding a pit. The entrance to a cellar perhaps? Bare earth surrounded the pit's rim, well-trod by boot prints. Williamson approached, wondering if the vicar was down there. On closer inspection he saw a wooden ladder descending into the pit, a shovel and pick abandoned on the ground behind it. He went cautiously forward, stepped over the wall and paused at the pit's perimeter. A melancholy moan rose up from the darkness, wind from an entrance deep underground. Williamson shivered.

"Hello?" he repeated, and, edging round the pit, lifted the pick by its wooden handle. The edges were blunt, bearing no residues of blood or hair. When he returned the pick, he noted an innocuous object on the ground. He leant, picked it up, and examined it in his palm. A circular chunk of green soapstone, thick at the middle and polished to a high degree. A rough star had been carved into the flat surface, at the centre of which a small squiggle was flanked by brackets. After examining it a few moments, he decided the brackets and squiggle symbolized an eye. He flipped it over, finding the opposite side blank.

"Hmm." Williamson looked toward the table. Could this be some archaeological find that had been dropped accidentally? He slipped it into his pocket for safekeeping. The pit moaned loudly, again. He took a sheepish step towards it and stared down. The darkness below appeared quite impenetrable. No one could be down there. Surely? A sudden, unexpected wave of vertigo sent him stumbling back, and

Williamson was forced to place a hand to the ground to steady himself. He looked around in embarrassment, but no one was here to observe him. The wind, rapidly picking up, made him shiver from head to toe. With a final, reluctant look around, he decided to return to the village.

Night had fallen by the time Williamson saw the village lights. He felt thankful he'd made it before darkness had blanketed the moors. With the poor path and no source of lighting, he might well have lost his way. As he approached the village outskirts, he encountered a large, solitary building. It took him a few moments to realize it was a church. The gable roof stood dark against the deep blue sky, as did the cross atop it. This was unmistakably the village's place of worship.

The vicar, he thought, and changing direction, approached the wall surrounding the church. He sent a rueful glance towards the village, walked through the open gate, and followed a cobbled path to the church. Rows of weathered, ancient-looking gravestones flanked his path.

He reached the entrance door and, foregoing a knock, turned the handle and pushed. Beyond the door stood a small, stone-walled antechamber, illuminated by white candles. A white marble font stood to his left, half-filled with holy water. Not being particularly religious, Williamson left it alone and stepped through the following door.

The nave stood beyond. The large chamber echoed as he closed the door behind him. Two rows of pews, centred by a red carpet, led to the pulpit and altar. A large gold cross stood mounted upon the whitewashed wall behind the altar. Yellow candles in tall iron holders illuminated the nave with a flickering, gentle glow. The light reflected off the stained glass windows in a myriad of different colours. It felt cold here, but not as cold as outside. It also appeared empty. *Where could this elusive vicar be?*

Williamson headed towards the pulpit, his footsteps echoing as he walked. He felt like an intruder, and shivered involuntarily. A door stood to the right of the pulpit's platform. He approached it hoping to find the vicar beyond.

"Can I help you at all?"

Williamson froze. He turned on his heels and found the source staring at him from behind the pulpit. The man had olive-coloured skin and piercing blue-eyes. Balding, his sparse brown hair lay combed over his scalp. The black robes indicated he was the man Williamson sought.

"I am Inspector Edward Williamson," he said. "I have been looking everywhere for you. You must be Reverend Cannon?"

"Yes, sir," the man replied, "You caught me in contemplation at the altar." He pointed to the cross. "In a bit of a trance you might say." The vicar stepped forward, and descended a small staircase set in the pulpit platform. A tall man; Cannon's thin body made him appear more so. They shook hands. The vicar smiled heartily, displaying a mouth of uneven white teeth,

"I visited the Roman ruins looking for you," Williamson continued, "I was hoping to question you over the body you discovered?"

Cannon's expression turned sad. "Oh... my apologies. I did not reach the ruins today, I had to return on some church business." He walked past Williamson and stepped through the nearby door. Williamson followed, into a warm, homely-looking room. It had a roaring fire, green carpet and yellow-papered walls. A writing desk stood to the door's left, with a large circular table at the room's centre. Maps and books covered the latter. The vicar paused at the table and offered Williamson one of the tall-backed chairs surrounding it. He walked forward, accepted the chair, and Cannon, sitting in another, shuffled it round to face him.

"There is not much to say about the body to be honest," Cannon began. "I discovered the poor man on the trail just beyond the carriage tracks. I found him unmoving, cold, and obviously dead."

Williamson nodded. "Thank you. I may still need to see the location, perhaps in the morning?"

"Of course, yes," The vicar agreed. "My flock is very afraid. I hope you get to the bottom of this."

"Yes, well-"

Something on the table caught Williamson's eye. Poking out from beneath a yellow, dog-eared map he noticed a pile of familiar green soapstones. Cannon, following his gaze, reached over and lifted back the map. Dozens of green stones were revealed, bearing an identical star-shaped carving upon their surfaces.

"What are they? I know they are from the ruins. I found one myself." Williamson reached into his pocket, producing the soapstone he'd found. "They do not look particularly Roman," he added.

"May I see that?" The vicar asked, and Williamson handed it to him. Cannon retrieved a magnifying glass from the table and scrutinized the soapstone.

"Hmm, yes. I found hundreds of these in the ruins, piled up

on the floor of an underground cellar." The vicar returned the glass to the table and held out the soapstone. "Keep it, as a souvenir."

"Thank you." Williamson accepted the stone and dropped it in his pocket. He checked his pocket watch and said, "I had better take my leave,now, but would like to continue things in the morning."

"Yes, of course," Cannon replied, and both men stood. "I will have to show you around the ruins tomorrow. If you have the time, that is?"

Williamson nodded. "Might be nice."

The vicar escorted him to the door. They entered the nave, and Cannon, following him out, continued speaking.

"A bloody battle occurred over that way you know, between the Romans and the locals." Cannon laughed. "They fought over the worship of a colourfully named deity called Hastur." His voice echoed as they stepped down the nave.

Here is a man who likes to talk, Williamson thought. *Shame he does not have more to say about the dead body.*

Outwardly, he asked,"A pagan god?"

"I believe so. References are vague. I am also attempting to deduce why the Romans buried those star-stones beneath the signal station."

They reached the antechamber. Cannon paused and offered his hand.

"Well. If you discover any skeletons in the ruins, be sure to inform me!" Williamson said as they shook hands. Cannon's face formed a brief, puzzled expression, then he grinned.

"Oh yes, ha ha, we shall be knee-deep in the dead if the Romans were involved!"

They parted ways with joined laughter, and Williamson, feeling newly energized, left the church to make his way back down to the village.

Williamson drifted awake from a deep, contented slumber. At first he thought he was dreaming, the loud rhythmic *tap tap tap* something his sleep-befuddled mind had difficulty processing.

"Master Williamson, sir!"

The sound of his name brought his awareness to the fore, and he sat up blinking.

"Sir," the loud, urgent knocking continued. He left the bed and rushed through the darkened room to the door. Opening it, he saw a young redheaded girl dressed in a dark blue maid's uniform. The girl curtseyed and smiled.

"Sir. I am so sorry to disturb you but they found another body in the village and they told me to come find you, as all hell is breaking loose and-"

Williamson shushed her. She'd spoken frantically, without taking a breath. "Where is the corpse?" he asked, speaking calmly to try putting the girl at ease.

She took a deep breath, "Over near the fountain sir. Laid there, all dead and unwholesome like."

"Very well. Now, what is your name?"

"Millie, sir."

"Millie. Can you go down there and see about keeping everyone away from it? And if Constable Foggitt is around, please request his assistance."

The girl nodded her head vigorously, her gaze lowered as she absorbed the information. Then she looked up and said,

"But sir, the dead body *is* Constable Foggitt."

"Oh bloody-" he began, then stopped himself from finishing the curse. "Just go down and do as I said, I shall be there in five minutes."

The girl nodded, turned and rushed down the corridor. Williamson left the door ajar and stepped over to the window, parting the curtains to bring light to the small, rustic-looking room. He dressed quickly. Remaining calm proved an effort, but he knew if he fumbled around things would take even longer.

Once dressed, he splashed water from the basin onto his face, wiped it dry with a cloth, and rushed to the door. Without pausing to comb his hair, he grabbed his hat from the hook and headed into the corridor. A left turn at the corridor's termination took him down a flight of narrow stairs. The bar followed, curtains closed and empty.

What time is it? As he stepped between the tables and stools, he checked his pocket watch. Just after ten. A terribly late start for him, and he recalled asking the landlady to wake him at nine. *No time to worry about than now, not with another murder right under my nose.* He hated to think of it this way, but a fresh scene would be a good thing, at least where finding evidence was concerned.

Williamson opened the front door, the bright light beyond causing him to blink. It took him a moment to recall his location in the village. He headed right, down a cobbled path in the direction of the fountain. He crossed the street, after once again unnecessarily checking for traffic, then cut down a narrow alley. As he neared the alley's termination a babble of voices reached his ears. Upon entering the square, he saw a large crowd near the fountain. He grimaced at the sight. Onlookers, in his experience, did nothing but get in the way and spread false rumours. Some anxious-looking faces spotted him, and the crowd parted at his approach, leaving a direct path to the fountain. A dark shape lay slumped against its rim. Millie stood guard before it, scowling at the crowd with her arms crossed. Williamson smiled. As he stepped between the whispering village folk, he noticed Georgie stood to the girl's right. Seeing his approach, Georgie sprightly cried, "Another corpse sir, a bloody dead body!"

Williamson paused, nodded to Georgie, and turned to Millie. "Thank you very much Millie. You have done a grand job." The girl smiled prettily and blushed. "Now could you go find the doctor, tell him to bring two stout lads and a stretcher?"

Millie nodded and rushed away. Williamson turned, raised his arms and addressed the curious, frightened crowd. "Everyone. I need you to return to your business. Please. I can only deal with this if you give me space."

Heads nodded, and voices muttered reluctant assent. The crowd took off and dispersed into smaller groups Satisfied he wasn't going to be disturbed, Williamson turned back to the fountain. *So this is Foggitt*, he thought, and kneeling, scanned the area before him. The dirt floor appeared dry, bearing no evidence of footfalls. From the corner of his eye he saw Georgie kneel beside him.

"Looking for clues sir?" the lad asked.

Williamson nodded, then crept forward. Foggitt was a large man, in a blue coat with a yellow carnation in the lapel. A white embroidered handkerchief concealed his face. Williamson guessed either Millie, or another onlooker, had placed it for decency. The man's back lay against the fountain, his legs spread. The heels of his black boots were caked in mud. Noting this, Williamson said, "Georgie, has there been any rain overnight?"

"Showers on the moors, sir, a little patter across the village as I recall."

"I see." He crept closer, braced himself, and removing the handkerchief placed it on the ground.

"Oh!" Georgie exclaimed.

A pale, weathered face stared blindly forward, the wide eyes clouded and grey. *This is why they covered the face*, he thought, and standing, reached over to clasp the head in both hands. He encountered resistance; the head appeared stuck to the fountain. A bit more applied force, and it came away with a disgusting, sticky sound . There on the fountain was a red spot of blood, and the head itself, icy cold in his grip, felt very light. *Another brain gouged out, damn.*

Williamson repositioned the head against the fountain, shuffled back a step, and began searching Foggitt's pockets. All were empty, excepting the inside pocket, from which he removed a small black notepad and pencil. He stood, turned, and saw Georgie crouched beside him, face as pale as that of the corpse. The square stood empty and quiet, now. Movement caught Williamson's eye, two men coming from the alley, bearing a stretcher. The doctor marched behind the pair, puffing heavily on his pipe. Britton-Jones waved. Williamson returned the gesture, then turned his attention to the notepad. A flick through the small square sheets took him to the final entry. He scanned it, and cleared his throat.

"Georgie," he said, and the lad stood to face him. "I think we may have found our man."

The church was locked, so their next stop, with Georgie walking dutifully by his side, was the Roman ruins. Georgie said he knew a shortcut, but it turned out to be the same path Williamson had used on his first visit. The moors were cold, the path damp underfoot. Britton-Jones had taken custody of the body, but Williamson had Foggitt's notepad, tucked in his inside pocket. The last page detailed Foggitt's suspicions concerning the vicar, and stated that he had planned to challenge the man last night.

Williamson felt a growing trepidation as they approached the ruins, a familiar feeling and, if he were honest with himself, a positive one. From previous experience, it meant he was on the right track.

Georgie, who'd been walking beside him in silence for a while, said, "Do you think he will put up a fight ,sir?"

Williamson nodded. "Possibly, but I really just want to speak with him."

The path ended and he stepped upon grass still damp with dew. It squished underfoot, and Williamson slowed his gait for fear of slipping. Georgie didn't have the same problem, most likely used to the moors interchangeable climate. He slowed down when he saw Williamson lagging behind. They crossed a ruined wall, and together approached the signal station's foundations. The vicar was nowhere to be seen.

"This way Georgie," Williamson motioned, and headed towards the mound. The fence remained still, no sign of a wind today. He couldn't hear the ocean either. A queerly quiet day, it felt like the moors and the sea were holding their breaths in anticipation.

"Look, sir!" Georgie exclaimed.

Williamson paused and turned. Georgie, having lingered a short distance behind him, stood pointing beyond the ruins. The pit. A flickering oil lamp stood near the edge, a needless illumination in the daylight. Williamson continued walking, stepping over the fence and onto the mound. He scanned the immediate area, his gaze returned to the pit.

He is down there, I know it.

The earth around the pit appeared muddy, treacherous. Upon reaching it, he placed his feet on the earth tentatively. It would be a terrible fate to slip and fall in. There were no sad, windy moans issuing from it today, but as he gingerly stepped closer, the detective thought he detected a flickering in the darkness. His eyes didn't deceive him, when he neared the rim and peered over, he saw a light at the bottom of the pit.

Is that the sound of stones being chipped? Yes, a sharp, rhythmic tapping. A soft squelching noise informed him Georgie was close behind.

"Is he down there?" Georgie asked softly.

"I believe so," Williamson replied, and after examining the pit a few moments, looked to the ladder. "I need to go down there Georgie. Can you hold the ladder while I am climbing?" He skirted the pit, looked to Georgie and found the lad staring into it intently.

"Yes, yes of course," Georgie said, snapping out of his fugue.

Williamson crouched and turned round. He pressed a hand into a section of earth that didn't look too muddy, gripped it, and found the top rung with his foot. The ladder seemed stable, thankfully, and descending two more rungs, he found the stile with his free hand. Georgie's shoes came into view as he descended, coated with mud both fresh and dry.

Williamson paused and looked up at his companion. "Thank you, Georgie." The lad nodded, and he started his descent in earnest.

Not knowing how deep the hole was caused Williamson some trepidation. Still, he comforted himself that it couldn't be too far. The chipping stopped, making him wonder if he'd been heard. He paused. His left hand, coated in dirt, bothered him so Williamson reluctantly wiped it against his coat. Marking his clothing was the better alternative to slipping. The pause gave him opportunity to look up. He saw a square of light above, Georgie's head in silhouette. Williamson waved, not knowing if Georgie saw the gesture, and continued down.

Suddenly, the ladder drifted away from the wall. Seized with panic, Williamson hugged the nearest rung. The ladder wasn't just moving, someone was actively shaking it from above. "Georgie!" Williamson cried as his feet slipped dangerously. He looked up and saw a mass of dark objects tumbling towards him. He gritted his teeth and lowered his head against the coming impact... A sharp stab of pain followed as something heavy cracked against his scalp. Stunned, he dropped helplessly through the darkness.

Williamson span through a nighted abyss without end. His screams returned a thousand-fold louder from the dark gulfs surrounding him. The sight of blue and red-lit chasms, filled with leprous-looking cities, made him yearn for the return of the darkness. He felt as though he were falling not just through space, but through time, mirroring the epic journey of some unseen, but very present, entity. Darkness, once more. After countless aeons, a pinprick of light showed ahead, that gradually resolved itself into a small, fiery ball, around which dark shapes orbited, There came a sudden acceleration and, finally, a massive floodlight burst so scintillatingly bright that his eyes burned from the assault. This was the most damned of places! As he tumbled further, and the blazing light consumed his vision, roaring voices, seemingly inside his head, cried, *Hastur!*

Williamson opened his eyes with a groan. He felt cold, and his head and left ankle ached terribly. *I am alive at least.* And this shadowy place... not nearly as awful as that terrible realm he had awoken from. Before him, the ladder ascended to the hole in the ceiling. Far above, he could see a spot of dark blue sky. Memory returned of his fall from the ladder. The drop couldn't have been a long one, obviously. Sitting up onto his elbows, he felt small objects clatter beneath him. He retrieved one, and found he'd landed on a pile of green soapstones.

Williamson let the stone slip from his hand. *Perhaps these cushioned my fall,* he thought. He climbed to his feet, favouring his right leg as he took a step towards the ladder. He looked up again. It would be quite a climb, considering his injuries. A sudden wind buffeted his clothes from behind. Turning, he saw a pitch-black tunnel opening in the wall of the pit, from whence that chilling wind issued. The recollection of those terrible dream cities made him cringe.

He had to go up. Williamson made his limping way to the ladder and mounted the rungs. Slow going at first, as he ascended, he found he could use his left foot if he didn't push too hard on it. And so he made progress... *as long as there isn't a repeat of the falling debris*, he thought grimly. With this in mind, he kept his gaze on the square of night above, gripping the ladder hard. Despite the cold, he was sweating by the time he reached the top. Clambering from the pit, Williamson pressed his hands into the damp earth at the rim.

The moon stood high in the sky, the light making the ruins eerily bright. He turned, sat up, and noticed the flickering glow of a nearby lamp. The circle of light illuminated two figures crouched before the table. The sight of Georgie alive relieved him, even bound and helpless as the lad was. It also meant he hadn't been the one to send him falling. Georgie stared at the ground unmoving. Beside him, trussed up and unconscious, sat the vicar. The sound of footsteps turned Williamson's attention to the right, and he climbed falteringly to his feet to face the two shadowy approaching forms.

"I knew you would survive," a familiar voice said.

The source of the voice filled him with surprise. The man from the carriage! "Stainsby," Williamson said. The man to his left was also familiar - Ravenscar's driver, Bimalinder.

"I am more usually referred to as Lord Ravenscar," Stainsby replied, in a gloating voice.

Williamson looked from Ravenscar's chubby, self-satisfied face to the Sikh. The former nodded, smiling widely.

"You. You are the murderer, Ravenscar?" More accusation than a question, Williamson took a wary step back.

"No, my boy, I am the acolyte." The two men stepped around the pit, facing him with the lamplight behind them. "I have been trailing you since the carriage ride, hoping to get you alone here."

The Sikh cricked his neck, moving his head side to side in a strange, rhythmic manner. Ravenscar looked at the pit.

"Cannon freed him by accident you know, the one I call Hastur. Though I was actually looking for him when I organised the dig." He tilted his head, indicating Bimalinder. "The first host. Quite unsuitable. You on the other hand..."

Williamson's guts turned to ice. The Sikh's skin had grown much darker, his face becoming riddled in cracks. Squirming black tentacles sickeningly bulged from his mouth, each pulsing obscenity tipped by a sharp talon. The head stopped moving, its bulging eyes turning terribly to Williamson.

"He requires more souls than this sorry little village can provide," Ravenscar explained. "He desires to explore this age, using a host familiar with cosmopolitan places." Bimalinder stepped forward, his monstrous face throbbing.

"You mean me?" Williamson asked.

"It is why I had those oblivious fools send you here. Even planted the note in our dear constable's pocket. You shall become host to the Feaster from Afar, the God of Ravenscar."

"Blasphemy!" an angry voice cried. Ravenscar and the monster turned in surprise. The vicar, now free of his bonds, charged towards them. He had the look of a maniac in his eyes. He barrelled into the Sikh, his momentum taking them both to the ground.

"No!" Ravenscar yelled, raising his hands to his face.

Williamson watched the pair struggle at the edge of the pit. Both men rolled and went plummeting down. Williamson flinched at the brutal sounds of impact. Ravenscar rushed forward, waving his arms in distress. He fell to his knees at the pit's edge and wailed. Williamson stepped towards him. "Lord Ravenscar!"

There issued from the pit a loud keening wail that halted

his words, accompanied by a fetid, reeking wind. The blast sent Williamson staggering backwards. Black, greasy slivers of smoke poured forth, something terrible lurked within. Williamson had a half-glimpsed, nightmare vision of flapping wings, of whipping tendrils attached to a deformed, withered body. An involuntary jabber of terror escaped his lips. The thing paused, hovering before Ravenscar. A second, powerful gust sent Williamson to the ground. As he fell, he saw the twisted horror shooting to the sky. Then it disappeared, and the moors were silent.

Williamson had landed on something soft, wet. When he tried getting up, the earth sucked at him greedily. With some effort, he pulled himself to his knees. Ravenscar remained crouched before the pit. Williamson stood and stepped towards him. "Ravenscar?"

The man made no acknowledgment of his presence. He walked forward, sent the pit a wary glance, then saw Ravenscar's face. "My god..." he gasped, and knelt for a closer look. A hole centred the man's forehead, red at the edges but with no signs of bleeding. His eyes were opaque, lifeless. It appeared his god had taken one last meal before departing.

The sound of falling rubble returned Williamson's attention to the pit. The vicar's corpse lay down there, Bimalinder's too, their bodies broken atop a pile of ancient green stones. Like the one in his pocket... *Perhaps these should have never been removed in the first place.* He retrieved the stone from his pocket, examined it in his hand, and tossed it into the pit.

"Help!" a voice cried. Georgie of course, still tied up before the table.

"Just a moment," Williamson replied and made his way towards him. The going proved a little slow, with his injured leg, but he soon reached the table and Georgie.

The lad grinned. "Vicar got loose sir. He could have untied me as well," he said and scowled.

"I think, Georgie, you were safer over here."

Georgie nodded in agreement. "What did you see there? I couldn't believe my eyes!"

Williamson said nothing, merely knelt, and began working on the ropes binding Georgie's wrists. "My lad," he said, and scrutinized the twinkling firmament. A shooting star appeared overhead, darting towards the horizon. He wondered to which distant star it might return, then turned back to the boy. "I have trouble believing it myself."

———

"You desired a story, Mr. Pickman, sir. I believe this one should suffice." Williamson retook his chair as a ripple of conversation rose around the room. Some nodded agreeably, though I caught the brief, and somewhat uncharitable, murmurs of "Well, he did hit his head, you know, so perhaps not fully *compos mentis*."

As always, my gaze turned to Pickman. His complexion remained pale, his lips tightly pressed together. For he knew, as well as I, that the white-haired, somewhat aged figure of Williamson had, when I last saw him a year ago, been a dark haired man in the full vigour of early middle-age...

We gathered about a large table.
Black drapes covered the windows

THE SHADOW OVER THE SEPULCHRE

JOHN DeLAUGHTER

"This is abominable, simply abominable! What type of club do they think this is? I feel I may take myself elsewhere."

"What's that, my dear Tredman?" I interjected.

"Oh, I asked the butler for a handful of cigars, to enjoy with a brandy. The pug had the audacity to inform me that their tobacco man was delayed in stocking up my favourite brand, the Havana brown import, the only one I ever smoke."

"Do they not have others, Tredman?" I replied.

"Yes, they have others, the fellow offered me them. But they simply won't do. They are pale imitations, rather like trying to smoke a finger of chalk. No, I won't hear of it!"

"What do you propose, my good man? Smythe asked us to meet him here today, to share his latest news. His letter was terse, in the gravest tones. I wouldn't miss his latest oration for anything," I said.

"Well, I suppose I can go without the calming smoke of my chosen cigars for one evening."

"That's the ticket, Tredman," I noted. "Stiff upper lip and all that. There's Smythe now. Roger! Roger! Over here!" I called to him. "My dear Roger, is that you? I know it's you, old man, for your friendly face is unmistakable. But, my God man, what happened to you? You look more like your father than yourself. Have you been sick, man?" I observed.

"Good Lord, old chap, you've never used a cane to get around before." noted Tredman.

I watched as Roger shambled with a noticeable limp across to the ring of majestic armchairs that encircled the club's fireplace. The club kept the hearth well-stocked with wood, this being a colder autumn than normal in His Majesty's isles. He motioned for me and Tredman to seat ourselves, then looked about nervously, as if expecting unwelcome visitors. Roger slid his mortal frame into the centre-most chair, like a man testing out the last lifeboat, or sizing up a coffin. It was then I noticed that he was missing his pinky finger, where his left hand rested on his cane. Smythe motioned with his other hand to be quiet, as the rest of the members gathered round.

"Gentleman," said Smythe hoarsely, "Where do I begin? What I'm about to tell you may well shock you. I warn you, leave me now, if you wish to retain your sanity and not get your name written up in the Almighty's list of those destined to damnation. I am in daily consultation with a pre-eminent bishop, in fear for my immortal soul."

I immediately thought Smythe was employing the cheap tricks that a sideshow barker uses to get people into his tent. At any moment, I expected him to turn his head toward the heavens, and send a pillar of fire from his lips like a fire-eater. But no, the startling change in Smythe's appearance lent gravity to his words.

"As you all know, my Uncle Cornelius died ten months ago, God rest his soul. It was sudden and without warning. A true gentleman and bachelor, he did not get his affairs in order with a solicitor, before his untimely demise. As my Uncle's logical heir, I and my confidants rigorously searched his spacious manor for either documents pertaining to his last wishes, or records pointing toward which institutions held his considerable assets," Smythe sighed. "But we found neither. His former solicitor from a civil matter, one Abraham Dowe, of Dowe, Dons, and McLartens, assumed the role of protective guardian of the estate, while further teams searched for Uncle Cornelius's assets. A sense of urgency plagued me, as months rolled by without any results. Since I needed resolution over his death, Mr. Dowe suggested a radical idea. He told of a spiritualist of renown, one Nigel the Unknowable, whose séances with the long departed had led to the actual reclamation of unknown assets of those same dead ancestors,"

Smythe paused for a moment, accepting and sipping from a glass of brandy. "That someone in the dubious occupation of a 'spiritualist' could provide concrete leads was something it took time for me to accept. My thought was then, *I dared not tell my friends, lest they brand me with the same shady soubriquet as Nigel.* A fear of blackmail also troubled me. But I felt as a man possessed, harried by the desire to close my Uncle's Estate. Dare I say, a spirit of greed darkened my every thought, a troubling motivation that was so distinct and apart from my normal constitution."

Smythe leaned forward as he spoke. "I need to ask you now, not to breathe what you hear to another soul. Swear that if you spread gossip about me, that the Almighty strike you down. Swear to it, I beg you" Smythe asked.

"This is preposterous, invoking the Almighty over a simple

tale," blustered Tredman.

The others in Smythe's circle glared at Tredman, a man prone to petty jealousies. Tredman's bravado immediately turned to hushed mutterings. The others, one by one, nodded their agreement to Smythe's request.

"Thank you, gentleman, and to you, my dear Tredman," Smythe replied. "Now, let me share the experiences that have left me a shell of my former self."

Yes, Nigel the Unknowable came highly recommended by my solicitor. But Dowe's opinion of the spiritualist had not prepared me for the regal and flamboyant nature of the man. Dare I say, that in my circles, such behaviours are shunned; they border on embarrassment. Of course, Nigel's business address was not located in a London district where a respectable business would maintain its storefront.

There are two Londons. There have always been two Londons and, pray tell, there always shall be. From its beginning as Londinium under Roman occupation to today, while the veneer of the place is fluid, the backbone of London remains the same. Whether a Caesar wore his reigning laurels or one from the House of Hanover wears his ruling crown, London remains timeless and eternal. I was borne and bred as a citizen, a noble of upper London and its palatial environs. Nigel set up his Obelisk to Olympus in the second, lower London, where all manner of devilry, debauchery, and deceptions are practiced in the open, celebrated as delicacies on the palate of human experiences.

It was dark, the time near midnight. I dressed as a

commoner and my carriage was a simple black affair without any marking of rank or relation to His Majesty. The driver was well-paid to keep his silence or face the swift removal of his tongue. The obelisk stood out from the ramshackle and rubbish that made up that district of Second London. With my sword cane in hand, and a sawed-off Brown Bess hidden under my shabby frock coat, I strode with one of my similarly armed agents, dressed as I was. Three knocks on the heavy door, a countersign exchanged, and the portal opened.

The place smelt of incense burnt on small altars positioned throughout the building. We passed by such a brazier near the hall's foyer, sinister and glowing, its outlines like a companion of hell, a familiar to do Nigel's occultic biddings. My companion and I crossed ourselves at the sight, as Nigel's assistant led us deeper into the spiritualist's lair. We gathered about a large table, large enough to seat a family. Black drapes covered the windows and black sheets hid everything else, so as not to distract a client from the ceremonies.

On the table sat the normal tricks of the trade - a gold bell, trumpet down, a large candle bedecked in Egyptian hieroglyphs, a large, skin-bound book, a small pewter pyre for burning exotic incense, a large crystal ball mounted on a tall amethyst pedestal, an obsidian scrying mirror, and a small, silver wand festooned with stylised stars and demonic faces. I silently hoped that this was my first and only session with the psychic counsellor. After the pre-agreed price was paid, the séance began.

Nigel's associate, a tall, pallid man, discussed the mechanics of the ceremony before his master's appearance. Nigel entered the room with a flourish of his black, sigilbedecked cape. He wore a small turban, fastened with a dazzling obsidian clasp.

"Do you have a personal possession that your Uncle cherished?" Nigel asked with a gesture of his hands, each adorned with rings featuring gemstones worth a kings-ransom.

"Here's his signet ring, worn by the male members of his side of the family for generations," I said, handing him the onyx ring bearing the Smythe family crest, a chimera beneath a crown. Nigel's associate snuffed out all candles save the large Egyptian one. The Spiritualist placed the palms of his hands face up, the right containing my Uncle's ring, the left empty. He began muttering in an ancient tongue, a proto-Latin that predated the Vulgate, when Rome's gods were flawed and feral. A gentleman made it a point to study such things, in the past, it helped discern who was a Romish Infidel and who was faithful to the Blessed Mother Church of England. God save the King!

Nigel reared back in his chair, his darkish eyes grew glassy, his Latin intonations became less self-pronounced, and more the frenzied utterances of a man possessed.

"No, NO!" yelled Nigel as he bolted upright.

Nigel's associate sprang toward his Master, shouting what I gather was an exorcism. With a strike of his forearm, Nigel sent his associate flying against a wall; the man's shouts dwindled to painful whimpers as he lay broken on the floor. My agent rose to confront Nigel, but I grabbed him and shoved him back into his seat.

"Not yet," I said, thinking the performance might be a ruse, part of Nigel's attempts to up the price. Nigel continued to chant in a frenzy of old Latin spells, while he raised his hands before his person as if to embrace someone. The Spiritualist's turban flew off his head, as his long silver hair and necromancer's cape rose around his person, as if he were a ghost taken to flight over a graveyard. Nigel's head became a grinning skull, his ribs appeared stark and skeletal! I crossed myself in unison with my agent, our hands clasped tightly on our weapons. Was Nigel being flayed alive before us?

The scrying mirror flew from the table into Nigel's grasping hands, the amazing sight of congealed flesh and blood appearing on its smooth face

"Almighty God, protect thy lambs!" my Agent swore.

I saw my Uncle alive as if I looking over his shoulder. The enigmatic signet ring glimmered on his left pinky finger. The light was diffuse, he was walking through a twilight world somewhere. Then he walked past something I immediately recognized, a particular tombstone marked with a skull and crossbones. An hourglass carved in the weathered granite sat above the *memento mori*. My Uncle was walking through Saint Gertrude's graveyard in the dark hours, approaching the Smythe family crypt.

Suddenly, he began running, looking back over his shoulder. My Uncle stopped at the crypt, trying to unlock the barred door. I saw all this from the vantage point of a bird of prey. Then Uncle Cornelius looked up, his face full of abject terror. He screamed silently, repeatedly. The picture drew back, as the dark outlines of a bat-like, horn-headed thing, as tall and broad as the Crypt, overshadowed him. Something like feathery jungle vines snaked down from the heights toward my Uncle, the tomb now a place of terror.

My Uncle slid down against the gate, his face ashen and

grey, his body immobile, his eyes glazed over in death. Simultaneously, Nigel dropped the scrying mirror and crumpled to the floor, his ghostly appearance replaced by that of a shattered man. He looked as though he'd been struck by lightning, his hands burnt black where he'd held the mirror. The mirror's crash broke the spell that froze my agent and I in our chairs.

Swiftly retrieving my Uncle's ring, we left Nigel's Obelisk with all due haste, my agent promptly informing the Bow Street Runners of the incident, and of Nigel and his associate's medical condition. Due to my involvement, George Ruthven agreed to keep the matter private, that the family may be spared any potential embarrassment. Strangely, my Uncle had officially died of a faint heart. That he might have died of fright seemed a conjecture arising from my own mortified imagination during the séance. Did I suffer from a case of mesmerism? No, my agent swore that he saw exactly what I did. So why wasn't Uncle Cornelius' body found at the Smythe family crypt, instead of in his bed, where he was said to have died in his sleep?

I gather that the occultic career of Nigel the Unknowable ended that night, his mind devoured by the psychic claws of an unknown shadow. He was, last I heard, a patient at the First Middlesex County Asylum, in Hanwell. His associate later died from the blows Nigel had delivered.

It took some time to recover from the episode, this being nothing I'd ever seen before. Fantastic, you might say, yet it all bore the marks of stark reality, literally getting inside the last memories of my dear Uncle. A practical man, I informed Mr. Dowe of my experience and the events that sent Nigel to the asylum. My description of the séance did not ruffle Abraham Dowe, he simply pawned Nigel's lunacy off as the eccentric frailties of a sensitive psychic. He asked what I planned on doing next, a surprised as it was I who paid him for the practical advice of a neutral third party.

That he had referred me to Nigel hadn't shaken my initial trust in him. In any case, I told him I needed time to gather my thoughts before considering my next move. I am not a simpleton, prone to follow the counsel of others without having my own mind on things, particularly given the new evidence about my Uncle's death. And though it originated in what amounted to a psychic Punch and Judy Show I most assuredly took that evidence seriously. I did begin to wonder, though. Had Dowe's agents moved my Uncle's body to his bed, during their search of the Smythe crypt?

Something else stuck in my mind, the discovery of an occultic thread that led back to my Uncle. During my personal search through his private possessions, I had found a small, padlocked room beneath an innocuous staircase in an older wing of my Uncle's manor. It contained a collection of bizarreries from his many trips to the more obscure corners of the British Empire. On the far wall hung gilded *khopeshes*, swords taken from the tombs of dynastic Egyptian pharaoh. There was an ancient ossuary, a limestone box once used in first-century Palestine, housing the revered bones of a noble descendant. It sat in a tiny alcove, surrounded by odd incense thuribles, empty of its calcified contents, the lid unceremoniously deposited on the floor. It bore the simple description, *St. John*. The bones of the Messiah's nearest disciple, holy relics of the Romish church, were nowhere to be found.

There were gilded icons from another age, some seemingly older than man. A skeleton, no doubt that of a demon, stood in another corner, tall and broad, having four dangling arms, and two heads, with rhinoceros-like horns protruding from the misshapen skulls. The bones appeared clear and glittered in sparkling colours, like a faceted gemstone in my candlelight. There was a pyramid's capstone, covered with Hieroglyphs. The remaining boxes in the room had the appearance of treasure chests. However, rather than being stuffed with jewelry and gemstone-encrusted scarabs, I found within them the mummified hands of six giants, all with six fingers and opposable thumbs. Strangely, all bore a signet ring like my Uncle's, though greater in size.

Were these the remains of the fabled Nephilim, the occultic powers behind each Pharaoh's throne? A weathered, vellum scroll, sat in another alcove, enscribed with the simple Latinised names of *Jannes* and *Jambres*. Otherworldly effigies occupied other niches in the wall. Among these eccentric and extraordinary items stood a statue of a winged devil, whose smallish shadow cast by my candle, fit the spectral outlines of the flying beast from my crypt vision. It was ugly and inhuman, vaguely anthropomorphic in its beastly outlines, having a shadow for a face, and obtuse horns ringing its head like a thorny crown. It had raptor-like taloned feet, talons among its wing pinions, and flowing tendrils like a sea delicacy's tentacles.

When I lifted the fetish to examine it, a small Lapis tablet dislodged from its base, its surface saturated with cuneiform sigils and seals. A rusty key also dislodged with the tablet. I knew at once I had an official document of state or commerce from the golden age of the ancient empires that once ruled the world. And what of the key, where did it fit into the puzzle? I resolved to learn the significance of the tablet.

The thought came to me that King's College had a language chair that may be able to unravel the tablet's mystery. Sir Henry Creswicke Rawlinson, a renowned orientalist, was a visiting scholar there. Somewhat bewildered, I re-padlocked the room and left with the Lapis tablet in hand and the key in my pocket. I began to wonder if Uncle Cornelius had embarked on his own study of the occult, particularly the Egyptian wizard-priests Jannes, Jambres, and their servants, the Nephilim. Had my Uncle opened a door to the occultic forces that brought about his death? What of the remaining Smythe dynasty? Had a weird curse from the dusty past been laid upon us?

At the college, I was told that the best way to locate Sir Henry was to look for the largest retinue of students between the classes. There, he could be found. I had forgotten about the hustle and bustle of collegiate life. I finally found Sir Henry on a bench at Chetwynd Court, surprisingly free of his entourage. He barely looked at me, as I introduced myself. However, when I produced the Lapis tablet from a small satchel, his eyes widened like saucers. He whisked me off to his office, bubbling with a thousand questions along the way.

"Let me have a look at that Lapis parcel of yours, Mister, Mister-" asked Sir Henry, as he pulled out a large magnifying glass and began to examine the cuneiform tablet.

"My name is Smythe, Roger Smythe," I said, tolerating the scholar's inattention. His office was small, barely larger than a closet, stuffed with books floor to ceiling, and toppling stacks of paper.

"Oh, Smythe, you say? Did you know your name originated among early Pictish Clans? I served with a gentleman by that name in His Majesty's Army. Might Harold Dustin Smythe be a relative of yours? He told me the full history of the name." said Sir Henry as he eyed the tablet, before jotting down notes. I settled into the lone chair situated before Sir Henry's desk. After half an hour of silence, the renowned orientalist looked up at me, his face aglow.

"My good fellow, do you know what you have here?" he finally asked, pointing at the tablet with his magnifying glass.

"I can't say that I do, Sir Henry, that's why I sought you out. Your reputation in my circles preceded you. I knew there was no better person to trust this family heirloom with than you."

"This is the earliest inscription." He continued to examine the piece. "Perhaps I should frame it this way. Besides its value as a historic relic, and a Lapis treasure... good God man!" Sir Henry exclaimed. "It's, it's-" Sir Henry went breathless. "It's in early Cuneiform, an ancient script of the Sumerians, later adapted for international use as a language of commerce." Sir Henry rattled off facts that, though interesting, left me in a fog.

"I see. But what has this to do with the Smythe family?" I asked, maintaining my polite posture.

"It's a wedding contract, between one Scota, daughter of the Egyptian Pharoah Cingris, and one Ciniod Rianorix Smythe," Sir Henry enthused. "They joined together in a pact of blood, swearing oaths to their pagan gods—specifically, Great God Anubis, God of the Underworld— that their love would never die. Heavens above, man! This is proof positive that the Egyptians visited and settled in the British Isles long before the Romans set foot on our soil. It confirms the contentions of the early Scottish chronicler, Walter Bower!"

Obviously excited by this discovery, Sir Henry told me he wanted to show the tablet to a wider circle of colleagues. I demurred for the moment, so he took wax impressions of the thing and made quick sketches. I bid my adieus to my noble friend, with a promise that he would see the Lapis tablet again.

Following this revelation, I decided it was time to explore the Smythe family crypt, for had not my Uncle died at its threshold? Perhaps the answer lay in its ancient, cobwebbed corners or among its interred corpses. I thought it better to go alone by night, and so prepared a satchel for what I may encounter ahead. The fact that Uncle Cornelius had delved into occult abysses weighed on my mind, let alone that other factor; the vision of his death at the claws of the wind-borne assailant. I had awakened many nights screaming from what I had seen in that hellish vision, so often, in fact, that my beloved took to sleeping in another wing of our manor.

I needed cabalistic weapons equal to the occultic bird of prey and whatever else my Uncle might have invoked. Besides my shortened Brown Bess, my sword cane, and a flintlock pistol, I carried on my person a canteen of holy water, blessed unknowingly by both an infidel padre of the Romish church, and a priest from the Mother Church of God-Fearing Englishman. I also carried an exorcist fetish bundle prescribed by a Latin translation of the heretical *Picatrix*, an ancient Arabian book of astrologic and occultic magics. A simple crucifix, my Uncle's signet ring, the Lapis tablet, and the mystery key rounded out the pack. Shouldering these reminded me of my days in His Majesty's Army.

I stuck to the shadows, and avoided open areas where the moon lit up wide swatches of land. The crypt was on family land, but shared with the commoners that served the estate. In time, I came to the tombstone marked with a skull, crossbones, and hourglass, the psychic marker that figured prominently in Nigel's vision. An owl hooted as I arrived at the rough stone face of the crypt, its barred door tightly sealed, a mixture of silvers and shadows enshrouding its oblong exterior. No-one knew of my moonlight visit, save my most trusted agent, who I had instructed to organise a search party, should I fail to return.

I glanced back the way I'd come and around the exterior of the crypt, and saw no indication that anyone followed or lay in wait. I unlocked the crypt's door, which rasped on rusty hinges, and entered, within. The place smelt of mould, dust, and rotting corpses—British embalming practices not being as precise as the Egyptian priests who prepared their Pharaohs for the afterlife. Perhaps portions of Uncle Cornelius' lead-lined coffin had been broken. As an honour due the dead, I would answer that question later. I lit a lantern and turned it on the foyer that housed the caskets of the most recent tenants. The gilding on some had tarnished, but otherwise, everything looked to be in order. I decided to search the distant quarters of the Crypt, the one less travelled. I could not call to mind anyone having stepped foot there, at least in my lifetime, excepting, perhaps, my agents searching for my Uncle's wealth.

Steeling myself for what lay ahead, I pressed on, entering

into a forest of caskets with wood rotted. The lining of coffins with lead was a recent practice. Every sense was alert as I walked between rows of stacked coffins, differing in size, as many children and wives had died young down the centuries in the Smythe family line. My footsteps violated the sacred silence of the sepulchre. Names on coffins, if such inscriptions persisted, slowly dovetailed from King James spellings to the pointed Saxon minuscules of the eighth or ninth century, then to the Latin script used by the servants of Hadrian.

As I rounded a heap of tomb rubbish and disintegrating bones, I spied a low, faint circle of light peering out from a forgotten corner. I hid my lantern behind the teetering stack to confirm whether the spectral light ahead originated with my light. Certain that it didn't, I put out the lantern torch and walked through the dark corridors toward the feeble light. It came forth from beneath a layer of dusty grave clothes, which hitherto hid the light.

Kicking them aside revealed a barred bronze lid, from whence the glow shone. A large, peculiar padlock sealed this egress to the underworld. Playing a hunch, I pulled out the odd key I found among my Uncle's effects. I fumbled with the padlock in the dim light emitted from around the trapdoor's seams. That the key fit was no surprise to me. Had my Uncle used this door to the abyss before? The padlock came apart after some effort. I laid it aside and attempted to lift the cover. Quite heavy for its size, I got it open three-quarters on its hinges, engaging helpful counterweights in the process, before it mechanically stopped.

Light spiraled upward through the aperture, blinding me for a moment. Below the rim, lay a circular vault and ladder.

One side led off into a tunnel from my vantage point. I tested the ladder, a curiously aged wood and stone affair. Proving itself sound, I descended its rungs to the chamber's floor, noting the litany of Romish and Runic warnings carved into the chamber's walls. The source of the light? For some inexplicable reason, the walls of the chamber glowed. I relit my lantern, muttered a prayer, and crossed myself before proceeding further, following the tunnel that led immediately off the chamber. I had no idea that catacombs lay beneath our family crypt. Strong timbers of considerable size buttressed the sides and ceiling of the tunnel. That I was descending deeper into the earth, there was no doubt, for I was walking down a gradual incline.

I estimate an hour or so passed before I reached an antechamber, crowded with two large Egyptian sarcophagi, each laid on an opposing side of the room. These were inlaid with lapis lazuli, silver, turquoise, and gold. Both lids of the prodigious coffins had been removed and set aside. I immediately lowered my satchel and withdrew the tablet. Yes, an inscription on one sarcophagus matched one of the names of the tablet, indicated by Sir Henry to read, *Scota, daughter of the Pharoah Cingris*. I fell to my knees at the revelation. There were occultic implications, no doubt, for the once-sealed caskets were empty. I sat on the floor for a time. That is until I felt the cold barrel of a Brown Bess pressed against the back of my head.

"Here now," said a fellow with a Welsh accent. "Hands up, sir, or you're a dead man."

I complied, slowly got to my feet and turned. There, in the torchlight, stood betrayer and solicitor Abraham Dowe, holding the Brown Bess on me, accompanied by two ruffians, paid muscle no doubt. They immediately stripped me of my weapons.

"So, look what you found, my dear Roger," Dowe said eyeing one sarcophagus, then the other. You could see him counting crowns with his eyes.

"Either of these is already worth a King's ransom," Dowe muttered. "Where's the rest of the treasure? Beyond this chamber, I bet? The Egyptians always liked to take it with them, wealth for the afterlife." Dowe grinned.

"I don't know, this is the first time I've ever been down here," I said.

"Then we'll see the Smythe clan's vast cache of lost wealth together, beyond the tunnel ahead. Move along." My once-trusted agent, shoved the Brown Bess against my chest.

"What do you stand to gain in this?" I asked.

My agent smiled and replied, "Now that's none of your business. Move along now."

I was shoved forward roughly with the Brown Bess.

As we moved, the air ahead hung heavy with an impenetrable stratum of shadows and gloom. Would this track lead to my own premature grave? As I tumbled into the next chamber of shadows, I heard a collective gasp of astonishment from Dowe and his henchmen. The cavern felt enormous and was dimly lit. Spread around its vast circumference hovered hazy pillars of greenish flame, vaguely anthropomorphic in cast and stature. In their faint light, my eyes fell on a confusion of features. A great oily river bisected the cavern, a slow-moving Styx that flowed from one shoreline of this underworld to the Dantean beaches of another. I heard oily splashes across the cavern void, as unseen abominations played in its greasy depths.

"Bert, why don't you do a walk-around with your torch, so we can better see where the treasure boxes lie," ordered Dowe, impatient at the emptiness he saw. One of the ruffians emerged from behind us and began to wander, flaming brand in one hand and a flintlock pistol in the other, towards the glistening river. He walked forward into the dim light.

"Go on, Bert, there's nothing to be afraid of." Dowe motioned to his lackey.

Bert stopped and looked at the foremost ring of odd stalagmites.

"Hello, hello, hello, this one's got a funny shape, sort of like my Gertie back home." said Bert, as he ran his finger along the pillar, then tasted it. "Hey, this here is a pillar of salt!" he exclaimed.

Pillar of salt, my focused mind observed. Now where before had I heard that?

Bert ranged out farther, his face and form fading in the distance. At one point, his light fell at the base of something large. It exposed black roots that spread over the cavern floor like a black walnut tree, only on an unheralded scale. The black bore of the tree disappeared into the dark heights of the cavern. *What was a tree doing down here, so far below ground?* I thought.

Bert held up his torch to see the extent of the tree's growth.

"That's no tree!" screamed Bert as he jumped back from the leering, multiplied faces. "It's a blooming stack of teetering skulls held together with spider webs! I ain't being paid enough coin for this job."

"Move along Bert, you'll have plenty of time for sightseeing once the job's done," Dowe yelled out. The remaining three of us moved forward into the abyss, following the henchman. Next, Bert came to the edge of the oily river. In the dim distance, there appeared a tall, immense door, hundreds of cubits high, grotesquely carved in motifs, glyphs, and sigils from across the ages and the known continents. Bert yelled from the near distance, "What do you suppose lies behind that door?"

Without warning, a falsetto scream pierced the darkness, a pistol blast echoed in the heights, and Bert's torch fell.

"Bert? Where'd you get off to?" Dowe's second lackey shouted across the expanse. The Brown Bess relaxed, no longer pointing at me. An intense foulness filled the air, as something reached down to grab the lackey's face, forcing it to tilt upward. In the ruddy light, there hovered above us one then another, then another, levitating monstrosities, each bearing the canine head of Anubis, and the multiple arms of a menacing Shiva, each carrying a weighing scale or a glistening scythe. The bodies were a tattered folly of bandages that spread toward each man like a Kraken's tentacles.

Firearms went off aimlessly, as Dowe and his lackeys screamed. One by one, each rose into the cavern heights, carried by putrid, constricting coils of bandages. One, two, then three bloodied skulls plopped to the floor around me. The decapitated head of Abraham Dowe stared blankly up at me, a rictus grin replacing his previous triumphant smile.

I fell to my knees, gathering up my fallen satchel, a torch, and my sword cane. I thrust the torch desperately upward, swatting away the descending strappings of another disciple of Anubis. I tried to retreat towards the tunnel while defending myself with fire, yet could not, for as I glanced behind myself,

I saw a knot of those ghastly figures blocking the opening. Sensing my distraction, one of the things swatted away my torch, effortlessly hoisted me into the air, and pulled me towards its snapping, canine maul.

"The master has need of thee," the thing barked hoarsely, its breath reeking of the carnal depths of hell.

I gagged at the stench. The dim contours of the cavern floor flew by below me as the thing carried me toward the enormous door beyond the oily river. I glimpsed odd, profane things mirrored in the slimy waters. I laughed nervously; my mind froze in fear over what I might soon face. I tried to extract my sword, but the thing held my cane at an angle where I could not withdraw it. Then the thing flew low to the cavern floor and tossed me sideways, as a common labourer might toss a sack of potatoes across a warehouse floor. Unhurt, but my senses jarred, I saw a small retinue of giants, a herald of Nephilim, gather around me, living models of the skeleton in my Uncle's hall of horrors. One took me up like a beggar's bundle, and carried me forward, as a deafening rasp of gears echoed in the cavern.

As I nervously sized up my newest gang of inhuman captors, they ogled me back, snarling. Some had two horned-heads while others only had one. I wondered if I were the main course in their next meal. Strangely, they produced a bizarre horde of ancient Egyptian instruments, as the knot of beasts ambled forward. Two played rattling sistrums, another played dissonant chords on a sambuke, and a third played slow blasts on a long-necked, silver trumpet festooned with occultic motifs.

Other beasts, demons, and loathsome monstrosities joined in the throng behind my entourage. From unknown portals to hell below, arose a litany of croaking, squealing, caterwauling, and wheezing voices that ascended from an untold horde of polyglotIc beasts, quasi-humans, living, amorphous heaps, animated demigods, and blasphemous chimeras. Beneath a myriad of countless torches, many marched proudly wearing sashes or belts of their feral conquests, sporting the skulls of nobles, warriors, and priests from the surface world. The cacophony of sounds was deafening as we neared the grand sigiled and glyphed door, lined with broken seals, some of which bore the unmistakable four-sided *signum manus* (or signature seal) of Charlemagne the Great. My mind reeled with my situation and its implications.

The chief Nephilim strode forward, lifting its four arms in adoration, all but one holding forth the headless corpses of my erstwhile companions. For some reason, one of its left hands was missing. Then, it dawned on me - one treasure box in my Uncle's bizarrerie bore six severed left hands of these malformed giants. It barked out something in old Latin that I dare not repeat, or it will draw down swift vengeance like lightning from above. That the melancholic and Mephistophelean spirits of the world gathered before my unbelieving eyes, I have no doubt. They stood there before the grand door worshipping in the abyss for what seemed hours.

I cannot say how much time past, my sanity hanging from a thread, as it was. Yet, at one point, the huge edifice opened, the noise drowning out the roaring beasts that celebrated before it. An immense onyx obelisk appeared. Three heads of Anubis with fiery eyes, snarled atop it, smoke poured from their nostrils. To its base, flew the living effigy, the one I'd found in my Uncle's lair. Here was the dark chimera whose shadowed presence had terrified my Uncle to death outside the crypt above.

To the side of the Black Obelisk, undulated a living gate, a protoplasmic portal to purgatory, transmutation, and beyond. It was enormous. Without head, limb, or other contrivance comparable to human outlines, its presence titillated my hominid senses, yet it made no sense, no rhythm, nor reason to my higher faculties. It mimicked in its immensity, a shoal of fish. A thousand spectral mauls all shifting in unison; budding, blossoming, and withering as one. Shards of inner lightning struck sporadically, revealing a flowing, confusing skeletal structure. That this was but the merest forepaw of a greater god-thing, was made plain by the odd flopping and flapping that resounded in the darkness behind it, beyond the door.

My heart almost burst at the sight.

Then, I noticed a seated gilded statue of Scota, daughter of the Egyptian Pharoah Cingris. In her face and eyes, oh her feral living eyes, I saw the countenance of the she-demon Lilith, the wife of Adam before Eve, crafty, cunning, a living curse on all mankind. Were her demonic devices somehow intertwined with the Smythe clan? The sight shuddered me to my core.

In a moment of lucidity, I thought; *here was a centre of the universe. Perhaps the centre of the Smythe clan's universe, surely part of its sorted history from near the beginning until now, but in the same instant, timeless and alien, wholly apart from the world of the clan. The well of the Smythes might dry up and whither, but this fountain would remain, seeking to devour all-comers, all those looking for eternal things beyond their temporary lives. They might spell an end to my world, but a beginning to another.*

The foremost Nephilim grabbed me by the left arm and dragged me forward. We passed through a knot of the other giants, each holding one of their left arms into my sight, each limb missing an enormous hand. I felt it analogous to a military bride and groom, passing through a tunnel of the groom's fellow officers, each brandishing their swords in a ceremonious blessing of the betrothed. Such was my jumble of thoughts. In absolute silence, the assembled throng of terror waited. The Nephilim that accosted me stopped and bowed before the seated statue of Scota.

"I am Ciniod Rianorix Smyth. " the Nephilim croaked as the assembled celebrants howled. "I am first Father of the Smythe Clan" it went on, hushing the trumpeting mob with a swift signal of its right hands. "Before the assembled today, I offer you, Roger Smythe, the chance to live forever, co-reigning over all that you see, for eternity. And to own an Empire greater than the King of England, for he himself does obeisance in his private chambers to Scota, otherwise, his line would not rule the ancient Pictish Isles." Ciniod said.

I lay in a heap at the monster's feet, staring up in unbelief at its words. "And at what price?" I asked.

Ciniod grabbed my left arm exposing my Uncle Cornelius's signet ring. The Chimeric throng roared in orgiastic abandonment at the sight of the ring.

"In life, you will become an agent of Scota, doing her will and working her wonders among the Sons of Man." Ciniod said. "And in death, you become as I and the other eternal Five Fathers of the Smythe clan, part of Scota's retinue of lovers. You must also pass through the ordeal of the gate to be deemed worthy." he continued.

"And what of eternal life in heaven?" I asked, my ability to say no, waning.

"What of it?" snarled the Nephilim, as if it spat out a curse.

A single idea surfaced in my mind. "What if I say no?" I said.

"Infidel! Then you will die eternally, like all the others who spurned Scota's love." Ciniod roared, revealing in a mocking vision, my fate; I saw a forest of rough crosses, where thousands of naked men hung crucified, straining painfully against thousands of nails, moaning in their endless, collective agony. In a swift move, the Nephilim stuck my hand between its toothy jaws and snapped off my left pinky, signet ring and all. I howled in agony, falling to its feet. I struggled while bleeding, searching in my satchel for the one item. Yes, there it was...I lifted high the Lapis tablet and threw it into the monstrous mob that attended the Nephilim and their Masters.

An untold pandemonium ensued with each blasphemous celebrant vying for the talisman. In pain, I ran toward the oily river that divided the cavern, dodging the maddening crowd whose attention was drawn elsewhere. I reached its shore and flung myself into its cold, murky depths. I hoped to die a death, apart from the power of the Nephilim, who would crucify me in that second death.

"And that, gentlemen, is my story." Smythe sighed as if a terrible weight were lifted off his shoulders.

"But, how did you live after jumping into that oily river?" Tredman blurted out.

"I don't know. Divine providence, I gather, though I'm not sure at this juncture, which pantheon to thank," Smythe replied.

"How incredibly preposterous! Do you really expect us to believe your story?" Tredman continued, in love with the sound of his own voice.

Smythe looked sternly around the circle. "I care not whether you believe me. It is my tale; I will stick by it. Yet..." Smythe said, becoming stoic.

"Yet what?" Tredman said.

"I am in constant fear for my life. It is apparent to me now, they want more than my pinky and signet ring. My Uncle's Manor burnt to the ground, occult collection and all. My estate has been struck by bizarre misfortunes. In every shadow, I fear the forces of hell gather and will soon come for me. I dare not go out after dark. At all hours of the night, in whichever room I happen to reside, I've heard the scratching of a wild beast at the window and, occasionally, a shadow across the pane, perfectly like to the one that caused my Uncle's death. I'm doomed, I tell you, doomed," Smythe muttered.

"Gentlemen," I said, tired of Tredman's bombastic badgering, "let us refresh our drinks and adjoin to another room, where perhaps another Pickmanite will share his tales."

I stayed by Smythe's side as the others left. Shouldering Roger's weakened frame, his cane in hand, we shuffled to a side room, a private space that afforded members some measure of seclusion, should such a state be desired.

A flickering street lamp, from beyond an opaque glass fronting a side alley, faintly illuminated our domicile. I lowered Roger into one of the three stuffed armchairs that dominated the spartan space. Members often used such apartments to sleep off their excesses. A knock came on the mahogany-panelled door, a butler peeked around the open portal, a lit candelabra swaying in hand.

"Is everything in order, sir? Do you require anything?" asked the valet.

"No, we are quite alright, my good man, thank you." I replied.

The butler disappeared and the door quietly closed. Roger looked up at me with thanks in his tired eyes. I sat down facing him, my back to the alley window, pondering what I should say. Abruptly, the room darkened, as a play of strange shadows shifted with life on the wall opposite me. There came a low, cautious scratching at the opaque window, and a muffled, disembodied chatter, beyond a doubt in *Old Latin*. Roger came to life, his face filled with terror at the sounds and shadows.

"Mother of God, they found me! The window! THE WINDOW!"

In the middle of that blasphemous group
stood a most singular individual.
Vaguely humanoid in shape,
and somehow misshapen

SHADWELL'S TALE

RUSSELL SMEATON

The night crept in, under the door, dank and cold. The servants had banked the fire up good, and it did a valiant attempt at keeping the fog at bay, but the damp of the Thames was not to be denied. Above the odour of cigars and the coal fire, I could smell the dampness that permeated the carpets, that faint tang of salt from the sea, even so far away. Gas lights spluttered, somehow making the room feel darker rather than dispel the gloom they were intended for. The leather of my chair creaked as I snuggled myself back. The brandy was warming me nicely and I felt the glow that only good brandy and company can bring.

As was our routine, we had gathered to recount our experiences for Pickman. I was feeling uneasy. I had still not ventured out to explore our great city, and all that lies underneath. My bones ached perpetually, and I preferred the comfort of my residence on Park Lane. So, I sat there, hoping that Pickman wouldn't turn his kindly gaze upon me in anticipation.

I needn't have worried. After a few rounds of gentle conversation, the room fell into a natural silence and it wasn't long before Shadwell cleared his throat, and we all knew he was about to tell us his tale. He wiped his mouth, and I noticed his left hand was bandaged, entirely covered. I vowed to ask him what happened at a more convenient time. The shadows of the room darkened, making the company look like shadows.

"Gentlemen," began Shadwell. "Let me tell you about a strange figure I encountered down at the docks."

At mention of the docks, a few of the company exchanged bawdy guffaws, quickly followed by a stern rebuke from Pickman. We all knew the reputation of the docks and those lonely souls who ventured there for a moment of physical comfort. The laughter soon died down, and Shadwell took another sip of brandy. Wiping his mouth with his bandaged hand, he looked long and hard at his glass, his eyebrows furrowing. An unfortunate effect of the shadows made Shadwell's eyes appear larger than usual, almost black as they swivelled inside shrunken sockets. I wondered when he had last slept, as he looked decidedly dishevelled.

"As I was saying, the docks are a fine place to wander during the day. You can experience the whole world under your very eyes just by strolling along the waterfront. Ships coming in from all corners of the world, bringing with them their own stories. Gentlemen, we are truly fortunate to live in such a glorious age."

A gentle swell of agreement accompanied this statement. The room seemed to shrink as Shadwell began to tell his tale.

Some days ago, I had tarried at the docks, savouring the sights, smells and sounds. It was like walking through many different countries, all located here in our wonderful London. Truth be told, I hadn't intended on spending so long there, but I found myself in a distinct reverie. So there I was, strolling around the docks, wide eyed as a puppy. In any event, dusk began to fall, and I decided it was time to retreat for home. After all, the docks are not necessarily the place a gentleman of means should be wandering around unaccompanied of a nighttime!

So, I turned heel and started in the direction of Fleet Street, where, as you probably know, I've been renting rooms. No sooner had I done so, when I noticed a rag tag bunch of street urchins running down a street. The way they moved stirred the feeling in me that they had a single agenda. Knowing of our meeting, I decided to follow, hoping for a tale to share with you fine gentlemen.

They moved fast, darting down alleys that made me regard my polished shoes with woe. My feet splashed through puddles that reeked of all manner of human despair , and I distinctly felt the damp seep through. Even now I can remember the cold, clammy texture. By that time, I was too invested in the chase to give up on account of having, pardon my pun, cold feet. So, I pressed on, even though I was by now hopelessly lost in a warren of hovels the likes of which I hope to never see again. Grimy sheets hung above me, grey and motionless in the night air. Rabid dogs snarled their territory, as they strained against mouldering ropes that I hoped would contain them. And still, the urchins ran on.

They moved fast as whippets, and I would have lost them if they hadn't made regular stops. The first was to collect a hand drawn cart, wooden wheels warped with age. I puzzled as to the purpose of this wagon, but the first mystery of the night soon revealed itself. Their next stop was a motionless body, slumped behind a particularly fragrant pile of refuse. My suspicions were confirmed as they bundled the body onto the cart. An arm flopped lifelessly out, which was efficiently secreted into the cart. In those god-forsaken slums, it seemed the dead were forgotten and left to lie where they died. I didn't have long to ponder the heart-wrenching sadness of this final lack of dignity for these poor souls, for the urchins were off again, onto the second mystery of the night – what did they do with these bodies?

As I followed them, my first thought was they were taking the body to one of the clinics where surgeons purchased fresh cadavers to practice their craft on. I knew of no clinics in those parts, but even so that was not their destination. After another stop to pick up another body, we carried on, until the street opened up onto an old, disused harbour. After the claustrophobic streets, their buildings so slumped with age that almost no sky was visible, the open space felt practically dizzying.

A full moon was barely visible in the night sky, a thin drizzle reducing it to a white smudge. It was quiet at that harbour, and I looked around in an attempt to get my bearings. This was a part of the city I had never visited before, and could get no sense of where I was. The only thing I was certain of was the mighty River Thames, lapping against a mouldering jetty. The urchins chatted amongst themselves, but so quiet I couldn't make out their conversation. The way in which they moved in small, fidgety motions made me think they were nervous, scared even. I wondered what they waited for, and in that murky moonlight, it was hard to make out just exactly what was happening.

In the gloom, I could just about see the group of children stiffen, almost like soldiers standing to attention, and, for some unknown reason, I felt my skin crawl. My senses became heightened as I strained my eyes and ears to try and make sense of what was happening. The children had stopped talking, and I could hear a creak of elderly wood and the gentle splashing of the river.

Soon came another noise to my ears. At first, I couldn't place it. A scratching, following by a twittering sound. Rats, and lots of them! I expected the children to run and hide, screaming in disgust as a veritable tide of vermin swarmed over the harbour, past the urchins and toward me. I stood my ground, but I'm not ashamed to admit I felt close to bolting. Instead, I gathered my courage and held fast as the rodents washed past me, as a stream flows round a rock.

Eventually, the swarm was over, and the harbour was once again wreathed in silence. The urchins remained motionless, and my ears pricked up as another sound slowly became obvious. Again, a scratching sound, but different to before. This was more like a clattering of forks on a plate. There soon followed a smell as of something dredged up from the dark deeps of the ocean floor, rank, like a whale carcass left to rot. I felt my stomach twist and spasm, as I fought to hold down its contents.

Still I couldn't see, so I stole closer, despite the nauseating stench. As I moved towards the children, I could see them, more clearly, drenched in fear, their pale faces frozen in place. Looking out over the harbour, over the inky darkness of the Thames I finally saw the reason why. The waters were shallow as the tide started to ebb, revealing dark, oozing mud banks.

There, coming from the river, a sight out of any nightmare, but I assure you I was wide awake, and this was no dream! A cast of crabs was scuttling towards us, but these were no ordinary crabs. It was hard to judge precisely, but I would hazard a guess that each was the size of a large dog. I was suddenly thankful for the gloom and lack of direct moonlight, as I didn't want to see just what was coming closer and closer, and yet I found myself transfixed.

In the middle of that blasphemous group stood a most singular individual. Vaguely humanoid in shape, the being was tall and somehow misshapen. Covered in rotting clothing, the thing walked with the aid of a long staff, something akin to a shepherd's crook. Before it could come any closer, the children burst into life, throwing the corpses they had collected over the side of the jetty, and onto the dark mud. Each corpse landed with a wet splat, and the crabs pounced on the bodies. I admit, it was at this point that I did look away, for I couldn't bear the sight of what was surely an unholy feast. Even so, as I turned my back, I could hear the sound of flesh being rendered and noisily eaten, and I believe my stomach finally gave way.

After what seemed like an impossibly long time, the repulsive noises finally came to a close, and the scuttling sounds receded back into the depths of the Thames. I dared to examine what remained, and felt my heart freeze. The tall being was still there, looking up from the mud-flats to precisely where I was stood. I couldn't see its face, but I felt sure it was looking at me. I felt as though freezing cold water had been thrown over me, and I found myself fixed to the spot, unable to move. Thankfully, the being slowly turned, and hobbled slowly back into the river, until it was no longer visible. Only then did the life return to my limbs, and I felt my entire body sag with relief. I started to wonder what it was that was down there on, and now in the river. How did it breathe? Was it human? Why did it walk surrounded by huge, corpse-eating crabs? My head swam with impossible questions that my brain could not answer.

I know not how long I stood there, pondering the imponderable. I was brought out of my reverie by a tugging of my coat sleeve. Looking down, it was one of the urchins. Her face was strangely beatific, especially after the horrors I had witnessed. Her accent was thick and coarse, speaking in a thick dialect that I shan't trouble you gentlemen with here. Our conversation went something like the following.

"What are you doing 'ere, mister?" she asked.

"Erm, well, I was following you," I answered truthfully enough.

"Why?"

"I was curious and then...well," and I found I couldn't finish the sentence as the recent ragged memory of those crabs came back to me.

"Ahhh, you saw *him* then," she replied, looking out over the river. Dawn was slowly breaking, and a mist was coming off the river. A few gulls flew overhead, squawking in their vulgar way.

"Yes, I did. And them."

"We calls him the Shepherd," she ventured.

"Him?" I asked, though I knew who she was referring to.

"Yeah. See, he shepherds those crabby things. We feeds 'em so they don't get too angry. We live near 'ere, and it wouldn't do for them things to get too angry."

I could see her logic. I shuddered as I imagined what those things would do if angry.

"So you feed them the dead?" I asked.

"Well, the Shepherd come to us, and promised us a new life if we did, but we didn't believe him. We knew if he didn't get what he wanted, the new life for us would be a dinner for the crabs."

There was some other conversation, and some of the others children wandered over to add their pennies of wisdom to the pot. I believe one of the older girls offered me some service of a more intimate nature, so I quickly made my excuses and, after paying them for directions, was able to make my weary way home.

As you can imagine, I couldn't rest or settle. My mind kept seeing those crabs, and thing they called the Shepherd. I started to ponder more and more on what the girl had meant by *a new life* that the Shepherd had offered. It seemed to me more than just a veiled threat to keep his flock fed, as I now considered those crabs to be. A strange, vile flock, but a flock nonetheless. I rested fitfully on the couch, barely able to eat or drink. My man brought some vitals, but my heart wasn't in it, and I merely pecked at the food like a chicken.

I vowed to see the Shepherd again, but why I couldn't say. My stomach still churned at the memory of the sound made by those distorted crabs feasting, and yet the Shepherd had taken hold of my mind and I could think of nothing else.

That night, I stole down to the docks once more and attempted to retrace my previous steps. By sheer luck, I found myself at that deserted jetty once again. Unlike the night before, the sky was clear, a swollen moon shedding its gibbous light over the scene. The tide was already out, the reeking mud-flats fully exposed. I could make out all manner of refuse, but the scene of the previous night's feast was clean. Not even a single bone remained in place, and I began to wonder as to my sanity. Had I imagined it all? After all, giant crabs being herded across the River Thames made no sense.

I sat down on the jetty under that yellowing, cankerous moon. Dangerous as it may seem, I think I must have dozed off, or dropped into a trance of some description, as I suddenly became aware of the stench from the night before. Senses instantly on guard, I realised with horror that the Shepherd was in front of me, closer than before. How long he had been there, I couldn't say, but there he was. Unlike last night, I could clearly see what was standing before me. Taller than the average man, but still humanoid, he leant against his crook as a few large crabs scuttled around his legs, no doubt in search of a tasty treat. His clothing was soaking wet, dripping a black ichor that stank of dead fish. I could see things moving inside the tattered robes, as he casually fished out a black eel, throwing it to the crabs who fought briefly for the morsel. His skin was pale and mottled, almost purple with dark blue veins marbling his arms. Seaweed and barnacles littered his clothes and skin, and small crabs scurried over his body.

As I looked up to his face, for the second time in as many days, it was as though a shard of ice pierced my very being. He was staring directly at me, and had probably been doing so for some time. His eyes were clouded a thick milky white, and I wondered if he was blind. Yet the way those scummy orbs followed me made me doubt this assumption. His mouth was a thin cruel line that opened into a smile, a smile I wish I hadn't seen. Thin teeth, like those of a shark crowded that mouth. And it was then he spoke.

Water trickled out of his mouth as he talked, and my brain reeled as I tried to focus on what he was saying. Alas, I cannot, or will not, recall that conversation. The only thing I clearly remember him saying was *The Shepherd needs his flock, but the flock has to change its ways to see the way"* His voice was somehow wet, gurgling, like a drain, and even now I can feel my skin crawl as I think of it.

Finally, he stopped his insane liturgy, and held a long arm out towards me. Without thinking, I reached out and he put something in my hand. I felt his skin then, cold and wet, just as I knew it would be. Even now I fancy I can smell his flesh on me, as when you've handled fish too long.

Without another word, he turned and walked back into the Thames as before, those peculiar strides taking him further and further out until he was no longer visible. The moon was still above, but had begun to sink down, stars twirling around it as it began its descent.

I stayed put on that jetty, trying to make some sense of my experiences. I looked at my hand and examined what the Shepherd deposited there. Coins, and no small amount. Larger than any I had seen, but green with age. Some were more corroded than others, but they all looked rare and expensive. I put the majority in my pocket, keeping one out that I examined in the waning moonlight. The damp chill air seeped into my bones, and my joints ached with it, but still I remained where I was, turning the coin over and over, willing it to tell me its secrets.

At the first light of dawn, I stood up with a groan, my spine protesting at the sudden movement. Seagulls were already voicing their displeasure at the morning, and a light mist rose from the river. As the day began, I sloped off to my residence. Making my weary way up the stairs, I couldn't even muster the energy to undress, merely collapsing on the bed. As soon as my head hit the pillow, I had fallen into a deep, dreamless sleep.

I know not what time I awoke. At some point, my man must have paid me a visit, as I was at least partially undressed and under the sheets. On the bedside table were the coins the Shepherd had handed to me, and I shuddered. For on waking I thought my encounter merely some fevered dream. But the presence of those damnable coins proved, once and for all, that the Shepherd was real.

It was here that Shadwell stopped and reached for his glass. His hand was shaking, so I picked up his glass for him and handed it over. Our hands brushed and he jerked back, almost spilling his brandy. He fixed me a glare with those beady eyes for a second too long to be comfortable, and took a hefty draught of his drink before lapsing into silence.

"Well, Shadwell," said Pickman after a moment, "That was a fine tale. Wasn't it gentlemen?"

A murmur of assent met this statement, and I found myself nodding along. Tales of street urchins, abandoned jetties, flesh eating crabs and a strange mysterious creature were indeed components of a fine tale.

"Can you remember anything of what the Shepherd said?" young John Dingman asked. We all leaned closer to Shadwell, curious as to what he might say.

Shadwell remained silent for a moment or two, his right hand absently rubbing his bandaged left. As I peered at him, I noticed once again his eyes seeming to be darker than usual, possessing an almost queer independent motion. It seemed he wasn't going to venture any more information that the evening, but after a moment or two, he continued.

"I can't be sure," he started, somewhat hesitatingly. "It seemed like such a long time ago, even though it was just a few days past. Alas, I don't remember, but here, take a look at these and see what you think."

He reached into his pocket and brought out a handful of coins that he scattered onto the small table by the fire. As he had said, they were large and mottled with a curious green staining. Olmstead wasted no time and picked one up, straight away putting it in his mouth to bite down on it. Examining his teeth marks, he gleefully exclaimed the authenticity of the gold coins. The rest of us followed suit, laughing and picking up a coin or two. Pickman abstained, and watched us quietly, a small sad smile playing over his lips.

"Keep them if you like, I have plenty," said Shadwell, "Besides, I don't think I'll need them anymore."

"Whatever do you mean, man?" I asked. It seemed damned cryptic, after all.

"Well, the Shepherd..." started Shadwell, and then paused.

"Yes," prompted Pickman, "what about the Shepherd?"

"Is a Shepherd a shepherd without a flock?" he answered, with a question that prompted no answers.

He would be drawn no more on the matter, and light-hearted debate as to who this Shepherd was, and the nature of those large crabs. Many theories were tested and expatiated, each more outlandish than the last. Soon, it was the turn of the next speaker, and attention focused once more on a single figure, stood before the fire, expounding their recent weird adventure.

For myself, however, I continued to reflect on Shadwell's story. It all seemed so far-fetched, and yet, Shadwell was not the sort for poetic fantasies. I must have drunk a little more brandy than usual, as I began to crave a drink of water. Specifically, lightly salted water. No sooner did I acknowledge this, than I thought back to that moment as Shadwell and I brushed hands. I had felt something rough on his hands, and it only then occurred to me what it reminded me off. Maybe it was the craving of the salt water, and memories of childhood trips to the sea, but his hand had felt like the rough barnacles one finds in rock pools or on the underside of an old boat. And then, the final horror settled into place. His hand, his bandaged hand... Even though it was fully swaddled in clothe, even now I fancied I recognised the shape obscured within. Not that of a hand, but that of a claw. The claw of a crustacean, impossibly on the arm of a man.

I shuddered, the hairs on my neck raising. The urge for salt water came back, and my hand felt the coin Shadwell had given, secreted in my pocket. As I took it out, did I spot a small white growth on my hand? A tiny barnacle? I thought back to what Shadwell had said.

"The Shepherd needs his flock, but the flock has to change its way to see the way..."

*I scarcely sleep and when I do, my rest is
haunted by unsettling visitations*

THE FITZWYRM LEGACY

JOHN HOULIHAN

The fire had burned down to its embers and the hour approached midnight when Mrs Sternblight at last received her invitation to speak from the chairman of the Pickman Club. There was a slight murmuring ,and at least one audible *harrumph* at her appearance, for not all members of the club were so enlightened as to be convinced of the considerable merits of the female of the species.

But Mrs Ermentrude "Irma" Sternblight ignored them, strode confidently to the head of the table, fixed the assembly with a stern eye and any dissension was soon quelled by the firmness of her gaze. A hush descended on the assembly, then slowly and deliberately, she took a brandy glass full to the brim and upended it, so that the white expanse of her throat was exposed. The contents were consumed in one long, thirsty pull. She reached into her décolletage and produced and lit a formidable cigar, coaxed it until the tip glowed, puffed away unhurriedly, cleared her throat contentedly and began.

"Gentlemen... I am honoured to have been so recently accepted into your august company, albeit with some reservations, I understand?" She arched a meticulously sculpted eyebrow, but none dared meet her stare, so she continued.

"It is therefore my great privilege to recount for you a most strange and unusual tale which occurred during a recent visit to the esteemed county of Yorkshire. What drew me there was a missive from a Mister Dudley Fitzwyrm, a new arrival to this country from his native homeland of British Columbia, Canada.

He spoke in the most flattering not to say reverential terms, referencing a mutual acquaintance, and being kind enough to acknowledge my trifling assistance in the Matter of the Missing Mi-Go. Mister Fitzwyrm begged my help in a most pressing and confidential concern and requested my attendance at his newly found country seat. It is with his express permission, that I now lay this tale before you, trusting to your good sense and sagacity, both that you may comprehend its lessons and, I must insist on this, that the details of which shall go no further than this very room. Am I to take it that will be the case?" A round of nodded assents assured her that it would be so.

"Very well, gentlemen, thank you. I hold you to your word and your honour. I will not trouble you with the details of my journey, but two day's excursion and not a little hardship eventually brought me to the hills and dales of God's own country. I proceeded to the nearby village of Birtleby, and hired a carriage to take me to Fitzwyrm Manor, although as it turned out, no amount of encouragement or financial inducement would persuade the driver to venture beyond the gates of the drive, nor disclose the reason for his apprehensive attitude.

Even though he would not speak against the place, his silence was thoroughly instructive, gentlemen, significant even I say, for these country folk's attitudes often reveal darker and more unwholesome truths about the object of their trepidation.

Fortunately, my extensive travels, both in this country and the wider world, have prepared me well and I am used to travelling light, so I shouldered my single valise and walked up through the heavily wooded driveway.

The day was waning but the light was still good, although curiously few native birds or animals disturbed my sojourn through this gentle midsummer's eve. The estate was heavily wooded, ancient, dense tree land, which was fairly typical of the region, although this plantation had a strangely oppressive feel to it and carried a faint air of decay and rotting vegetation.

It was a mile or so until I caught my first glimpse of Fitzwyrm Manse itself, a moated Elizabethan manor house of some three storeys, constructed in the local yellowing sandstone. It retained much of its original charm but had been much expanded by subsequent generations, although now it was a little dilapidated and careworn, a green shroud of ivy winding around its ancient turrets and towers.

A strange knocker of unusual pagan design was mounted upon the formidable oaken doors – an unsettling portent – but I grasped it firmly and its knock resounded through the hallway. Footsteps approached and it was not long before a retainer answered my summons.

"Yes, madam?"

"Mrs Sternblight to see Mr Fitzwyrm."

"Mr Fitzwyrm did not inform me he was expecting guests," said the butler, a tall, creaking, rather haggard looking fellow, with thinning auburn hair and mutton chop whiskers. Despite his apparently humble manner there was an insolence in his rheumy eyes that I did not take to. He seemed on the point of shutting the door in my face, but I thrust an ankle boot over the threshold.

"Is he obliged to keep his servants abreast of his plans, then?"

"No, madam but..."

"Mrs Sternblight! You came! Oh, I am so glad to see you." Behind the butler, a younger man materialised and said, "Show Mrs Sternblight in, at once."

"Of course, sir. This way madam..." the portal was opened, but it seemed to me with great reluctance.

"You will take tea, or coffee perhaps, Mrs Sternblight?" the young man enquired.

"Coffee, and please, call me Irma."

"Then you shall call me Dudley. Have some coffee brought to the sitting room, please."

"Yes, sir," said the butler solemnly and withdrew, apparently much inconvenienced.

"This way, Mrs..."

"Irma."

"This way, Irma."

We proceeded through the entrance hall, a shadowy expanse rich with red-oak panelling and laden with the dust of centuries. A grand staircase swept up to the apartments above and the walls were hung with a surfeit of pictures, presumably the preceding generations of Fitzwyrms. One in particular caught my eye, a portrait hung on the first floor landing which dominated the hall. It was of a dark haired woman with a prominent nose, clad in an Elizabethan dress and ruff, her face severe but sensual, her hand displaying a ring with a most particular smoky jewel. The eyes were dark, like jet, hard and unyielding, her thin lips suggestive of sensuality, but most of all, she projected a sense of proprietorship as if she were mistress of all she surveyed.

Coffee was brought by an anonymous maidservant and followed in quick measure by a passable supper. As we consumed it, a pensive Dudley Fitzwyrm laid out the reasons he wished to engage me. I will not recount the entire conversation, but summarise its most salient points for you, gentlemen. Dudley Fitzwyrm was the scion of a distant Canadian branch of the family and was due to inherit the entire estate following the death of its previous owner, a Mrs Patience Fitzwyrm. He had received a telegram some two months ago, urging him to journey here with all haste, but had arrived shortly after his aged relative's demise. Subsequently, he discovered the terms of her will were most unusual, not to say downright peculiar.

"For you see, the Fitzwyrms are an old family, Irma. We were once great explorers and are scattered widely across the globe. There are branches in many of the distant colonies, several in Australia, more in South Africa, and a positive gaggle in India.

"Why my aged relative chose me to be her successor, I do not know. My parents died when I was young and I have made my way in the world creditably enough, earning a modest living as a ranch hand. The prospect of inheriting an entire English estate and its associated income was simply too enticing a prospect to resist. A real stroke of luck, or so I thought."

As he spoke, I sipped on a palatable glass of Bordeaux and examined my prospective client's physiognomy and demeanour. He was a tall, dark haired fellow in his middle to late twenties and a strapping young specimen too, in the prime of his life, with an impressive physique honed by the arduous outdoor life. Yet, despite his apparent vigour and all the advantages of youth, here was a man labouring under a great burden, and a recently acquired one too.

His body was hunched and his manner withdrawn, his face pale, his brow sunken, and the virile moustache which adorned his upper lip wilted and drooped. Most troubling of all were those dark soulful eyes which were framed by grey hollows and rimed with misery. A troubled young man, when in his situation, troubles should there be none.

"It is a strange legacy," he said, returning to his subject. "I am to be sole heir with a not inconsiderable income of some three hundred pounds per annum, but all is dependent upon my solving a most perplexing mystery. In order to inherit, I must recover the Fitzwyrm signet ring before the next full moon, or all shall be lost and the estate pass to another. It is a silver band, set with an unusual jewel and has been passed down generations of Fitzwyrms, apparently."

"I see and this is why you require my assistance? You are aware I am a renowned occult investigator, Mr Fitzwyrm, not a player of find and seek?" I said, trying to remain kindly.

"Nor would I presume to trouble you with such a trifle, unless there were weirder and more outré developments surrounding this matter. For you see, ever since I arrived here, I have felt troubled, haunted you might say, my mind given no rest or recourse, my spirit weighed down, subdued by an unnamed dread. Someone, something, an unseen force of utmost malevolence wishes me ill and works actively against me. I feel it has designs upon my peace of mind, indeed, upon my very life itself!"

"What would cause you to believe such a thing?"

"My days are dreary and restless, full of omens, portents, and unusual phenomena which no material science could explain. Objects fall, seemingly of their own accord, I hear voices which call to me and when I follow them, I find but empty rooms. I seem to drift between this world and others, experiencing strange and terrible visions during my waking hours. I scarcely sleep and when I do, my rest is haunted by unsettling visitations. I feel as if I am constantly watched, as if some dread intelligence directs its malevolent attentions at me."

"And what of your search for the heirloom?"

"Fruitless, hopeless, pointless. I hardly know where to begin. The only note I received was cryptic, 'Your destiny watches over you, embrace it.' I have pondered its meaning, tried searching its truth, indeed I have scoured this mansion from top to bottom but without result. And..."

"And?"

"The month is nearly up. Tomorrow night the moon waxes full again and the chance to claim my inheritance will disappear... and with it perhaps my life itself."

"Perhaps the two phenomena are linked? Have you thought to seek aid or information? "

"The servants are no help, indeed are more of a hindrance, full of evasions, half truths, incomprehensible mutterings, if not outright gibberish."

"And your neighbours?"

"No-one in the locale will come near this place for fear of incurring the wrath of what they call, 'dark powers'. One confided to me it has been a hotbed of paganism, witchcraft and sorcery for centuries, and that none would dare set foot in the place. Then she simply slammed the door in my face. From what little I can discover, these legends began with Avice Fitzwyrm, an Elizabethan sorceress. She was said to consort with demons and otherworldly powers, and was condemned by John Dee himself, She was apparently condemned to be burned at the stake for witchcraft."

"Indeed? I believe I have made her acquaintance already."

"What?!" he said, confounded.

"The portrait in the hall," I replied, trying to calm his obviously frayed nerves. "She wears this smoky signet ring you seek?"

"Ah, yes a most vivid and unsettling work. I was minded to have it taken down, but the servants baulked at the prospect and would not hear of it. The butler had the boldness to remind me I am not the master of this house yet: his unspoken thought, that I never would be."

"Most enlightening."

"So, will you help me, Mrs Sternblight... Irma?" I am at my wits end and fear for my lucidity, indeed my very soul itself."

"Would you consider leaving? Renouncing this legacy and going back to the life you led before?"

"I would in an instant, if I thought it might do any good. But I cannot bring myself to leave this place, some strange force compels me to stay and see this thing through to the end, for good or ill."

"Very well, then, Mr Fitzwyrm, I am resolved. I will do my utmost to help you in this matter, although be warned, I fear the consequences may be very grave indeed."

"I don't know what to say, nor how to express my gratitude, Irma! From the very bottom of my heart, thank you!" He grasped my hand earnestly, and at that moment a little hope began to bleed into those sable eyes.

"Perhaps it's best you do not thank me yet," I said.

"Believe me, this is the best news I have received since I came to this hellish place. I had begun to think death would be my only release."

"Hmm, well let us hope that will not be the case."

The next morning I awoke early, rested and refreshed after my arduous journey, and lay in bed awhile, contemplating the strange matter in which I had become involved. Although my sleep had been untroubled, it had not been undisturbed. The enchantments, charms and amulets which I routinely employ to protect me from malign influences had been at work and while their mystical defences had not been breached, their boundaries had been sorely tested. It confirmed my suspicions. Dudley Fitzwyrm had not been imagining things, some malicious power was at work here.

It was mid-afternoon before I was reunited with the troubled heir, for he had endured another distressing night and looked gaunt and hollow-eyed upon our meeting, and in some degree of distraction. In the meantime, I had used the opportunity to explore the house and grounds a little further. It was easy to discern why the place had such a disagreeable reputation, for the rolling hills and dales were choked by woodland and it felt secluded, cut off from the real world, harbouring some long concealed malice which festered here. Ravens and other carrion feeders flocked in the trees and their harsh calls pierced the otherwise eerie silence. Strange fungal growths clung to the trunks of fallen trees and rot and decay seemed all pervasive. Most pertinently of all, unseen eyes seemed to dog my progress and I felt my presence not only noted but actively contested.

"Well, Irma, have you had a chance to ponder a course of action?" enquired Fitzwyrm.

"I have and I think we should begin at the source."

"The source?"

"Your relative, Patience Fitzwyrm. She has not been buried yet?"

"No, she is laid out in the family mausoleum, and will not be interred until the next successor is chosen. Another quaint old family tradition apparently."

"Very well, then. Where is this crypt?"

"A little way to the east, I believe."

"You have not visited her yet?"

"No, I did not think to."

"Then let us proceed."

An hour's perambulation brought us to the edge of the estate and a large semi-circular outcropping of ancient limestone, which must have been formed millions of years ago. Placed in front of these crags was a graveyard where presumably the estate's retainers had been laid to rest down the long centuries. I do not grace it with the term cemetery, for this was no Christian burial site, but a wild and pagan expanse, where cairns and mounds predominated rather than the headstones and crosses one might expect.

It was a bleak and forlorn place too, half reclaimed by nature and overgrown with rampant moss and ivy, with foetid stems and curling roots which rose from the earth to grasp it with their tumorous tendrils. At its centre, a mausoleum had been raised, a circular edifice made of yellowing lichen-encrusted sandstone with a domed roof and a pair of barred windows set below. Coupled with the maw-like entrance, it gave the impression of a great face, screaming in torment or perhaps ecstasy.

"A most forbidding place," Fitzwyrm said, quailing visibly.

"Indeed, but let us cleave to boldness. We will not solve the problem by inaction, and time is of the essence," I averred.

Inside, an almost stygian gloom enveloped the tomb's shadowy circumference and a series of horizontal niches were carved into its walls, although oddly, they were tenantless. Most curious. A dim, greenish shaft of light plunged down from the dome shining on a central stone plinth upon which a woman's body had been laid out. Patience Fitzwyrm wore a plain old-fashioned dress and her arms lay by her sides, her fists clutching sprigs of mistletoe. Her visage was spotted with age, and the prominent Fitzwyrm nose concealed under a light veil, but unusually her hair remained dark and lustrous under its evergreen crowning wreath.

"So that is my forebear?" said Fitzwyrm.

"I presume so. There is a marked resemblance."

"So she is the source of all my anguish?"

"Perhaps."

"Well, without her death, I would not have been

summoned, not have embarked upon this strange quest, would not be haunted by this unwelcome legacy!"

"Curious, here she lies, but the gate is left wide open with no protection against foxes or other predators..."

"Hah! None would dare disturb the rest of... that particular body!" a voice cackled and Fitzwyrm vaulted a foot backward, which drew more wheezing laughter.

The owner was a curious looking fellow of middling build, nonchalantly hefting a large scythe. He wore long boots with gaiters, heavy trousers, a waistcoat with a watch chain and his shirt sleeves were rolled back to reveal brawny arms. Mischievous eyes peered from beneath the cloth cap which covered his forehead, and his face was adorned with a large handlebar moustache beneath its bulbous nose. His manner was fey, almost mocking, and an archness played around his features, colouring his high, rather flute like voice.

"And who pray, are you?" I asked.

"I wouldn't be praying round here, reckon the old un 'ud take against it. I'm the groundskeeper, missus." His eyes twinkled. "Pleased to make your acquaintance."

"Do you have a name?"

"I do." He winked as if party to some joke of his own, but refused to elaborate further.

"And this was your mistress?"

"Oh, aye ... Mrs Fitzwyrm was mistress of us all... and more."

"Did you know her well?"

"Yes missus, we was very close," he chuckled. "Like peas in a pod."

"You don't seem much affected by her loss."

"Oh, aye, a sad day, but then it comes to us all, even me, 'ventually, I suppose. But I'm a believer in the life eternal, the perpetual resurrection an' all. I know we'll see t'other again one day. Maybe sooner'n I think." This thought seemed to amuse him greatly and he could scarce contain his mirth. There was something peculiar about him, something I couldn't quite lay my finger on, but my instincts were aroused and I was nearly upon the point of making some significant breakthrough when Dudley Fitzwyrm piped up.

"Do you know the whereabouts of her ring? The Fitzwyrm signet which she wore?" he asked, and the groundskeeper frowned, a shadow crossing his face.

"Don't rightly know. 'spose it might be in her lair."

"A most peculiar phrase," I said, raising an eyebrow.

"Argh, don't mean anything by it. 'ats just what we call the folly, us *serving* folk," he leered.

"This folly? That sounds promising. How would we find it?" said Fitzwyrm.

"Oh, just walk outside and follow your nose, or the path to the west... missus used to retreat there often, when she felt the call."

"The call?" asked Fitzwyrm.

"Oh, you know, mister. And if you don't, you soon will. Hah!"

"What do you mean by that?" Fitzwyrm demanded.

"No offence meant, mister. But you're her blood, her kin, aren't 'ee? Her legacy awaits you, whether you will it or no."

"I..." Fitzwyrm blustered.

"Well, I'd best be off," said the groundskeeper. "No rest for the wicked, an' things won't tend to 'emselves, now will they, heh? Be seeing you." And with that, he tipped his hat and stalked away.

"A most singular fellow," I opined.

"Odd, not to say downright peculiar. What do you think he meant by *her legacy*? The way he phrased it had most sinister sounding connotations."

"Possibly, or perhaps he was trying to unnerve you? There was something odd about him though..."

"What is one more peculiarity amongst so many..." said Fitzwyrm and, as he recounted his troubles, my mind began to wander, trying to make connections, striving to identify the eccentric groundsman's idiosyncrasy that had exercised me so much. Lost in cogitation, a bad habit, sadly, to which I am all too prone, I at first failed to notice a most profound change occurring. Even though it was scarce past mid-afternoon, a darkness had begun to bleed into the day, the light changing, dimming, as if we were undergoing a minor eclipse.

"...and I'm not certain how much more of it I can take..." Now Fitzwyrm noticed it too, and his words trailed into silence.

The light outside the tomb was positively gloomy now, and an awful stillness settled over us. I felt the hairs on the nape of my neck rise as if a thunderstorm approached. A great force had begun to exert itself upon us, a darkling shroud which brought with it a horrible pressure, numbing mind and chilling soul. There was movement from the trees, branches bending and snapping before the passage of some gigantic presence.

"What the devil?!" exclaimed Dudley.

"Something worse, I fear. Stay back and whatever you do, do not go near the entrance."

I ran to the portal and, keeping my back to the woods outside, hastily began to inscribe the inner threshold with some chalk. I made a sign, muttered an imprecation and then it was complete. I could only hope it would hold.

Back inside, we pressed ourselves against either side of the entrance portal and awaited the dread thing's coming. The echo of heavy hoof-beats reverberated inside the dome and the darkness thickened, swallowing up all the light. There was a sticky sound, as of something rubbing and oozing together and a disgusting snuffling, grunting and truffling. A foul odour pervaded our nostrils, a rotting, putrid smell which made the nose sting and the senses reel.

Fitzwyrm was plainly terrified, knuckles clasped white with terror but he could not help himself and started to inch toward the corner.

"I implore you, do not look upon it!" I cried and my fervent entreaty, perhaps just the sound of my voice, broke the compulsion and he pulled himself back. Fitzwyrm closed his eyes and slid down the wall, rendered almost insensible by this terrible manifestation.

Something moist slithered at the entrance and there came an inhuman, high-pitched squealing which was truly awful to hear. A loud, heavy impact made the stone shake and, for one awful instant, I thought it would bring the walls down about our ears. Another shocking blow, and the thing screamed again, like fingernails dragging themselves across your soul. Just as I was certain it must charge inside and devour us both, it halted, then retreated, moving away until its heavy tread was lost amidst the gloaming.

After I had recovered my composure, I went outside to

examine the aftermath. The darkness had stolen away with it, dreary afternoon light slowly ebbing back in. Monstrous, elephantine tracks led off toward the undergrowth and the stone was slick with disgusting viscous fluid.

"What was that thing?" Fitzwyrm asked, leaning against the stone as he tried to force air back into his lungs. The strain of the encounter showed: his voice quavered, his face was ashen and he was clearly in severe distress.

"It is perhaps better that you do not know."

"And those symbols you inscribed?"

"Wards against the foul things of this world and others. And yet it did not attempt to breach them."

"What was its purpose, then?"

"I do not know, though why it hesitated and then retreated when it had us at its mercy, I..."

"So what must we do now?"

"Perhaps we should seek this 'lair' the groundskeeper spoke of?"

"Are you certain? I am not sure my heart would stand the strain of another such meeting."

"Stalwart hearts and steady heads, Fitzwyrm. Let us journey there and see what we may see. Besides, what other choice is there?"

Despite Fitzwyrm's misgivings we were not accosted any further on our journey to the folly, however he remained in a state of agitation and continued to glance around, starting at every snap of a twig or uncommon bird call. The blood had drained from his face and there was an unusual cast to his eye. I feared for his composure and the equanimity of his mind.

Afternoon had given way to evening, the air was alive with a sweet, sickly pollen and the drowsy drone of insects as we journeyed through the woodland. Although there was no sign, it was difficult to escape the feeling that we were observed by unseen eyes.

We followed a winding natural path which led us deeper and deeper into the woodland. Small cairns had been raised at irregular intervals and, as we drew closer to our destination, posies and nosegays of brightly coloured flowers were strewn across the trail. On the trees' lower boughs pagan symbols had been cut into the wood, and they were hung with strange figurines of intertwined rushes and twigs. Some were stylised depictions of what might have been an earth goddess figure, and there were cruder and more primitive effigies. But no life-affirming fertility symbols these, rather disturbing hints of something more ancient, darker and inhuman.

Glimpsed through the boles of the trees, we caught the first sight of our destination, the folly, which lay in a natural amphitheatre within this ancient demesne. Yet, this was no classical recreation of a Greek temple nor stylised ruined castle as one might anticipate, but a circle of nine standing stones surrounding an enormous central slab.

The outer ring consisted of lichen-shrouded menhirs and in the eerie light underneath the trees they could almost be human forms, maidens caught dancing in wild abandon. The forest floor was carpeted with strange fungi and other cankerous growths, but it was the central fallen stone which most drew the eye. Laid upon its end, this vast lump of rock was shot through with deep runnels, its uneven surface encrusted with dark, mysterious stains of an unknown origin.

It was surrounded by more wreaths and wooden figures with an outlying radius of black candles completing the bizarre tableaux.

It was easy to imagine that weird, unwholesome ceremonies, dark sabbats, and unspeakable rites had been enacted here, and maybe not just in ancient times either, for this profane grove showed signs of more recent use. Fitzwyrm seemed much afeard, and even I was unsettled by this ungodly place. It was only using all my powers of persuasion that I could eventually coax him to breach its outer confines.

"This place has an evil air, Irma.."

"You may be right, but I have a feeling we have been directed here for a purpose. Though what that purpose is, I cannot fathom. Sit awhile and rest, while I look closer."

Unconvinced, Fitzwyrm sat down on a log and began to mop at his brow with a handkerchief. His skin was pale and his eye frantic, his whole posture stooped and withdrawn, like a cur that expects to be whipped.

The pagan ephemera did not intimidate me, so I made straight for the slab where I felt the most significant evidence might be ascertained. The surface was old and weathered, but smooth in places as if worn down by frequent use. There were sets of deep parallel gouges, irregular indentations made in groups of three, where something had cut deep into the stone's surface. Most sinister of all, almost lost amongst the garlands, I found fragments of hempen rope with dark stains upon them. They had been cut clean through, as if severed by the sharpest of knives. Informative, if not to say a trifle harrowing.

"You would do well not to linger here." I heard Fitzwyrm's

intake of breath and turned to see who had voiced this sentiment. The newcomer was a sharp faced, middle-aged woman in a black dress with a long white apron and starched collar. Her hair was gathered up beneath a bonnet-like cap and her lips were pursed in an expression of disapproval. Jet-black eyes regarded us scornfully.

"We were directed here by the groundskeeper," said Fitzwyrm.

"The groundskeeper, hey?" She seemed pleased by this and a flicker of a smile ghosted across that severe mouth.

"And who are you, pray tell?"

"I am the housekeeper."

"And your name is...?"

"Not important. Know only that I serve... served Patience Fitzwyrm and those who came before her."

"You have lived here for a while then?"

"Yes, a long time."

"Then you will know what this place is called?"

"It is called Fitzwyrm's Folly by the ignorant, but it has other names as well, in languages that are no longer spoken. It is a place of power, a conduit between this world and others. All the Fitzwyrms, from Avice onward, have come here to worship, give praise, make sacrifice."

"This is no church, no holy place," said Fitzwyrm. The housekeeper turned a gimlet eye upon him.

"Not all deities are confined within walls of stone, Dudley Fitzwyrm. This is a sacred place... a natural abode, where the true nature of the world is revealed and appreciated... it is said Avice discovered it, though in truth... she merely awakened it."

"And what of Avice?" I enquired. "Her name continues to crop up in this chronicle. Why is she so important to the Fitzwyrm story?"

"A singular woman, both wise and powerful. It was she who truly founded this family, this dynasty. Her origins are obscure, lost in the veils of history. Some say she was a mere peasant girl with the gift, but she was a wise woman and a talented one too, and caught the eye of Sir Walter Fitzwyrm, one of the great Elizabeth's courtiers. They married and when he died, she inherited the title in trust for their only son, Stanley. An astute and canny woman, she sent ships to the colonies which brought back mercantile goods and other riches. She used this wealth to rebuild the house and grounds, expand the estate, lay down the foundations for the entire dynasty."

"An impressive legacy, yet from what little I could learn from my researches, she came to an unhappy end. Accusations of heresy, witchcraft, sorcery?"

"Lies!" Those sable eyes flashed, then subsided again. "She merely exercised a different kind of power. She was observant, knew how to expose people's secrets, accessing knowledge that others preferred to remain hidden. When she came to court, the Virgin Queen was entranced by her beauty and her gifts. Elizabeth made Avice one of her favourites and the two grew close, too close perhaps."

"None of this is in the official histories."

"No, for the Virgin Queen was a jealous woman, recognising one who could rival, perhaps even surpass her power in the fullness of time. Perhaps... Avice overstepped her bounds, but the Queen had Sir John Dee investigate her and that old mountebank probed lesser folk with confessions and torture, invented lurid revelations, stories and half truths that damned her. By the time he had finished fashioning his calumnies, she was condemned as a witch and sentenced to be burned at the stake."

"But this did not happen?"

"No, for remember... Avice had the gift and saw what was to transpire, She disappeared before they could arrest her. None ever saw her again."

"And what happened to the estate?"

"Avice was condemned in absentia and Sir Stanley Fitzwyrm eventually succeeded to the title. He was a sickly child, but inherited his mother's looks and it was said, some of her power and spiritual strength. Her loss affected him greatly and when his majority came, he refused to attend court, withdrew from public life and confined himself to this estate for the rest of his life. Like his mother, he revered the old ways and sired many heirs to honour them and keep the Fitzwyrm name alive."

"And so this is my legacy?" said Fitzwyrm.

She looked upon him like a cat that had discovered a particularly flavoursome mouse. "Oh, yes. You will inherit this and much more. The Fitzwyrm legacy is yours if you can claim it."

"Then where I might find the ring? The Fitzwyrm signet that will ensure my succession?" Fitzwyrm said and again the housekeeper looked pleased, as if harbouring a secret of her own.

"Your destiny awaits you in the manse. As to where you will find the ring? Well, I would begin my search in her private library. For it is there that much may be discovered."

"Her library? I found no such room when I searched the house."

"Perhaps you were not meant to find it *then*. Perhaps you *are* meant to find it now?"

"But where to begin?"

"I cannot be expected to give up all my... mistress's secrets. You are a Fitzwyrm, if you are worthy you will discover the way. But you must start with Avice, all things spring from her."

"Avice?"

"I can say no more. I must leave you now." Peering intently at Fitzwyrm, the housekeeper gave one last supercilious sneer and then removed herself. As we watched her depart, Fitzwyrm said, "We must return to the house then, it seems."

"Yes, although I have a feeling that may be a little more difficult than it sounds," I replied. For as the housekeeper's form receded into the surrounding forest, an eerie haze had formed and begun to close in upon us. Its tendrils curled and wound their way through the trees, swallowing up the trunks, restricting visible space so that we were soon hemmed in. As it enveloped the stone circle, I advanced and touched it with a finger to try and ascertain its substance. It was icy to the touch, and almost solid in form. When I pushed against it, it resisted, becoming more tangible, barring any hope of escape.

"Trapped!" wailed Fitzwyrm when I relayed the news.

We heard something approaching. Vast wing beats rent the air and in a few breaths they were upon us, three unnatural forms circling in the skies above. Their long, slender bodies were outlined against the pale moon, vaguely humanoid in shape but with curved horns, barbed tails, and clawed feet. There was something diabolical about them but also a fluid, sinuous grace, and when the moonlight struck them it revealed a grey, oily pelt like leathery whale skin. Most disturbing of all there was just a smooth featureless mass where their face should be.

One by one they peeled away and began to dive, making no sound as they swooped at Fitzwyrm. With a piteous cry, he flung himself to the floor only just managing to escape the swish of their razor-sharp talons. Their wingtips missed him by a fraction and he curled into a foetal ball to escape their repulsive attentions. Foam frothed on his lips as he writhed in shock and horror. Seeming to sense his distress, they renewed their attack, revelling in the terror they inflicted upon him.

The repugnant creatures paid me not the slightest attention, which seemed significant, but it allowed me space to form a plan of action. Quickly, I gathered what materials I could, taking twigs and leaves, swiftly twisting and weaving them into a very specific shape. Once the icon had been fashioned, I whispered the protective charm, imbuing the form with the necessary power. For a moment, I thought I must have miscast, but then the talisman began to glow with a golden light.

In the time this had taken, Fitzwyrm's remaining mental defences had collapsed and he now lay prone on his back, eyes rolling back into his head so that only the whites showed. The creatures had not yet touched him, but seemed to be tormenting him for their sport. Swiftly, I ran over to his recumbent form and stood astride him, raising the talisman toward them. As the first wheeled to renew its attack, I raised the symbol high so that its light suffused the night air.

Its effect was immediate and mid-way through its dive, the first fell creature recoiled as if struck, flinching and then banking away, physically repulsed by the sign's power.

Another tried but received the same result, and it whirled, physically pained by the talisman's effects. If it had possessed a mouth I'm certain it would have screamed, but the language of its body was unmistakable, displaying disgust and revulsion. The third, perhaps sensing the futility of renewing its assault, did not even attempt to rejoin the fray but banked and rose to join its unholy companions. Soon all three were flapping away in unwholesome unison, until their forms were lost amidst the evening gloom. As they retreated, the confining mist began to dissolve and I discarded my improvised amulet and attempted to revive Fitzwyrm.

It took all my skill and not a little patience to restore him to his senses and even when he had come to, his mind had received a terrible shock from which it struggled to recover. For a while he was simply a vacant space, then slowly, slowly, he began to mewl and whimper, incoherent, until finally words were formed.

"The faceless things! Aiiee! No! Save me..." He was shaking and panicking and I was forced to administer a stern slap to the face which sobered him quickly enough.

"I apologise for striking you, Fitzwyrm, but you must collect yourself."

"But... I..."

"Here drink this, it will revive you." I poured half the contents of my hip flask down his throat and he coughed and spluttered as the fiery liquid met flesh. After a few moments the brandy began to do its work and he became more coherent again.

"What were those things? Why did they attack me?"

"Steel yourself, Fitzwyrm. Those were Nightgaunts and this was no mere accident, but design. Why? Well I suspect what is at stake is not only your sanity, but your very life itself. But there is no evading it now. We must survive, endure, and overcome. The crisis point is yet not reached, but it will be soon and be assured we will weather it together. Come."

Avice Fitzwyrm did not seem ready to yield up her secrets just yet. If anything, her face seemed entirely set against us, scowling and more severe than ever. Many of her features now appeared to have bored themselves into my brain, the sable eyes, the prominent nose, the utter disdain on that cruel visage. A Tudor rose curled in one hand, exhibiting the smoky, jewelled signet of the Fitzwyrms, but our utter bafflement appeared to amuse her, for her mouth contained just the faintest flicker of a smile.

"How are we supposed to find this secret library from a painting?"

"Give me a moment to think, Fitzwyrm."

Dudley Fitzwyrm remained in a state of extreme agitation. The recent shocks had not been beneficial to his health, and his skin had an unhealthy pallor, like stretched vellum, his eyes roved wild and his jaw had developed a most pronounced twitch. I knew we must bring this matter to a conclusion, and soon, or his mind would not take it.

"The answer must lie here somewhere," I said aloud, contemplating the portrait, "if not with Avice herself, then perhaps... wait... look... the mansion behind her!"

"What of it?"

"There are one too many windows. I swear it does not correspond with the doors upstairs."

"An extra room, then?"

"Precisely, but how to open it?"

I mused for long moments. We were so close, surely the answer must be here somewhere? Avice's portrait seemed to glower and leer at me now, intimidating and hostile, which meant I must be close...

Then I saw it, and could have given a leap of joy. The rose, the Tudor rose! The hand she held it in had a single finger extended upward. A stylistic flourish? No, a sign! I followed it to its source, an unusual brooch pinned to the brocade of her dress. It was an enamel of a stylised tree with multiple trunks and tendril-like branches and on closer inspection what might have been multiple mouths. Following my instinct, I depressed its surface which gave way reluctantly but I was rewarded with the sound of an audible creak and a door swinging open on the landing above!

Even for one such as I, who was used to the atmosphere of uncanny places, the library was a remarkable and most unsettling place. Indeed, what the housekeeper had termed a library could scarce qualify as such in the conventional sense, for it was more of an organic open space. There were books, yes, and I recognised the spines and covers of many arcane, not to say blasphemous, volumes, but there were many more scrolls, manuscripts and vellum heaped up in overflowing piles. Sloped writing in several different hands rambled across its dusty, crumbling walls and, at its centre, a five-pointed star had been inscribed upon the floor, surrounded by a circle of esoteric symbology.

Nature had run rampant through this place, with fronds of ivy, mistletoe and other less easily identifiable plants of obscure and sinister nature winding and twisting their way throughout. All manner of small creatures scurried through the chaotic undergrowth, skittering into shadowy nooks and corners at our coming. An unusually large dormouse perched upon the vast desk which dominated the far end of the room, its eyes bright, whiskers twitching, with frayed, matted fur and a unicorn-like horn in the middle of its forehead. It got up on its hind legs and contemplated us thoughtfully for a moment, before it too scurried away. Above the desk, a portion of the roof stood open to the skies, for now true night was upon us. Cold stars shone down, though the heavenly vault was populated by strange constellations, unknown suns in strange configurations which made the eyes swim and the mind giddy.

But there, there on the table, lay a great tome, a bound volume in dark leather and upon its surface was a circular band gleaming in the starlight!

"Good Lord, is that it?!" said Fitzwyrm, lurching forward, blundering obliviously through the circle to the other side of the desk. Stepping more cautiously, I followed him. The ring comprised a tarnished silver band supporting that unusual smoky jewel which seemed to burn with a weird internal light. Sparks of gold coalesced into a design resembling a tree with multiple trunks and branches which formed the family crest. Fitzwyrm held it up to the light, and while he regarded it open mounted, I read the gold-lead lettering on the mouldering book's cover which said, *The Servants of Shub-Niggurath*.

"Before you..." I began.

"So, you have found it, Dudley Fitzwyrm. My congratulations." The butler appeared from the shadows, though whether he had been there the whole time or just materialised, it was impossible to say. Dark eyes, laden with meaning, regarded us disdainfully, but Fitzwyrm did not jump nor start this time. Instead he held the band up and stared through the ring's circumference, entranced by its allure.

"And are you ready to embrace your legacy?" enquired the Butler in a contemptuous tone.

"I am," said Fitzwyrm, slipping the circlet onto his finger before I could caution him against it. If I was expecting fireworks or some great revelation, there was no such occurrence, although Fitzwyrm seemed different from before, calmer, more rational, the manic look had disappeared from his eye.

"Then, turn the page and become who you were always destined to be!" the butler smirked, in a curiously high pitched voice which did not seem entirely his own. There was a glint, a cast to his eye that was at once both familiar and distinctly unsettling, but it was too late to share the revelation, for Fitzwyrm had grasped the book's cover and flung it open.

For an instant, nothing happened, but then a sporous cloud engulfed us, sending me reeling, coughing and gagging, as I gasped for air. The noxious emission penetrated my nose, throat, and lungs, irritating them to a marked degree, and I leant heavily against the desk, legs trembling, eyes itching, swooning in extremis. Then I was falling and the last thing I heard was Fitzwyrm's body hit the ground before mine own.

My mind spun and whirled through the dark of aeons, tumbling and turbulent, as ages passed and the lives of men rose and fell consumed by the vicissitudes of time. Bodiless, weightless, I came to a halt, hazily casting around me in the corona until I eventually recognised the Fitzwyrm manor house. But this was of another time, for armed men in ruffs and long boots strode toward it, intent on apprehending someone, torchlight reflecting on their naked swords. I flew on and over them, out into the woods and beyond, into the night, drawn to another place, a circle of light within the circle of stone. Fires burned and painted bodies and pale flesh writhed in ecstasy and supplication, dancing forms circling in and out of the menhirs around a captive bound on the central pillar. There I lingered or was held, watching as the music, played by an unseen orchestra of flute, pipe and drum grew louder, more intense, a sensual, otherworldly melody whipping the dancers into new heights of frenzy.

Now, other forms materialised, shadowy, corrupt satyrs and worse, half-human, half-beast like things which cavorted and gambolled, mingling flesh in inhuman congress, mating with each other in their orgiastic lust. The music reached a crescendo as their high priestess appeared, wearing a headdress of bone and feather, but otherwise naked as the dawn. It was not hard to recognise Avice Fitzwyrm. She raised a copper knife aloft and suddenly the music was stilled.

"Ai, Shub-Niggurath! Dark Goat of the Woods, I call to thee! Answer me, my mistress!"

A great shadowy phantom which had hovered upon its

fringes now bled into the clearing, a diabolic goat with a dozen legs, ebon hooves and tendril-horns which curled into a writhing mass across its back. Three crimson eyes with elongated elliptical pupils burned in its nightmarish face, regarding the sorceress with an unknowable expression. The witch spoke again, her voice high and piercing.

"With this sacrifice, I seal my compact with you, life unending, life eternal, life dedicated to thy service, down the ages for as long as I will be of use, until you claim me again!"

With that Avice Fitzwyrm plunged the knife into the chest of the victim, slashing, ripping at the flesh, lifting his heart up as an offering toward the nightmarish demon. She bit deep into it, blood running down her chin and over her breasts as her body began to shimmer and phase, flowing back and forth, becoming one with the unnatural form of the Black Goat of the Woods.

I swam hazily back up to consciousness, still reeling from this blasphemous revelation, my limbs heavy, body leaden and unresponsive. Dimly, I perceived a low chanting, hushed words and whispered sounds, but my eyelids steadfastly refused to open. Having experimented widely with mystical herbs and vision-granting fungi, I am naturally resilient to the effects of poison and other toxins. Yet, I still felt forced to reach inside my dress for a vial I kept for just such occasions, a concoction prepared by a practitioner from New Orleans skilled in the esoteric arts. Its taste was bitter, vile, but I felt its efficacious effect almost immediately and began to slough off my torpor.

I prised open an eyelash to find I was in the mausoleum again. The hour was close to midnight, and I had been deposited away to one side and left in an unruly heap. At its centre, Dudley Fitzwyrm was laid alongside his deceased relative upon the slab. The three servants, groundskeeper, housekeeper and butler, were arrayed around the pair in a triangle, candlelight illuminating their features, concentrating as they intoned strange words and mystic syllables. An unusual aura, like inky fire, clung to the groundskeeper and as I watched, it passed from him to the housekeeper and then the butler, alighting on each in turn before moving on again. As it did so, their facial features changed, transformed, taking on a similar look, as they were possessed by the ghostly force.

Their tone grew faster, more urgent and slowly, stealthily, I raised myself to the vertical again, hoping to evade detection.

"Do you seek to frustrate my mistress, Irma Sternblight?" said the housekeeper, turning those intense sable eyes upon me.

"Oh, I think we can dispense with this pretence of yours... Avice Fitzwyrm," I replied, and her eyes flashed and she gave an acerbic laugh. The dark aura leapt again and now it was the groundskeeper who addressed me.

"So, you have seen through my little deception, then?"

"Oh, indeed, for in rendering Dudley Fitzwyrm and I unconscious, you inadvertently revealed more than you intended, your thoughts crossing with mine own. In truth, I had already suspected it with all these convenient little encounters you had arranged for myself and Mr Fitzwyrm. You should have been more careful, Avice, your aura was showing."

"Well, aren't you the regular detective," said the butler as the focus shifted again and she took control of his haughty features.

"I prefer the term occult investigator, but the methodology is much the same, I'll grant you. But satisfy my curiosity on one point."

"Very well, perhaps you have earned that privilege."

"You are able to transfer your consciousness between persons, as you transfer it now between your servants. So why Dudley? Why entangle him in your machinations when it seems you have plenty of eager participants to receive your consciousness?"

"Why, the bloodline of course, as I'm sure you know, or must guess. I can exist in other willing vessels temporarily, but for no more than the passage of a single moon. To be reborn, to truly live again, I must reside in one of the blood. It is part of the compact, the agreement I made with *her*. The woman the world knew as Patience Fitzwyrm, was just the latest in a long, long line, through which I have passed down the centuries. Fitzwyrm succeeding Fitzwyrm, propagating and infecting my own antecedents, one after the other."

"So why delay? Why bother with the creature which stalked us here? Why the Nightgaunts? Why this strange quest? Do you enjoy tormenting your prey?"

"I admit I do, but that is not the whole reason. The recipient's mind must be prepared, weakened, pushed to the very brink of insanity. When it hovers there, whilst its defences are at their lowest, it is only then that I may enter unopposed."

"Which is what you intend to do now?"

"Indeed, but not just yet, for the time is not quite ripe to dissolve the bond which binds mind to body. It soon will be, but that is one eventuality you will not live to witness." Avice leapt to the groundskeeper, who convulsed rhythmically, then reached down and shouldered his large scythe. He advanced toward me making some experimental swings, the keenness of the blade whistling as it cut through the air.

Now, it is axiomatic that one may employ all manner of protective charms, mystical shields and defensive arts against supernatural foes, and true, that any of those methods might have been effective here. However, I also believe in more practical methods. and so I had come prepared with a little item from a certain Mr Henry Nock, esq. of Nock, Jover & Co. master gunsmiths. You may not be familiar with the pepper-box revolver, or pepperpot as is sometimes known, or indeed you may even hold the antiquated notion that ladies should have little truck with such deadly firearms. But I can assure you it has proved a most efficient and trusty companion on several perilous occasions.

I slid the pistol from my bodice and, taking careful aim, shot the groundskeeper in the chest, much to both his and Avice's surprise. The scythe clattered as he collapsed, a dark stain spreading across his waistcoat and, as he did so, the aura drained away from him, flowing through the ether and into the housekeeper, who cried out at the unexpected intrusion. Evidently, such an unanticipated entry brought a degree of pain to both the recipient and the spirit, an unlooked for but most welcome development. Features contorting into a horrid new configuration, the housekeeper hurled herself at at me, raising a large and very sharp kitchen knife with murderous intent.

One of the most practical and useful features of Mr Nock's finest is its revolving barrel and, with a quick click, another round was chambered. This time the ball drilled clean through her forehead. The housekeeper crumpled, the aura streamed once again, and the butler gave voice to further agonies as he was possessed. Now, it was his haughty features who bore down on me, eschewing all weapons, meaning to throttle the life out of me with his bare hands.

Yet, he too had overplayed his hand, perhaps believing that like a shotgun, two barrels would be the sum of my output. Not so, for the pepperpot is a three-barrelled revolver! And so it was, with a look containing both surprise and disgust, that the butler too perished, shot clean through the eye, if you'll forgive a slight boast about my feat of marksmanship.

Now, I would like to tell you that was the end of the matter and that with the final servant's demise, our business was concluded, for with her three servants mortally wounded, the spirit of Avice Fitzwyrm should have had nowhere left to go. Alas, I have to report, this was not the case!

Lacking a suitable vessel, Avice's restless spirit swooped and circled, first trying to invade my own person, but my wards and charms protected me from her unwanted advances. Howling like a demented banshee, Avice's spirit bounded around, and finally sought refuge in her former domicile, the shell of Patience Fitzwyrm! The old woman rose unsteadily from her slab, bones creaking, sloughing skin, as she jerked into unnatural life. Nearly a month in the domain of death had given her body the rigidity of rigor, and she jerked and staggered forward in a horrid semblance of life. Yet, in that aged, wrinkled face, the features of Avice Fitzwyrm now twitched and twisted with unbridled fury.

"You will regret your interference, Irma Sternblight!"

croaked the old lady's voice as she lurched forward, limbs warming, anger lending her an inhuman strength. But I am not so easily taken, for during my travels I have mastered the techniques developed by Ng Mui, the Shaolin nun, and was easily able to evade her clumsy attack. Her momentum carried her forward, and I used my leg to trip her so that she sprawled headlong into the ground, wreaking further havoc on that unfortunate body. As she struggled to right herself, I was in motion again, moving quickly and with purpose. By the time she had risen to her feet, I was prepared.

"I will rend you limb from limb and feed your soul to the Mighty Mother with a Thousand Young!" cried the unliving corpse, drawing eldritch power from inside herself, summoning all her hatred and spite, so that her skin rippled with dark energy. Unnatural, tendril-like horns sprang from her forehead, her legs transformed into fell hooves, demonic teeth sprouted over her lips and her eyes boiled with black rage.

I waited calmly, poised, balanced and my tranquillity only seemed to infuriate her further.

"Well? Have you anything to say, before I destroy you?"

"Just this..." I said holding up my pocket watch. "Time is of the essence, Avice Fitzwyrm, and you have run out of it. Midnight is here, and with it your doom." I displayed my hunter's face, revealing the minute hand reaching its zenith. In the distance there was a faint refrain as a village bell tolled, chiming the hour.

"*Noooooo!!!*" screamed the witch as she abandoned Patience's form and sought to enter the body of Dudley Fitzwyrm. But the sands of time had elapsed, a barrier formed, and now she could not find ingress.

"Are you missing something, perhaps?" I said, holding up the Fitzwyrm ring which I had removed while she floundered. Howling and screeching, the amorphous, shifting aura flowed toward me, but could find no sanctuary there and off it went again, bouncing from the walls like an errant firework wailing in its distress.

As the last chime of the distant clock died away, there came another sound. Foliage parted, branches snapped, thunderous hooves advanced, echoing outside. I dared not look for fear of my sanity, but a darkness, a void, a thing of evil loitered there on the threshold, I could sense it. Avice could too, for her movements grew more frantic, more desperate. Then abruptly she stopped, frozen, hovering over the inaccessible body of Dudley Fitzwyrm as she screamed, "*Ai, Shub-Niggurath, ai!* No, great mistress! It is not my time! I can still serve... I..."

But her entreaties were in vain, for a great roar reverberated around the space, as an almost indescribable, inhuman sound, somewhere between the bellow of a giant bull and the diabolic tittering of a demon gave answer. The thing that had been Avice Fitzwyrm was drawn inexorably toward it, dragged screaming into the great well of darkness that lurked outside. Despite her attempts its overwhelming pull, patches and fragments of her began to tear away as she was slowly subsumed into the essence of the outer goddess. She gave one last piteous wail and then all that remained of Avice Fitzwyrm was sucked out into the eternal night and consumed in a gnashing, grinding frenzy. The last I saw of her was a glimmer of those sable eyes, not filled with hauteur or malice now, just primal unreasoning fear, a wretched look which will haunt me to the end of my life."

Having concluded her tale, Irma Sternblight swallowed another large brandy and lit a fresh cigar. A low but growing hubbub of voices greeted her account's finale, a mix of curiosity, consternation, disbelief, and incredulity, as the shocked members of the club discussed the details and veracity of the tale. Yet this soon gave way to a wave of generosity, admiration, appreciation and a good feeling which overrode any lingering scepticism and doubt, for the mood of the members had swung to approval, and they let it be known most fervently. A few isolated claps rang out, then firmer applause and finally an appreciative wave of acclamation engulfed the room. There were even some whoops and cheers, and rather disrespectfully, a whistle or two from the younger, drunker and more enthusiastic members.

Irma Sternblight acknowledged the acclaim with a wave of her cigar and when it had died down sufficiently, she took little persuasion to conclude her tale.

"Gentlemen, I thank you. I am honoured and not a little humbled that you now endorse me as one of your own. I hope that my accession will pave the way for many more females to join your ranks within this most august of portals (here, a stern eye dared any to defy her wishes). "I wish I could tell you that this tale had a happier ending, but alas it was not to be. Dudley Fitzwyrm was much burdened by his experiences in that bizarre place and had no wish to linger there. He entrusted me to purge the library of its foul secrets and its many manuscripts and tomes now remain under lock and key in a place of safekeeping. I and one or two of my trusted associates will study them more fully and when they are rendered harmless, I mean to donate at least some of the texts to the club library.

"On my advice, Fitzwyrm also commanded that the stone circle be pulled down and the mausoleum demolished, so that their malign influence may never be felt again. Once fully exorcised of any remaining evil influences, the manor house will be sold, but only to a person of impeccable character who will safeguard it against falling into ruin and depravity again. Perhaps some members of this club may care to submit bids next year? A broken but immensely richer man, Dudley Fitzwyrm returned to his native land immeasurably chastened by the experience and vowing never to set foot on British soil again.

"I, however, intend to take what I have learned about Shub-Niggurath, the Black Goat of the Woods, sorcerous witches and the artificial transmigration of souls through the generations during this most trying episode and set it all down for perpetuity. I intend to write a pamphlet, if not a short book, so that others may learn and benefit from my experience and recognise the signs of sorcerous possession and cross-generational necromancy. Thus I hope to warn others about the eternal, enduring lessons that made up the totality of the dreadful Fitzwyrm legacy."

*With a deep breath, gagging as the
stench once again grasped at my
gullet, I peered over. All I saw was a
bottomless black hole*

THE TRUTH ABOUT DOTHEBOYS

SHELLEY De CRUZ

Newman Noggs shuffled forward to stand in the light of the hearth. Despite the turnaround in his fortunes, years of unwilling yet obligatory servitude to the contemptible Ralph Nickleby had left its mark in the melancholic slope of his shoulders, pained expression across his furrowed brow and gnarled, fidgeting fingers. Although he was now a man of sufficient resources, he still favoured plain and simple clothing, as though having already once lost a fortune had left a permanent scar on his psyche, and the fear of a recurrence of said loss counselled his every consideration when it came to the matter of expenditure.

His coat, whilst well fitted to his slight frame, showed signs of wear at the cuffs and a missing button – a sartorial expression of his refusal to believe he deserved the acceptance of his friends and peers. His fall from a well-to-do family to the status of nothing more than a menial clerk, through the ever-descending labyrinthine passages of drink and injudicious speculation, meant redemption was still a difficult concept for him to endure.

"Come, come, Noggs," Pickman gestured to the gathering, correctly interpreting the man's unease. "Every man here is on equal ground. Status and means hold no sway in this court. As a respected member our little assembly, you will be heard without prejudice or ridicule. I see you came prepared." He nodded in encouragement towards the wrinkled sheets of paper in Noggs' hands.

"Yes," Noggs admitted reluctantly. Then more boldly, as if only just making his mind up at that very moment, he held the letter up so that all gathered could see. "Yes. I have here correspondence that will never reach its recipient. I will make sure of that, and you will come to see why. The contents will prove too distressing to the young gentleman and his family, their identity most of you will be familiar with, and of the tragedies and abuses imposed upon them by the machinations of Mister Ralph Nickleby."

At the utterance of that name, there was a collective drawing in of breath and much tutting and shaking of heads.

"But –" Noggs faltered "– the truth cannot lie in the bottom of a dusty drawer."

The group, as one, leaned forward, their collective interest piqued. Noggs cleared his throat and perched a pair of grimy pince-nez upon his rubicund nose. At his lowest point in life, he rarely spoke in sentences of more than three or four words. Now, addressing a room full of expectant faces, no matter how familiar, in a state of sobriety was a terrifying prospect causing the muscle under his left eye to spasm. Yet, he was committed and pressed on.

"You will all be very aware of the circumstances of my previous engagement, and the downfall of my employer? Yes, of course, it could not have passed unremarked. However, you will not be in the possession of the events that occurred concurrently to the collapse of his financial empire. Ralph Nickleby was a man of secrets, and not just those belonging to his victims which he harboured and exploited, but his own secrets – a long history of dishonourable and despicable behaviour conducted with free will and a severe lack of conscience. The man, in a word, was a monster."

Noggs sighed, the weight of his regret at his involvement in recent affairs, however peripheral, pressing his shoulders even further down. He shook out the sheets of paper and cleared his throat.

"I should preface the reading of this letter by introducing its author. A good man of a stout and earthy nature, who knows right from wrong and proved to be a loyal friend to the young gentleman in question. John Browdie is a corn merchant who made the acquaintance of Nicholas, Ralph's nephew, whilst he was stationed at Dotheboys Hall. Not knowing the whereabouts of Nicholas' residence in Devonshire, he made the calculated and accurate assumption that I was still responsible for closing down Ralph Nickleby's business affairs in London. This letter was addressed to our offices in Golden Square, and fortuitously arrived the morning I was due to shut the door for the final time and hand over the keys to the land agent. Browdie, not having enclosed his correspondence to Nicholas under separate cover, had simply written instructions in his opening lines for the letter to be forwarded in its entirety at my discretion."

Noggs twitched his head and blinked furiously, hoping that he had provided adequate justification for reading a communication not directly intended for his attention. There was no indication of disapproval on the faces arranged before him. Pickman made a noise in the back of his throat and looked pointedly at the letter. Noggs, in return, raised the papers closer to his face, tilting the pages towards the hearth so that the firelight could better illuminate the words scrawled upon them. His lips trembled, mouthing silent words until he reached the passages he sought.

...It was an unexpected but grand and welcome sight to see you at my door, Nicholas. Mrs Browdie and myself were beyond pleased to receive you and to hear your news. Whilst grieved at the passing of poor young Smike, I cannot say I am not thankful to hear that your uncle will no longer play his wicked games and treat his relations so poorly. Why, if he had not taken matters into his own hands and brought the sorry affair to an end himself, I am not at all sure that I would not have taken the next coach up to London and beaten him black and blue, much in the manner of the hiding you delivered onto that wretch, Wackford Squeers.

As you know, I rode out to Dotheboys Hall to see how the news of the master's well-deserved misfortune was being received at the school. And I returned with a tale of how the boys had brought about their own rebellion and delivered a severe punishment upon the remaining Squeers family, driving them from that evil place.

What I did not report was the discovery of such imaginable horror that I have not, until now, been able to find the words or the courage to put pen to paper. But what I saw, Nicholas, and what I heard... I described the Hall as evil, but that does not even begin to paint a true depiction of what I witnessed. Hellish and wicked and sinful, it was. Even now, Mrs Browdie wakes me in the night, claiming that I scream and bellow loud enough to wake the dead. I can clearly recall the dreams that cause this extreme reaction and spend the next day in a state of deep anxiety and dread, as if some horror lurks just outside the width of my sight... a dark, brooding shape looming just over my shoulder to make me doubt that I did enough.

I arrived at the Hall to be greeted by the most uproarious scene. Boys were running wild, with much yelling and whooping. Mrs Squeers and her brood of two were amongst the thick of it, wailing and weeping.

It was amid the riotous confusion that I became aware of a small, cold and bony hand grasping my fingers. I looked down to see such a scrawny, miserable boy – more dirt and rags than child – staring up at me with eyes as round and dull as two old pennies. He pulled on my hand, with no more strength than a day-old kitten, and I could tell that he wanted me to go with him. I followed, my attention peaked by the intense nature of the boy's expression and his haste to get to our destination.

He led me to the old stables, long abandoned and used for storing furniture and a collection of broken things. It was a dark and damp place even though rods of light came through the weather-damaged roof, so I pulled to doors open, as wide as I could, and entered. It took me some minutes to realise what I was looking at. Stacks upon stacks of mouldering trunks and cases and crates. Some still had labels tied to the handles. I looked at a few and read names, boys' names, but none that I recognized.

Curiosity took hold, and I lifted the lid of one box. There

was not much in it, a small wooden horse, and a book of the Gospels. I turned the cover and saw an inscription on the first page. Kind and sorrowful words from a mother to son, wishing him happiness at his new school and encouraging him to make the best of this singular opportunity. It fair made my heart want to burst with anger.

I turned to the boy and asked him if this was his trunk. He shook his head and pointed to the farthest corner of the stables. I wondered if the owner of the book was hiding there and moved forward to fetch him into the light. But when I reach the far end, there was no one there, just more crumbling boxes and, at odds with the rest of the building, a swept space on the floor with a sturdy trapdoor set in. I wondered what new cruel punishment Squeers had conjured up, and made to pull on the brass ring attached to the door. The boy made a strange, frightened sound and fled as fast as his stick thin legs could carry him.

Hefting the door open, I was greeted with the most terrible stench. It was rotten and raw, like a stagnant pond newly dredged, and scraped at the back of my throat. Peering into the hole, I could see stone steps, only a few before the darkness swallowed them. I looked about and saw an oil lantern hanging on a nail in the wall, a flint and strike-a-light sitting on a nearby ledge. Once the lamp was alight, I descended the stairs, taking care as I approached the bottom of the flight for they were slick and oily. I held the lamp aloft and spied wall sconces holding old iron torches. With care, I lit those nearest to me and turned round to survey the room.

I can barely describe with enough words what I saw. There, in the centre of the room was what I took to be a well, for it was a low wall in the shape of circle. Some intuition told me not to cross over and look down into the hole. Instead, I swept my gaze about and took in the room. The rough-hewn stone walls were marked with dark blotches and streaks. The far side of the room was still in darkness, so I ventured forth.

As I drew nearer, a shape loomed into view, a shape that glowed soft and white in the lamplight. But it was not until I was upon it that I recognized, with a start, a pile of bones standing some six or seven foot high. I admit I laughed at my own foolishness and without reason, kicked at the pile. For whatever nonsensical reason, Squeers had kept the bones from all the meals he had eaten. Perhaps to make the meagre gruels and meatless broths they fed the boys?

The bones shifted and slipped. Something small and round detached itself from the mound and rolled to my feet. I looked and barely suppressed a yell of shock. It was a skull, but not of any animal. It was the skull of a child.

It was as that moment, I heard it. A soft, scratching noise akin to rats in the walls. Only no rat could pass through these solid rocks. I came to realise, with a growing horror ,that the sound was echoing up from the well. Now, I am not a timid man, as you know, but will freely admit to being sore afraid that that moment. Bracing myself, I forced my reluctant feet towards the brick wall surrounding what I was now suspecting was no well at all. With a deep breath, gagging as the stench once again grasped at my gullet, I peered over.

All I saw was a bottomless black hole. Extending my arm out so that the lamp could shine its feeble light into the abyss, I still could not see anything, and yet the noise continued and seemed to be coming closer. Something hissed and, startled, I dropped the lantern. It span away into the hole, the flame extinguishing, but not before I saw something. Something I have never seen before or thought to exist, and something I pray I will never see again.

Eyes. Glittering, blinking black eyes looking back up at me, set into pale grey, misshapen faces. I stumbled back many paces, banging clumsily against the rock wall and slipped, coming down heavily on the bottom few stairs. Winded, I righted myself to a sitting position and shook my head, sure that my imagination had taken ahold of my sanity. When I had fallen, I had struck out my hand to soften the landing. I became aware that my hand was now wet and sticky. I lifted it into the torch light and at first thought I had injured myself but a quick examination proved this not to be the case.

I stood, took the nearest torch from the wall and lowered it towards the step. There was blood, dark blood, not fresh but not yet dried in this damp cellar. My gorge rose but my revulsion was overtaken by the awareness of a new sound. I turned to see a head and shoulders rising above the rim of the well. One thin, leathery arm, then two, swung over the lip and, defying their apparent feebleness, gripped the brickwork and hauled the rest of the creature's body out of the pit.

And I mean creature, for although vaguely human in shape, there were so many things unhuman about it. It stood facing me, its breath harsh and rasping, ribs expanding and collapsing, visible under wrinkled and hairless skin the colour of wet London clay, and yet I did not believe it could see me clearly. The long whiskered snout that protruded from its face quivered, as if to scent me out. Its long grey tongue flicked out between fiercely sharp fangs, tasting the air, its large, pointed ears swivelled about as if to hear me. I instinctively knew that for as long as I stood still, it would not be able to locate me. but I could not stay in that underground room forever.

My mind was made for me when more heads started to emerge from the well. The creatures had started to keen as one. A nerve-shredding wail punctuated with grunts and yelps. My courage was failing fast and I knew I had to act before even one of those monsters got within a few feet of me. I had seen the pile of bones and instinctively knew what my fate would be.

With a scream, I ran at the first beast, brandishing the torch ahead of me like Jophiel's flaming sword. I had understood enough in that small amount of time that light was not their friend. The creature grunted and lashed out, but the arc of fire danced around it, confusing it. With as hefty a lunge as I could managed, I thrust the torch into the brute's chest. It screeched and staggered backwards. Another thrust and it toppled over , back into the well, its shriek piercing the inky gloom. Like a madman, I set about the other creatures, swinging and whacking at any extended body part that was attempting to exit the well. They each fell back, disappearing into the blackness, but one of the damned monstrosities grabbed at the torch, wrenching it from my hand. Fortunately, as it did so, it lost its grasp on the brickwork and also tumbled away.

But I was to have no respite. Although I had managed to force the miscreations to temporarily withdraw, I could hear the rage in their growls and barks, and knew that they would be back within minutes. I cast my eyes about and uttered a prayer of thanks when I spied a cluster of jars of lamp oil. I caught one up and, having no time to open it properly, smashed the neck against the wall. I poured and splashed the contents into the well, making sure to cover the inner face of the hole. I snatched up a second bottle and repeated the action, and a third and fourth time. The screeching had turned from anger to protest and then back to anger. I knew I had only seconds left. Seizing two more torches from their sconces, I threw them into the midst of the seething mass as it slipped and scrabbled to exit the shadowy pit.

The noise was something I never wish to hear again. As if all the devils in Hell had raised their voices as one to sing a demonic chorus. The room was now brightly lit from the burning well, and I noted only then not just one mound of bones, but several,pushed into the darkest recesses.

How many? I asked myself, as the realisation dawned as to what hideous activity had taken place in the depths of Dotheboys Hall. How many boys had been despatched to Greta Bridge and how many parents had been told their sons had died or run away? How many, like that poor, brave lad Smike, had been abandoned at the school to never be missed or considered again?

I sat there until the flames had burned out, until I was sure that I was the only living thing in that hellhole of a cellar. And, I am not ashamed to admit this to your good self, I sobbed for all the lost boys. My despair turned to fury as I came to think of those who perpetrated this heinous crime. There is no doubt in my mind that your uncle was involved, given that he actively sought out families with troublesome dependents and made a tidy profit from it. But he is now beyond the arm of human justice and I can only hope, God forgive me, that he burns as fiercely in Hell as those creatures in the pit.

I took up the last remaining lit torch from its sconce and

with all haste, staggered up the stairs, slamming the trap door behind me. Without hesitation, I set the torch upon the nearest stack of boxes, piling armfuls of straw around it, watching the fire catch hold. Very soon, the barn was ablaze and folding in on itself, burying whatever may have remained of those creatures in their underground tomb to choke and die.

I stood in the yard for a moment, watching the thick, grimy smoke billow away into the sky, before turning back to face the hall. I could see the lads had done their work, windows were broken, furniture lay smashed on the cobbles, doors tilted drunkenly on their hinges. Scores of boys were running across the fields, hooting like wild geese, free of the misery inflicted upon them over the years. Others, now spent, stood huddled and mute. I herded them together and sent one of the oldest to fetch the town constable and the good folk of Greta Bridge to do their Christian duty to these poor wretches.

As for Wackford Squeers, let me just say it is a remarkable coincidence that Mrs Browdie has a cousin working as a crewmate on the transportation ships...

Hands dropping to his side, Noggs bowed his head, exhausted from the effort of his narration. Not a sound could be heard from his audience, just the rumble and crack of the fire as it burned in the grate.

Pickman, who had listened with a strange expression on his face that darkened as the tale progressed, finally broke the silence. He rose from his seat, giving a soft grunt as he pulled himself upright. He poured a glass of brandy and took it over to Noggs, who shook his head. Realising his mistake, Pickman muttered his apologies and passed the glass to the nearest person seated behind him.

"So, then what?" asked Pickman.

Newman Noggs gave a shuddering sigh that rattled through his entire body.

"I wrote to Mr Browdie explaining that Nicholas can never be made aware of the events he has described. The boy is too gentle a soul, it would score him to his heart to know that he was ignorant of such atrocities and that the same fate could have befallen his cousin, Smike. I appealed to Browdie's good nature to bear this heavy load upon his own shoulders and he, being the stout and reliant fellow I believe him to be, replied with a promise I trust him to keep. And so that concludes my business in London. Through the unwarranted charity of my friends, I have the use of a small cottage close to where Nicholas and his family now live. I leave for the West Country tomorrow. This–" he spat with some vehemence, "–will not be leaving with me."

He lifted up the letter and stared at it with an expression of determination. With a flourish, he crumpled the pages into a ball and flung it into the fire, whereupon it bloomed red and black before collapsing in upon itself and disappearing into the flames.

I thrashed mindlessly, bellowing hoarsely like a beast at the slaughter, frantically grasping around me, my clawing fingers finding only unyielding earth

KING OF TIDES

ROBERT POYTON

Many and multiform are the dim horrors of Earth, infesting her
ways from the prime. They sleep beneath the unturned stone;
they rise with the tree from its roots; they move beneath the sea
and in subterranean places.

- The Necronomicon

All stories told, the assembled fell into an uneasy chatter that swept around the room like a chill autumn breeze. The ambience was broken by the chinking of a fork on a glass. It was Pickman who now stood, hand raised for quiet. As I mentioned before, he appeared to have lost weight and his expression, usually one of avuncular warmth, jocularity and verve, was drawn and haggard. The word *haunted* came to mind, though I know not why. You see, Pickman was an avowed materialist, a follower of the latest theories of galvanism and evolution. Despite his enjoyment of "strange tales" he professed no belief in the supernatural or the ultra mundane, a fact that had been the prompt for many a lively discussion at club meetings in the past.

Odd, then, that I should ascribe that particular word to his appearance. Odd but accurate, as his subsequent story confirmed. A hush settled across the group. I imagine all of us thought he was about to thank everyone, give his usual speech about the past year, the future of the Club and so on. None of us expected Pickman to actually relate his own story, something that, to the best of my knowledge, had never occurred before.

I have described Pickman as a collector, and that he was, content to listen, as a man may be happy collecting butterflies without ever once going out into he field himself. So you can imagine our surprise when Pickman informed the assembled that he had his own tale to tell, and more than once I saw him glance nervously at the windows as he did so. Here is what he said.

"Dear friends, let me first thank you all sincerely for you contributions tonight. As always, none has disappointed and I am grateful to have spent another evening - another year - in such fine company. Might I also reassure those of you who have expressed concern over my appearance, that I remain in good health. Physical health, at least. Sleep comes fitfully. The slightest sound awakens me. I dare no longer sleep in the dark, and yes, I do have a loaded revolver beside me at all times. Even then, when I close my eyes I see *him* again... But I ramble. Let me start at the beginning. Let me start with the summons."

———————

I

It was a quiet day at Tweedie & Prideaux, the solicitors at which I had been employed for not a few years. My primary role was in an investigative capacity, mostly covering insurance claims. These ranged from the relatively mundane, through to rather more serious cases, such as the potential poisoning of a well-insured spouse. Still, what I was to be drawn into was neither of those, in fact it was something quite different. *Very* different. A liveried footman appeared in the office one morning, asking for me by name, handing me an envelope. Within, on extremely fine paper, was a letter requesting my attendance on none other than the Duke Of Wellington. You can imagine my surprise! Naturally, I immediately conferred with Mr Tweedie, who nodded vigorously and said, "Ah yes, it quite slipped my mind to mention it! It seems you have been recommended to his Lordship by a past client. Well then, don't dally, off you go!"

I subsequently followed the footman into a waiting coach, and within half an hour, we came to a halt outside Apsley house, where I was ushered into the presence of the great man himself. He rose from his desk as I entered his office, bidding me good morning, and motioning for me to take a seat. As another footman wheeled in a tea trolley, the Duke, with characteristic directness, explained immediately the purpose for my summons.

"Tunnels, Pickman. This is all about tunnels. You've doubtless heard of the Thames Tunnel project? It's the brainchild of Brunel. The man is a genius. French, but we won't hold that against him. In fact, it was at my instigation that he was released from jail and his debts cleared. No sense in us losing such a good man, what?"

"Indeed, your Lordship," I nodded, accepting the china cup and saucer proffered by the manservant. "I believe I read something of the project in the newspapers."

"Good. " The Duke remained standing, hands behind his back. I could easily picture him standing so, resolute and proud, amidst the cannon smoke at Waterloo. "But there is a problem," he continued. "And I'm told you're the man to solve it. Is that right?"

"I am sure I can do my best to investigate any issues that may have arisen," I stammered, somewhat on the back foot.

"Capital! That's that settled, then! Wyndham here will give you all the details and see you out. I look forward to reading your report."

"I - ah - oh, thank you, yes, indeed," I once again stammered as the footman took back the un-drunk tea and pressed a large, manilla folder into my hand. Scant seconds later, I was back in the carriage, wondering, as you might imagine, what had just occurred!

That particular mystery was solved on my return to the office. Mr Prideaux popped his head around my door to assure me, in his usual cheery way, that I was to focus the totality of my professional intent on the Wellington Case, as it had now been named, and that I would receive no other work until its conclusion. "This is a great opportunity for the firm!" he beamed before leaving. Still in something of a daze, I opened the file and began to read.

The outlines of the situation were as follows. The Duke had invested a far from negligible sum of money in the formation of the Thames Tunnel Company. The scheme involved digging a tunnel under the Thames, from Rotherhithe to Wapping, in order to create a crossing point. Obviously, with the sheer volume of ships, not to mention their size, the creation of a bridge was entirely impractical - unless someone could invent one that lifted like a drawbridge! Still, to create such a tunnel was no mean feat, and Monsieur Marc Brunel had been brought in to apply his considerable intellect to the problem. He had come up with an ingenious idea, essentially a reinforced shield of cast iron, with small compartments at its front, in which miners would dig. Periodically, the shield would be driven forward by large jacks, and the tunnel surface behind lined with brick. Some claimed Brunel's inspiration for this unique device had been the humble ship-worm, *Teredo navalis*, which has its head protected by a hard shell as it bores through ships' timbers.

So far, so good. A huge, brick shaft had been sunk on the bank at Rotherhithe, its centre excavated, and the shield constructed some fifty feet below the surface. For some months now it had been in operation, and was running on schedule. Brunel's son, Isambard, was over-seeing the project and, expected issues aside, all was going well. Then, according to the file before me, the problems began. Small things, at first. Tools going missing, items of machinery sustaining damage overnight. These may have been put down to casual pilfering or vandalism from local ne'er-do-wells, but the site was strictly guarded. Sabotage by rivals was mooted but, again, even with an increase in the number of watchmen, the events continued. Then came the deaths.

It is a sad fact that, in any such endeavour, there will be casualties. It may sound callous, but such tragic losses will be built into the fabric of the project, with funds already put aside to compensate the families of the lost. There had been one major incident early on, when the river had broken through the thin crust above, and poured into the workings. Fortunately, all escaped in time and no lives were lost.

The deaths came rather as a result of the intense miasma within the excavation. According to the report, not only was there the stench from the river itself, but digging often uncovered large pockets of decaying vegetable matter, with the subsequent release of toxic gasses into the work area. In one such case, two unfortunates were overcome by fumes, to the point of suffocation. Now, you might say, such a thing would surely be expected. Indeed, I would whole-heartedly agree. What was totally unexpected, however, was that their corpses, laid out overnight for removal in the morning, would vanish without a trace.

The second, and, to the Duke, more disturbing incident concerned the young Isambard Brunel. Apparently, he had stayed in the tunnel late one evening, no doubt engrossed in some engineering problem or refinement of the apparatus. The watchman, on his rounds, had seen him tapping away at one of the pumps and continued on his way. It was on the watchman's return that he'd found the young man in a virtual catatonic state on the ground, his face a mask of fear according to the report. With some difficulty, he'd helped the lad back up to the surface. However, the state did not wear off, and Brunel junior was taken to a sanatorium, suffering from what was described as *acute shock*.

The combined effect of both these events was to bring work on the Thames Tunnel to a halt. As you can imagine, with such vast sums of money involved, pressure to complete the project on schedule is immense. And so my brief was revealed; to investigate the circumstances surrounding these events, to advise the Duke of my findings and, dependent on those, to push the project once more into life. To my mind, at that time, this all seemed straightforward enough. A simple accident, unfortunate but not entirely unforeseen, and a young man who, overcome by the demands of the immense task fallen upon his shoulders, succumbed to a nervous episode. Ah, as the old adage goes... ignorance truly is bliss.

It seemed entirely proper to begin my investigations at the site itself. The file included a letter of authority from the Duke, and explained that the overseers of the project had been informed of my likely appearance and subsequent nosing around. I began with the watchman who had discovered Brunel junior, a local by the name of Michael Geggus. Following enquiries, I found him that evening in the nearby Three Compasses and stood him a pint as he told me what had happened.

"Well, I seen the young gent there, bid him *Good Evenin'* as you do, then went on with me rounds. As you know, sir, what with all the bother what's been going in, we were told by the guvnor to keep a sharp eye out. So, I done me full round and was working back to the pumps again. That's when I seen him, slumped on the ground. All pale and quiverin' he was, like he was havin' a fit or sunnink. So, course, I went over, got him sat up, made sure he was alright. Then I blew me whistle - we all has one, like the Runners," he laughed and showed me the whistle on a chain around his neck. "Couple of the lads came down and we carried the young gentleman back up top. That was it, really."

"Did you see or hear anything unusual?" I asked.

He supped his pint and thought for a moment. "Comes to

think of it, there was sunnink odd. A shadow of sorts, cast up on the side of the pump, like someone was moving through the gap between 'em."

"A person? Tall? Short?"

He shrugged. "Hard to say. Looked sort of hunched over. I took a quick butchers, but there was no-one there. Trick of the lamplight, I reckon."

I thanked Geggus for his time and decided next to visit the tunnel itself. The watchman on the gate was well informed and expecting me, calling up one of the foremen from below to escort me down into the bowels of the earth. Although digging work had stopped, he informed me that a skeleton crew was still in place, maintaining the tunnel, keeping an eye on things and carrying out some of the fixings and finishings on the work already done. The spiral staircase down seemed endless, and the air grew more dank, rank and chill as we descended. At the foot of the shaft, the excavation opened out into a large cavern, dimly lit by gas lamps. There, I was greeted by the Chief Engineer, one John Armstrong, a pale looking man afflicted with a racking cough.

"This damn air," he spluttered after one particularly violent spasm. "It'll be the death of me if I stay here much longer."

I could only concur. Even my thick muffler and the application of a perfumed handkerchief did little to mitigate the effluvia that assaulted the senses; the sharp tang of human ordure combined with that of damp earth, rot, soot and sweat to create a truly eye-watering experience. Nonetheless, I followed Armstrong into what he termed his "office," an alcove carved into the side of the wall. Drawings and charts covered the desk, Armstrong bid me sit and poured a welcome livener.

"I'm told I must give you all due assistance, Mr Pickman. So please ask me anything, and I will do my best to answer."

Truth be told, he could tell me little more than what was contained in the report. The two dead men, Collins and Ball, had been laid out in an adjoining chamber, to be taken back to the surface on the morrow. Yet, both corpses had mysteriously vanished at some time during the night. It was as we were discussing this matter that another figure loomed in the doorway. Balding, quietly-spoken, of slight build and possessed of the most piercing blue eyes, he introduced himself as Inspector Calhoun of the Thames River Police. We both rose to greet him, as he explained his purpose for being here.

"Two cadavers gone missing, so I've been told?"

"Indeed," Armstrong responded. "Though, if you'll forgive me, Inspector, isn't your jurisdiction above, on the water?"

Calhoun raised an eyebrow. "On the Thames or below it, that's my patch." He withdrew a pipe and a strike-a-light from his coat pocket, eliciting a panicked response from Armstrong.

"Hells teeth man, don't strike that light, this place is full of gases!"

Calhoun grunted and returned the items. "Thing is, we've had a spate of these reports. Bodies going missing. Not that we have any shortage of 'em, what with all the badgers operating round here." He spoke of the local gangs of ruffians who were not averse to robbing a chap, murdering him, and disposing of the body in the river. "The victims eventually turn up to us, if you get my drift." He gave a somewhat macabre smile at his own pun, and I shuddered at the thought of a job that entailed fishing bloated corpses from the reeking waters above our heads. "We take them to one of our cold rooms prior to investigation, and there they stay. Unless someone steals them it seems, because, as we all know," the Inspector smiled again, "corpses don't just get up and walk off by themselves, do they, now?"

There was no arguing with that, and following my next request, Armstrong took us to the makeshift alcove morgue. The place was certainly chill enough, and I pulled my muffler tighter around my neck. Armstrong explained the pair had been laid out on the bench before us and covered with a sheet. An Irish brogue sounded as we stood examining the scene.

"Tis surely strange what happened to those two chaps, there." We turned to face an older man in rough, working clothes, stained with mud.

"This is O'Brien, one of the gang leaders," Armstrong informed us.

I made a perfunctory examination of the space, and could find nothing out of place. The earth was soft, and may have shown footprints, but any such had long been combined with those of the workmen.

"Can you take us to where the men were found?" I asked the workman, and the Inspector and I were led to the huge workings at the far end of the cavern. There, the large tunnel had been lined with brickwork, and things were a little less damp. Holding a lantern aloft, O'Brien led us to a spot further in, closer to the digging face and the great shield that stood against it.

"There she is," O'Brien patted the device with obvious pride. "Ninety tons, and over twenty feet high. Like a big pastry cutter she is. Allows thirty six fellers do dig at once, so it does. It's a marvel, of that there's no doubt."

Calhoun rolled his eyes. "All well and good, but where were the bodies found?"

O'Brien moved us to a smaller side tunnel running parallel to the main one. As we went I slipped, almost putting my foot into a roughly dug drainage gully half filled with foul smelling water. But for the steadying grasp of Armstrong, I would have stood knee-deep in the filth.

"Mind the gap," Calhoun smirked.

The side tunnel contained a series of bricked archways used for tool storage, men to rest and the like. Indeed, a few fellows were sat round as we approached, munching on bread and cheese. O'Brien kept up his monologue.

"Found just over there, they were. Overcome with fumes, it looks like, they must have staggered back to this spot and keeled over. Poor fellers, working down here late at night. Shouldn't really be happening, but time is money and all. There, that's where they got to before collapsing."

Armstrong stood back as Calhoun and I made an inspection of the area. Nothing obvious presented itself, at least not until Calhoun pointed out something a short distance away.

"This earth, here. It's a different colour from the rest. Looks fresher." The earth in question was piled in a low mound around the base of a heavy bench.

O'Brien shrugged. "Lots of rats round here, digging their own tunnels. Some say the place is riddled with them, sir. Rats, or worse."

"Worse?" I ventured.

O'Brien fell uncharacteristically quiet for a moment. "Just

some of the lads talking sir, you know how they will. *Pookas* and the like!"

"Alright O'Brien, that's enough. Get back to your duties," Armstrong rebuked, and the old man left us, mumbling under his breath.

"Superstitious lot these Barks," muttered the Inspector. It did enter my head that *Calhoun* might well be a name of Irish origin, but I kept the thought to myself.

"Beggin' your pardon, sir?" One of the men sat eating knuckled his forehead and stood. I noted the empty sleeve pinned to the front of his jacket. He obviously caught my glance.

"Lost it at Waterloo, sir. Aye, I were there with the Duke." He stood proud, chest out. "That's how I came to be workin' here, see. It were his Dukeship who got me the job."

"How heart-warming," was Calhoun's response and I must admit I was beginning to form a dislike of the man. In my view, one should not disrespect those who gave service to King and country. The old soldier, oblivious to any sarcasm, continued.

"I know as how some might speak against the Duke, but he looked after his old troopers, I'll give him that."

I nodded. "Yes, indeed. But you were going to tell us something pertaining to the current situation, mister, erm..."

"Sam." He replied. "Sam Small, sir. Private Sam Small, 30th Foot. Well, yes, you see I heard what the gentleman here said about our Irish friends and, with respect mind, I'd say there's more in heaven and earth, as the Great Bard wrote. It were after the battle, y'see, a group of us wounded were lying there, waiting for stretchers. An eerie silence had fallen over the battlefield. The only sound were the faint whispering of the wind and the moans of the afflicted. Heaps of dead lay around us, Frenchies for the most part. Oh yes, we made 'em pay alright. Certainly, we had dead of our own, but the square held against those devils on horses."

I coughed, not entirely voluntarily in the heavy miasma, to spur Small on a little. He took the hint.

"Anyway, as I lay there, my arm shattered by a cannon ball, I seen them. Furtive figures, shadowy, crouched low. I thought 'em locals at first, here to plunder the dead of watches and coin, or the like. But then I saw that they were lifting the fallen and draggin' them off. *Orderlies*, I thought, though they didn't seem to be wearing uniform, or even clothing come to that. It weren't until some actual orderlies came up, with lanterns shining and guns at the ready, that they all scarpered. I got a quick glimpse of one in the light. Big bugger he were, all hairy. There were summat queer about his face, but about that time I passed out. From the pain, like."

He paused for a moment, as if reliving the moment. On a whim, I handed him my flask for a snifter. He took an appreciative swig and handed it back. "When I come round I were in th'ospital, minus an arm. Ran a fever for a few days. While I were there I got chatting to the sawbones, he'd been around, let me tell you. I asked him about what I'd seen. You know what he replied?" Sam leaned forward, drawing us in, then whispered. "*The eaters of the dead!*" He sat back, staring around the dank tunnel.

Inspector Calhoun was not impressed. "That's it? While in a wounded, feverish state, you think you saw a large, hairy man, a looter, no doubt, and that explains our missing corpses?"

Sam straightened, bristling. "You may scoff, sir, but none of us here goes round in less than threes on night shift. And I allus carry this." He produced a large bayonet from inside his jacket. "It saw off old Bony, it'll see off whatever's down here!"

II

I arose later than usual the next morning. I must admit, my sleep had been disturbed not only by an irritating cough - an effect of spending time in that odious tunnel, no doubt - but also by disturbing dreams of vague and threatening shapes. Still, a hearty breakfast dispelled my collywobbles, and I resolved to spend that morning visiting Brunel and son. By the time the Sedan chair deposited me outside Brunel's residence, I was feeling much more myself. Brunel was a much smaller man than I expected. I suppose I'd had a vision of the mastermind of such a grand scheme being something of a grand fellow. Still, petite he may have been, but he greeted me warmly, with the hint of a French accent, and welcomed me into his study.

As with Armstrong, he had no real further information to impart other than that contained in the Duke's files. And so, I asked if I may see his son, now being nursed at home. Brunel led me to an upstairs bedroom. Inside, reposing on the bed, lay Brunel the Younger, his youthful face peaceful in sleep. I wondered at the curtains being opened, but was informed by the father that his son would become extremely distressed at being left in the dark. Brunel motioned to the grim-faced nurse in attendance, who glared at me on leaving, and I sat on the bedside, shaking the young sleeper gently by the shoulder.

Presently, he came around, his eyes somewhat cloudy, his expression confused. "Father?" he croaked.

"I am here, *mon gars*," Brunel leaned forward. I took the glass of water from the bedside table and held it to the young man's lips as he drank. "This is Mr Pickman," the father explained. "He'd like to ask you a few questions." To me he then whispered, "The doctor has administered laudanum tablets, so he may be a little unfocussed."

I nodded and turned back to the son, now sitting up, looking a little more bright-eyed. I began with some general chat, talking about the weather, asking him some light, personal questions. Then I asked about the tunnel. The change was instantaneous. From a bright, pleasant, if somewhat hazy young man, his face immediately contorted into a mask of terror. His hands grasped the bedsheets like claws, a tremor afflicted his whole body. I felt Brunel Snr stiffen beside me, but pressed, gently but firmly, on with my line of questioning.

"What did you see that night, Isambard? What was it that shocked you so?"

The trembling continued, and the sobbing began. At the prompt of Brunel senior's hand on my shoulder I stood and made to leave. It was obvious the young man was in the grip of a fear that paralysed his mind.

I sighed and comforted his father as best I could with a few words. Yet, as I moved to the door, a single phrase burst from the young Brunel's lips. A phrase that he repeated as the now even more scowling nurse, pushed past me to administer to her ward. Four words, over and over.

"The Hounds of Hell! *The Hounds of Hell!*"

I must admit to having been at something of a dead end, the irony of which, given the tunnel below did not escape me. On the previous night, Armstrong the engineer had admitted himself stumped when it came to an explanation. Inspector Calhoun had put the corpse disappearances down to resurrectionists, though how they had affected entry and escaped unseen while carrying two bodies, he had no account for.

In normal circumstances, had it just been about the bodies, life would, I imagine, have largely carried on as normal. People go missing in London every day, the bodies of two labourers were small beans in the scheme of things. But the fact of the scale of this, currently suspended, project, and the involvement of the Duke, cast a different light on matters, and so I resolved to deepen my investigation. The remains of the two unfortunates had vanished from the tunnel. Brunel junior had experienced something queer in the tunnel. To the tunnel I must return.

I had established that, while the watchmen were on duty all night, the maintenance crew below were finished long before midnight. My plan of action, then, was to sit it out in the tunnel, to see if some person or other may make an appearance, perhaps for sabotage, or some other nefarious purpose, in which case I might apprehend them, or at least discover the cause of recent events. If only I had known, my friends. Life was never to be the same again.

On the last check of my my watch it was fifteen minutes past one. I had sat here in the cold and damp for close on two hours, now. The watchman had supplied me with a lamp and, judging from his expression, clearly thought me mad.

"Wouldn't catch me staying down there overnight," was his parting comment as I trod down those interminable steps once more. I must admit to feeling somewhat more nervy on this occasion. Last time, I had the company of fellows, the cavern below had been lit. Now, all lay shrouded in darkness, which, if anything, lent the foul air an even more oppressive nature. I walked around a little, then sat for a time. At times, I covered the lamp, steeling myself against the total blackness that resulted. *It's only the dark,* I repeated to myself.

Nothing happened. There were the usual strange sounds one hears in any place or building at night. Creaks, drips... the brief scurry of rats gave me a start. But upon uncovering the lamp, I saw the few scattering forms were nothing but the normal rodents one encounters along the shores of the Thames. No, it wasn't until after a quarter past one that I heard the other sound.

It was distant. A sort of scraping, as of something on wood. Then, a dragging noise and a dull thud. My heart was in my mouth. This was no river rat. The silence that followed was almost overwhelming in its tension. I had the distinct sense of a presence somewhere out there in the dark. Did I uncover my lamp? No, I'm somewhat ashamed to say that I did not. Rather, I pressed myself back into the corner behind me, crouching down beside one of the pumps. There I waited, scarce daring to breathe, as that presence lurked somewhere unseen in the darkness beyond.

Can you imagine my fear, my friends? Can you imagine the primal terrors that flooded my brain, sat in absolute darkness, seventy five feet below the surface of the Thames, at the heart of the greatest city in the world yet, at that moment, so totally alone.

Next, a scuffle of feet. Again, too loud for rats. The clatter of a shovel falling to the floor gave me such a start that I feared my heart would stop. I jammed my fist into my mouth in dread that my ragged breathing would be audible to.... to whatever it was out there. A rank stench came to my nostrils, bestial, foul, rotten. A stronger sense of the presence came with it, lingered, then mercifully receded.

More scufflings, then a repeat of the dragging sound, and that final dull thump again. I'm not sure how long I crouched there in the stygian darkness, drenched in a cold sweat, the blood pounding in my temples. Yet, after hearing nothing more, I eventually stood. Now it was that I raised the lamp, to reveal, in my little of circle of light, only that which I had seen before.

Upbraiding myself for my cowardice, I moved to where I thought the dragging sounds had come from. That brought me to the arch we had examined the night before, where Calhoun had spotted that odd, small earth mound at the side of the workbench. Lowering the lamp, I could now make out drag marks, and signs of the earth having been very recently disturbed. A sudden thought took me and, placing the lamp on the bench, I grasped its corner in two hands and attempted to straighten my back. Nothing resulted, other than a very slight lifting, followed by an immediate dropping as my strength gave out.

A new determination gripped me. By God, there was a mystery here, and I'd be dashed if I was going to give up at the first hurdle! I gripped the bench again and, rather than lift, instead pushed it to the side. It moved a little, then a little more. I stopped to regain breath, then applied myself once more, to the task. My efforts were rewarded with a shifting of the bench a few feet to one side. As I retrieved the lantern, a thought struck me. Granted, I am no longer a young man, and though relatively inactive, am far from unfirm. However, it took all my efforts to move this bench even a scant distance. Someone had, it seemed, lifted it with ease, and from what position? They must be endowed with positively Herculean strength!

My question on position was answered with the lifting of my lamp for, revealed by the moving of the covering bench, there came into view a hole, a large hole in the heavy clay beneath my feet. A tunnel within a tunnel, that led down and away to who knew where? Would that I had stopped there, would that I had done the merest of my duty and reported my findings to the Duke. But, no.

The old curiosity, I suppose, got the better of me, and I leaned forward, lamp poised, to peer into the pit below, to see if I could ascertain anything of its construction or origin. And that is where the soft clay at the lip of the hole crumbled and gave way, and that is where I fell, tumbling, into the yawning blackness below. Tumbled, span, cannoned from wall to wall, or perhaps floor, in a flurry of arms and legs, lantern falling, the stench of the earth overwhelming me, until at last I crashed into something solid and passed into oblivion.

III

I came to. My hat was gone, the lamp smashed, my body battered and bruised. Once again, I found myself in pitch black.

But not now the blackness of the cavern, of a large, open space. No. This was the absolute darkness of the tomb. I felt as one interred before his time, with dank earth clogging my nose and mouth, with no sense of up or down, of time or place. I admit, panic overtook me then, and I thrashed mindlessly, bellowing hoarsely like a beast at the slaughter, frantically grasping around me, my clawing fingers finding only unyielding earth. I wriggled and crawled, like some vast grave worm, somehow making my way along that passageway.

It was the glow that saved me, and restored me to some semblance of sanity. It was the faintest luminescence, sickly green in hue, yet, at that moment, it was as beautiful to me as the most glorious of sunrises. Like a moth to the flame, I continued my scrabbling, half falling, half sliding into the cavern that was the source of the glow. I must have passed out again.

When I awoke I found myself slumped in the centre of what appeared to be a natural chamber, some twenty feet across. The source of the glow were the numerous fungal growths that dotted walls and floor. By their light I performed a quick self examination. Despite numerous aches and pains, I had escaped serious injury. My clothes were in somewhat of a state, being torn and smeared with dirt. My watch had been broken in the fall.

Glancing around, I saw a number of tunnel openings in the walls of the chamber, all similar to that by which I had entered. But here came my dilemma. Which tunnel had been the one I entered in by? In the faint light, it was difficult to find any sign of my ingress, and my sense of direction had been totally annulled by the manner of my arrival. I patted down my pockets, finding my pipe, also broken, and, thankfully, my striker. My muffler was wool, and so, useless for burning. My cravat, however, was of fine lace, which should go up nicely. With a few, tremulous strikes, I was able to get a flickering flame at one end of the cravat, and lifted it to swiftly examine each tunnel in turn.

Even with the extra light, I could find no trace of my scramblings. However, the flame flickered a little at one entrance, and I fancied I could feel the merest touch of a breeze on my face. Wishful thinking perhaps, yet I was certain that the flame had flickered, as it rapidly approaching my fingers. Without delay, I made my way to the tunnel mouth. Before my makeshift torch was dropped by my burnt fingers, I made out some detail of the passageway. It was circular, the floor slightly flattened. I am no expert, but the place did not look natural. I cannot say that it had the man-made smoothness of a secret passageway, such as we meet read about in *The Castle of Otranto* or similar melodramas, but, at the same time, it appeared far too even to be natural - unless perhaps it had been carved out by water. That thought brought with it the unwelcome prospect of an impending flood, yet the floor and walls appeared to be bone dry.

Bones. Hah! For that is what I found in my fumblings. With no light, and the fungal glow far behind, I found myself once again in total darkness, though at least this time I was walking, for the tunnel was just high enough to accommodate me, with a slight stoop. And so it was that, stumbling on an object underfoot, I crouched to place a hand down, feeling the touch of something smooth and round. Curious, I lifted it, running my hands along its smooth length. The object bulged out at each end, and I suddenly realised I was holding a bone of some description, a long bone. With a gasp, I dropped it to clatter amongst its fellows.

Gingerly, I stepped around the pile and continued on my way, hands outstretched like a blind tinker. Just past that point, the tunnel widened beyond my outstretched arms, forcing me to stay close to one wall. It was here that the foetid animal odour from before assailed my nostrils again. I confess, I wavered, and considered going back, reversing my course. Yet no danger emerged from inky darkness and, gripping the stem of my broken pipe firmly between my teeth, I pressed on.

I found myself once more in that timeless state. The further I went, the more I felt the press of the dirt and rock above me. Was I still below the river? I felt that I had been walking for hours, yet it may have been mere minutes. Was I ascending, or descending further into the bowels of the Earth? The faint breeze had not grown any stronger, was it even still there? Yet, the memory of it brought the merest smidgen of hope. It was to this smidgen that I clung on my Hadean sojourn, this and the thought of finding again even the merest speck of light. And so I was rewarded, by another glow ahead, and, I admit that I gave a sob of relief as I quickened my pace towards that light, striving for it as the thirst-ridden desert traveller hastens to a sweet oasis.

Once again, I burst out into a cavern. Larger, this one, and with no doubt that it had been constructed, for large flagstones covered the floor. The source of the ruddy glow was a burning sconce set in the carved rock wall. The chamber was hexagonal in shape and at its centre sat a large object. While the floor was worked stone, that object was a natural boulder, black in colour and standing some five feet high. I felt a natural aversion to it, though was immediately distracted by the strengthening of that faint breeze..

Its source was one of the five tunnel openings in the room. The dimensions of each was the same as that I had entered in by, but only the dark opening before me emitted the breeze which, I fancied, carried with it the scent of the river. I moved hastily towards it, only to be brought up short by two things - the sudden, reoccurrence of the beastly odour that assailed my nostrils, and the appearance of a pair of baleful, yellow eyes in the depths of the tunnel ahead. I came to a faltering halt, unsure whether to stand or flee, as a low, guttural voice issued forth from the pitch black.

"Master Pickman? Welcome. I have been expecting you."

IV

Before I could make any decision, a figure born of nightmare emerged from the opening, like a spider from its lair. Long, sinewy arms and legs presaged the arrival of tall, man-like creature. I estimated the height as well over six feet, perhaps approaching seven. Wisps of red hair covered a mottled and misshapen cranium that showed pale white. The face was of a similar complexion, thought the features could scarcely be imagined in even the most deranged opium delirium. They called to mind the features of a great hound or jackal. Black lips writhed over large canines. The snout bristled with short, wiry hairs. The dark nostrils twitched as if scenting. But, if you can believe such a thing, the greatest horror were the eyes, for they appeared to be fully human.

The gangrel body was semi-clothed in a ragged slip which did little to hide the bony frame beneath. The long arms ended in claw-like hands, and the legs, God help me, the legs terminated in queerly-cloven hooves. To say I was rendered speechless would be an understatement. Never in my life have I known such crushing terror. Now I knew what the faun must feel when faced by the wolf. I do believe I shut my eyes and prayed for this all to be some fever from which I would soon awaken. An unexpected noise forced my eyes to re- open. The creature was laughing, a low, rumbling sound that, to me, had little humour in it.

"I understand." It spoke again. The voice was deep, harsh, yet unmistakably English. "You find my appearance disturbing. Fear not, sirrah, for you are in no danger. At least while you are in my company."

The creature moved to stand by the boulder, beckoning me forward with a gesture. My limbs moved of their own volition and I stood before it, as it inspected me with those cognisant eyes, sniffing the air as it did so. Eventually, I found my voice.

"Where am I? Who are you? Wh-what are you?"

"You are in what we call the Crawls. These warrens run beneath the whole of London. And beyond, in some places. My name?" Those yellowed fangs were bared again. "In another time I had another name. But now, you can call me King of Tides."

"Tides? A strange title." Then realisation dawned. "The river!"

"Indeed. Yes, and even your somewhat lacking human

faculties can no doubt scent it. For that tunnel leads to the river, to a certain spot we term Dead Man's Hole. For it is there that Mother Thames is most generous with her provision."

I felt cold beads of sweat break out on my brow. I reached to mop it with my handkerchief, noting the tremor in my hand. "You mean... you mean you feast on..." I could not bring myself to speak the unspeakable. The monster raised a sardonic eyebrow.

"Dead flesh? Do not we all? And yet, Master Pickman, unlike your kind we do not slaughter to feed. The tides provide... for the most part. Ah yes, *but nature should bring forth, of its own kind, all foison, all abundance, to feed my innocent people.*"

Somewhere in the back of mind I recognised those words, yet my faculties, under such stress were, as you might imagine, most severely compromised. The creature continued.

"As to what I am... that is a long story and not so easily explained. You are familiar with *Beowulf,* that most epic of English poems?"

I nodded mutely, somewhat confused at the direction this conversation was taking.

"Well, there are those who speculate," the thing continued," that Grendel was one of our kind. For we have been here for quite some time. There are hints in folklore, of course. But I believe the current term, derived from the Arabic, is *ghul.* Yes, what you see before you, Mister Pickman, is a ghoul."

My brain continued its feeble attempts to assimilate this information. "But this is madness," I stammered, "Such things are the stuff of myth and fanciful stories."

"Ah, fanciful stories." Those canines flashed again. "And are not men's lives built on fanciful stories? Is not London still full of theatres?" The creature struck a dramatic pose. "Do not the descendants of the Lord Chamberlain's Men still strut the boards, proclaiming the words of the Great Bard?"

"I - that is, yes I suppose they do." My mind was reeling now, I felt as though reality were slipping slowly from my grasp. "You know of what happens above?"

The thing turned to regard me with tilted head. "I do. And I see all that has changed in my city."

"Your city?"

"Well, perhaps not of my birth. But of my re-birth. And of my fortune when I was as you."

"You are... were, human?"

A cloud passed briefly over the creature's visage. "No use to speak of the past. It is to the future we must look. And that is why you are here, Master Pickman. But first, I must show you something. This way, if you would?"

He gestured to an archway on the far side of the chamber. Having found the light, I felt extremely reluctant to leave it, particularly in the company of such a being. My hesitation must have been clearly apparent.

"I assure you again, you are safe. My subjects have instructions not to harm or hinder you. In fact, you passed one of my kin in the passageway on your way here. He could have reached out and..." a large hand was raised, the taloned fingers clasped suddenly shut. "Ended your life with no more thought or effort than snuffing out a candle."

My expression of alarm instigated another barking laugh. "Fear not. Besides, we generally prefer our meat... less fresh.

Now, after you, sirrah."

I am honestly unable to say which was the most terrifying of my peregrinations in that underworld: my first involuntary tumble into the abyss and the subsequent panic; my walk alone in total darkness; or that third journey, once again in deepest night, with that monster at my shoulder. The carrion stench of it was reminder enough of its presence, but every now and then a large paw would rest on my shoulder, guiding me gently towards one or other unseen branch in that network of tunnels. No word was exchanged until, having followed a distinctly downward slope, we entered another chamber, the largest yet and, I somehow sensed, the deepest and oldest.

V

I thought that my mind had reached the limit of its ability to absorb and manage shock, yet those limits were tested to the extreme by what occurred next. I found myself seated on a cold stone bench in what I can only describe as an auditorium. A small brazier had been lit, for my benefit I imagine, atop what I surmised was a large altar stone, of similar material to the boulder I had seen earlier. This rock, though had been shaped, and contained many carvings along it sides. Of what they depicted, I shall not speak. I had a sense of a large space, though very little was visible beyond the brazier's ruddy glow. The King was a lurking presence somewhere in its outer fringes. He had already bid me to "stay within the light," and I had no intention of disobeying. My wonder at this subterranean structure must have been obvious.

"Roman," the King muttered. "At least parts of it. But the

chamber and altar itself are much older. My people have observed ritual here for many, many generations."

I could vaguely make out movement in the shadows, and glimpsed the white of many bones. Strewn across the floor they were, including a rib cage, virtually intact, though almost wholly detached from its previous owner. A small thing moved within and around it. With a choke I realised it was a baby, a pup, a cub, playing with... *things*... as my own children had played in their cribs. I swiftly averted my gaze and was about to ask another question when there sounded the dolorous toll of a bell. Three times it rang, the deep peals reverberating around the chamber and out into the passageways beyond.

"The Summoning," explained the King.

In a moment of near-hysteria I chuckled at the fact that his answers only provoked more questions. He turned to look, in that tilt-headed way again, at my outburst of jocularity.

"We summon the tribe. My people, the Tides Clan. To the north, the Hill Clan, to the south, the Downs. But we have little to do with either. Matters of import are put before the clan." He turned away as scufflings sounded in the dark.

Yet again, my conscious mind reeled at this knowledge. Not just one or two of these creatures made their hellish abode in this subterranean realm, oh no, of course not! There were whole clans! And they were organised! My laughter continued, to be cut short by a growl.

"Silence, if you value your life!"

I became aware of more shufflings, the click of hoof on stone, and of movement beyond the light. How many forms emerged, I could not say, though those I had glimpses of bore the same lineaments as the King. Eyes flashed in the dark, I felt the hatred and oppression of their glare.

The King began to speak, as though he were some some great stage orator, and not the leader of a pack of cave-dwelling cannibals. I understood little of what followed, though that may have been due to my somewhat parlous mental state. The creatures conversed in a curious mixture of gutter English, guttural barks, growls and meeps. For a time I drifted into a dream state, where I was sat in the audience of a plush theatre, enjoying the drama, hearing the gentle ripple of laughter from the assorted gentlefolk around me.

It was drama that brought me crashing back to reality. Not that of a powdered actor, however, but the marrow-freezing spectacle of a ghoul at least the size of the King hovering at the edge of the nimbus. The tone of language was distinctly hostile, and while the words were difficult to make out, the sentiment was all too apparent. Given that my continued existence here relied entirely on the protection of my host, I sat up and paid close attention to the exchange. A few words became clear amongst the growls.

"Work with humes? Mad!" the newcomer snarled, thin lips curling back.

"Times change, no choice!" responded the King.

The answer was a sinister bark of laughter. "Of course." The rebellious ghoul, naked I noticed, his rough fur bristling along his spine, swept hands the size of dinner plates aside and made a mocking bow. "Course Your Majesty. We all knows, don't we." He raised a taloned finger to point at the King. "Raised by 'em, he was. Why, he's no more than a half-breed!"

There was an audible intake of breath from the assembled, followed by a tense silence. The King bowed his head. I thought he was going to turn away, to submit to the challenge of this upstart. Instead, with a speed that defied expectation, the King leapt, claws extended, canines bared.

The resulting affray was like nothing I have seen before. The most brutal of dockyard fights paled into insignificance compared to the sheer bestial fury before me. This was naked savagery, a primal battle for survival that brooked no mercy and offered no quarter. The pair locked and writhed, their movements too fast for my eyes to follow. I shrank back in terror at the ferocity on display, sickened as there came to my ears a terrible crunch and a ripping. The challenger emitted a howl of agony, one elbow bent at an impossible angle.

The King did not relent. He surged forward, misshapen jaws clamping around his opponent's neck. With a feral wrench, he tore out the creature's throat, spitting away a bloody gobbet to the flagstones. The challenger fell back, eyes wide with fear of impending death, dark blood spurting, glistening in the brazier's glow. He had barely hit the ground when the pack descended. Emerging howling, from the gloom came a pack of the things, to fall upon their fallen kin, rending, biting, tearing.

My gorge rose in revulsion as the previously terrifying beast was transformed into a collection of broken limbs, gobbets of flesh and greenish - yellow innards that slithered obscenely to the stone. Crunching, snapping, gulping, I covered my ears as the King stood above it all and let vent his howl of triumph, the scratches and wheals showing on his pale body, his white maw bloody and red. The previous humanity in his eyes had vanished completely, replaced by the abysmally vacant, impersonal stare of the true predator.

My brain at last surrendered. I slipped from the stone bench into merciful unconsciousness.

Of the following events I have but the vaguest recollection. I came round to a whimpering sound, which I ashamedly realised was mine. I was in a small room, curled in a corner on a foul smelling blanket. The chamber was lit by soft candlelight, I could make out a shelf filled with leather-bound books, and a small desk. Was I back on the surface, perhaps in some office or library? I gave a sob of relief. It was cut short by the figure of the King coming through the archway. He squatted by the desk and observed me closely.

"Can you hear me? Can you understand me?"

I nodded mutely. The spark of intelligence had returned to his eyes. This close, in the better light, I noticed a jagged scar above the right one, not fresh, not from his recent fight. He returned my nod. "Then all's well."

"Your foe... you killed him!"

"Indeed. For their must always be a Reckoning." He grinned again, then turned to the desk. Next to a quill and inkpot rested a parchment. He quickly glanced over it, rolled it up, fixed it with a ribbon and handed it to me. Yet more amazement, though by this time I think I would not have blinked had the Emperor of China ridden past on the back of an elephant! I meekly accepted the proffered scroll, though another question escaped my lips.

"You called my name. In the tunnel. You called my name. How did you know who I am?"

The King shrugged. "We know much of what goes on in the Above. London is riddled with our burrows, our hiding places, our hidey-holes. We are ever at your shoulder. So it was that I marked you out, on hearing of your appointment by the Iron Duke. This is a man, I thought, who may prove of use to me."

"Of use? As what?"

"As a messenger. I would speak to the Duke personally but my appearance may cause some alarm." Another grin. "As it was, the attempt by one of my kin to speak with your Mr Brunel proved... unfruitful."

"Speak? About what?"

"About progress." He sighed. "For over two hundred years I have dwelt here, yet have never witnessed such a pace of change as in the last score of years. Progress, Master Pickman. Others of my kind resent it, would ignore or fight it. Your burial places are being transformed, modernised, meaning that our old feeding grounds are disappearing. Your engineerings and delvings have brought your people into our world, giving us a stark choice: accept, or die. But if we are to accept, there must be an... understanding. Hence the message," he motioned to the scroll, "which you are to deliver personally to the Duke."

"You can write?" I ejaculated, immediately following up with, "I meant no offence!"

A low rumble of laughter. "Yes, I can write. Some said I was..." He gazed upwards as if lost in memory. His eyes snapped back onto mine. "Yes, and that was but one of the skills that propelled me into becoming an agent for certain powers. But that was another life. And so. You will deliver the message?"

I glanced down at the scroll. "I -I shall. But will the Duke believe me?"

"He will. There are certain secrets mentioned within that

scroll that will confirm its authenticity. As I said, little of what occurs in London passes us by. He will believe."

"What if he sends troops down here? What if he determines to exterminate your kind?"

The King sneered. "A thousand troops could not drive us from the Crawl. And we can strike from the shadows at any time. Should we so choose, none would be safe. But I have heard that the Duke is a practical man. He will see the sense of my offer. After all, he is also a man of progress."

"Your clan? There seemed to be some disagreement."

"Yes. Much disagreement. And already some have attempted to impede the work on your tunnel."

"I see, it was they who stole the bodies?"

The King shook his large head. "No. I am somewhat abashed to say that was due to the actions of my aforementioned 'ambassador'. I fear the temptation proved irresistible. But still, the malcontents are for me to deal with. Your job is to hasten to the Duke, for the quicker an agreement can be brokered, the sooner the more vociferous of my people can be placated. Come, *tempus fugit*, we have tarried long enough. You should leave."

We rose and I followed the stooped figure out of the room, back into that warren, where I recognised little and would have been hopelessly lost without my guide. To my horror, after we had been walking for some time, a clamour arose behind us, a chorus of howls as if from some infernal pack. The King urged me on.

"Hurry," he growled. "Up that way, to the Chamber of the Stone."

We began a trot, my breath ragged in that confined space,

fear lending wings to my heels. The clamour grew, howling, barking, the undoubted sounds of pursuit.

"Go!" urged the King, pushing me forward, then turning to disappear into the dark. I faltered, curiously concerned at the fate of my host. "Go!" he barked again, then vanished.

I stumbled on, closing my eyes to the terrible sounds of strife behind me. Thankfully, the glow appeared ahead and I hurried to it, bursting into the boulder chamber like a shot out of a cannon. Scarcely pausing for breath, I plunged into the upward tunnel, the fresh breeze on my face filling me with hope, as the clamour behind faded into obscurity.

Onward I pressed, regretting my somewhat sedentary and epicurean lifestyle, sweat stinging my eyes, pulse pounding in my temples. *Light, blessed light!* With a final, vigorous effort, I surged towards the light, towards life, towards sanity. As the breeze grew stronger, as my eyes were dazzled by even that soft glow, I slipped in the damp mud underfoot, tripped, fell, and knew no more.

VI

They tell me I was found unconscious on the banks of the Thames by a pair of toshers. I will be eternally grateful to those good people, for there are those riverside dwellers who would have robbed and stripped me, and rolled me into the waters. And I now know full well the fate that would have befallen me there. I came to on a couch in the parlour of a local doctor. My clothes, despite their rips and unmentionable smears, were clearly that of a gentleman, hence my delivery to the good doctor. Though I did wonder afterwards, whether all of these people were not somehow connected to, or agents of the Duke, such is my state of paranoia these days. To my great relief the scroll, if slightly flattened, was still in my inside jacket pocket. I pressed on the doctor my urgent need to visit the Duke, and he was kind enough to have his carriage take me there without delay.

Despite the early hour, for dawn's rosy glow had but barely touched the roofs of London, the Duke was already at his desk. I was shown in with some urgency, the Duke arose, obviously shocked at my bedraggled appearance. He waved away my apologies, no doubt he had seen worse on the battlefield. I presented him with the scroll and he bade me sit, a footman rushing in with welcome tea and buttered pikelets which, I'm not ashamed to say, I demolished with some gusto.

As I ate I watched the Duke's face with interest. He began with a frown, but any fears I had of my being laughed out of the office were allayed when I saw his expression blanch and his fingers tighten. He sat back for a moment, as if gathering his wits.

My word. I could scarce guess the manner of revelation or secret that could rattle the Iron Duke so. Of subsequent events, there is little to tell. I was taken to a room to wash and change, following which I feel into a deep sleep for many hours. I never saw the Duke again, his people transported me back to my dwelling. By all accounts, he was pleased with my work, at least according to Messrs Tweedie & Prideaux. Certainly they were most appreciative of the pecuniary reward which followed shortly after. I gather the young Brunel recovered, and the excavation of the Thames tunnel has recommenced. My part in this endeavour was done.

"And so, dear friends, here ends my tale." Pickman motioned Hodgson for another brandy, drained it and sat heavily. If anything, he look more pallid and unwell than before. A low murmur rippled around the company.

"Good God, man!" Le Blanc eventually exclaimed. "You mean these dreadful cannibal things are scurrying around beneath our very feet, and the Duke knows about it? Why have we not heard of this?"

Pickman waved a weary hand and mopped his brow with a kerchief. "You have not heard of this because of the arrangement. And, I would ask you all, as friends, to share not a word that I have spoken to you tonight with anyone. Not even your closest family."

"Arrangement? With these foul creatures? Why, that's unbelievable!" Treadwell muttered.

"If only it were," Pickman continued. "For, as has been relayed to me since, *what is the life of the odd urchin or beggar or tavern wench compared to the marvellous engineering achievements which will transform our fair capital city?*"

"They plan to feed the things?" Weems, as many of us, stood aghast.

"Only with the dead, I am told. At least, for now. Who knows what the future may bring.? Which is why, my friends, I have an announcement to make."

A hubbub immediately arose, silenced only by Hodgson clinking loudly on a glass. Pickman stood, faltering and spoke with some emotion.

"I fear this shall be our last meeting, my friends. Truth be told my mind had already been made up, but hearing your tales tonight has only confirmed my decision and strengthened my resolve. I shall be leaving London. The Pickman Club shall be no more."

A clamour broke out once more, this time old Hodgson was forced to resort to the dinner gong to restore order. Pickman continued.

"You see, I once thought our metropolis the greatest place on earth. Our jewel in the crown of Empire. Of course it has its dens, its rookeries and the like. Yet it also has wonderful parks, magnificent architecture, museums, galleries and the most civilised society in the world. Yet, as has now been revealed, London is nothing more than the hollow shell of a resting body, rendered presentable, even beautiful, by the art of the undertaker. Beneath the powder and rouge lies foulness and rot. Our city is as riddled with vermin as the most rank and putrescent corpse. Hidden from our eyes, the mortal remains of our beloved are taken, despoiled, devoured."

"They shall lie down alike in the dust, and the worms shall cover them." Reverend Dyer quoted, and all turned to stare at him. He gave a small cough. "Well, that would be the natural order of things."

"But this is profoundly unnatural, and with the full cooperation of the authorities," Pickman continued. "And I have my family to think of. The thought of my loved ones suffering such a fate. My wife... my dear departed wife." His voice caught, and not a heart there failed to soften at our host's obvious distress. Still, he mastered himself to go on.

"No, my friends. I'll subject neither myself, nor my children, or their children to such monstrousness. To that end we are leaving London. We sail for the Americas on the morrow."

"But where will you go?" I asked.

"New England," came the reply. "I have family there, cousins who left these shores many years back. Indeed, he for whom I am named was among the first of our family to settle there. We shall create a new home in Boston. As you all know, my late, dear wife was of an artistic nature, and our children have inherited her tendencies. I hear Boston is a thriving centre of the arts, with many new opportunities, unrestricted by the social conventions that tend to stifle the creative mind in England. There, we shall be far away from this city, away from this charnel house, this perfumed cesspit, this city of ghouls with its ancient secrets. And so, with a heavy heart, I bid you all farewell."

There were nods and hearty responses from around the room, though I fancied many of us were still in shock, both from the implications of the night's revelations, and at this unexpected end to both the evening and the Club.

What more can I say? Following Pickman's announcement, the meeting slowly drifted apart, as the incoming tide softly dissolves the stoutest sandcastle. I fancy that more than a few of us might have well been considering a similar move, given the evening's tales. I myself certainly avoid dark passageways and graveyards after dark, and wonder if the pitter-patters of the small hours are merely rats, or something worse.

As for Pickman, he and I were the last to leave the club that night. He shook my hand at the door, gave me a brief smile and departed. The last I saw of him was a lonely figure walking slowly away along the moonlit cobbles.

BIOGRAPHIES

GLYNN OWEN BARRASS

Glynn Owen Barrass lives in the North East of England and has been writing since late 2006. He has written over two hundred short stories, novellas, and role-playing game supplements, the majority of which have been published in France, Germany, Japan, Poland, the UK, and the USA.

TONY BRADBURY

Tony is 61 yrs old, and lives in Norfolk England. In real life he is a factory manager and makes cardboard boxes. He is currently tying to build his skill up for when he finally retires and can do this on a more regular basis. Tony loves horror and *Warhammer 40K* novels and is currently learning to play the Delta Blues but is finding that it's a lot more subtle than it sounds.

GAVIN CHAPPELL

Over the last twenty years Gavin Chappell has been published by Penguin Books, Horrified Press, Nightmare Illustrated, Death Throes Webzine, Spook Show, and the podcast Dark Dreams, among others. He has worked variously as a lecturer, a private tutor, a tour guide, an independent film maker, and editor of *Lovecraftiana: the Magazine of Eldritch Horror*. His influences include Robert E Howard, Michael Moorcock, HP Lovecraft, and Terrance Dicks. He lives in northern England.

B HARLAN CRAWFORD

B. Harlan Crawford is a lapsed musician, sub-par artist, would-be writer and purveyor of the sort of low-brow schlock that is ruining this country. He festers loathsomely at his home in Tennessee with his wife, two cats and two dogs. More of his fevered scrawling can be read at
https://thelibraryoftheschlocklords.blogspot.com

SHELLEY De CRUZ

Shelley wrote and illustrated her first book at the age of four. Then she had to go to school, grow up and get a proper job. Undeterred, she still manages to produce illustrations, posters and cards. There is also a stack of sketchbooks under the bed full of doodles looking for their own story. Somewhat unusually, for the female of the species, she does not like chocolate. www.facebook.com/graveheartdesigns

JOHN DeLAUGHTER, M. Div., M.S.

John has appeared in *The Lovecraft eZine*, *Aphotic Realm*, *Samsara: The Magazine of Suffering*, *Tigershark eZine*, *Turn To Ash horror zine*, *The Atlantean Supplement*, *The Eldritch Literary Review*, *The Chamber*, *Horizontum* (Mexico City), *Círculo de Lovecraft* (Spain) and *Vastarien: A Literary Journal*.

John's fantasy novels in the *Dark Union* series are available on Amazon. He lives in Pennsylvania with his wife Heidi. Follow John's latest publication news on Twitter @HPL_JDeLaughter, Facebook @HPLJDeLaughter, or Instagram@HPL_JDeLaughter

MIGUEL FLIGUER

Miguel Fliguer lives in Buenos Aires, Argentina. His self-published first book, *Cooking With Lovecraft*, is a collection of gastronomical weird tales. His short stories and collaborations are featured in the *Ancestors & Descendants*, *Weird Tails*, *Portraits of Terror*, and *Corridors* anthologies from Innsmouth Gold; *Vastarien* (Grimscribe Press); *Strange Aeon 2022*; and in *The Necronomnomnom*, *Lovecraft Cocktails*, and *The Necromunchicon* illustrated cookbook grimoires (Mike Slater, Red Duke Games). He dwells on Twitter as @cookingwithHPL, and as himself in the *Book of Faces*.

JOHN HOULIHAN

John Houlihan is a British sci-fi and fantasy author and has been a writer, journalist and broadcaster for over 30 years. He's best known for his *Seraph Chronicles* and *Mon Dieu Cthulhu!* book series and recently published a new collection of sci-fi stories called *The Constellation of Alarion*. He currently works as a narrative designer, video game consultant and script writer and creative lead on the *Achtung! Cthulhu* RPG. www.john-houlihan.net

TIM MENDEES

Tim Mendees is a rather odd chap. He's a horror writer from Macclesfield that specialises in cosmic horror and weird fiction. A lifelong fan of classic weird tales, Tim set out to bring the pulp horror of yesteryear into the 21st Century and give it a distinctly British flavour. His work has been described as the love-child of H.P. Lovecraft and P.G. Wodehouse.

Tim is the author of over 100 published short stories and novelettes, nine novellas, and two short story collections. He has also curated and edited several cosmic horror-themed anthologies. Tim is a goth DJ with a weekly radio show, one of the organisers of *The Innsmouth Literary Festival*, and the co-presenter of the Innsmouth Book Club Podcast & Strange Shadows: The Clark Ashton Smith Podcast. He currently lives in Brighton & Hove with his pet crab, Gerald, and an ever-increasing army of stuffed octopods.

timmendeeswriter.wordpress.com/

ROBERT POYTON

Robert is the founder of *Innsmouth Gold*, set up as an outlet for his music and literary projects. A long-time fan of weird fiction and Sword and Sorcery, Robert is a keen musician, and an experienced martial arts instructor, having published a wide range of books and films on Chinese and Russian arts. He is co-host of the Innsmouth *Book Club* and *Strange Shadows* podcasts. raised in East London, Robert now lives in rural

Bedfordshire, where he enjoys making a noise and swinging sharp objects around.

MIKE SLATER

Mike is the author of *The Necronomnomnom*, purveyor of infernally bad puns, and designer/mastermind behind games of all sorts. He is a lifelong fan of Things Not of This Earth, and at this point, is ready to loose some of his ideas upon unsuspecting readers. When not hiding from the Evil Day Star, he can be found hiking, writing, gaming, or waiting to kindle the fires of Burnhenge.

RUSSELL SMEATON

Born from an egg on a mountain top, Russell has spent the past 40-something years doing stuff and things. After spending a decade travelling around the world he has now settled down in the North of England. He lives with his lovely family and a few errant cats, who know far more than they should. Luckily they're not telling.

LEE CLARK ZUMPE

Lee Clark Zumpe has been writing and publishing horror, dark fantasy and speculative fiction since the late 1990s. His short stories and poetry have appeared in *Weird Tales*, *Space and Time* and *Dark Wisdom*; and in anthologies such as *The Children of Gla'aki*, *Best New Zombie Tales Vol. 3*, *Through a Mythos Darkly*, *Heroes of Red Hook* and *World War Cthulhu*. His work has earned several honourable mentions in *The Year's Best Fantasy and Horror* collections.

As entertainment editor for Tampa Bay Newspapers, his work has been recognized by the Florida Press Association, including a first place award for criticism in the 2013. Lee lives on the west coast of Florida with his wife and daughter.

Acknowledgements

We would like to give thanks to everyone who helped make this book possible. To our authors and artist for sharing their talents, and to all those who backed the project and helped spread the word, including:

Alec Smith
Aref Dyer
Brian Hicks
GhostCat
Gideon Clarke
Jennifer LeBlanc
Joey O'Connor

John Dingman
Lisa Gargano
Mindy Geres
Shane Ardley
Thomas Kirby
William Loudon

Chris Halliday
Matthew Carpenter
Patricia Erdely
Ruth Beaty
William Stowers

Adam
Alexander Nirenberg
Ana E
Andrea
Andrew Ferguson
Anthony Deming
Balki
Bobby D.
Brian
Brian Hanes
Brooks
Bruce Ellis
Bryan Colman
Charles Denno
Chris Chastain
Chris Jarocha-Ernst
Chris Kalley
Darin Hlavaz
David Batson
David Chamberlain
David Chrichard
David Griffith
Denis Wildschütz
Derek Egerman
Ed Matuskey
Eric Priehs
Ernie

Esa Eriksson
Francisco Vera
Gina Kern
Grobe
Izaak
j william berger
Jacob Lewis
Jamie Turner
Jason Ramer
Jean-Luc Ruvera
Jeffrey McMahan
Joe Kontor
Joseph Kozik
Joshua Long
Julia Morgan
Karl
Kenneth T. White III
Kristina
L.E.D.
Lee Carnell
luciano
Magegunner
Marek Girwicz
Mario Santos
Mark Hughes
Martin Kilby
MasterZinja

Mathias
Matt McCormick
Michael DeCuypere
Michael Flores
Mike James
Nicole Bunting
Paul Motsuk
Peter Halls
Philip C. Robinson
Red Duke Games
Rhydderch
Roger Strahl
Rumplestiltskin6
Russell Jurney
Ryan Kasprowicz
Sam
Simon Mark de Wolfe
Stefan Hoyle
Steinar
Therese Öberg
Tim Lonegan
Timothy Lowe
Tobias Gasser
Tony Ciak
Walter Koegel
Yvonne Budden

Abe
Abel Teo
Adam Alexander
Alejandro
Alexander Jung
Andrew O'Leary
Asenath Waite
Ben
Ben Gasparini
Beth Honeycutt
Boris Veytsman
Brad
Brandy Ybarra
Brian D Lambert
Bruce tribby
Cam
Christina B
Ciera
Damon & Peni Griffin
Dan Arbiture
Daniel Sandholzer
Duane Warnecke
Ed King
Elliott Malone
Fjjj
Frank

Frederick Siem
Geoff G Turner
GMark C
Harm Willem
Henry Lopez
Ian F. Bell
Jaap van poelgeest
James TD Smith
Jared 'pirate' Foley
Jeremy W. Sherman
Jim Kosmicki
John Haines
John M. Portley
john potter
John Ver Linden
Jonathan
Klikke Sietel
KorvusRock
Laura McGuire
Leo Lele
Lucinda Duvall
Mark Carter
Mark Froom
Matthew Plank
Matthias Ackerl
Meredith Carstens

Michael Fitzpatrick
Mike James
Myles
Myron Fox
Nathan
Nathaniel Adams
Paul Adams
Philippe Gamache
Phyllis Gibson
Randy Martin
Richard O'Shea
Richard Souza
Ricky Broome
Robert L. Vaughn
Robin Komarica
Ryan
Scott
Simon Hunt
Stephane Gelgoot
Steven Darrall
Stewie
Talon Conant
Thomas Sutton
Todd Ellner
William Buthod

If you have enjoyed this book, please
post a review on Amazon. Thanks!

www.innsmouthgold.com

For the latest info on new releases, special offers and events,
sign up to our *Innsmouth Whispers* newsletter.
You'll get a 20% discount voucher on joining!

http://eepurl.com/hysilb

INNSMOUTH LITERARY FESTIVAL

Sat. 30th September 2023 10am -5pm
King's House, 245 Ampthill Rd,
Bedford MK42 9AZ

A festival celebrating 100 years of Weird
Tales magazine and weird fiction in general.

Full program of events, including:

Author signings and panel discussions in the Theatre

Film screenings in the Picturehouse

Readings in the Cafe

Trade stands in the Chamber of Commerce

Gaming in the Play Zone

Competitions and photo ops

Post Festival pub meet

Guests include:
David Hambling
TL Wiswell
Chris Lackey
Mike Mason
Ann Smith Spark
Greig Johnson
Simon Bleaken
Thomas Campbell
Russell Smeaton
Paul Fricker
Zoe Burgess-Foreman
Alexandra Beaumont

**GUEST OF HONOUR
RAMSEY CAMPBELL
LIVE ZOOM Q&A**

Full details at
http://www.innsmouth.uk/

ANCESTORS AND DESCENDANTS

This anthology explores prequels and sequels to Lovecraftian tales. You will discover the dark history of the de la Poers, read of the early days of the artist Pickman, and learn the secrets of Erich Zann. From downtown Arkham to distant Venus, this unique illustrated collection expands and explores the rich legacy left to us by the Father of the Weird Tale.

Lovecraft loved cats! So we gathered together new weird stories with a distinctly feline theme!

WEIRD TAILS

From unearthly Ultharians to the humble house moggy, from temple guardians to witch's familiar, you might never look at your cat in the same light again…

Portraits of Terror

New tales of the weird and the Lovecraftian, all based on the theme of the Arts. From doomed musicians, to magical paintings, from lost Shakespeare plays to unworldly sculptures. Thirteen tales that may well change your perspective on Art and Creation…

CORRIDORS

The world changed. Now, we live underground in labyrinthine complexes, our lives overseen by the Ministry. For only they have access to our Ruler… The King in Yellow.
13 tales in a new setting based on the King in Yellow mythos of Robert W Chambers.

FEAST OF FOOLS

This anthology continues the tradition, of Robert E. Howard, with eleven new sizzling *S&S* tales. The yarns within feature a cast of lucky thieves, avenging barbarians, bold swordswomen, and temple plunderers, not to mention sorcerers, necromancers,and a range of horrors that would freeze the blood of all but the bravest warrior.

THE DUNWICH TRILOGY

A MODERN MYTHOS TRILOGY!

THE DUNWICH NIGHTMARE

DC Marcus Hinds and journalist Suzy Bainbridge get drawn into a mystery following a series of grisly murders on Dunwich beach. Could there be a connection to the nearby top secret research facility?

THE DUNWICH CRISIS

The scale of the conspiracy is revealed as Marcus and Suzy are drawn deeper into the nightmare. Meanwhile, an ancient evil stirs in the depths of the North Sea and the world is about to change forever!

THE DUNWICH LEGACY

The true purpose of the Geneva CERN facility is revealed and Marcus plunges into the "world beyond" in order to save his friends and avert global catastrophe.

"A must read for all Lovecraftians. Check your sanity at the door to the dark realms of Robert Poyton's Lovecraftian Worlds." - Amazon review

INNSMOUTH BOOK CLUB

If you are a fan of Lovecraftian books and films, check out our podcast the **Innsmouth Book Club!** Exclusive tours of Innsmouth's cultural sites, including the museum, library and Gilman house, where we talk weird fiction book, film, RPGs, and music ,and chat to Lovecraftian creatives.

Also take a look at **Strange Shadows**, a podcast devoted exclusively to the weird fiction of Clark Ashton Smith!

www.patreon.com/innsmouthbc